BEYOND REPAIR

Sass and Steam
Book 4

CATHERINE STEIN

For everyone in the LGBTQIA+ community,
whether open or not, and all those still searching
for an identity. And especially for Theo.
I love you as you are.

1

St. Louis, Missouri
May 10, 1906

OWEN CASSIDY HAD WOKEN to the sight of a pretty woman before. This was the first time, however, that he'd woken to find said pretty woman gripping his severed limb.

"Jesus Fucking Christ!" he screamed. Or tried to. It actually came out more of a breathless, "Guaaaargh."

Seemed his voice wasn't working. Nor were his muscles. A tiny twitch of his head was all he could manage. The world was a blur of harsh, bright light, a shimmering halo around the terrifying siren standing over him.

"I told them one injection wouldn't be enough for the likes of you," the woman said, a rueful little smile playing across her lips. She shook her head, tossing her chin-length, red-blond hair.

The likes of me? Owen's muscles would have clenched in anger, if his body was working. He'd heard that same damn thing so many times, these days usually from people who would be mortified if they realized who he was. Who the hell was this woman to be spewing such contempt with a smile on her face?

She was rich, that was absolutely certain. Not a hint of a tan, so if she ever ventured outdoors it was beneath the shade of a parasol. And only a woman of means could get away with her unfashionable short hair and avant-garde clothing. Her loose, brown trousers sat low on her hips, held up by a leather belt with an array of tools dangling from it. A white shirt much like one Owen might have worn covered her torso, topped with a corset-style cropped tweed vest laced snugly across her breasts. Definitely an I-wear-whatever-the-hell-I-like outfit.

"Don't move," the woman warned, as if such a thing were a possibility.

Owen lifted his gaze—at least his eyes worked—to study her face. Pointed chin, dainty nose, peculiar blue-green eyes. What a bizarre color. He fixed his attention on it, trying to discern whether it was only a trick of the light.

A good thing to focus on, those odd but pretty eyes. Kept his gaze from wandering. Kept him from looking at...

She moved, pulling his attention back to the arm she held clasped in her hands. His arm. Disconnected from his body. Owen tried to scream, but again his vocal cords produced nothing but a pathetic choking sound.

The woman fiddled with a wire, and he saw his disembodied fingers twitch. *Felt* them twitch.

"Hmm," she murmured.

Fuck!

Taking as deep a breath as his frozen body could manage, Owen allowed himself to take a proper look at his detached limb. His not-quite-detached limb, it seemed. Oh, the flesh and bone was all severed, certainly, but a series of wire filaments ran from the end of the arm to the stump of whatever was left of his shoulder. He couldn't quite see because he couldn't turn his head. Blood flowed through thin, transparent tubes. The strange woman moved another wire, nodded, then set the arm down beside Owen—on the bed, or whatever this was he was lying on.

Who the hell are you? he wanted to demand. *What are you doing to me?*

She crossed the room, as calmly as if nothing the slightest

bit unusual was happening, rummaged inside a drawer, and returned with a syringe in her hand.

"No," Owen tried to say.

Either she didn't understand or she didn't care, because she jabbed the needle into his not-dismembered arm and pressed down on the plunger.

When he next woke, he was whole. More or less.

Nora's patient twitched in the slightly too-small hospital bed. Her surgery at home would have been more comfortable for both of them, but she couldn't complain too much. Several electric lights allowed her to illuminate the small room to suit her needs. The hospital provided access to the necessary tools and supplies, and here in the sanitarium wing, everything was quiet and spotlessly clean.

The man on the bed twitched again.

"Good morning!" Nora smiled down at him, pleased with how well his body was adapting to the biomechanics. The swelling around the splice points was minimal, and the skin less red and tender than it had been last night. He would only be a three-weeker. Probably because he'd been so fit to begin with. The hard muscles of his bare torso attested to that.

She was curious to meet him. Clearly he worked for a living, yet the suit she had cut from his wounded body had been bespoke. Wealthy, but not afraid to get his hands dirty. Interesting. The sort of man she could respect.

His eyes fluttered open, and she took a moment to peer into them. The light-brown irises were clear, pupil dilation normal, no signs of redness. Excellent.

"Who the hell are you?" he demanded. "What have you done to me?" He jerked, trying to sit up, but his body failed to cooperate.

"Please try to lie still," Nora said, trying to inflect her voice with both comfort and authority. "The drug takes time to wear off."

"Who the hell are you?" he repeated. Rather irritable, this one. Most of her patients suffered from a bit of bewilderment after surgery, but they usually weren't angry.

"Dr. Eleanor Taylor." Nora declined to extend a hand, not wanting him to attempt to lift his right arm yet. "And you are?"

"None of your damned business. What have you done to me?" He grunted and tried again to move, managing to lift his head a bit.

"Your muscle function will return more easily if you relax and allow your body to adjust little-by-little," Nora explained. "You're coming out of two days' sedation. I suggest you begin with gently wiggling toes and fingers, then—"

"I suggest you answer my goddamned question!" he snarled.

Nora put her hands on her hips. "I am a skilled biomechanologist, and it is thanks to my work that you still have both your arms. If you can't speak to me with a modicum of respect, I will be happy to sedate you once again."

His eyes narrowed. Who was this man that he would respond to a healer and helper with nothing but fury and suspicion? Had he been mistreated in other ways? She knew nothing of him, and nothing of how he'd come to be lying in the street, his shoulder torn to pieces by a nasty splatter-bullet. He'd had no money, no identification, and he'd been too insensible up until now to give so much as a name.

"What have you done to me?" he repeated, the words soft, but clipped, his teeth clenched.

"You were found with a grave shoulder wound, too severe to heal properly with ordinary medicine. For you to live, the arm would have needed amputation. Fortunately, I was there to offer an alternative. All the damaged tissue has been removed, and your shoulder replaced with a mechanical joint. After recovery, you will have full use of the arm."

"And what if I didn't want to be turned into some sort of machine?"

"Would you prefer to be missing an arm?"

He paled. Several seconds passed before he spoke again. "How was I wounded? What happened?"

"Gunshot. The bullet fragmented on impact. A weapon meant to maim in the event the shot isn't lethal."

"Who? Why?"

"I have no idea. It had already happened when we stumbled upon you. Now, might I have the pleasure of your name, sir?"

"No." He wriggled and managed to sit up. Impressive. "No, you're going to do the talking, Dr. Taylor. You're going to tell me exactly where you found me, who you were with, how you got me here, where the hell 'here' even is, and every other scrap of information you think might be useful. And then I'm going to go home."

Nora couldn't help the laugh that escaped. "Home? I'm afraid, Mr. Furious, you are not leaving this room or that bed for the next three weeks."

His eyes widened. "Three weeks? Are you mad, woman?" He tried to push himself up further using his right arm, but the newly repaired limb wouldn't respond. He pushed with the left instead, straightening his spine and swinging his legs around to dangle over the side of the bed. "I have work to do. And apparently an enemy to find."

"Don't attempt to stand up, please," Nora cautioned. "It won't be pretty."

He glared at her. "I've had quite enough of your help, *Doctor.*"

Nora shrugged at the sneer he put on her title. Fine. If the jackass wanted to demonstrate how little brains he had in his head, that was his prerogative.

He shoved himself from the bed, teetered for a few seconds, then collapsed.

"This is why you ought to listen to your doctor," she scolded, just before his eyes rolled up and he lapsed into unconsciousness.

2

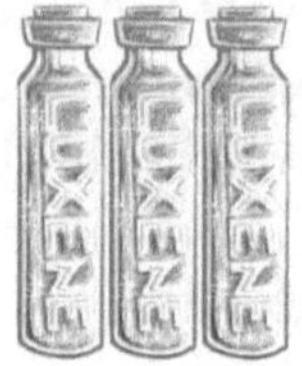

"Good morning, Mr. Cassidy."

Owen blinked several times, trying to adjust to the too-bright light of the newly-opened curtains. Why was this doctor woman so perpetually cheerful? Did she *enjoy* chopping bits off of people and stuffing them full of God-knew-what sorts of machinery?

"You know my name," he replied. *You dolt. Obviously she knows. She just said it. Once again, you're showing yourself to have a head full of rocks.*

"When stories began to circulate that a luxene magnate had gone missing, I suspected it might be you," she explained. "My brother is a prominent lawyer here in town, and it didn't take many calls from him to find someone who could positively identify you."

Owen pushed himself into a seated position. His "repaired" right arm still didn't work correctly, despite her claims to brilliance. "You speak of me as though I'm dead," he grumbled. "And I prefer 'tycoon' to 'magnate.' It comes from Japanese, you know. 'Magnate' is just from Latin, which makes it worthless, as every Gaius and Sextus went around slapping 'Magnus' onto the end of his name." There. Let her think him a fool *now*.

"How very scholarly for someone who dropped out of school at age thirteen."

Owen flinched. Damn. Had she gone and researched his background?

"I dropped out because it bored the shit out of me, not because I couldn't read." And because his family had needed money. His father had died and his baby brother had been a newborn. They'd needed the income the muscle of a strong lad could bring in.

"Apparently. And then you discovered luxene and made a fortune."

"Yes." *The summary of my life, as told in the magazines, with the caption "The American Dream" beneath my grainy photograph.*

Owen tried lifting his right arm again, only managing to get his hand a few inches off the bed.

"You're doing well," the doctor said, the right side of her mouth hitching up in a half smile. "But it will be two weeks or so until it really feels normal. I have a series of exercises that will help ease the process, if you're willing to heed my advice."

Two weeks. Dammit, he didn't have two weeks. He might not remember what had happened to land him here with the pretty but annoying biomechanologist, but he knew what it meant. The strange "accidents" and "errors" in his mines and his refineries recently were deliberate sabotage. He was needed back at work immediately, and he wouldn't rest until he'd discovered who was responsible for putting his men and his company in danger.

"Didn't you say three weeks before?" Did she think he wouldn't notice that her arbitrary timeline had changed?

Her smile twitched. "That was a week ago."

"What?" Owen's head swam, an all-too-familiar sensation. Good God. All those times he'd slid in and out of consciousness, those dreamy moments when he'd been unsure what was real and what wasn't... "No."

No. It couldn't be. That was one night of stupor. Not a week. Not a full goddamn week.

"The first several days are the most vital to your body's

adjustment to the biomechanics. Keeping you from moving about and harming yourself has proven challenging."

"Harming myself," he repeated through his clenched teeth. Who else had been harmed in the meantime? What damage had been done to his property? How deep into hiding had the bastard who'd shot him gone?

"Indeed. You are an extremely fit and vigorous man." She gave his well-honed torso a pointed look.

Desire surged in his groin. Good. That part of him wasn't damaged. Not that this was the time. But it had been some time since he'd scratched that particular itch, and he had an especially attractive woman gazing upon his half-naked body.

Wait. If he'd been here a week, who had given him food and drink? He wasn't dehydrated. Who'd been helping him relieve himself?

"You're not the only doctor here, right? There's a man helping you somewhere? Can I speak to him?" Maybe a male doctor or assistant would be more reasonable about this whole two weeks thing.

All evidence of happiness washed from her face, leaving her mouth drawn tight and her blue-green eyes hard as a frozen lake. "*I* am the only doctor. I need help from no one, man or woman." Her glacial stare caressed Owen head to toe, extinguishing his lust as surely as a dunking in a tub of ice. Then, as if she'd read his mind, she continued, "And, yes, I helped you with everything. I've seen every bit of you. Touched every bit of you. And in case you're getting any ideas, this…" She waved a hand over him. "Doesn't interest me that way. Not a bit."

The doctor spun and walked toward the door, leaving him alone feeling angry and not a small amount foolish. He was done with this. No more wasting time. No more listening to her high-and-mighty proclamations.

The moment the door to the small room closed, Owen

swung his legs over the side of the bed. No dizziness. Good. He wasn't about to repeat the incident from last… week.

Biting back a growl of frustration, he inched himself to the edge of the bed, letting his feet brush the floor, giving his legs a moment to adjust. He moved slowly, testing his muscles, shifting his weight from the bed bit-by-bit until he was standing under his own power.

He'd done it. He could stand.

He paused a moment, then rocked to test each leg separately. Shaky, but not dangerously so. Stiff from disuse. He took several laps of the room. Yes, he could walk. His legs protested the change in situation, but they were sturdy enough he wouldn't fall. He would adjust quickly.

Owen's eyes flicked to the closed door. Dr. Taylor was stubborn. Demanding. Convinced she was right. But she was also much, much smaller than Owen. And even one-handed with wobbly legs, she couldn't physically restrain him. Not without more sedatives, and he wasn't eating or drinking a damned thing that had passed anywhere near her.

No. He was leaving. Now.

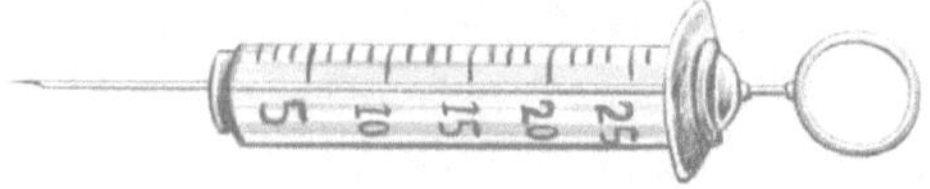

3

H_{E'D GONE OUT} the window.

Nora ran a hand through her hair. The stubborn oaf. He was going to set the healing process back by days, if not weeks. And if he managed to do real damage to the shoulder, the arm might never work correctly again.

She yanked the window closed, gathered a bag with a few supplies, and set out. He couldn't be hard to track down. People would notice a large, shirtless man wrapped in a blanket.

Nora nodded to the woman at the desk near the entrance to the sanitarium. The staff had been kind to the strange woman doctor who had barged in with a bleeding man and demanded a room. She appreciated each and every one of them. Nora had paid to rent the space for a full month. She'd be back soon, with one grouchy man in tow.

And then she'd have to figure out a plan for keeping him there. She didn't want him to remain fully sedated. He needed to begin exercising the arm, working it incrementally up to full strength and range of motion. She had a plan. She had a plan and he was messing it all up.

Much to Nora's chagrin, finding Owen Cassidy proved more difficult than she'd expected. No one on the street claimed to have seen him, though how anyone could miss him she didn't understand. He was six and a half feet tall and must have weighed something near to two hundred fifty pounds.

Men like that were obvious when they *weren't* half-naked and sporting a biomechanical shoulder. After half an hour of fruitless searching through the neighborhood, she headed for her brother's office.

"How's the luxene mogul?" Trevor greeted her, standing to look at her over his mountains of papers.

"He prefers the word 'tycoon' and he's missing." Nora plopped down into a chair. "He climbed out the window."

Trevor's eyebrows arched. "Out the window? I thought your patients usually liked you. What did you do to this one to make him flee?"

"It wasn't me. It was him. From the first he was angry and frustrated and unwilling to listen. I don't think he believes me about the necessity of recovery time, and if I don't find him, he's going to lose function in that arm. And since it's his dominant hand, he might not be too pleased about that."

Trevor shrugged. "Sounds like he's bringing the trouble on himself."

"True. But I wasn't recognized as top biomechanologist in the country by letting my patients ruin perfectly good work. I did it by helping people to the best of my ability." And by hiding her gender behind initials when submitting testimonies about her work, but that was an entirely separate problem. "I need to know where he might have gone. His home address. The locations of his refineries and mines. If I can find him, I can prevent any disaster."

"Uh, Nora? He's not noted for being especially... accommodating. Set in his ways, I guess you'd say. Runs his facilities with strict discipline and rigid structure. Doesn't like outside intrusion. Stubborn as an ox, to put it bluntly."

Nora grinned at her brother. "And I'm not?"

Trevor shook his head. "I'm just warning you. The two of you might be like those funny sheep with the big horns who smash their heads together repeatedly."

"I look forward to the challenge. The address, please?"

Owen Cassidy lived in a stately brick townhouse in a gorgeous, tree-lined neighborhood. The lawns and gardens along the street were perfectly trimmed, and every house was in excellent repair. Fashionable ladies strolled the park across the street with small fashionable dogs, while governesses chased their fashionably-dressed children. Now and then, a luxury steam car rumbled down the street.

It was all precisely what Nora expected.

The butler who opened the front door, however, was not. His clothes were appropriate for his duties, and he stood with a stiff formality as he peered down at Nora, but his face was craggy and weatherbeaten, his gray hair long and shaggy, and he was missing an eye. She could have helped with that last if the injury had been recent. She suspected it wasn't.

"Is Mr. Cassidy in?" Nora asked, squaring her shoulders and adopting her professional tone. "I am a physician and must consult with him regarding his recent injury."

"I'm afraid he is not at home." The butler's nose turned up a bit and he moved to close the door. The staff had been warned about her, she guessed.

Nora stuck a foot between the door and the jamb. "It's a matter of some urgency. If Mr. Cassidy is to heal fully, he must complete his period of rest and therapy. It is essential for a successful surgery."

The butler's smug expression morphed into a scowl. "Seems to me you shouldn'ta operated on a man without his say-so."

Nora fought back a sigh. "I am a doctor. I found a man unconscious and in danger of losing at least an arm and likely his life. I had to make the decision I believed was in the best interest of the patient, and I had to do it right that moment or he would've bled out in the street. Sometimes that is the nature of my occupation. If living a life with biomechanics is stressful to Mr. Cassidy, I can recommend the name of a consultant who specializes in talking patients through traumatic life experiences."

"Sounds like bunk," the butler snorted.

So many people thought so. It irked Nora to no end how little care people gave to emotions and one's mental state in relationship to health. Didn't they realize the brain was an essential part of the body? A wildly complex one science had only begun to explore.

Her own brain was a perfect example of the mysterious nature of the human mind. For years she'd thought herself broken or deficient because of her lack of sexual or romantic interest in… well, anyone. Her body didn't seem to have those tendencies. At least, not usually. There'd been a few times during her youth when she'd felt stirrings of interest in people she was close to. And there'd been the one time a friendship had blossomed into something different. When she'd dreamed of kisses and longed for even the slightest touch.

She'd never experienced anything like it since. It was only when she'd finally discussed the matter with Lina that Nora had truly begun to understand herself. She wasn't broken. Her brain simply worked differently. And so, so many people everywhere had their own brains that differed from what was considered typical.

If only everyone would pay attention to experts like Lina. The work she was doing could make the world a better place for all.

So frustrating. This was why Nora preferred to be alone with her patients, doing what needed to be done. Explaining things gave her a headache.

"Well, whatever you and your employer might think, and whatever the circumstances that brought us here, the fact remains that Mr. Cassidy needs my assistance and advice in order to ensure he will be able to continue working in the capacity to which he is accustomed. I would be grateful if you could inform me of his whereabouts so I might ensure his continued wellbeing."

The butler blinked several times. "You've got a fancy way with words, don't you, Doctor?"

Nora didn't reply, not sure if he was insulting her or complimenting her.

"Mr. Cassidy's gone to the mines. He's needed there. Not a place for a fancy-talking lady."

"Thank you." Nora removed her boot from the doorway and gave the butler a nod. "Good day to you."

The mines. The worst possible place he could have chosen. Naturally.

4

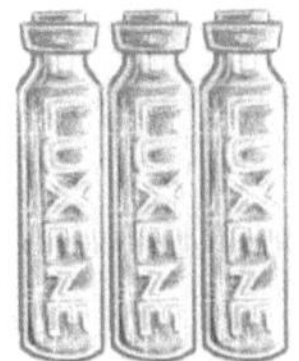

Owen tore his gaze from the mangled machinery. Another sprayer lost. A pipe had burst and taken one side of the trellis-like structure with it. Already the rock walls were drying out. And a dry tunnel was a dangerous tunnel in the world of luxene mining.

"I'll have to bother Leslie again," he muttered.

Owen hated to beg yet another favor from his childhood friend. Leslie Atwater may have started off building mining equipment, but these days his manufactory churned out a constant stream of new machines for an ever-growing number of clients. He was busy. And while he would always be happy to make time for Owen, that didn't assuage the guilt. Atwater had better things to do than make irrigation machines.

"Cassidy?" The booming bass voice of Louis Cardot, Owen's mining supervisor, echoed down the corridor.

Owen turned to greet Cardot. The diminutive Black man hardly cut an imposing figure, but he had a knack for keeping the men in line with his voice alone. Like Atwater, Cardot had been one of Owen's first collaborators in this venture. When he had something to say, Owen listened.

"What's the trouble?" Owen asked. He adjusted the sling propping up his useless right arm. It was worse now than when he'd left the biomechanologist, and he'd been trying not to dwell on that too much. He'd told the men he'd been injured without giving any specifics.

"There's a woman here. A woman in trousers. Wandering the grounds beneath a lacy parasol."

Owen cursed.

Cardot's mouth curved slightly. "Someone you know, I gather?"

"She's a doctor. Helped out with my shoulder."

Cardot eyed Owen's injured arm. Noticing the way the shirt stretched and bunched over the biomechanics, no doubt. "Right. You gonna explain that?"

"Yes. When we have a moment in private. Right now, don't wanna talk about it. Seems I have a lady to scare away first."

"Don't know if she'll scare. She's comfortable as a lady at tea, from the little I saw. All smiles and politeness, greeting sweaty, dust-covered men as if they were the finest of gentlemen."

Owen grimaced. No, she wouldn't scare easily. Not when she'd handled his severed arm, calm as anything. Not when she was so determined she'd trekked fifteen miles from downtown St. Louis to his mine to chastise him.

But maybe he could talk to her. Maybe she could offer him some therapy for the arm that he could do while he worked. Because he wasn't going back to the hospital. He was needed here.

Owen followed Cardot up and into the sunshine, past men hauling the raw luxene ore from the caverns for transportation to the refinery.

"Watch that sprayer," he cautioned one young man. "Won't do any good if the water runs all over the ground instead of the rocks."

"Yes, sir." The worker nodded and adjusted the nozzle.

"Can't be too safe with all the trouble going on here of late," Owen muttered.

Cardot nodded gravely. "Been thinking of hiring an

investigator. We'll talk about that, too, after you shoo away your lady friend. She's just over there."

"She's not a fr—" Owen stumbled, not at all prepared for the sight of Dr. Eleanor Taylor smiling in the spring sunshine.

Her clothing style hadn't changed from what he'd seen before, though this pair of trousers was black, and her short corset-vest was blue satin instead of sober tweed. She held a lace-trimmed, lavender parasol tilted over her left shoulder, shading her from the sun's scorching rays. Their eyes met, and her cheery smile turned wolfish. She'd found her prey and was ready to pounce.

Owen's whole body tightened. He'd be only too happy to let her devour him.

"Not a friend?" Cardot chuckled. "Maybe close your mouth, then."

Owen snapped his jaw shut. So what if she had all the swagger of a riverboat card sharp? Who cared if she didn't back down from a challenge and instead met it head-on and smiling? What did it matter that she possessed those wild turquoise eyes? She was still a nuisance.

Besides, she'd informed him she wasn't interested the way he was interested.

Owen stalked toward her, letting his frustration at almost every aspect of his life rise inside him. It wasn't fair, to make her the focus of his anger, but she was the only difficulty he could remove from his life at the moment.

"What do you think you're doing here?" he demanded.

Dr. Taylor continued to smile. "Familiarizing myself with the premises. Since you insist upon being here, I have no choice but to join you to see you are properly rehabilitated."

"Rehabilitated sounds like something you do to a criminal."

"Yes, well..." She let the unspoken words and her smirk state her opinion of him.

Owen scowled. "You're not welcome here. Mine's no place for a lady."

"Nonsense. And I have no particular interest in the mine. I only mean to ensure you limit your activities and perform your therapeutic exercises for the next two weeks. Firstly, you must remove your sling. It's holding the arm in entirely the wrong position and likely doing damage. You'll be very lucky if you haven't set the healing process back."

He had, he suspected, but he'd be damned if he'd admit it. He'd see her gone, then remove the sling and start working on those exercises. But he wouldn't stay in bed or any of that nonsense.

"Give me a list of the exercises and get back to the city. I don't need a nanny."

She twirled her parasol and shook her head. The way her short hair bounced whenever her head moved mesmerized him.

"Apparently you do." She stared at his shoulder, one hand reaching down to fiddle with a tool in her belt. "Can you even wiggle your fingers?"

"Of course." He demonstrated, but they were stiff and responded slowly.

Her blue-green eyes locked with his, wide and full of pity. The expression made Owen's stomach clench. He was no weakling. He'd made do his whole life and he didn't need help from her or from anyone.

"Get lost," he snarled. "I have work to do."

She faced him with shoulders square, her feet spread in a stable stance, ready to push back if he tried to force her off his property. "So do I."

Owen could pick her up with his good arm and throw her over his shoulder. She was barely half his size, after all. But he wasn't one to manhandle women.

He tried once more to convince her. "Look, as much as I would like to have a nice, long break, I've already been away too long. We're having troubles lately. I've had to shut down a portion of the mine entirely due to machinery malfunctions."

Her defensive stance relaxed. "Oh. Maybe I can help."

"What?"

She pulled a small wrench from her belt and spun it around in her hand. "I'm a doctor, but I'm also an engineer. That's what it means to be a biomechanologist. I can fix ordinary machines in my sleep."

"I have people for that."

"Yes, I'm sure you do, but an extra pair of hands might be just the thing to help alleviate some of your troubles. And then *you* can focus on recuperating."

"I don't need any damned recuperating. I just need some time, and a bit of…" He wiggled his fingers again, willing them to work. "Of practice."

"You need a doctor. It was a traumatic injury and a complicated surgery. And don't think I can't see those stress lines around your eyes or how tightly you've clenched almost every part of your body. You're exhausted, you've overworked yourself, and you're damaging your biomechanics."

At these last words, a number of nearby heads turned to stare. Goddammit. He did not have time to explain this. He stepped toward Dr. Taylor and gripped her arm, his big hand easily circling her biceps.

"I am escorting you off the premises right now," he growled.

"Release me," she demanded. She dropped the parasol and dug into a pocket with her free hand. "Or you'll regret it."

Owen forged ahead, pulling her with him. "I'm afraid you've left me no choice."

Her hand swung at him, a loaded syringe in her fist. Owen started to dodge, but before he could move even an inch, an explosion ripped through the air and the ground gave way beneath his feet.

5

NORA LEANED OVER Owen Cassidy's large body, feeling the warmth of his breath on her cheek. Breathing steadily. Pulse strong. Thank God.

She emptied the syringe and tucked it away. He hadn't gotten a full dose when she'd jabbed him during their tumble into the sinkhole, but he'd be out for at least the next quarter of an hour.

"You all right, miss?"

Nora looked up. A slender man gazed down at her. Nearing his fortieth year, she guessed, and dressed in sturdy, well-tailored clothing. Dark eyes. Dark skin. Hair shaved short, much like Mr. Cassidy's was. Or had been, when she'd first seen him. Now he had a head of short fuzz and scraggly whiskers.

"We're not hurt," Nora replied. "But Mr. Cassidy is, er… sedated. I'll need some assistance to get him out of this hole."

The man's brows narrowed. "I think you and I and Mr. Cassidy need to sit down together and have a nice long talk. But after we take care of this trouble." He extended a hand. "You're a doctor? Come with me. There may be injuries."

Nora took his hand and allowed him to help her out of the crater. He directed several men to assist Owen, then beckoned for Nora to follow.

The trouble wasn't hard to find. Smoke still rose from a collapsed section of mine not far off, and the acrid smell pricked

Nora's nose as they approached. Men scurried here and there, pulling hoses and carrying buckets of water, dampening the entire area around the accident.

"Mr. Cardot!" A man rushed up to Nora's escort. "A few injuries, sir. No fatalities. The accident occurred in an unoccupied section of the tunnel. I can't say for certain, but it looks as though the irrigation machine may have broken down. Was dry as a bone. We're hosing it down now."

Mr. Cardot nodded. "This young lady is a doctor. Please escort her to the wounded men and see she is given whatever supplies she requests. I will take over the investigation."

"Yes, sir. This way, please, miss." He squirmed. "Um, sorry, Doctor."

Half-a-dozen men had sustained injuries ranging from superficial to serious, and within minutes Nora had thrown herself into her work: cleaning, stitching, setting bones, and wrapping wounds. Time passed unheeded, and when she at last tucked away her supplies and looked up, it was to find Owen Cassidy staring down at her, wearing an expression she'd never seen on his face before. It almost looked like… respect.

"Thank you, Dr. Taylor, for assisting my men. You may send your bill to my office in St. Louis. It will be attended to promptly."

Nora's brows rose. "There is no fee."

"Nonsense."

"It was an emergency situation, I was a medical specialist at the scene. It was my duty to assist, and I need no further reward than seeing the injured men bandaged and on the mend."

"A do-gooder, are you?"

The sarcasm in his voice made her scowl. "And what, pray tell, is wrong with that?"

"Nothing," Owen replied. "If it were genuine. But I've found through the years that most people are only looking out for themselves. And those who claim to do things 'for the good of humanity' are the worst of all."

"Hmm." Nora placed her hands on her hips. "And you have oh-so-many years of experience."

"I'm thirty-three," he retorted, "and I started this business when I was eighteen. I have experience enough."

"Well, I'm thirty-seven, so I have more."

His brow furrowed. "You can't be thirty-seven."

Nora rolled her eyes. Supposedly she ought to be pleased when people underestimated her age, but in truth she merely found it annoying. "I have an exacting skin-care regimen." Which was true, but it was because she found the moisturizing lotion soothing. Looking good was nice, certainly, but feeling good was better.

Mr. Cassidy made a harumphing sound and folded his arms across his chest. "Very well, Doctor. You've lived longer. But a long life of luxury is a far cry from one of honest hard work. If you value work, you understand its worth and you'll take my money."

"Fine." She'd let him have this. It couldn't hurt anything and he had the funds to spare. "But it could be some time before I'm able to attend to such business. I was only in St. Louis to visit family before I stumbled upon you. I live and work in Savannah, but I won't be able to return to my regular practice until I've seen you through your full recovery. It could be some weeks, yet. Perhaps a month."

His jaw clenched and his eyes narrowed. "Give me a list of the damned exercises. I'll do them. But I have work to do."

"Perhaps I can help." She'd keep offering until she wore him down. "Explain to me what's been happening and point me in the direction of the problems. Perhaps you might have a moment's peace if you give me a suitable task."

He stared into her eyes for a long moment, and she watched the expression on his face shift from frustration to calculation to acceptance. "Very well. Come with me. You and I and Mr. Cardot are going to have a long talk."

Nora smiled. Victory. "Excellent. While we do that, you can begin exercise number one."

6

OWEN HAD LEARNED a thing or two in his years of business, and one of those things was not to waste time and resources fighting losing battles. He had other priorities right now. If Dr. Taylor insisted on helping, he'd let her. She'd patched up his men, after all, and there was a chance she would make herself useful elsewhere. If not, eventually the mining operation would wear on her rich-lady sensibilities and she'd leave.

The site of the explosion had been safely hosed down by the time the trio arrived on the scene. Owen tapped out the doctor's exercise pattern against his thigh as he surveyed the damage. Bits of twisted metal—remnants of another irrigation machine—lay scattered amidst the rubble where a portion of the ceiling had collapsed. The yellow-green rock walls were charred and blackened. He could find no obvious signs of further imminent collapse, but given the unstable nature of the terrain, this portion of the mine would have to be shut down until braces could be installed to stabilize the tunnel.

More money spent. Fine. He had plenty of that. But the time, resources, manpower; such a waste. It would hurt their production rates. They'd not meet the demand from the luxene distributors, and the fallout would hurt his workers.

"We need to stop this before we lose the Pure-Lux contract," he fumed. The powerhouse distribution company was Owen's biggest customer, and many smaller distributors mimicked its every move.

Cardot nodded. "Tagget has the resources to open his own mining operation if he's not satisfied with ours. And word is he's still got some mad notion about running motorcars on luxene."

"Luxene. The fuel of the frivolous," Dr. Taylor muttered.

Owen glared at her. While he didn't entirely disagree, this was his livelihood, and a growing industry that employed thousands. "That frivolous fuel provides jobs and feeds families, Doctor, and I'd thank you not to belittle my life's work."

As always, she met his angry stare with unflappable calm. "Try to lift your arm just a bit higher while you do that exercise. Here."

She gripped his arm and bent the elbow, then pushed his artificial shoulder back into a more relaxed position. Every touch sent shivers of delight through his body. Had the biomechanics made the arm more sensitive? Or was it her? Perhaps merely a reaction to his recent near-death experience? Regardless, it was damned inconvenient, this senseless lust. Owen gritted his teeth, trying to think of anything but her.

"Is it uncomfortable?" she asked, a little puzzled frown puckering her lips.

"No," he bit out, stepping away from her and resuming the finger exercises.

She turned away. "Why is it so wet in here?" Another timely change of subject. Smart woman.

Cardot offered the explanation. "The raw luxene is a soft, powdery rock. The dry dust is highly explosive. But when dissolved in water, it becomes stable and safe. We use sprayers to keep the mines and the ore moist during digging and transport to the refinery."

"So this sprayer malfunctioned." She nudged a bit of the broken irrigator with the toe of her boot.

"Or was sabotaged," Owen snarled. "Far too many breakdowns in the past month to be coincidence."

"And the machines have all been recently inspected," Cardot added. "Not a case of old hardware or incomplete repairs."

Dr. Taylor nodded. "Do you have any idea who might be tampering with the equipment?"

"Ghosts."

Owen and the doctor both looked at Cardot with raised eyebrows.

"That's what the men are saying," he explained. "Ghosts or spirits of men who died in these caverns. Some say the mines are cursed, or you are."

Owen's fists clenched. Or, rather, his left fist did. The fingers on his right hand only curled a bit. "Superstitious nonsense."

"Mmm. But the question is: would you rather they believe in ghosts and curses, or believe a very human someone is trying to ruin the business and kill you?"

Owen swore under his breath. "We need to stop this, and we need to stop it now. I'll hire an investigator to deal with the… incident in St. Louis. Here, we need to tighten security, again, and do full inspections on all the machinery."

"I can help with mechanical inspections and repairs," Dr. Taylor offered. "I have a good eye for small flaws and delicate repairs from my biomechanical work."

"Fine," Owen grunted. He didn't want her around, but it seemed he needed her. Already his fingers felt more nimble. With more of her exercises, maybe he could have his arm working in a matter of days. The trouble would be in convincing the men having a woman on site wouldn't add to the recent string of bad luck. "Follow me."

It quickly became clear that despite her perfect skin and pristine clothing, Dr. Taylor did not possess any rich-lady sensibilities. Clearly blood didn't bother her, but neither did dirt, sweat, foul language, or gawking working-class men.

She flung herself into the work, handling oily machines with care but no squeamishness or hesitation, inspecting each piece in minute detail before making adjustments to screws, bolts, hinges, and more.

Owen couldn't keep up. He'd done every job there was to do here, but his true skills lay in directing, organizing, and running the business. He was good with plans, logistics, and money. Today, with his right arm hanging broken at his side, he'd become little more than a useless observer. Worst of all was her knowing smile as he struggled to help as much as possible one-armed and left-handed.

"My findings," she announced hours later, as he walked her toward the exit gate. She handed him a crumpled, grease-stained slip of paper with an indecipherable scrawl on it.

Owen stared at the paper for a minute before looking at Dr. Taylor. The setting sun bathed her pretty face in a warm glow, highlighting the red in her pale hair. If she'd been any other woman in any other place, he might have asked for a kiss. Instead he asked, "What the hell does this say?"

She pointed at her writing, heaving a sigh. "Missing screws or bolts: fifteen. Loose screws or bolts: twenty-five. Hairline fractures: four. Bent or warped springs, gears, hinges: seven."

Owen nodded, able now to make out some of the words.

"What it doesn't say there is that all of these issues were from recently inspected machines, and located in natural weak points," she continued. "The most delicate and intricate parts of every apparatus were the faultiest, meaning something as simple as a bump or even normal operation could cause a catastrophic failure. I have not the slightest doubt someone tampered with your equipment. And whoever it was is an engineer. They know machines."

Owen nodded, trying to tamp down his impotent fury. Who would do such a thing? Who would endanger his men? And why?

"Thank you for the report. Cardot is arranging for

additional security so it won't happen again. We may have to set up a tighter inspection schedule. And I'll have to go to the refinery tomorrow and begin an even bigger inspection on the equipment there."

"I'd be happy to accompany you."

That sugar-coated smile. Owen wasn't sure whether he loved it or hated it. He flexed the fingers of his right hand. "I'm sure you would."

"Tonight you should rest. You've been much busier than is good for you. You'll need a nutritious dinner and a long night of sleep. Tomorrow we can begin the next series of exercises."

"Right." Much as he didn't like to admit it, Owen was exhausted. His entire body ached, he couldn't suppress his yawns any longer, and his concentration had begun to slip. It was time to head home. After all, what was the purpose of his nice house on Lafayette Park if he never used it? "Come with me, Doctor. You're welcome to ride with me in my motorcar back to the city. My driver will be happy to drop you wherever you wish. Where are you staying during your visit?"

"Well, I *was* staying with family," she replied. Her smile turned impish.

"You were." He frowned at her, his stomach churning with apprehension. He wasn't going to like what she said next. "And now?"

"Now, I'm staying with you."

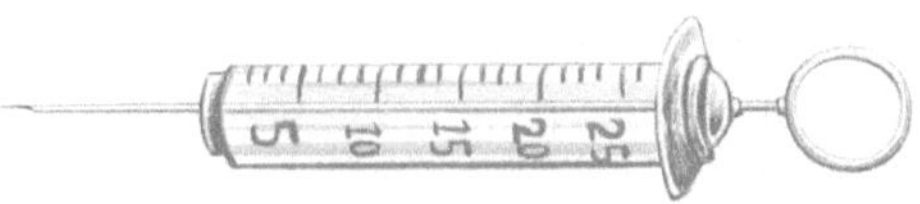

IT TOOK NORA several startled seconds to remember she wasn't in a hotel.

Oh. That's right. I invited myself to the home of one of the richest men in St. Louis.

And for some reason he hadn't protested.

No one had. Her brother hadn't sounded the least bit surprised when she'd telephoned and asked to have her things sent to Mr. Cassidy's home. Her family had long ago accepted her eccentricities. She was too old and too unusual for anyone to care where she went and with whom. New York society was hundreds of miles away. Too far to make her a source of embarrassment for the family members who moved in those elite circles. Besides, no one here knew her. Even if whispers of scandal started flying, they'd vanish once she resumed her normal life in Savannah. This would have no effect on her future work.

Nora stretched, taking a moment to survey her surroundings. The room was beautifully appointed, the strange bed comfortable, with soft sheets. Everything from the furniture to the draperies appeared of the highest quality, though none of it was opulent nor gaudy.

Owen Cassidy was a man of contradictions. He sneered at the wealthy, and styled himself a working man, yet here he was, living in a fine house in a fine neighborhood, and filling it with beautiful, expensive things. Clearly he didn't eschew all trappings of wealth.

His money was well-spent, certainly. Nora's own tastes ran along similar lines. She liked well-made things and didn't mind paying a high price for them. What she didn't like was anything made simply to show off. She wanted to be known for her work, not her money.

"Mr. Cassidy and I are quite similar in many ways, I think," she said with a smile, climbing from the bed to greet the dawn.

Despite the way they'd clashed, she'd already begun to like him. She could imagine them becoming friends. Nora would wager that he, too, liked to rise early and begin working promptly. Today, though, he'd be asleep for some time.

She dressed for the day, then took a leisurely breakfast in the dining room, attended by Owen's efficient, but suspicious staff. Like their employer, they were terse and gruff. They met Nora's smiles with tight lips and narrowed brows, flirting with rudeness without ignoring her completely.

The morning papers made no mention of the explosion at the mine yesterday, nor of any other recent troubles. She read the entire paper through without finding a single mention of Owen Cassidy or his company. Interesting. Did he deliberately work to keep his name out of the news, or was he simply too uninteresting to mention now that he was no longer "missing and feared dead"?

Nora didn't find him uninteresting in the slightest. In fact, she found him rather fascinating. His business meant everything to him, but why? For the money he acted as if he didn't want? How had he come to have an enemy who wanted to destroy him, and who was that enemy? What other secrets lay beneath his hard, mistrustful shell?

A broad grin spread across her face. Getting to know Owen better would be a delight. She'd always liked a good mystery. She read far too many true crime reports and sensational police news stories. And some of her previous patients had been pirates and smugglers.

"Why the hell didn't anyone wake me?" Owen's voice reverberated off the walls as he stormed into the room. He poured himself a large mug of coffee, snarled at it for being lukewarm, and then turned his angry gaze on Nora. "Did you tell my staff not to wake me?"

A young woman bustled in with a tray of food, placing it on the table near Owen. He didn't sit.

"You never said we were to wake you, sir," the girl said. "And Trask said you looked like you needed the rest. Sir." She nodded and scurried off.

Owen cursed and grabbed some of the food from the plate, still not sitting. "It's half past nine, dammit. I should have been at the refinery hours ago. God knows what's happened there without me."

"You don't trust anyone, do you?" Nora asked.

"What are you talking about? And what the hell do you think you're doing here, Doctor? Do you think I run some sort of hotel?"

"You said last night I could stay."

"A moment of weakness," he grumbled.

Nora shook her head to hide her smile. "You won't stay in bed and recuperate, so I intend to follow you until at least the first three weeks are up and I'm certain you've adjusted to the biomechanics. In the meantime, I'm happy to help you investigate your troubles."

"You're the most aggravating woman I've ever met." He grabbed a bit more breakfast then turned and walked out of the room, eating as he went.

Nora abandoned her newspaper and followed him out the front door. Owen tapped his foot impatiently while a driver pulled up in a Studebaker electric motorcar. Owen held the door for Nora, then climbed into the backseat beside her, muttering something under his breath.

"Are you annoyed by my presence," she asked, "or are you annoyed you can't drive your own car with your arm not fully healed?"

"I'm annoyed that I'm late," he snapped. His eyes, though, were fixed on the steering wheel. He wanted to drive. He took pride in this vehicle. He could probably deliver an hour-long lecture on why electric power was preferable to steam.

"Next exercise," she offered as a distraction. "Pinch your thumb and first finger together. Then the next finger and so on. Try to squeeze tightly, as if you were grabbing something. By the end of the day we want you able to hold something tightly enough in your fist that I can't pull it out."

He grunted, but started the exercise. Nora wouldn't say anything about it, but he wasn't as unreasonable as he acted. He did listen to what she had to say and was even willing to change his mind, so long as his own concerns remained the priority. Stubborn, but not obtuse.

The luxene refinery was situated at the edge of town, right along the river, with easy access to both steam barges and the railroad. Outside the building, busy men loaded massive barrels of fuel into shipping containers for transport to distributors across the country.

"Does anyone buy the luxene directly from you?" she inquired.

"No. The distributors all run it through purifying machines these days, ever since Tagget came up with the idea to save his hide after the Dynalux fiasco. They package it up nice and clean in fancy bottles in sizes people can afford."

"What will happen when your mine runs empty?"

He shrugged. "I'll open a new one. I own luxene-rich land all up and down the river."

"Oh. Is it more common than people believe, then?"

"I only know of it in caves and rocky formations along the Mississippi. But my guess is it's like gold. People will find it elsewhere and we'll get one rush after another."

"Hmm. But no one currently owns any competing mines?"

"Not yet."

"No possible enemies there, then. Any issues with the distributors?"

"None. They turn a good profit and so do I. No changes to any contracts lately, no new customers, no loss of old ones."

"And your workers? Are they part of any labor union? Have they ever threatened a strike?"

His entire six and a half feet stiffened in outrage. "Absolutely not! I pay a fair wage with reasonable hours and safe conditions. If any union man has a gripe with me, I'd thank him to come down here and have it out face-to-face. I have never and will never exploit my men."

"Even so, it's always possible to have a disgruntled worker. Someone who doesn't fit in well with your system, perhaps, and interprets his discomfort as your wrongdoing."

Owen took her arm to help her from the car, practically hauling her off toward the main refinery building. "Come with me. You can see for yourself we don't have those sorts of troubles. Men who don't fit in don't get hired."

"Ah. Perhaps a disgruntled applicant who was turned away."

"Who is smart enough to gain access to the premises, knows enough about machines to tamper with them, and hates me enough to want me dead? I don't believe it."

Nora shook her head. "If you follow crime at all, Mr. Cassidy, you'd know that motive plays a vital role. I am speculating, of course, but if we can determine what might drive someone to do these things, we might in turn be able to pinpoint the villain himself."

"Owen!" a young man's voice called. "I expected you here hours ago."

Owen froze. A man who could only be a relation of some sort strode swiftly in their direction. He was nearly as tall as

Owen, though lankier, and possessed of the same clear, brown eyes and the same strong jaw.

"Timothy. What are you doing here?"

"I came to help inspect the machinery," the young man replied. "I heard you were doing that today. But I expected you sooner. I've been here over an hour."

"Heard from whom?" Owen growled.

"The men at the mine. I stopped by yesterday evening, just after you left, apparently. Wanted to check on things, after all the strange mishaps."

"That mine is no place for you."

Timothy rolled his eyes. "I'm not a porcelain doll, big brother." He put the slightest sneer on the last two words.

"I don't want you there. And I don't want you here, either. Go back to school."

"School is a dam—" His eyes flicked to Nora. "Dashed waste of time. Even the advanced engineering classes are below my level. I'm not learning anything new. I'm dropping out."

"Like hell you are!" Owen's right arm twitched. He reached to grab Timothy with his left arm instead, but the younger man darted out of reach.

"You did."

"I had to. You don't. I didn't work all these years to give you a better life so you can throw it all away."

"I'm not—"

"Enough. We're not discussing this now. Go home. I'll come by this evening to see you and Mother."

Timothy merely smirked. "So you're not even going to introduce me to your lady friend?"

A muscle in Owen's jaw twitched. "Timothy, this is Dr. Eleanor Taylor, biomechanologist. Dr. Taylor, this is my very much younger brother, Mr. Timothy Cassidy."

Nora smiled at the boy. "Pleased to meet you, Mr. Cassidy."

"Call me Tim." He grinned, the gleeful expression almost shocking on a face that looked so much like Owen's. He had dimples. Did Owen have dimples? Did Owen ever smile? Or laugh? The man needed more happiness in his life.

"I'm Nora. You're a student of engineering?"

"Yes. I've been tinkering since I was a child and I ought to have a job by now, but my brother is rather obsessed with 'proper education.'" Tim offered his arm to Nora and they began to walk toward the refinery, leaving Owen scowling behind them. Tim lowered his voice. "I think he may have picked me up and literally thrown me out if you weren't here, so thank you."

Nora chuckled. "Don't be too hard on him. He's had a rough week."

"Oh?" He edged closer. "Tell me everything. He never does."

Nora glanced back at Owen. His scowl hadn't changed, but he moved his fingers in the new exercise pattern as he stormed after them. "He can be reasonable if you give him a chance."

"Yeah, right. You're too optimistic, Nora."

She'd heard that so many times in her life. *Too optimistic. Too idealistic.* As if finding the good in people and striving for a better world was a bad thing. She believed in good. She believed in hope. She believed she could make a difference.

Today that difference would come from ensuring the safety of the equipment and keeping Owen on the path to recovery. Those would be easy compared to her third, more ambitious goal: make Owen Cassidy smile.

8

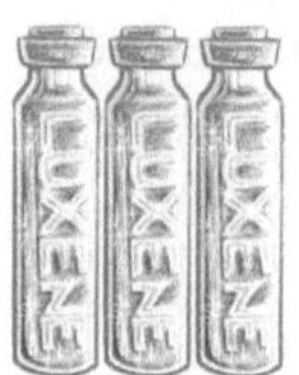

I SHOULD HAVE sent him off to Harvard.

No, no. Too far. Timothy would have grown bored there, too, and be running amok without Owen nearby to keep an eye on him. Right now, though, Owen understood the appeal of far distant schools. Maybe the University of California. Or the Sorbonne.

The rascal was brazenly flirting with Dr. Taylor. Grasping her arm, whispering, laughing. For the love of God, she was nearly twice his age! Had he no shame?

The worst part was that they looked good together. Natural. At ease. Far more companionable than she'd ever been with Owen.

Nora. The nickname fit her so well. Cute. Bouncy, like her short hair. But there was something strong about the name, too. Determined and independent, but sweet and happy.

"Nora."

It felt good on his tongue. Much better than the stiff "Dr. Taylor." It rankled that she'd never offered him the name. Not that he'd given her any reason to. Maybe she'd be hanging on his arm now if he'd smiled and made use of the long eyelashes he'd been teased about as a boy.

Owen didn't have the luxury of flirtation. He had no time for frivolous wooing. He had responsibilities. A family and a business to look after. And wasn't the whole point to allow Timothy to have the life Owen never could? To let him have those young and carefree years? It was the promise Owen had given to his dying father. He would be the man. He would be the adult who made certain his mother and baby brother had everything George Cassidy could no longer guarantee them.

Besides, you have no right to be snarling like a jealous lover.

Theirs was a temporary business arrangement. Surely Nora could lure any man she desired. She was intelligent and hard-working. Fearless. Bold enough to barge into his home uninvited. Much too much for a naive youngster like Timothy. Perhaps it was best to part them after all.

"The machinery is quite ingenious," Tim was saying when Owen caught up to them. "As you can see, the raw luxene ore is loaded here, where it passes through a series of grinders which break it down into a fine dust."

"Slurry," Owen corrected. "Dust is too volatile. We keep everything wet throughout the entire process. When it comes out at the end, it's a thick paste."

Timothy scowled at him. "The *paste* is then transferred to the next machine, where it is fully dissolved in water, in the exact proportions to make the fuel people use every day."

"None of the machines appear to be running," Nora observed.

"I had them all shut down," Owen explained. "Full inspections first. I won't have a repeat of the mine explosion here."

"Sensible. Well, let's get started. Tim, why don't you begin here, and I'll start at the opposite end. We can meet in the middle to discuss our findings."

Nora jogged off to begin her inspection, Owen right on her heels.

"Whose refinery do you think this is?" he demanded.

"You agreed to allow me to help. I'm helping."

Owen glanced back at his brother and lowered his voice. "Helping by letting a child participate, against my obvious wishes?"

She crossed her arms beneath her breasts. Her corset today was of a more conventional style, and it thrust her bosom up in a manner Owen couldn't have failed to notice unless he was dead.

"He's hardly a child, Owen. And he seems highly intelligent."

"He is. He's brilliant. But that doesn't mean he has a lick of sense in his head. He needs to be in school."

"I think you need to give him a chance to prove himself. All I had to do was glance at him to know he desperately wants you to see him as a man, not a boy. Now, if you'll excuse me, I have work to do." She dug into her pocket and withdrew pen, paper, and a screwdriver. "And I believe you have some exercises to continue."

Well, I'm not going to make him smile this way, Nora thought, giving a rueful shake of her head. How unfortunate that they always seemed to be at odds. She was sure they could find common ground if only they could make their way into a civilized conversation.

Someday. She wouldn't give up on him.

Nora ran her fingers over the smooth metal of the dissolving machine. "Is it empty? We will need to inspect the inside as well."

"It should be empty," Owen replied. "There are blades inside each compartment to circulate the water. The tank opens at the top. I'll fetch a ladder."

His relief at having a way to be useful was palpable. Nora made a mental note to jot down ideas for tasks he could take on during his recovery. Putting him in a positive emotional state would make the recovery feel faster.

She let her eyes rove across the refinery as she waited for him. The men moving carts and barrels worked steadily and efficiently. No one showed obvious signs of discontent, and the facility was clean and safe as far as she could tell. Nothing suggested a possible labor union issue. It seemed she could trust Owen's word on that, even if his perspective as the business owner might be biased.

The workers were a varied group. Some were as young as Tim, others older and grizzled. Men of different races worked side-by-side in harmony. Did anyone object to that? She'd witnessed incidents of racial strife in Savannah. She could believe someone might want the business to fail over a refusal to segregate. She added the idea to her list of motives, though it was no more likely than the others. Thus far her investigation seemed doomed to failure.

Nora finished her inspection of the outside of the tank while Owen fetched and positioned the ladder, then climbed up to take a peek inside. Unlike at the mine, she spied no cracks and no loose or missing fasteners.

"I'm seeing no signs of tampering," she said, hoisting herself out of the tank and scrambling down the ladder. "Is security here tighter than at the mine?"

"The building is always locked when the last shift leaves for the night," Owen replied, "but the mines are fenced off and locked, too. Breaking into either is hardly impossible, but it's not easy."

"Hmm. Perhaps easy with the right tools. I've heard of mechanical devices that can open locks faster than a master thief."

Owen's dark eyebrows arched. "That so?"

"Yes. I've known a few pirates in my lifetime."

His brows climbed even higher. "Pirates."

"Indeed."

He shook his head and grabbed hold of the ladder, easily

moving it to the next section of the machine with his single good arm. "Sometimes I wonder about you, Doctor."

Nora set one foot on the bottom rung. "Oh, good. Because I wonder about you all the time."

He said nothing further as she climbed up to continue her inspection. A silent sort of man, was Owen Cassidy. Nora didn't mind, but she did wonder what it might take to get him talking, and whether it would be more or less difficult than getting him to smile. Achieving both at once would be a true victory.

"We should remind Tim to pay close attention to any parts that are delicate or intricate," she suggested. "Most of the flaws in the mine machinery were in such places."

Owen made a grunting noise that conveyed neither approval nor disapproval.

Nora looked down at him. "Shall you tell him, or shall I?" When he didn't reply, she started down the ladder.

"I'll tell—" Owen's words were lost beneath a sharp crack from overhead.

A chunk of metal clanged to the floor.

"I didn't do it!" Tim cried.

Before anyone could reply, a section of the ceiling gave way, raining debris on the unprepared people below. Nora covered her head and screamed as the ladder fell away beneath her.

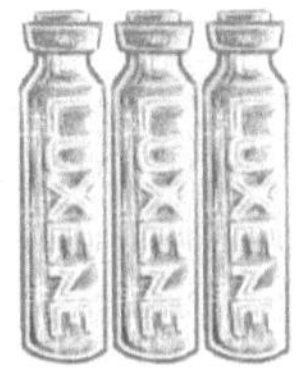

9

For an instant, Owen forgot his arm didn't work. Unfortunately, it was the same instant he attempted to catch Nora as she toppled from the ladder.

Instead of gracefully plucking her from the air and sweeping her beneath the protective shield of his body, he got one arm under her, jerked in bafflement when his right arm didn't move, and crumpled in a tangled heap with her atop him.

As shards of metal and wood cascaded from the sky, Owen dragged Nora underneath him, curling around her and ducking his head to protect himself. Another instant and it was over, the air silent, the world still. Owen didn't move. His body stung in places where he'd been struck by the falling debris, but nothing felt severely damaged. Nora trembled in his arms. Alive. Thank God.

He pushed himself up with his good arm, looking her over for signs of injury. A sliver of metal jutted from her left arm, blood staining the white cloth of her sleeve around it.

"Don't move," he ordered. "I'll get a doctor."

She started to sit up. "I'm fine. It's just a small gash."

He reached to push her back down, his hand freezing mere inches from her breasts. Dammit. He couldn't touch her like that. How was he supposed to keep her from getting up and harming herself? Doctors made terrible patients, he'd been told.

"Stay down," he barked, clambering to his feet.

Timothy jogged over, his cheeks red, but apparently unharmed. "Nora, are you hurt? I swear I didn't do it. Something cracked above me while I was atop the machine, and…"

His eyes lifted to the ceiling. Owen's gaze followed. Above them, a perfectly square hole gaped in the roof, as if someone had cut a skylight. Clear, deliberate sabotage. The villain wasn't even trying to disguise what he'd done.

Owen shook with rage. He spun toward his brother. "I told you this was no place for you, dammit! You could have been killed!"

Timothy gaped at him. "Wha—"

"Out! Get out! And don't come back!"

Yes, he was being high-handed. Unreasonable, even. But, by God, he was going to keep his brother safe from this mess. Owen whirled away before Timothy could protest, motioning to his men. He spared a glance for Nora, who had ignored his orders and had risen to her feet, clutching her injured arm to her chest.

"Any other injuries?" he asked.

"No, sir," a worker replied. "You three were the only ones in the immediate area when the collapse happened."

Owen nodded. He looked to one of his foremen. "Shut down the entire building. Send everyone home. I'll have a repair crew on site as soon as possible. Please excuse me. I need to take Dr. Taylor to receive medical attention."

Without another word, he gripped Nora's right arm with his left, and began to escort her off the premises. Her silence said as much as her pale complexion: she was unwell. By the time they were halfway to his car, she was shaking.

Owen scooped her up in an awkward, one-armed carry, bracing her on his hip as if he were a mother carrying a small child. Maybe the men were right. Maybe he *was* cursed. It would explain why every physical interaction between himself and Nora involved one or the other of them wounded or in danger.

"It's like one of those 'be careful what you wish for' warnings," he muttered.

"What is?"

She wasn't insensible. That was a good sign. Except now he had to explain his thoughts.

"I wished for the touch of a beautiful woman. Unfortunately, we can only touch when one of us is afflicted with grievous bodily harm."

Nora laughed. "It's not grievous. It's only a little gash."

Right. A little gash that had her on the verge of passing out. Still, her laugh was a beautiful thing, and he warmed a bit inside to think he'd drawn it out of her at a trying time.

The "little gash" took a dozen stitches to close, and the surgeon who patched her up warned her to rest for several days to recover from the wound and the blood loss. From the expression on her face, she was as pleased by those instructions as Owen was by her demands he remain abed for two weeks. As they departed, Nora stubbornly marching on her own two feet, he felt a chuckle rumbling deep in his chest.

He turned to grin at her, his left hand poised to assist her should she falter. "Well, my dear Doctor—"

She staggered to a halt and Owen grabbed her arm to keep her upright, all traces of amusement vanishing.

"Are you all right?" he asked.

"You were smiling," she gasped. "Do that again."

"What?"

"You were smiling! Why were you smiling? Do it again. I want to be sure I wasn't hallucinating."

Owen assisted her into his car, uncertain if he would be able to recapture the moment of happiness he'd experienced before she stumbled. "I was smiling because I was thinking how much you and I…" And there it was. This time he laughed aloud.

"You're a hypocrite, Doctor. You berate me for my stubborn refusal to sit still and heal, when you are exactly the same."

"Lovely," she muttered. "I finally make you smile and it's only to poke fun at me. And here I was, hoping you might actually possess a sense of humor."

Owen chuckled again. "Ah, but how do you know I don't? Perhaps you should try telling a joke." His expression grew serious. "I do owe you an apology. I've been a terrible patient, and I'm seeing things from your perspective now. You will understand why I can't abandon my work at the moment, but I promise to better heed your advice, and I hope you will look to your own recovery as well."

She harrumphed, but her lips twitched upward. "Why, Owen Cassidy, are you certain you didn't take a blow to the head when that roof caved in?"

"Ha ha." His smile broadened, enough that his dimples would show. Were they becoming friends?

When was the last time he'd smiled like this? He was teasing and being teased in return. He couldn't even remember that happening before. Strangely enough, he liked it.

But it's all with a woman who has declared herself one hundred percent uninterested, he reminded himself. *You can befriend her, but no making advances.*

Silence descended once again as they rode back to his townhouse, and along with it came a bone-deep exhaustion. She'd been right, dammit. Even with the extra sleep this morning, his body wasn't ready for the stress and exertion of today's events. Right now he wanted nothing more than to lie down and sleep.

Unfortunately, he couldn't properly rest until the crisis was over. His production was now entirely at a stand-still. His men would be safe at home, but without the business running, their livelihoods would be in jeopardy.

Nora appeared content to sit and rest as long as he remained within her sight, so he had a comfortable chair brought into his study for her, and he set to work making phone calls. She didn't interrupt, not even to remind him about his finger exercises, and he found himself wishing she would say something. Anything. She was tired, too, and involved now in a mess that should have had nothing to do with her.

Owen lifted the phone receiver again, tempted to call the train station for a one-way ticket to Savannah, Georgia. Instead, he requested a private number in New York, one very few people had access to. Owen had never liked needing help, but he knew when he did. And this time, he needed someone he could be absolutely certain valued the continued prosperity of Cassidy Mining.

The phone call took several minutes to go through, but at last a man's voice said, "Good afternoon, Mr. Cassidy. What can I do for you?"

Owen hadn't given his name, and he didn't want to think too hard about how he had been identified.

"Mr. Tagget," he replied. "I need to consult with you on a matter that affects both our businesses."

IO

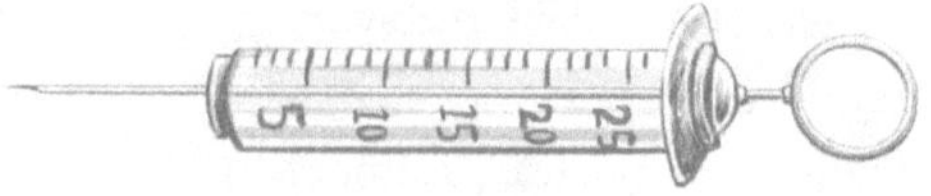

NORA COULD NO LONGER tell where the hole in the ceiling had been. She walked through the refinery with her head tipped back, eyeing the new equipment that had been installed. Owen hovered behind her, prepared to catch her if she tripped and fell, she suspected. He had a savior complex. Always wanting to rush in and protect everyone. Which did make sense for a man who had taken on the role of provider for his family at such a young and impressionable age. Lina would probably have even more to say on the matter from her psychotherapist perspective.

None of which Owen was likely to heed, unfortunately. Nora couldn't blame him too much for that. She wouldn't like it if anyone laid all her faults bare and made her confront them, either.

"Are those cameras?" she asked, pointing at one of the boxes that a Tagget Industries man was busily affixing to a ceiling beam.

"Yes. They will be positioned to capture images of any intruders who might tamper with the machinery. There should be one at the entrance to my office low enough for us to examine, if you'd like."

"Please."

Owen crooked his right arm to escort her. He'd yet to recover full range of motion and his usual strength, but he'd made great strides during the past several days.

They'd settled into a companionable sort of partnership since her injury. Not quite a friendship, perhaps, but a mutual respect and civilized collaboration. Nora found herself growing more fond of him with every passing day. Whatever his faults, Owen was a man who cared for others.

As repairs and inspections were conducted and security measures implemented, Nora and Owen watched and supervised. They sat and rested as much as was practical, following the proper procedures for the care and rehabilitation of their injuries.

She hadn't caught him smiling again, but she'd been contemplating jokes she might try out on him. She *would* bring back that smile. It was far too glorious a thing to be so rare. Wide and playful, with big dimples and shining eyes. He had a face made for smiling and it saddened her to think life had made him all seriousness and responsibility.

"Here we are," Owen declared. "Appears to be in place and operational."

Nora turned her attention from his countenance to the camera. An ingenious device, compact and well-built, with a small, wide-angle lens and an array of sensors she would have liked to dissect and examine.

"A good design," she observed. "More of a deterrent or a way to identify the villain after the crime than an actual preventative, though."

"Yes. They are meant to work in tandem with some of the other devices being installed today. I'm hoping to view those as well. I know there are vibration alarms on the roof and at the windows."

"The ones used at that Paris art exhibition? They made all the scientific journals."

"Yes. Those exactly."

"I'd like to see them. Are they powered with luxene?"

Owen's mouth twitched into a near smile. Too wry to count, in Nora's opinion, and it didn't display his dimples at all. "Yes. So I'd best get production up and running again. I've exhausted nearly all of my reserves fulfilling recent orders and any disruption in the supply chain will drive prices up."

"That's why I don't use luxene in any of my biomechanics. Too rare, too expensive."

"Yes. The fuel of the frivolous. You've told me."

She steered the conversation back on track to avoid any argument. "What of other security measures? No guard dragons?"

Owen shook his head. "Tagget thinks guard dragons are useless. I'm working entirely on the recommendation of his security team."

"And his engineers were the ones conducting the equipment inspections and repairs the last few days?"

"They were."

Nora crossed her arms over her chest. "I don't mean to criticize your decision… Actually, yes, I do. How can you give a security contract to a man who installed spy devices in every telephone office in the country?"

"If my business fails, Pure-Lux fails. It's to his advantage to assist us."

"What if he's the villain? What if his nefarious plan is to drive your company into the ground and then buy it for pennies so he can have his own mining operation without doing any of the work of starting one?" She dug into her pocket for the small notebook where she had begun to organize her crime notes. "It's by far the best motive of any we've thought up."

"It *is* an excellent plan," a voice with a distinct northern accent said from somewhere behind them. "Delightfully nefarious of me."

Nora whirled around. Evan Tagget was as handsome as in his photographs, though shorter and slenderer than she would have guessed. He held himself with an air of supreme confidence. Combined with his stark black, exquisitely tailored suit, it made him nearly as imposing as Owen, despite being barely half his size.

"Too bad it's not true," Tagget continued. "It would do wonders for my reputation."

The woman beside him—with dark hair, golden-brown skin, and a flouncy, knee-length dress of swirled blues and purples—jabbed him in the ribs with her elbow. Tagget tilted his head and grinned at her, his smile so full of genuine adoration Nora rocked back on her heels in shock.

Tagget's sudden and surprising marriage had been in all the papers, naturally. They'd said it was a love match. Now that Nora saw the evidence with her own eyes, she absolutely agreed.

Tagget took his wife's hand, interlacing their fingers as if it were the most natural thing in the world. "But I've neglected introductions," he murmured. "Vi, my love, this is Mr. Owen Cassidy, the force behind luxene, and Dr. Eleanor Taylor, esteemed biomechanologist. Mr. Cassidy, Dr. Taylor, this blossom of utter perfection is my wife, renowned artist Violet Dayton Tagget."

Mrs. Tagget rolled her eyes at her husband's flowery compliment, but her smile held the same deep affection his had.

Nora wasn't sure which was more disconcerting: that Tagget knew exactly who she was or that he and his wife were so clearly passionately in love.

Nora didn't understand romantic love any more than she understood sexual attraction. From a scientific standpoint they made sense of course, but on a personal level they remained an enigma.

The memory of her one significant attraction played through her mind. At that time, she'd thought, *At last! This is what everyone talks about!* Until the one-sided nature of the affection had come crashing down on her with sudden, agonizing finality.

She'd consoled herself that she was better off without such

feelings. Who would want to be falling in love all the time if it were as awful as her one disappointing experience? And what use was sexual attraction except an inconvenient urge one couldn't satisfy without risking pregnancy or disease?

Seeing the Taggets, however, roused old questions in the back of her mind. What would it be like, to feel that way and have those feelings reciprocated? What would it be like to look at someone and feel the desire to kiss them and touch them and know you could?

Nora was so lost in her thoughts that a long moment passed before she realized the conversation had continued on without her.

"…Will be departing soon," Tagget said. "I have a friend up in Michigan who's been dying to meet Violet. We'll be returning to Paris after our visit. I don't think New York is quite ready to welcome me back with open arms."

"Scandal still hasn't died down?" Owen's brows lifted in surprise. "With Pure-Lux doing so well, I thought your reputation had improved."

"It's not that," Violet explained. "Evan recently publicly humiliated a rising New York politician. Ruined his campaign."

Tagget smirked. "Considering what he called you and what he called me, I'd say his punishment was rather lenient." He turned his attention back to Owen and Nora. "But enough about me. I stopped by to bring you a new innovation." He withdrew a small, rectangular device from his coat pocket. "It's a thermal sensor. Sensitive enough to detect a cow at two hundred yards."

Nora and Owen looked at one another. Owen shrugged, then looked back at Tagget. "A cow."

"We were in Australia. Surrounded by farms. Regardless, two hundred yards. But the sensitivity can be adjusted to whatever suits you with this knob. It will easily catch an intruding human sneaking about in the dark when a camera would not suffice. It can be wired to an alarm or to trigger a device of your choosing. At the moment, I only have the one, so I suggest you install it to watch over the front door of your home. When more have been manufactured, I will send men along to install them here and at the mine."

Owen took the small machine, then shook Tagget's hand. "Thank you. I appreciate your business."

"And I yours. Good day, Mr. Cassidy." Tagget extended a hand to Nora, but when she grasped it he bowed to kiss her knuckles instead of shaking. "And to you, Dr. Taylor." He took up his wife's hand again and they strode together toward the exit.

"Well, that was interesting," Nora remarked when the Taggets had disappeared from sight.

Owen studied the thermal sensor. "Do you still think he's my villain?"

"No. Unfortunately. He did have the best motive. Let's finish our inspection and then return home. I'd like to study this sensor he gave you, and I can handle the installation."

"We can use it here. I don't need devices on my house."

Nora gestured at his biomechanical shoulder. "That says otherwise. You've looked to the safety of your facilities and your people. Now look to your own. You've an enemy out there. And my guess..." She pointed at the security camera. "He won't like what you've done."

II

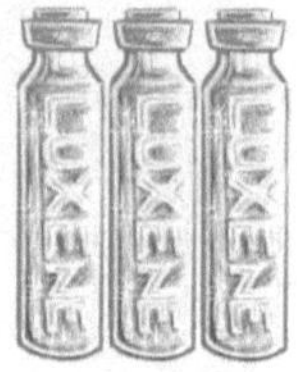

Nora was looking at his mouth again. Owen kept his face locked in a neutral position. It had confused him for a time, her preoccupation with this portion of his anatomy. She'd claimed no physical attraction to him, and he'd seen nothing to indicate that her statement was anything but truthful. But why stare, then, if she wasn't thinking of kissing?

It had made no sense until last night, when she'd laughed aloud at something she was reading. When he'd asked what was so funny, she'd given him that impish smile of hers and replied, "Oh, you wouldn't be interested. You have no sense of humor." The epiphany had hit him like a thunderclap. She was watching for him to smile.

And now that he knew, he wasn't going to give her the satisfaction until it suited him. Not when teasing her was so much fun.

Today, though, remaining impassive had been surprisingly difficult. All security installations were finished. Both the mine and the refinery were up and running. His tour of the facilities that morning had been quick and satisfying, and for the first time in weeks, he truly felt he could take an afternoon to rest and relax. He'd take a nap, spend some time with a book or perhaps a game of chess if Nora was interested, and then a nice dinner. Maybe he'd take Nora out.

He remained disappointed she didn't return his romantic interest, but he hoped they might cultivate a friendship regardless. He'd grown to enjoy her company over the past few days and thought she might return the sentiment.

Something rubbed against his leg and purred as he ascended the front steps of his townhouse. He jumped—an automatic reaction to a lifetime of allergies to anything with fur—startling Nora. But not the cat, it seemed. It purred again, still rubbing his leg.

"Er, Dr. Taylor, do you think you might—" His words trailed away as he looked down at the cat. Or, rather, the dragon.

The tiny mechanical animal was both the size and shape of a kitten, topped with a pair of delicate wings that fluttered as it nuzzled him. Owen bent and scooped up the creature, pleased to not have to beg someone else to move it away from him.

"What are you doing here, little one?" he asked it, petting its metal head. He glanced around for a potential owner. "Where do you come from?"

Owen hopped down the steps and set the kitten-dragon on the sidewalk, giving it a nudge. "Go on home, little fella."

The dragon toddled off, and Owen turned back to his house, not realizing he was smiling until Nora had already caught his eye. He quickly schooled his features, but she only laughed.

"I saw that! I knew you were a protector, but that was something more. You, Owen Cassidy, are all soft on the inside."

Any last vestiges of a smile dissolved into a scowl. The kitten-dragon had been adorable. It was a simple empirical fact. His reaction had nothing to do with... anything else.

"Men aren't soft," he grumbled.

"And women aren't biomechanologists who cut their hair short, wear trousers, and invite themselves into the homes of unmarried men."

He winced at the scorn in her tone. "I meant no offense. You are an extraordinary woman."

"I am a woman who has the luxury of a wealthy and understanding family. It softens many of the repercussions of going against convention. And while you may not mean offense, you give it. To every man and woman who is or who wishes to be other than what they are told. You do yourself no favors, forcing yourself into that mold.

"That isn't the Owen I wish to befriend. I want to see the real Owen, the one beneath your protective shell. You know he's there. But if you continue to suppress him, you'll only become harder and risk losing the parts of you that make you a good man."

Owen could only stare at her. He wanted to tell her she was wrong. That he was exactly as she saw. That he contained no traces of the carefree boy who had once laughed and smiled often, and who had wept when he couldn't have a dog because it made him ill. But he couldn't bring himself to lie to her.

"The dragon was cute," he admitted. "I like cute things."

A hint of her smile returned. "See? Was that so difficult?"

I like cute biomechanologists who aren't afraid to scold me.

But no matter what she said, he couldn't afford to be soft. Not while he had the well-being of those he cared for to think of.

"Enough standing about on the doorstep. The clouds are getting dark, and if it's going to rain, I'd prefer to be inside."

"Agreed. And you could use a nap."

He rolled his eyes. "Yes, Doctor." To show off just how far he'd come, he lifted his right arm and pressed his hand to the metal plate beside the doorbell. The mechanical lock clanked and opened.

"I was wondering if that's what that was. Glad to see you comfortable using it. After your nap I have a new exer—"

"Owen!"

He whirled around at the sound of his brother's worried voice. Timothy jogged toward them, face flushed with exertion.

"Thank God I found you," he gasped. "I'd gone to the refinery, but they said you'd left for home."

Owen quickly ushered everyone inside. "What's wrong?" Dread twisted his gut. "Is Mother okay?"

"She's fine. She's visiting with her ladies' card playing group. But the house… Someone broke in last night."

12

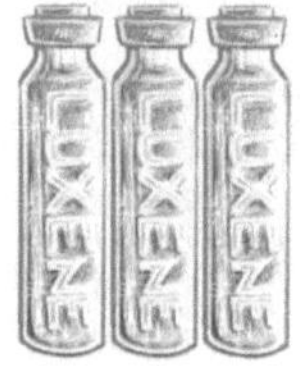

OWEN DRAGGED HIS BROTHER into the study. Nora followed, implacable as ever, closing the door behind her before settling into what had become her customary place. Owen was too agitated to sit, and so too was Timothy, it seemed. The young man walked directly to the liquor cabinet and poured two glasses of Owen's best Kentucky bourbon.

"Nora, would you like a glass as well?" Tim asked.

She hesitated a moment, then replied, "Just a splash, please."

Tim filled a third glass half as full as the others, then distributed them, before taking a seat. He shifted nervously, swirling the drink and staring at it, but not lifting the glass to his lips. Nora sipped tentatively at hers, frowning. Owen downed most of his drink in a single gulp, then began to pace.

"Tell me everything," he demanded.

Timothy didn't lift his eyes from the bourbon. "This morning we found the lock to the rear door destroyed, possibly by a mechanical contraption. Drawers and cabinets throughout the first floor had been opened and rifled through. I'm not certain yet if anything is missing. The break-in must have occurred during the night, but we heard nothing, saw nothing. I questioned the household staff, but no one noticed anything unusual before turning in or during the night. I can only assume it was a thief and that the silver or something else of value will be gone." He looked up suddenly, his expression fierce. "I'm not afraid. But I don't want Mother to worry. I think she should stay with you for a time, until I can replace and upgrade the locks."

Owen finished his drink. "Mother will stay here. And so will you."

Timothy scowled. "I knew you would say that. I can take care of myself. Someone should stay there to protect the house."

"Absolutely not. You'll stay here."

Tim's eyes darted to Nora. "Won't I be disrupting your... friendship?"

"We are not having an affair," Owen snapped. "There's nothing to interrupt. For Mother or for you. You will stay here."

"Fine. But I want something in return." He held up a hand before Owen could object. "You keep me informed. You tell me everything the police say about the burglary, tell me what sort of locks you're installing, let me know about security upgrades. I want to know what's going on at my own house."

"That's fair," Owen replied. He'd been hard on Timothy lately. Hopefully letting him feel involved would soothe some of the animosity between them. "I need to see the house. I want to talk to the staff about closing up and see that you and Mother have your things brought here. Have you reported the incident to the police?"

"No. I thought you would want to see it for yourself first."

Owen nodded. "Let's go."

· · · ᴑᴑᴑ · · ·

Owen didn't even think about the fact that Nora came with them until Timothy whispered, "Why did you let her tag along?"

The question startled Owen. She'd been following him everywhere for so long now it seemed natural. He wouldn't have forbidden her from joining them, even if she'd bothered to ask. He wanted her thoughts on what had happened here. Having another set of eyes could only be a help, especially when they were accompanied by a mind as sharp as Dr. Nora Taylor's.

When he didn't answer, Tim said, "Tell the truth. You two are involved, aren't you?"

"She's treating my arm. She's not interested in anything else."

"But *you* are." Tim slotted his key into the lock and opened the front door. "Follow me, please, Dr. Taylor," he said in a louder voice. "I'll show you where the break-in occurred."

This townhouse was quite a bit smaller than Owen's house, due to his mother's preference for a more modest living space. Even so, it was located in a nice, quiet neighborhood, where neighbors knew one another by name and crime was almost unheard of. Had this burglar entered other houses last night as well? Owen didn't like to wish misfortune on others, but a rash of crimes would indicate an ordinary criminal. A targeted break-in, however, could well be the work of his mystery villain.

The small household staff had temporarily barricaded the rear door. Owen cleared the boards out of the way and opened the door, checking its solidity, as well as that of the jamb. Nothing appeared damaged. The lock, however, was a mangled mess. Nora knelt in front of it, her blue-green eyes focused intently as she ran her fingers over the ruined metal.

"Definitely a mechanical device," she opined. "You can see the scratches where it sat around the lock. From these rounded gouges, I would guess the device drilled straight into the lock in multiple places, until it fell apart completely."

"A drill that size wouldn't make enough noise to wake anyone upstairs," Timothy added.

Owen nodded, trusting their knowledge of engineering above his own. "I will ask the police if other recent incidents show a similar forced entry."

Nora stood, brushing dirt from her trousers. "I don't

understand why the thief would use such a crude device in the first place. The lock-picking apparatus I know of hardly leaves a mark, and the lock remains intact afterward. A house can be robbed with no one the wiser. And if you're a thief without access to such a sophisticated piece of machinery, why not use traditional lock picks? Again, it hides your crime."

"Maybe he simply didn't care," Owen suggested. *Maybe he wanted to be seen. Maybe he wanted* me *to see.*

Done with their perusal of the door, they closed and barricaded it once again, then followed Timothy into the house to assess the internal damage.

Nothing Owen saw had been destroyed, but many drawers and cabinets were open, their contents tumbled. He walked from one to the next, trying to think what had been inside and what might have been taken.

"We've made up a list of what's missing, Mr. Cassidy," said the housekeeper. "All the good silver, a pair of candlesticks, the crystal decanter, and the painting from young Mr. Cassidy's study."

"Mother's jewelry?"

"No, sir. Upstairs was undisturbed."

"Thank you. I will give the list to the police."

"A criminal with a crude break-in device who doesn't even bother to search bedrooms for jewels?" Nora's eyebrows arched skeptically.

"He didn't want to risk waking anyone?" Timothy guessed.

"He didn't care about stealing. If he had, he'd have looked for an empty house. This is a staged burglary."

Owen's heart thudded. Just what he'd feared. He folded his arms across his chest, regarding her with a dispassionate expression. "Because he entered an occupied house?"

"In part. The ruined lock and open drawers indicate no interest in hiding the crime. The timing of the crime to when everyone is home suggests a desire to scare or intimidate the occupants rather than stealing to earn money. A thief after coin would prefer a house where he could find jewelry, a safe full of money, or other valuable, portable goods. Instead he stole art. Ridiculous. Selling stolen art is nearly impossible because it's so easily identifiable. Any one of these things might be disregarded. But taken all together? No professional thief would do such a slapdash job."

Her deductions confirmed all his fears, but even so a smile tugged at the corners of Owen's mouth. Nora's nimble mind and no-nonsense attitude delighted him. She observed, she analyzed, and she stated things precisely how she saw them.

"You have an exceptional intellect, Nora Taylor," he said, letting the smile come. "I'm grateful for the opportunity to get to know you, and your companionship and advice is rapidly becoming invaluable."

She beamed. The broader her smile grew, the wider his own became in response.

"Now you can officially say you made me smile," he teased.

"Victory!" He thought she might laugh, but her smile abruptly faded. A startled, almost worried expression passed over her face before she settled into her usual calm. "You should contact the police," she said, once again all business. "You can tell them my thoughts, but I expect they will come to similar conclusions. Shall Tim and I head back to your house?"

Owen's brow crinkled in puzzlement. "Yes. That will be fine. I will finish here, then fetch my mother and join you for dinner."

"Good, good." She backed toward the door, her eyes not leaving him, her mouth twisted into a half-frown. "I will see you then." She nodded and darted off, not waiting for Timothy to follow.

Owen stared for a long moment at the space where she had been. What the hell had just happened?

13

"TELL ME, MISS TAYLOR... Or is it Mrs. Taylor?"

"Dr. Taylor," Nora corrected, the lack of irritation in her voice made possible only by years of practice.

"Ah." Owen's mother's gaze drifted down to Nora's hands, searching for another way to answer her question. Though lack of a wedding ring could imply widow as much as spinster. "Tell me, Dr. Taylor, as a woman, what is the appeal of wearing trousers such as you have chosen this evening?"

Chosen today. Nora hadn't changed for dinner like many people did. Like most people did, she suspected, when they went out to a restaurant with someone as wealthy as Owen Cassidy. He hadn't changed, either, of course, being far too practical to dirty multiple suits in a day.

"I don't like dresses," Nora replied. "I never have. As a girl I would discard them and borrow my brothers' clothes instead. I find trousers are much more practical. They are comfortable, they have pockets, and they do not restrict my movement."

Practical was her number one concern in clothing choice. Which was why she most often chose her cropped vests over a more traditional corset. They laced snuggly across her breasts without constricting, preventing her from bouncing without hampering her ability to move. Today she'd chosen the lavender vest that matched her favorite parasol. Trimmed with satin ribbon and beads, it was pretty and feminine, even paired with trousers and her men's-style shirt.

"Ah. I see," Mrs. Cassidy murmured. "I confess I do not understand young ladies these days, with their bicycles and unusual clothing and desire to go off to college."

"The desire for independence and equality has always existed. It has simply become more visible over the years."

Nora's lips curved in a genuine smile. This was a nice, safe topic. She could expound on it for the entirety of dinner, if necessary. It would distract her from Owen's compelling presence.

Even though he sat around the corner of the square table, his nearness made her squirm. She kept her gaze riveted on Mrs. Cassidy, yearning for further conversation. She couldn't bring herself to look at him.

What had happened back there at Timothy's house? Owen had complimented her, genuinely, and he'd smiled. The first smile she'd drawn out of him all on her own. Nora remembered the feeling of warmth spreading through her stomach, the pleasure that her deductive reasoning had impressed him. In that instant, she'd known they'd moved beyond reluctant partners and become friends, and she'd smiled back, happy with this new development.

And then she'd thought about kissing.

She'd been staring at his magnificent smile. It was boyish and happy and free—all the things Owen wouldn't let himself be. *That's the Owen I want to get to know better,* she'd thought. *The secret Owen who pets mechanical kittens.*

His comment about liking cute things had replayed in her head, making her smile grow wider. Cute things like Owen's dimples, she'd thought. He had lovely dimples. And a nicely plump lower lip.

That's when it had happened. She'd wondered what it might feel like to kiss that lip. A shiver of excitement had run through her at the idea of pressing her mouth to his and tasting that lip. Followed immediately by panic. Why him? Why now? This was not the sort of complication she wanted in her life and she had absolutely no idea how to handle it.

Nora was so lost in her thoughts she nearly missed what Mrs. Cassidy was saying. Something about if women all became doctors, who would have the babies?

"My career has in no way barred me from motherhood," Nora explained, hoping her companion was indeed looking for an explanation and not an argument. "Many professional women marry and have families, and I could have done so had I been so inclined. Education and careers don't prevent children."

"I agree," Owen added. "They simply give women more options and more knowledge. If she's not desperate to marry to provide for herself, a woman can exercise more care when choosing a spouse and raising children. And there have always been women who did not want such things."

Nora edged her chair away from him. Was her face turning red? Because now she *really* wanted to kiss him. How was she supposed to live under the same roof with him for another week? Would everything he said and did only make her body react more strongly? There had to be a way to get these ridiculous feelings under control. Perhaps she could pick a fight with him. Steer the conversation to a topic where they disagreed.

"Where did you conduct your studies, Dr. Taylor?" Owen asked.

Nora took a steadying breath before looking at him to answer. "Boston University. A number of prominent women have earned—" She halted mid-sentence when she spied a member of the waitstaff hurrying toward their table.

"Mr. Cassidy," the man said to Owen. "You have an urgent phone call, sir."

All eyes at the table cast concerned glances in Owen's direction, but he nodded calmly and rose. "Excuse me. I will only be a moment."

Nora watched him go, her muscles tightening. What now?

Not another mishap at the mine or the refinery, she hoped. Thoughts of kissing faded under the weight of this new worry. Not at all the way she would have chosen to cool her desire.

She made a few bland comments about her time in Boston. Tim and his mother nodded and made appropriate short replies, but the mood had turned somber. Their gazes drifted often to the exit where Owen had disappeared, waiting. Eventually the conversation dwindled to nothing.

Much of the tension drained from Nora's body the moment Owen walked back into the room. She told herself it was only the relief at soon knowing what the trouble was and not any other sort of reaction to his presence. He crossed the room quickly and sank heavily into his chair. His expression was calm, but the tightness around his eyes and at the corners of his mouth betrayed his inner turmoil.

"What happened?" Nora asked.

"A shipping boat sank. The crew escaped unharmed, but two dozen barrels of luxene are now lying at the bottom of the Mississippi."

"I'm so sorry. Thank goodness no one was hurt."

"Yes. I'm afraid I will have to cut our dinner short, however. I should return home and make more phone calls. I would rather hire divers to retrieve the barrels than let all the fuel go to waste. And it must be done promptly, before they drift too far."

"We'll all come home with you, dear," Owen's mother said. "We don't mind a quiet dinner in the house."

"Thank you."

In short order they made their apologies to the restaurant staff and departed. Back at the townhouse, Owen paused at the bottom of the stairs, staring up at a point above the doorway. "I'll have Tagget's thermal sensor installed here tonight," he sighed. He rubbed the back of his neck with his right hand.

"That is wonderful range of motion for this stage of the healing process," Nora said, wanting to give him something to ease his unhappiness.

He gave her a small smile, but it was nothing like the earnest grin he'd shown her before. Sadness lurked in his wide, brown eyes. "Guess I'll be rid of you soon, then." Even the teasing words fell flat.

Nora had never been much of a hugger. Now, however, the urge to wrap her arms around Owen was nearly overpowering. She longed to hold him. To stroke his back and whisper that things would turn out well. To soothe away the helplessness and frustration with her body.

Instead, she stepped aside to allow him to climb the steps and trigger the automatic lock. She followed him into the house, but let him walk off alone to his study.

"I'll be around as long as you need me," she said to his retreating back.

Had she just stated her intention to remain here indefinitely? Or had she given him an excuse to send her packing whenever he desired?

More to the point: how did she *want* him to interpret her words?

14

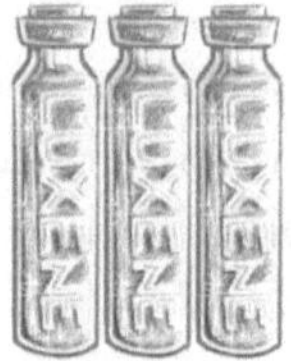

Owen pumped the tiny weight in his right hand, repeating the series of exercises even though Nora hadn't told him to. He was so damned tired of feeling broken and useless. He couldn't do anything but watch as the machines hauled barrels of fuel from the river, but he wouldn't let the time go to waste. If these exercises could bring him even a bit closer to his usual self, he'd do them night and day.

Nora made no comment. She stood at the edge of the dock, her attention on the salvage operation. All day she'd seemed distant. She hadn't avoided him, exactly, but their conversation lacked its usual liveliness, and she rarely looked at him for more than a moment.

Ask her what's wrong.

Owen's fingers tightened on the weight. That same thought had run through his head at least a dozen times now. But theirs was a business relationship. They weren't friends, and he certainly wasn't courting her. Personal issues were none of his business. She was here, overseeing his rehabilitation, and that was that.

A bubbling on the surface of the water heralded the appearance of another barrel. The salvage machine rose from the murky river, and the workers on the dock rushed to free the barrel from the claw and roll it down to the waiting truck.

When the barrel had been extracted, the claw closed and retracted before the machine began to descend back into the water.

"Interesting machine," Nora commented.

"Why, thank you, miss," came a slow Southern drawl.

Owen turned toward the familiar voice. Leslie Atwater bounded toward them, a mischievous grin lighting his face and the morning sun burnishing the gold in his dark-blond hair.

"Owen Cassidy, you scoundrel," Atwater said in mock annoyance. "How could you neglect to tell me you would be accompanied by such a vision of loveliness?" He flashed a smile at Nora before returning his attention to Owen. "Kind of you to offer a distraction from looking at your ugly mug."

Owen shifted the weight to his left hand and extended his right for a handshake, but Atwater ignored the hand in favor of an enthusiastic bear hug.

Owen returned the gesture with a brotherly thump to his friend's back. "Glad to see you haven't changed in the months since I last saw you."

Atwater released him and stepped back. "I never do."

"We need to meet for lunch or coffee one of these days, instead of..." Owen waved a hand helplessly at the salvage operation. "I'm sorry to bother you. I'll make sure to pay a bonus."

"What hogwash! You know I'm happy to help. You'll get your usual discount, and that's final. The salvage machines are always ready. You're hardly the first to suffer such an accident, nor will you be the last."

Owen's jaw tightened. If this had been an accident, he'd eat his hat. He resumed his exercises, gesturing at Nora with his left hand.

"Allow me to make introductions. This is Dr. Eleanor Taylor, biomechanologist. Dr. Taylor, this is Mr. Leslie Atwater of Atwater Manufacturing. He's the brains behind most of the machinery in my refinery and the inventor of these salvage devices."

"A pleasure, Mr. Atwater," Nora said, extending a hand.

Atwater shook hands, smiling. "A biomechanologist? No wonder you find my contraption interesting. I regret you cannot see the entirety of the working while it's beneath the water, but I would be happy to describe it for you. Do you see that man at the end of the dock with the panel of switches?"

Nora nodded.

"Those control the position of the machine. The divers report the location of the salvageable item, and he makes the necessary adjustments. The machine walks on four legs, slow and lumbering like a large animal. The claw in the center makes more refined movements and can also be manually adjusted by the divers. Once it closes, the rise to the surface is automatic."

"Lovely. It must be quite useful here along the river."

"Indeed. And I'm pleased it was not otherwise engaged when my friend had need of it."

"As are we all." Nora smiled at Atwater, though the expression didn't reach her eyes. What was bothering her? Were all the troubles becoming too much for her? Did she fear the possibility of danger? "Is there anything we can do to help the operation?"

"Oh, no, no," Atwater replied. "Everything is running smoothly, and Mr. Cassidy has dozens of loyal minions dashing about keeping an eye on things, as usual."

Minions? If Owen had a moustache, he would have been tempted to twirl the ends of it and cackle. Only tempted, though. He'd put silly behavior behind him years ago.

Although, perhaps that sort of silliness was what Nora needed to bring back her true smile. Owen couldn't shake the feeling he was somehow to blame for her unusual aloofness. He could think of nothing he'd done that might have caused it, but the yearning to fix the problem irritated him like an itch he couldn't reach.

"What brings you here to observe the salvage, Dr. Taylor?" Atwater asked, gracing her with the flirtatious smile that had charmed many a woman. Owen could hardly blame him. Nora looked particularly fetching today, in a vest that matched the unusual color of her eyes and snug black trousers with subtle pinstriping.

"I am working with Mr. Cassidy on the rehabilitation of his arm and shoulder," she replied, coolly dismissing any amorous advances. "You've heard, I assume, that he sustained a recent injury."

"Indeed, though the papers mentioned little else. I hope the healing is progressing well?" He cast a glance at Owen.

"Seems to be," Owen answered. He lifted the fist with the weight, suddenly conscious of how ridiculously small the one-pound bar looked in his big hand. "Doing my best to keep up with all the doctor's exercises."

"Excellent. I'm sure you'll be right as rain in no time."

"Thank you. For everything. We'll let you get back to your work." Owen offered Nora his arm. "Dr. Taylor, shall we continue our rounds?"

The touch of her hand sent spikes of desire throughout his body. He'd accepted by now that he was never going to get over this hunger for her. Not acting on it had become just another part of his daily life.

He led Nora along the dock, to where the recovered barrels had been loaded onto a truck. One of his employees stood beside the vehicle with a clipboard.

"Five barrels so far, sir," the man reported. "Only minor damage noted, no leakage."

Nora dropped Owen's arm to peer into the truck. The abruptness of the movement bothered him more than the loss of her touch. Perhaps she *was* avoiding him. Did he make her uncomfortable? He'd tried to be friendly without pressing any unwanted attentions on her. Maybe he was fooling himself. Maybe his lust was too obvious.

"I hope my apparatus has delivered the barrels in satisfactory condition?"

Owen looked back at Atwater, unsure if he'd followed because he had something to discuss about the salvage or because he wanted to flirt with Nora.

"They look fine to me," Nora replied, stepping aside to allow the men to look into the truck. "But Mr. Cassidy would know better than I."

Atwater twitched his eyebrows. "I trust your word, Doctor. As a biomechanologist, you must have an eye for perfection."

The shake of her head set her hair to bouncing. "Mr. Atwater, I'm afraid your charm is wasted on me. While I appreciate the compliments, I must dash any hopes you have of romance."

He laughed and executed a gallant bow. "My poor heart is broken, Dr. Taylor. Thank you for letting me down so gently."

This time when Nora smiled it looked genuine. "I expect you will recover quickly enough."

"Perhaps. But I fear my only hope is to depart at once and pray the next lovely lady I meet finds me more her type." He turned to Owen. "I trust the operation looks to be proceeding well? You're satisfied with the divers and the machine?"

"I am, thank you."

Atwater held out a hand. Owen hadn't shaken hands since the injury, but if anything was amiss with his grip or his technique, Atwater didn't comment.

"You're welcome. I'll be at my factory if you have further need of me." Atwater bowed to Nora again, then departed.

Nora watched him walk off before turning to Owen. "How is it that all your business associates seem to ooze charm while you specialize in surliness?"

"Are you teasing me, Dr. Taylor?" he asked, genuinely uncertain whether she was or not.

She took a step away from him. "I... I'm sorry. You have

plenty of reason to be in a less-than-happy mood recently. We should concentrate on your work and the arm."

Owen's mouth turned downward. "It wasn't a criticism, Nora. I'm not so humorless a man that I can't take a bit of good-natured ribbing. I had thought we were becoming friends. Was I mistaken?"

Several seconds of silence passed before she replied. "No. You weren't mistaken."

He let out a long, slow breath. "Good. Then, as a friend, might I ask: Is something bothering you? Have I done anything to upset you?"

"No, you've done nothing wrong."

"But something *is* troubling you? Can I help?"

She stared at his face, her brow creased in thought. No, he decided after a moment, not his face. His mouth in particular.

"Well..." Nora turned the word into a heavy exhalation. "You could kiss me. But that might make things even worse."

15

*Y*OU COULD KISS ME. Nora nearly smacked her hand into her own face. Was she out of her damn mind? Why had she said that?

Because it was the truth.

All day the thoughts had been tumbling around in her mind. She wanted to kiss Owen. She couldn't deny that. Nor could she deny that the sensation left her confused and anxious. She didn't know what to do about it. She'd never kissed anyone before. Not once. And rarely even had the urge to try it.

Most people, from what she understood, experienced varying degrees of attraction to a wide range of potential partners. They learned in adolescence and young adulthood how to handle the feelings and what sorts of attributes made a person more or less attractive to them. For Nora, though, the experience was so infrequent it left her as lost as a ship in a fog. Worse. Ships had instruments.

Owen's lower jaw still hung slack. His light-brown eyes had opened wide. He had pretty eyes. Clear and bright, with enviably long lashes. This was an empirical fact, certainly, and one Nora had noticed upon first meeting him. Now, however, those eyes did things to her insides.

"I should return to the house," she babbled. "You've done plenty of exercises for the day. We can talk again later. After dinner. I'll go. Let you get on with your work."

He snapped out of his stupor and caught her arm before she could back out of range.

"No, wait. Please." He glanced around at the men working on the salvage operation and steered Nora to the opposite side of the truck, giving them some amount of privacy. Once they were out of sight he released her. "I'm sorry, I'm confused. You want me to kiss you? To help with something? Or you don't want me to kiss you? Have I been bothering you?" He rubbed a hand over his closely-shorn hair. "Christ, I thought I'd managed to restrain myself. Do I make you uncomfortable? With the way I look at you or anything of that sort?"

Oh, what a mess she'd made. She ought to have told him nothing was wrong. And absolutely not mentioned kissing. "No. Nothing like that. You've been entirely gentlemanly and a proper friend. This is me. I'm... different."

He looked her up and down. "You do have an unconventional style and an unusual profession for a woman. But I fail to see how that is connected to this, er, issue."

"It's difficult to explain," she began, groping for some way to convey what to him would sound nonsensical. Even Lina with all her psychological studies had struggled to understand when Nora had tried to explain to her.

"Perhaps this isn't the best location, then. Where would you be comfortable? My study? The parlor? Or perhaps somewhere away from my home is better, if I'm part of this problem."

"It's *not you*," Nora insisted. "Your home is fine. Anywhere we can sit and talk."

"I'll have the car brought around."

The expression of confusion remained on Owen's face the entirety of the silent drive back to his townhouse. By the time they entered his study—still not talking—Nora feared it might have become permanent. Unsurprisingly, he headed straight for his liquor cabinet.

"Would you like a glass of bourbon as well?" he asked.

"No, thank you. I didn't like it." So. Apparently they could speak, provided half a room separated them.

Owen turned, the bottle in his hand. The furrow in his brow had only deepened since entering the room. "Didn't like it? Do you mean this particular bourbon was not to your taste? Or do you mean when you had a glass yesterday… it was your first taste of bourbon?"

"The latter. I don't partake of much alcohol. Strong spirits aren't especially healthy and I require a clear head and a steady hand for my work. Still, I like to sample drinks when given the opportunity, because I like to know what others are imbibing and it allows me to have a knowledgeable opinion on the matter. I'm not a fan of most liquor I have sampled, but I'm always open to new experiences."

Owen nodded. "An entirely valid practice." He turned back to the cabinet and poured his drink. "Shall I send for tea or coffee, then?"

Nora toyed with a bit of thread on her trousers. "Nothing, thank you."

Owen closed the cabinet, took a gulp of his drink, then walked to his desk, where he perched, half-leaning, half-sitting atop it. His eyes locked with hers. "Now, about this, ah, issue you raised."

"Yes." Nora wasn't much of a blusher, but her cheeks felt hot beneath his unflinching gaze. All of her felt hot. She'd opened her mouth and told the truth, and now she wasn't sure what would come of it except extreme embarrassment.

Owen took another generous swallow of bourbon. Nora remembered the way it had burned as it ran down her throat, and the peculiar taste that mingled sweet and smoky. She would taste it again if she kissed him, but would it be a strong flavor or a mere hint?

Curiosity dampened some of her discomfort. Perhaps she'd been thinking of this in entirely the wrong way. Hadn't she just said she was always open to new experiences? Maybe all she needed to quell her desire was to try it. She pushed herself up out of her chair and strode across the room until she was close enough to smell his shaving lotion.

Goodness, but he was a large man. Even slouching against the desk he was quite a bit taller than her. At this distance, she noticed every part of him. His shoulders, his chest, his hands. A single step could bring their bodies into contact. When he raised his glass to his mouth to drain the last of his drink, she licked her lips.

His breath hitched. "You want me to kiss you."

Nora's pulse hammered. "Yes."

He set the empty glass on the desk behind him without taking his eyes off her, and lifted his right hand to brush lightly against her jaw. "Why? What changed?"

"I..." Her voice had a strange, breathy quality. "I don't know."

Owen's thumb swept over her lower lip, a whisper of a touch that nonetheless sent a tremble clear down to her toes. Only days ago, such a gentle, controlled motion would have been impossible.

Really, Nora? she chided herself. *You're thinking like a doctor at a time like this? Try to be more romantic.*

Nothing came to mind. The things she associated with romance—flowers, poetry, love letters—were of no use. And the stroke of Owen's fingers against her jaw had done something to her brain. The only truly coherent thought was how stunningly soft his big, work-roughened hands were.

"Nora," he murmured, his head dropping toward hers.

She tipped her chin up, her whole body shivering with anticipation, desperate to feel his lips on hers.

Warm breath washed across her skin. His lips moved over hers in a slow caress, soft and tender like the hand that now shifted to cup her cheek. Her whole body jolted into hyper-awareness. She could feel the fullness of his lower lip, moving with soft motions that made her own lips tingle in response.

Prickles raced across her skin, and her nipples stiffened beneath her vest. She swayed toward him.

Nora gasped at the sudden collision of their bodies, his so hot and hard and muscular. Owen's tongue slipped between her parted lips and his hands dropped to clutch her to his chest. Without warning, the kiss turned from sweet to ravenous, a plundering exploration. It was too much. Too strange.

Nora pressed both hands to Owen's solid chest and shoved herself away from him. She shivered, not knowing whether from nerves or from a carnal longing she wasn't ready to face.

"Nora?" A worried frown curved the mouth that only moments ago had been kissing her as if he meant to consume her.

Kissing her. Her hand lifted to her lips before she could stop it.

"I'm sorry," she blurted. "I think we should stop. Please excuse me." She spun away and rushed from the room, desperate for time alone to sift through her muddled thoughts.

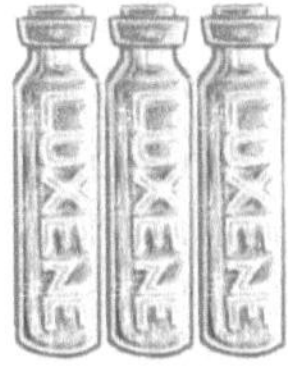

"I THOUGHT I WAS a better kisser than that," Owen grumbled into his mug of coffee.

His mother looked up from her breakfast. "What was that, dear?"

"Nothing."

"You look distressed. Is the shoulder injury bothering you? You should have the doctor look at it."

Owen rolled his shoulder. He still avoided looking at the biomechanics in the mirror, but the mechanical joint no longer felt foreign. He hadn't given it a thought this morning until his mother had raised the subject. Though that could be due in part to his obsessive brooding over what he'd done wrong with Nora.

"It's fine." The last thing he needed was to do anything requiring him to remove clothing in Nora's presence.

He glanced at the door again. No sign of her, and he'd been sitting here for twenty minutes. Either she'd slept as poorly last night as he had and was still abed, or she'd risen even earlier than usual in order to avoid him. Dammit. What could he possibly have done wrong?

Owen tried to turn his attention to his breakfast, but the fork didn't even reach his mouth before the sound of footsteps made him freeze. His head jerked to look at the doorway.

Not Nora. Timothy.

Tim rushed into the room, coffee in one hand, a newspaper in the other. "Owen. Have you seen this morning's paper?"

"No." He'd been too busy fretting. He needed to scan the police reports, though, for news of any break-ins that resembled the one at his mother's house. He still clung to the scant hope the perpetrator was an ordinary thief and not his mystery tormentor.

"You need to see this."

Timothy spread the paper on the table and pointed to an article in the center of the front page. Owen read the headline, blinked several times, and read it again. Much to his dismay, the words looked no different on the second reading.

Luxene Production Fueled by Unsafe Environment?

The string of recent accidents attached to the luxene-mining operation owned by St. Louis tycoon Owen Cassidy are not a matter of happenstance, according to an inside source. Instead, this former employee reports, they are the product of long-standing negligence and disregard for employee safety in pursuit of the almighty dollar.

"The machines are in constant disrepair," our source told us. "Mr. Cassidy spends no money to have them upgraded. In answer to the most recent malfunctions, he brought in a woman who is not a licensed mechanic and allowed her to toy with the machines at will. He neglected to even inspect the work she had done."

"The terrain where the mining operation is located is naturally unsafe," says a local geologist. "The area is known for hidden caverns and sinkholes, and all underground tunnels are in danger of flood and collapse when the Mississippi rises."

The fuel, too, is hazardous, as evidenced by the safety concerns that shut down Dynalux in autumn of 1904. Even the dust of the raw ore is highly combustible. More than a dozen casualties resulted from the explosion two weeks ago.

Our attempts to gain access to the facilities to further illuminate the conditions at Cassidy Mining were thwarted by recent security measures undertaken specifically for the purpose of barring the public from seeing beyond the gates. Robber Baron Cassidy, it seems, is determined to prevent any effort to thwart his exploitation of his workers. After all, a safe and wholesome working environment might subtract a few dollars from the millions in profits he reaps every year on the back of his downtrodden laborers.

"Goddammit," Owen swore, even though his mother was sitting at the same table.

"Language, Owen," she chided. "Nothing can be so terrible it necessitates using the Lord's name in vain."

Yes, it can, he wanted to reply. *Especially since right now I want to strangle this bastard so badly I'm clearly bound for hell anyway.*

"Didn't think any of your employees seemed resentful." Timothy shrugged. "But sounds like one of them didn't appreciate the way you run things."

"It's a bunch of da— dashed lies."

Tim sat down and plucked an untouched piece of toast from Owen's plate. "Any idea who might be responsible? Has anyone been fired recently? Or left on their own?" He smeared some jam on the toast and took a bite.

"Not that I am aware of, though I'd have to check employee records to be certain. Certainly no one has left who would have seen Nora—Dr. Taylor—working on the machines. And get your own breakfast."

"You weren't eating it."

True.

Their mother pulled the newspaper across the table and read the article, shaking her head. "What a nasty piece of writing.

You should telephone the paper and demand a retraction. You have never been cruel to your employees in your entire life. Surely this is only a vicious reaction from someone who is jealous of your success."

Owen pushed his eggs around on his plate. Plenty of people were jealous of his success. He had a personal net worth of over seven million dollars. Nothing on the order of the Evan Taggets or Andrew Carnegies of the world, but more than any rational man could possibly use in a lifetime.

"This is more than jealousy," he said. "This is mania. Whoever is doing this has a vendetta against me, and I haven't a clue why."

"Well, you can be an ass," Timothy replied, unhelpfully. "But not so much as to make anyone hate you. Nobody hates you. It's annoying, actually."

Owen shoved his plate over to his brother, who happily seized the fork and dug in.

"I'm going to call in the Pinkertons," Owen sighed.

"Is that a good idea?"

Owen's head swiveled at the sound of Nora's voice. She stood in the doorway, looking perfectly well-rested. She was dressed in the little tweed vest again, its cropped style emphasizing her ample breasts. Damn, damn, damn. And fixating on her face didn't help him in the slightest, because it only brought back the memory of the taste of her and how nicely her mouth had fit against his own.

Where had he gone wrong?

"What else can I do?" he asked, and for a moment he wasn't sure whether he was still talking about his business troubles.

"It's only that if you do have disgruntled employees, they might see the hiring of Pinkertons as an act of aggression. People haven't forgotten what happened during the Homestead Strike."

Owen cringed. He'd been a young man with a fledgling

business at the time. Even now, the thought of the violence during the contentious steel-workers strike gave him chills.

"I'm not strikebreaking," he argued. "I want their investigational skills. And Pinkertons know how to get to the heart of a troublesome business matter. What other option do I have anymore? Something must be done to stop this before all my workers end up without jobs. Or someone is killed."

Nora's blue-green eyes stared unwaveringly at him, and it took him several seconds to realize she was looking at his shoulder. He'd almost forgotten how close he'd been to being that someone. He rolled the shoulder again.

"I'll call the Pinkertons," he declared, his decision final. "Then I'll set up a meeting with Cardot and Jameson to discuss the matter. If you'll excuse me, I need to get to the telephone."

Nora stepped calmly away from the door so as not to bar his path. Even so, she twitched as he passed her. Her cool demeanor was no more than a thin veneer. She was as unsettled as he was.

He paused just inside the entranceway. "New exercises after I make my phone calls?"

She tipped her head in the slightest of nods. "Yes. From now on we're simply building strength. You'll be all done with me in no time."

Done with her? Not a chance. She could leave today and he'd still be thinking about her and that damned kiss for a long time to come.

Owen forced himself to look away from her and tromped off to his study. Whoever was behind the attacks and that newspaper article was determined to destroy him in one way or another. He wished he knew who. He wished he knew why. And he wished he had something—anything—besides more bad news to distract him from Nora.

17

"FLEXION. TEN REPETITIONS," Nora commanded, willing herself not to think about what had happened the last time they were alone here in Owen's study.

He lifted his arm straight up. He knew all her terminology now. This was good. This was something she knew and understood. Walking him through the new set of exercises restored some semblance of control in a life that seemed to have turned entirely upside down in the past few weeks.

She circled around him, scrutinizing the position of his arm as he stretched. "Good. Now hold both arms above your head and pass the weight slowly back and forth. Ten repetitions. How does it feel?"

"Not terrible. The right arm is growing stronger."

"Excellent." She watched him finish the exercise. "Horizontal abduction. I'll be applying resistance today, and I want you to push me out of the way if you can. Ready?"

Owen held his arm straight out in front of him, and Nora placed both her palms against it. She pushed as he swung his arm out to the side, testing his strength, making him work a bit harder each time.

"How did your phone calls go?" she asked, trying to distract herself from the sensation of touching him, even if it was through layers of clothing.

"As well as I could expect, under the circumstances. The

meeting is scheduled for this afternoon. You'll join us, I assume?"

Nora was so startled she forgot to brace herself and nearly toppled as Owen swung his arm again.

"I have no reason to join you," she replied stiffly, steadying herself. She repositioned his arm. "Again."

Owen pushed, but this time Nora was ready and it took him some effort to move her. "No reason." He gave a short huff of a laugh. "As if that matters. You've involved yourself in my business since the moment I met you. Why would you stop now?"

Because I don't trust myself around you. Because I'm afraid to repeat the painful embarrassment of the last time I felt anything like this.

Owen stepped away from her, both arms dropping to his sides. "It was that kiss, wasn't it? Whatever I did wrong, I apologize for it. I promise I won't touch you again. I would never subject you to unwanted attentions."

"It wasn't your fault. I was, uh, unprepared."

The memory of the kiss replayed in her mind, as it had so many times. It had started out so soft and tender that she'd been caught entirely unaware when it turned suddenly intense. Perhaps if she'd been experienced it wouldn't have startled her. But it had been her first kiss and all the theoretical knowledge in the world couldn't turn her into a worldly woman.

Poor Owen. He was staring at her again with that confused furrow in his brow. He'd probably thought she had a string of lovers in her past. After all, she worked in a man's profession, wore trousers, and had taken up residence in his home without an invitation, let alone a chaperone. She was bold and scandalous. Anyone would think it ludicrous to assume she remained unkissed at thirty-seven.

"But never mind that," Nora added hurriedly, before he could speak. "We have more important matters to attend to. Two more days of therapy and you should be clear to resume all your previous activities. Then I can return to Savannah and you'll be able to continue on without my interference. Now, what's next? Ah. Rotation. Internal and external."

Owen began the series of exercises, but the crease in his forehead didn't diminish, and his lips remained pressed together in a slight frown. "You aren't interfering," he said at last. "You've been a help. And if I've been less than gracious, I apologize. I'm unaccustomed to having friends outside my business. I suspect that makes my manners rather cold and authoritative. I shall strive to do better."

"You're not cold."

Quite the opposite. Controlled, certainly. And reluctant to share anything of himself. But those things didn't mask his passionately held convictions and sincere devotion to his family and to the workers under his supervision. That was what drew her to him. He made a true and loyal friend.

"If you'd like me to join you for the meeting, I will," she said.

He paused in his exercises. "I would appreciate it. You've witnessed as much as I have these past weeks, and you may think of some detail I've missed."

"I'll gather my notes when we finish here."

Three hours later, Nora sat at a table with Owen, Cardot, the head refinery supervisor Noah Jameson, and a pair of Pinkertons. One detective was Black, one white, but they both sported close-cropped hair, tidy moustaches, austere gray suits, and tinted spectacles obscuring their eyes. Were they trying to look intimidating? Or perhaps trying to distract from any distinguishing features with their near-identicalness? Being a generic man could certainly be helpful in their line of work.

Discussion was straightforward, facts presented with no embellishment. The Pinkertons took a few notes, but mostly they listened, their expressions unreadable behind their dark glasses. Nora contributed where she could and passed on all her notes from her inspections of the machines. Even so, she grew increasingly discouraged as the meeting wore on.

Cardot and Jameson could think of no potential suspects among the workers, though they did provide detailed descriptions of all damage and repairs as well as a list of employees who had left the business or been fired within the last year. Owen rattled off names of dozens of men he'd done business with, but none seemed to be at odds with him. And in the luxene business, he had no true competitors. No motives, no suspects, no progress.

When at last the interminable meeting came to a close, Nora plodded from the building, eyes on the ground ahead of her. "I'm not cut out for life as a detective," she sighed. "Criminal investigation involves far too much boredom and frustration." She shook her head and glanced up at Owen. "From the expression on your face I'm guessing you're feeling at least as deflated as I am right now."

His brows lifted almost imperceptibly. "You can read my expressions? And here I thought I never looked anything but grumpy and obstinate."

The right side of Nora's mouth hitched up. "Owen Cassidy, was that a joke? Let me feel your forehead. I want to check you for fever."

A slight smile touched his lips, not enough to show his dimples, but much more than Nora had expected under the circumstances. "I wanted to make you smile. If you can do it to me, I can do it to you. And your smile has been all too rare these past few days. I hate to think I may have contributed to squashing your joyful spirit."

"You haven't. I'm simply unaccustomed to so much waiting and not knowing. In my profession there's no end to the doing. Building, repairing, creating, strengthening. I'm good at that. Besides, even the cheeriest of us can't be a perpetual ray of sunshine."

Owen regarded her for a long moment. "Sometimes I think that's exactly what you are."

Nora opened her mouth, trying to think up some reply, but he turned away before any words came out.

"I'll fetch the motorcar," he said, striding purposefully off. No one looking at him now could have guessed that less than three weeks ago he'd been near death. It was good to see him driving, lifting things, resuming all his typical activities. Physically, he'd adjusted to the biomechanics as well as anyone. Mentally and emotionally, it was more difficult to tell, especially with the stress of all his business troubles.

"I hope those Pinkertons have better luck," Nora murmured. "They're trained for this at least." Truth was, she didn't want to leave Owen while he was beset by troubles. She couldn't do that to a friend. But once his rehabilitation was complete, what logical reason could she give for remaining in St. Louis?

"Hell," she muttered.

"Saucy language for a fancy lady," snickered a low voice from somewhere behind her.

Nora whirled to see who had spoken, but before she could get all the way around, a hand seized her around the waist. A large palm clamped down over her mouth, cutting off her scream of protest.

"You'll be coming with us, missy," the voice commanded. "And don't bother trying to fight."

The sting of a needle jabbing into her arm cut short her attempt to wriggle free. Damn. Taken down by her own preferred defensive technique.

Bastards, came her last coherent thought before the drug took effect, *Owen is going to tear you to pieces.*

18

THE ROOM SEEMED TO SWAY beneath her as Nora slowly came to. She lay on a hard cot in a darkened chamber. A rhythmic thrumming echoed in her ears. She ran through a list of common drugs and their effects in her head. What had her captors given her that would make her feel this way?

A shrill whistle from somewhere up above her jarred her from her dazed recitation. The feelings weren't drug-induced after all. Her senses were responding to external stimuli. She was moving.

Nora pushed herself into a seated position, pleased to discover she didn't feel ill or lightheaded. The cot she'd been placed on had been wedged at an angle into the small chamber. Empty shelves surrounded her on all sides, and the only illumination came from the cracks above and below the door in front of her. A storeroom of some sort, hastily converted into a prison cell.

She put a hand to the door and shoved, but it didn't budge. Solid. And securely locked.

Where am I? And when?

Nora patted down her pockets. Her defensive syringe had been taken, but her pocket watch remained, steadily ticking away. Good. If the watch hadn't wound down, a minimal amount of time had passed since the kidnapping.

She popped the watch open and bent down to hold it

near the sliver of light coming from beneath the door. Seven minutes past six o'clock. Evening the same day, most likely. She suspected she'd be groggier if the drug they'd given her had been powerful enough to keep her out until the next morning. She wound the watch anyway. Best to keep it going, since it was the only tool she had at the moment.

Good. She had her when. Next was where. The sway of the floor beneath her combined with the engine noise suggested a steamboat. On the Mississippi, then, and not too far from St. Louis. The engines didn't sound like they were running all-out, so even traveling with the river she doubted they'd gone more than thirty miles. And that was assuming they'd set sail immediately after capturing her.

Nora pounded on the door with a fist. "Let me out! You have no right to keep me here!"

The chances of her shouting making any difference probably hovered somewhere near zero, but it was an improvement on doing nothing. She pounded again.

"Let me out!"

"Ah, Dr. Taylor. How nice to see you have awakened."

Nora turned so quickly at the sound of the voice she bashed her shin on the cot and cursed.

"Such colorful language for a lady." The voice, coming from somewhere above her and to the left, was distorted and mechanical.

"Who are you?" she demanded. "What do you want with me?" She stepped up onto the cot, feeling along the ceiling for whatever device was projecting the sound. Her fingers found a rectangular box with a conical bell, a sort of mini gramophone. The small machine was firmly affixed to the ceiling, and Nora guessed wires ran from the back of the device into a room above, where the person speaking would talk into a mouthpiece like on a telephone.

She prodded gently at the device. If she could somehow open it up, she might be able to remove the piece distorting the sound. The fact that her captor needed to disguise his voice suggested he feared she might recognize him by it. Meaning he was someone she'd met.

"I don't want anything with you, my dear Doctor," the villain replied, "other than for you to wait patiently in your chamber."

"You kidnapped me for no reason?" Nora scoffed. "Seems a rather elaborate scheme simply to lock a woman in a closet."

"Come now, you know you are not just any woman. It's obvious you mean something to Owen Cassidy. Removing you from his presence serves my purposes."

"And those purposes are what? Harassment? Are you trying to annoy him to death?"

"I am merely repaying him in kind."

Nora snorted. "Oh, yes. I'm certain he's kidnapped many people's friends in the past."

"He likes that insolent mouth of yours, no doubt. I, however, have no interest in your haughty attitude and misguided defense of the scoundrel. Enjoy your stay with us, Doctor. I anticipate it will be of some duration."

The transmission ended with a soft click, leaving only the hum of the engine and Nora's angry exhalations. She dropped heavily onto the cot. The bastard. He knew Owen would come after her. He may have misinterpreted the exact nature of their relationship, but regardless she was a business partner and something of a friend. Owen would see her as one of his own, and he protected his own. And in doing so he would put his life in danger.

"Dammit," she muttered. Hadn't she just said to him she didn't like waiting and not knowing?

I'll have to fight back, however I can.

She slipped off the cot and sat on the floor, running her hands along the metal frame beneath the thin mattress. If she could snap or pry off some small bit, she might be able to use it to unscrew something or pry off a larger, more useful piece.

Anything she could manage would be progress, and the activity would keep her sane.

As her fingers pushed and pulled, her mind worked on the other half of the puzzle. Who was this villain and what was his goal?

He makes no sense, Nora thought to herself, unwilling to speak aloud in case he was listening. *Why attempt to kill Owen weeks ago, then never again? All the attacks I've seen have targeted his business, not his person, but the two can't possibly be unrelated.*

Except for that one incident, the end goal appeared to be to destroy the business, disrupt Owen's personal life, and overall to make him suffer. Whoever this enemy was, he believed he'd been wronged.

Forget the why. Focus on the who. Someone who thinks you might recognize him. Someone you've met.

Nora had encountered a sea of new faces over the past few weeks, at the mine and the refinery. She immediately dismissed the idea it might be one of the working men. They wouldn't have the means to orchestrate this complex scheme. Meaning it was someone higher up. Someone with money. Which narrowed down her list of suspects to few enough men she could count them on one hand. And all of them were close to Owen.

"Dammit," she muttered again. This betrayal was going to hurt.

19

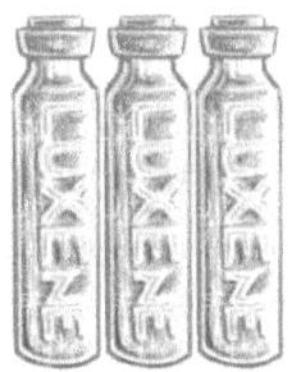

"I AIN'T THAT DAFT."

Owen stared out from the prow of the riverboat. The hazy form of the craft ahead of them was rapidly fading into the shadows of the onrushing night. His muscles clenched at yet another refusal. On a boat full of conmen and gamblers, not one was willing to assist him?

"Me neither," said the man on Owen's opposite side. "Smacks of piracy. I ride these boats to stay clear of the law, not to invite them in for tea and cookies."

Owen's fingers tightened on the rail as he struggled to keep his expression and voice neutral. He was offering damn good money for a few hours' work. More than they'd earn at cards in a whole night. And judging by the patches and loose threads on their suits, these fellows needed the money.

"We're staging a rescue, not plundering their treasure," he growled.

"A rescue?" The gambler snickered. "You some kind of vigilante, then?"

"You need Darling," the other man opined.

"Darling?" Owen repeated. Was that a name? A nickname? A woman of ill repute they thought might distract him from his purpose?

"Yup," agreed the second man. "Darling'd do it. They don't call him Mad Malcolm for nothing."

Mad Malcolm. Fantastic. The only person who might help him was reputed to be out of his head. "Where do I find him?" Owen asked.

"Top deck, throwing down cards with the snob-nobs. Can't miss him."

"Thank you." Owen turned from the rail and started for the stairs. He'd take whatever help he could get.

The man guarding the door took one look at Owen's bespoke suit and waved him in. The top deck, reserved for those with money to burn, glowed with the warm, yellow light of abundant electric lights. The scents of spiced meats and expensive cigars wafted through the air, and drinks flowed freely, encouraging the revelers to empty their pockets and indulge.

Owen scanned the tables, watching as reckless men gorged themselves on rich food and strong drink, cards fluttering and dice bouncing on the baize. Every table was the same. Every watch fob gold, every diamond cufflink genuine.

The ages of the men varied from boys hardly out of the schoolroom to hunched, bald octogenarians with cards clutched in their gnarled hands. Some of these men were professional gamblers, but Owen couldn't guess which at first glance. Nowhere did he see a man who would warrant a, "Can't miss him."

"Looking for a seat?" asked a passing waiter. "There are a few open places in the back if you would follow me? Can I get you a drink? Something to eat?"

Owen shook his head. "I'm looking for a man called Darling."

"Ah." The waiter's gaze traveled upward—an entire foot upward—to lock with Owen's. "Er, you're not looking to raise a fuss, are you? Darling's no cheat. Whatever he took your employer for, he won it fair and square."

"I have no vendetta against the man," Owen replied, his

voice even. This wasn't the first time he'd been mistaken for a brute, and it wouldn't be the last. "It's a matter of business."

"Ah. He's over there. Corner table. Don't go looking for trouble."

Too late. Trouble had been following him for months and showed no sign of stopping.

Owen wound a slow, but deliberate path through the room to the corner table, where four men sat engaged in an intense game of five-card stud. Drinks sat untouched, and towering stacks of chips suggested high stakes. Owen looked at each man in turn, wondering which was Darling. The thin man with the stony face? The young buck with the flamboyant waistcoat? The slick pretty-boy in all black...

Owen's brow furrowed as he paused to give the man further consideration. Unlike his companions, he showed no sign of tension or serious concentration. He looked entirely at ease, and it wasn't because he was holding a winning hand. Owen stood in the perfect position to see his cards.

This had to be Darling. Owen didn't often find the adjective beautiful suited to a man, but Darling absolutely was. He had the look of a mythological Apollo: high cheekbones, ice-blue eyes, and white-blond hair tousled just enough to give him a wicked edge. Still, he wasn't so remarkable Owen would consider him instantly recognizable.

And then Darling turned his head to meet Owen's stare.

The right side of his face may once have matched the left for beauty, but now a wide swath of puckered scar tissue slashed across his cheek. Smaller scars dotted his brow and jawline, as if whatever had caused the damage had splattered him.

Darling's left eyebrow arched. "You plannin' to make my next wager?" The Southern accent was affected. He hailed from somewhere up north.

"Are you Darling?" Owen asked.

"Sure am, doll. You wanna be dealt in next hand or you just lookin' for an autograph?"

Owen reached inside his coat and flashed a stack of bills. "I have a business proposition for you."

"My favorite sort. Be right with you."

Darling finished out the hand, then gathered up his chips and his drink and excused himself from the table. He gestured for Owen to follow him outside.

"Well, then," Darling drawled once they were alone, leaning on the rail and taking a sip of his drink. "What can I do for you?"

"You see that boat ahead of us?"

Darling glanced over his shoulder. "Barely. Getting dark."

"At the speed we've been going, we'll pass it maybe two hours from now. There's a little lifeboat here equipped with one of those newfangled motors. I mean to use it to get on that boat. I need someone who knows riverboats to accompany me."

"Interesting. What's on the boat that's so important?"

"A woman has been kidnapped. I intend to free her." If she was even on the boat. A single eyewitness had said they'd seen a woman carried off toward the docks. A man at the docks had said she'd been carried onto the riverboat that Owen now planned to storm. This was a gamble worthy of an accomplice nicknamed Mad Malcolm.

Darling drained his glass. "Well. Not somethin' you hear every day. What's the job and what's the pay?"

"The job is to accompany me to the boat and help me find where she might be imprisoned. I don't know boats. I'd wander around lost and never find her. You can lead me to good locations to search and help ensure I don't get caught."

The gambler nodded, tapping a single finger against the now-empty glass he held.

"Payment is one hundred up front," Owen continued. "Five hundred after if we succeed."

"I can cash in the chips I just took from the table for twice that."

"Yes, but how much of that was the money you started with?"

Darling laughed. "Most of it. Gotta play big to win big."

"If this goes well, I may be moved to sweeten the pot. You have any use for luxene?"

Darling's left eyebrow twitched again. "You're Owen Cassidy. They weren't kidding when they called you a giant. Never figured you for one prone to midnight capers, though."

"The kidnapped woman is my friend. I protect my own."

"Ah, yes. 'A bold spirit in a loyal breast.'"

Owen frowned at the peculiar compliment.

"Shakespeare. Richard II." Darling held out his right hand. The back of it bore the same nasty scars as his cheek. "You have yourself a deal, Luxene Man."

20

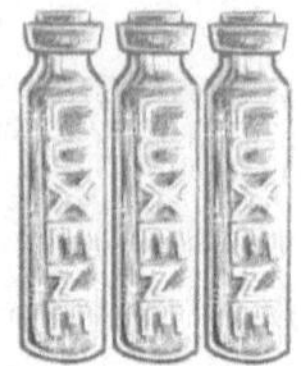

Owen nearly jumped out of his skin at the bleating sound of an unseen animal. He glanced at Darling, who appeared to be little more than a shadow in the darkness.

"You could've warned me there'd be goats," Owen hissed.

Darling shrugged. "Main deck's the cargo deck," he replied, loud enough that Owen winced. "Animals, feed, crates and barrels of any goods you can think of."

The goat bleated again. Thank God it was dark. If the thing were visible, Owen would probably be swayed by its cuteness into forgiving it for the noise.

"I'm allergic to furry things. If I start to sneeze…"

"Anyone who can hear us over the engine is close enough to see us. C'mon."

Darling waved a hand and Owen followed, for lack of anything better to do. This was the most foolhardy thing he'd done in years. Maybe ever. The longer they wandered the unpopulated areas of the steamboat, the more certain he grew that they'd be caught. And if he were thrown in prison for trespassing—or worse, piracy—he'd never see Nora again.

The thought sent a shiver of dread down his spine. Nora. He'd grown to care for her, and not merely because he was a lusty man who hadn't bedded a woman in ages. She was spunky and smart. Determined. Stern when necessary, but always kind.

A good person. Better than he was, certainly, and in no way deserving of the trouble she'd stumbled into.

He would find her, dammit. He'd find her and free her and take her home. And once he had her warm and rested, belly full of good food, he would beg her to let him kiss her again, with the promise that this time he would do the thing right.

Darling led the way up a secluded staircase, moving ever closer to the rear of the boat. *Aft*, Owen corrected himself. The engine noise grew louder with every step, the repetitive drumming echoing in his head. The interior of the boat was lit with electric lights, strung on wires hastily tacked to the ceiling. Fire hazard. Owen would never allow such shoddy installation in his own facilities.

Darling held up a hand and Owen froze. Footsteps sounded above the mechanical hum of the steam engine. Owen's entire body went rigid. A man appeared from around the corner, his face contorting into a frown of suspicion when he spied Owen and Darling.

"Leave this to me," Darling whispered.

"You gentlemen got turned around?" the man asked, his hand dropping to the revolver at his hip.

"Looking for a quiet place to have a smoke," Darling replied, all nonchalance. "Too windy outside."

"Well, this here's no place for it, either. I'm going to have to ask you to leave."

"Of course. We'll find somewhere else." He glanced back at Owen. "Won't we?"

Before Owen could even open his mouth, Darling's fist flew, catching the unprepared man in the side of the head with a blow that left him reeling. Quick as lightning, Darling landed two more jabs and the man crumpled to the floor.

"Who the hell are you?" Owen blurted.

"I'm Malcolm Darling, doll. Gambler. Did a bit of boxing back in the day." He bent down and rummaged through the unconscious man's pockets. When he straightened up, he brandished a key. "He would be your guard. I'd wager somewhere down that hall is your lady."

Owen accepted the key, and they hurried down the corridor and around the corner where the guard had come from. Up ahead, the steam engine clacked and whirred, pistons moving up and down while the boiler hissed in the background.

"Storage closet," Darling murmured, gesturing at a narrow door.

Owen's heart hammered in his chest. Had they really found her? If the closet turned out to be empty, or if the key didn't work, then what? A man was lying on the floor not far away, and it wouldn't be long before he woke up or someone found him.

The key slipped easily into the lock. Palms sweating, Owen turned it, convinced it would stick and he'd be out of luck.

The lock clicked. His breath rushed out in a sigh of relief. He pulled on the handle and the door swung open.

"Nor—"

Before he could even finish saying her name, a heavy chunk of metal came hurtling at him, and all he could do was yelp in alarm as he spun away from the blow.

21

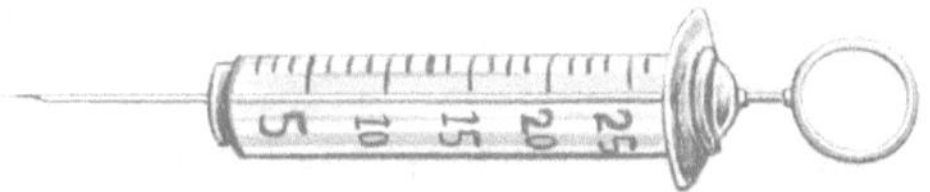

NORA CRIED OUT and dropped her makeshift weapon, the clank of metal on metal still echoing in her ears. She should have known something wasn't quite right when she'd heard muffled noises outside her cell, but she'd been too focused on escape.

The light in the corridor wasn't bright, but it was enough to pain her dark-adjusted eyes. She squinted, trying to see if she'd inflicted any damage.

"Owen?" she asked, the wince evident in her voice.

"Ow," he replied.

"I'm so sorry."

"Don't be. Let's get out of here."

Nora kicked the steel bar into the closet, beneath the cot that now listed on its three remaining legs. She pushed the door shut behind her. Owen motioned with his right arm for her to follow. Good. She hadn't injured him too badly.

"I *am* very sorry. I thought you were one of them, coming to deliver the food and water I'd demanded. Thank goodness you're so tall. I'd meant that blow for the head."

"Thank Zeus that Hercules there opened the door instead of me," drawled a blond man with a scarred face standing behind Owen. "I don't have fancy metal body parts to withstand a lady on the warpath." He tipped his wide-brimmed, western-style hat. "Evenin' ma'am. Malcolm Darling, at your service. Right this way, if you please."

Nora glanced at Owen with raised brows, but he only shrugged and gestured again for her to follow along.

Around the corner, a man lay on the ground, half-conscious and moaning. Darling bent to relieve him of his pistol, then continued on as if he did such things every night.

"Friend of yours?" Nora whispered to Owen, nodding in Darling's direction.

"Riverboat gambler," Owen replied. "Word is he's mad."

"Oh. Lovely. And now he's armed."

Owen looked over his shoulder at the man lying on the ground. "He took that goon down with his bare hands. Don't think it matters."

"Ah," Nora said, because shouting, "Are you out of your mind?" wasn't the most sensible of options just now.

She'd known Owen would come after her. The speed with which he'd done so and his less-than-respectable methods stunned her. He'd hired some slick-talking ruffian to escort him around the boat in the middle of the night and punch out any enemies they encountered? Such behavior didn't fit at all with the prim-and-proper businessman she'd first met. This was the impassioned Owen hidden beneath. The "protect my family with my life" Owen.

And what did that mean? Had she become a close friend? Something else? Her stomach churned, either from the unsettling thought or the lack of food.

Nora followed Darling through the corridors, wishing she'd kept the leg from the cot. Owen's enemy may not yet have stooped to outright murder, but he'd shown himself to have little care for the lives of others. The fact that none of Owen's employees had died was due to a combination of random chance and Owen's immediate response to halt production and search for other dangers. A less concerned employer wouldn't have fared so well.

Darling reached up over his head and yanked hard on a string of electric lights. A section of the wire came free, tumbling to the floor. Glass tinkled. The lights flickered once, then died.

Owen tensed beside Nora. "Gonna set the damned boat on fire."

Possible, but Nora preferred the darkness. The life of a crime-fighting detective was definitely best left to experts. Sneaking was nearly as bad as waiting.

After what seemed eons, the trio reached a narrow staircase and made their way down to the main deck. The smells of animal cargo hit Nora's nose an instant before the unhappy bleat of a goat made her flinch. She glanced at Owen. In the dim light his expression was inscrutable, but his body radiated tension. She clenched her fists against the urge to lay a comforting hand on his arm. She'd already established that touching him under ordinary circumstances was a bad idea. Who knew what sort of reaction her body might have during a time of stress?

Darling froze so suddenly Nora nearly crashed into him. Owen caught her arm to steady her, jerking his hand away the moment she'd regained her balance. Her heart thudded in her chest. Every breath sounded too loudly in her ears.

"Spread out," a distant voice commanded. "Don't let her leave this boat."

Darling whirled around, pushing Nora and Owen ahead of him. Instead of heading back up the staircase, he clambered over a stack of crates, saying nothing, expecting Nora and Owen to follow.

Owen cupped his hands to make a step and boosted Nora up onto a crate. She climbed over, dropping to the ground on the other side as quietly as possible. Cold sweat trickled down her neck. Owen's boots hit the floor beside her, his two hundred fifty-ish pounds shaking the deck beneath her feet.

The smell of animal was stronger here, and Nora could hear shuffling and low snuffles under the whining of the one irritable goat.

This was madness. Trailing a questionably-trustworthy

guide through the cargo space of a riverboat while armed thugs hunted for her? How had she ended up in such a mess? She squeezed between bags of feed and past cages of squirming creatures that might have been piglets. Behind her, Owen stumbled, his large body unsuited to the tight quarters. He jerked and made a soft noise that sounded like a muffled sneeze.

Nora forged ahead through the crowded and increasingly foul-smelling cargo, trying to keep pace with Darling, who slithered through the clutter as if he were born for this. The bleating goat had fallen silent, and off in the distance, the footsteps of her pursuers pounded on the deck.

How much longer until they reached their destination? There had to be an escape vessel of some sort. She assumed Owen and Darling had come by boat, though it was possible they'd been dropped from a dirigible. She scrambled over a large cage, pretending not to notice the scuttling beneath her of whatever was inside. Hopefully not something that would bite.

Up ahead, the crates and barrels began to thin out, and she slipped to the ground with a renewed sense of hope. If they could get to a lifeboat, or any sort of seaworthy craft, they could float away into the darkness.

And then, Owen sneezed.

The sound tore through the silence. A second, more powerful sneeze followed, and Owen toppled from his perch atop the cage with a resounding crash. Startled animals let loose a flurry of hoots, yowls, and other ear-splitting noises.

"Sorry," Owen gasped, before sneezing a third time.

"In the cargo!" an angry voice shouted.

Darling swore in a language that might have been French and broke into a run. Owen barreled after him, propelling Nora along as he shoved boxes and bags aside. The crack of a gunshot split the air and Nora screamed.

"Hurry!" Darling shouted. "We're almost there!" He raised the gun he'd taken from the fallen guard and fired off a shot into the darkness. More furious voices and heavy footsteps joined the clamor.

The moment they reached the rail, Owen grabbed Nora and hauled her off her feet, swinging her up and over into a small boat with a motor affixed to the back. He climbed down beside her, still sniffling, though the sneezes appeared to have stopped. Darling fired off several more shots, then dropped into the boat with enough force to set it rocking dangerously.

"You owe me *at least* five hundred," he said, scrambling to start up the motor while Owen yanked on a mooring line.

The motor roared to life, and the boat jolted forward, knocking Nora to the floor. Gunfire erupted from the riverboat, bullets splashing in the water to their right and left. Nora ducked low and clung to the seat. Owen huddled beside her, while Darling shielded himself behind the motor as he steered. Nora didn't much care where he was taking them, as long as it was away.

"Make that one thousand," Darling amended, his voice eerily calm.

"Done," Owen replied. "Just get us to safety."

The gambler tipped his hat. "Aye, aye, Cap'n."

22

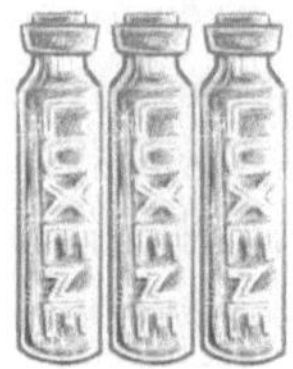

GRAND TOWER, ILLINOIS. Population eight hundred seventy-six. Home to an iron foundry and a ghost, apparently. The chatty man behind the desk was eager to rattle off the entire history of the small riverside city. Owen wasn't interested in the details. The town had a hotel, a train station, and a telephone. Good enough.

They'd stumbled into town near dawn, soaked to the bone from the rain that now sheeted down the windows like the never-ending cascade of Niagara Falls. Owen had seen the Falls once, briefly, as he passed through the area on some tour of business he could no longer recall. He wanted to return someday to linger, but he was always busy with work. Too busy.

At the moment, he couldn't remember what the point of all that work was. He was exhausted, shivering, and his head had begun to throb. He'd actually thought for a moment the concierge had said something about pirates. Absurd.

"…Your room key, Mr. Cass."

Owen blinked at the iron key with the attached tag bearing the number seven. Was it meant for him?

An elbow dug into his side. "Your key, *Mr. Cass*," Darling echoed. "Take your wife and go upstairs to rest before y'all catch your death."

"Right." Owen grabbed the key and took Nora's arm to

escort her up the stairs. She moved stiffly, but he couldn't tell if her cold, wet clothing was the cause or if she disliked his touch. "Whose asinine idea was this?" he mumbled.

"Darling's. He swooped in, introduced us as Mr. and Mrs. Cass and requested a room for us and a room for himself. He used his own name, though."

"Which might not be real in the first place."

Nora shrugged one shoulder. "Not sure why he would *pick* the name Darling."

"Not sure of much of anything about him, but he helped me when no one else would, and he managed to find us a place to dock before the last of the fuel ran out, so I'm inclined to think well of him."

"As am I. You're shivering. We need to get you out of those wet clothes. And I want to have a look at your shoulder."

"Mm-hmm." Owen trudged up the stairs and somehow managed to get the key into the lock. The modest-sized room was lit only by the low-burning fire in the hearth, but it was warm and dry. He locked the door behind them and began to shrug out of his sodden clothing, keeping his back turned to Nora, assuming she was doing the same. "If you toss me a blanket, I can curl up here by the fire."

"Don't be daft," she retorted. "There's a perfectly good bed. You can wedge a pillow between us if you're terrified of me."

"I'm six and a half feet tall. I won't fit in that bed."

"Oh. I hadn't thought about that. I'm sorry."

Some article of her clothing hit the ground with a wet plop, and Owen squeezed his eyes shut. Which did nothing to block his mental picture of a naked Nora.

"At least the doorways here are tall enough I don't bash my head. They aren't always."

"That must be frustrating. And of course you have to get all your clothing custom-made."

"Yes. Fortunately, I can afford it." He hadn't always been

able to. In the years before he'd discovered luxene, his mother had spent hours sewing and altering garments to fit him.

Soft cloth brushed his bare back, and he flinched, his eyes flying open. Nora wrapped the quilt around him and patted his mechanical shoulder.

"Don't panic. I've seen you naked before, if you recall. And please come to the bed if you're cold or uncomfortable, even if you have to curl up. I'll make room." She yawned. "I'll inspect your shoulder after we've had a nap."

Owen answered with an inarticulate grunt. He tugged off the remainder of his clothing, spread everything out to dry, and sat in front of the fire, pulling the quilt tightly around him. Rubbing his aching temple did little to relieve the pain. He stared into the coals, as if they could burn away his imaginings of Nora lying naked in the bed only a few feet away.

It only took a few minutes for exhaustion to overpower him. He surrendered and stretched out on the ground, until his fantasies faded into dreams.

When he awoke, the only indication time had passed were the coals that had burned down. The room remained dark, the sliver of sky visible between the curtains still an unrelenting gray. Rain continued to drum a steady patter on the roof.

Owen lifted his head from the pillow someone had wedged beneath him. A second blanket covered him now, along with the quilt. Nora, tending to his well-being.

"You were shivering," she answered his thoughts. "Never feverish, though. Merely wet and cold. Welcome back to the land of the living."

Welcome back to the land of resolutely not turning around.

The sizzle of a flaring match was soon followed by a warm, yellow glow illuminating the room as Nora lit a lamp.

"I'd like to take a look at your shoulder, if you don't mind."

Owen sat up and let the quilt fall away from his upper half. For the first time, he took a long look at the steel and brass joint keeping his arm attached to the rest of his body. Without a mirror he could only see so much, but what he did observe no longer repelled him—it impressed him.

Nora's skills were remarkable. For the rest of his life, every time he saw himself undressed, he'd think of her and what she'd done for him—a stranger—out of the goodness of her heart. Because helping others was so much a part of her she couldn't even imagine not doing so.

Christ, he was falling hard for her, and right when they were set to part ways. His rehabilitation was finishing and the trouble with his business had become too dangerous. When he made his phone calls, he'd be arranging for her train tickets back to Savannah. It was the least he could do, since he knew she wouldn't accept payment. And best he let her go now, before he completely lost his head.

Nora had wrapped sheets around herself in a fashion reminiscent of a Roman toga. She knelt beside him, manipulating his shoulder while she poked and prodded at the workings. Her movements were as brisk and professional as usual, but a stiffness remained in her posture. The urge to apologize again surged within him, though he still hadn't determined what his transgression had been. In all likelihood, he would never know.

"Good." Nora released his arm and drew back. "Nothing looks damaged. I guess I don't hit as hard as I think I do."

"Or you underestimate the strength of your biomechanics. You do remarkable work."

A slight flush crept over her cheeks and she scrambled to her feet, clutching the sheets around her. "Thank you. You may cover up again now."

Owen pulled the quilt over his shoulders and pushed himself off the floor. He was done with this. He wasn't going to spend whatever time he had left with her with this strain between them.

"Nora…" He stopped himself from taking a step toward

her. At his size, he had to do whatever he could to appear less intimidating.

Owen paused to gather his thoughts, and a knock sounded on the door before he could decide what to say.

"That would be our breakfast," Nora said. She crossed to the door and opened it a crack, then swung it wide, stepping behind it to shield her undressed state from the young man bearing a tray of food. "Thank you."

"You're welcome, ma'am," he replied, setting the tray on the small table in the center of the space. "I'm to tell you they're still searching for clothing. Hard to find something appropriate. No one's working, it being Sunday and all." He gave a nod and ducked back out the door.

"Sunday," Owen murmured. He'd completely lost track of time. He couldn't even guess at the date. "Then I suppose I should thank God we're all alive and well."

Nora took a seat, carefully adjusting the sheets covering herself, then lifted the lid off a plate of food. The scent of freshly cooked sausage and hot coffee hit Owen's nostrils with such force that his stomach growled in reply. He plopped down into the second chair, failing to keep his coverings around him as elegantly as Nora had done.

For a few seconds, he struggled to cover himself, before noticing she was paying no attention to anything other than her breakfast. He grabbed for a fork and dug in, ready to make up for twenty or so hours without a bite.

When he next looked up, his plate was empty and Nora was watching him, her head tilted slightly in that way of hers when she was lost in thought. An entire piece of toast and two small sausages remained on her plate.

"Is something wrong?" he asked.

"Hmm?" She gave her head a slight shake. "No, nothing's wrong. Why?"

"You haven't finished." He gestured at her food.

Nora chuckled. "Ah. I've had plenty. I'm quite full, in fact.

I'm rather smaller than you are, you know. Feel free to have the rest if you want it."

Owen hesitated until she pushed the plate across the table to him. He was still hungry. And if she truly had no intention of eating more, he hated to let it go to waste.

"When you finish we might want to return to bed," she suggested, her words punctuated by a yawn. "We can't do anything until our clothes dry or we're brought something else to wear, and we could use the rest."

Owen swallowed a bite of sausage and regarded her for a moment. Her eyelids drooped, she had dark circles beneath her eyes, and her shoulders sagged.

"Didn't you sleep yet?"

"No," she admitted. "I wanted to make certain you weren't ailing and to arrange for something to eat." She yawned again. "But it's okay."

"Like hell it is." He abandoned his food and sprang to his feet. The quilt fell away, but he no longer cared. He was not going to let Nora run herself ragged taking care of him. "You're exhausted. You're going to bed."

She averted her eyes and scrambled from her chair. "I'm fine. I can get to bed myself."

Owen muttered a curse under his breath and hurriedly covered himself. "Dammit, Nora, I'm sorry. I'm not... I don't..." He took a steadying breath. "I promise I won't touch you or kiss you again. Not unless you want it."

She crossed both arms over her chest, folding in on herself. "I don't know what I want."

Her statement made no sense to Owen, but tired as she clearly was, he couldn't be too surprised.

"It's easier when I'm being professional," she went on, staring out at some random point on the wall. "I know how to do that. I don't know how to..." She waved a hand helplessly.

"You should sleep. Everything will be easier when you've

rested." He took a single step toward her, then another when she didn't back away.

Nora's gaze flicked toward him, and he tugged on the quilt where it gaped open across his chest. She laughed, the sound a mixture of humor and despair.

"No," she replied. "No, it won't be."

"What can I do to help?"

"I don't know."

Another step and he was at her side, painfully aware of how much he loomed over her. "May I help you to bed, at least?"

She peered up at him, and for a few seconds he feared she'd never say a word to him again.

"Maybe…" she started. "Maybe a hug."

That, he could do. He opened his arms, allowing her to lead the embrace. When she sagged into his chest, he drew her closer, tightening his grip to support her. Slowly, her body relaxed against his. Her head fell to rest over his heart, and she let out a weary sigh.

"Let's get you to bed," he murmured.

He steered her to the bed and tucked her in beneath the one remaining blanket. Not wanting to give her time to accuse him of neglecting his own well-being, he crawled into the too-small bed beside her and draped the quilt to cover them both. When she snuggled close, he hooked an arm around her, holding her until she drifted into a sound slumber.

Things would be awkward when they awoke, he predicted. At the moment, he didn't care.

23

Waking in Owen's arms was unexpectedly delightful. He was warm, his protective embrace soothing, and Nora was content to remain cuddled against him. Until a persistent knocking triggered two jarring realizations: she had to answer the door because Owen was stark naked, and this incident would have repercussions.

She couldn't predict what those repercussions might be, but they were unavoidable. One didn't snuggle with a naked man without *something* coming of it. As far as she knew.

The same boy who had brought the breakfast waited outside the hotel room door, a large bundle of clothing and personal grooming items clutched in his arms. Nora relieved him of the burden and carried it to the bed, where Owen now sat upright, the quilt pulled up to his chin. The hunger in his eyes almost made her stumble. He looked at her now the way he'd looked at his breakfast while his stomach growled audibly. Like she was the only thing that could satisfy him.

"They've found us something to wear," she said. Surely that raspiness in her voice was a natural result of having just woken up and not a sign of arousal. Wasn't it?

"Good." He didn't move, but his gaze remained fixed on her. Her bedsheet wrapping suddenly felt less like a dress and more like a deliberately provocative undergarment.

Nora yanked a hairbrush and a pale yellow garment she

was fairly certain was a woman's evening gown from the pile of clothing. "I'm heading to the washroom to clean up and dress. I'll, uh, leave you time to do the same."

"Of course."

Nora clutched the dress to her chest and hurried from the room, thankful that the ladies' bathing chamber was only a few doors away and no one was present to witness her inelegant dash. Their waterlogged arrival was peculiar enough already.

Washing with tepid water and giving her tangled hair a thorough brushing calmed her nerves, but the anxiety began to creep back in as she stepped into the yellow gown. When was the last time she'd worn a dress? Years ago, probably. Perhaps the last time one of her siblings had married.

This particular gown was clearly meant for a ball or other party, not for a casual dinner in a small hotel, but at least it would allow her to leave her room for a time. She hoped Owen's clothing was sufficient for him to do the same.

His nakedness hadn't bothered her in and of itself. Her profession made her well-versed in the anatomy of the male body, and she'd seen Owen unclothed during her time caring for him. She'd even seen him fully aroused, presumably when something in his dreams had led to sexual excitation. It was entirely natural and not in the least bit distressing. Only her body's new reactions concerned her. Even the *thought* of him was causing a bit of a quiver at the junction of her thighs.

Ridiculous. She splashed some of the now-cool water on her face, then set to work adjusting and fastening the dress. It was on the small side, and she didn't have a corset. When it was fully buttoned, the tops of her breasts protruded from the neckline in a fashion she never would have attempted, given the choice. She turned to the mirror, expecting to appear scandalous and of sallow complexion.

Much to her surprise, the dress flattered her. The neckline didn't expose nearly as much as she'd felt it did, and the color was pale enough to bring out the rosiness in her cheeks.

Perhaps she could go down to dinner and not feel awkward after all. Until she inevitably stepped on the hem and tripped. Or someone noticed her bare feet.

She returned to her room to find Owen and most of the remaining clothing gone. A single pair of stockings lay folded atop tidy blankets. Nora laughed aloud. Only a man like Owen Cassidy would make his own bed in a hotel room. She quickly pulled on the stockings and headed downstairs, still unshod, but reasonably presentable.

Just as she reached the last step, a familiar voice called out, "Well, ain't you the prettiest thing this side of the Mississippi."

"Mr. Darling." Nora gave him a nod. "I really don't see how you would know such a thing, seeing as we only recently crossed the river."

"I've traveled all over, m'dear, and you are without a doubt the loveliest of women."

Nora couldn't help but smile. "Your compliments are as false as your accent," she teased. "You're not from anywhere in the South that I'm familiar with."

"C'est vrai, mademoiselle. I'm Canadian," he replied in what she assumed to be his real accent. He tipped his hat, which was still a bit squashed and soggy from last night's adventure. His clothing looked damp as well. "I'm hopping a wagon out of town. Best of luck to you and your luxene man."

"Oh," Nora blurted, startled by the news. "But—" But Darling was already halfway to the exit. She watched him slip out the door, then headed for the dining room. Owen would surely be hungry again. They could talk over dinner and make plans. Without the awkwardness of the confining bedchamber.

She swished into the dining room, managing not to get her legs tangled in the skirts, her confidence rising with every step. Yes, she was overdressed, but she could take on the world even in a too-tight yellow ballgown.

And then Owen spied her. His jaw dropped. He scrambled to his feet, almost knocking his chair over in his haste. His gaze darted up and down, and she realized with a hot rush of embarrassment that he was trying not to stare at her breasts. Before she could stop herself, she glanced down to make sure she hadn't popped too far out of the dress.

So much for not being awkward. This was why she preferred her usual style. Her vests were cute, comfortable, and supportive, and she never had to fear accidental exposure.

"Thank you," Nora said as Owen pulled out a chair for her. Unaccustomed as she was to adjusting her skirts, she particularly appreciated the gesture.

"You're very welcome." He sat opposite her, too far to touch, but near enough to see every twitch of his mouth and every movement of his eyes. "You look lovely tonight. The dress is different than your customary style, but I think it suits you equally well."

"I think it overexposes and undersupports my rather large chest."

Owen coughed. "You are perfectly well-proportioned, and you are not at all exposed. Simply, er…"

"On display?"

She wouldn't have thought Owen a blusher, but a definite pink tint colored his cheeks. "I'm sorry. I'm a cad. This is wholly inappropriate. I only meant to say that the dress looks well on you."

"No need to apologize. I steered the conversation that direction. And things are bound to be a bit strange after…" She stopped before she could dwell too much on the way his body had felt against hers, even through the double layer of sheets. "Well, Darling has left, so one of us could take that room tonight."

"Yes." He drew the word out slowly.

"If it's safe, of course," Nora hastily added. Now that the idea was out there, separate rooms sounded less appealing. She'd enjoyed her nap in Owen's embrace, and she valued his companionship. Perhaps this was what she needed to safely explore her attraction: gentle, soothing hugs and quiet cuddling. Nothing wild like their single kiss.

"Of course," Owen echoed.

"We do have an enemy chasing us, and even shooting at us."

Owen rubbed his chin. He hadn't shaved, and a shadow of stubble lined his jaw. "I do wonder if the gunfire was meant to kill us or only scare us. They didn't even hit the boat. Still, it's safest to act as if he means us harm."

"I agree. Since it's possible he's tracked us here, we might be safest together."

"True. And of course we'd have to explain to the hotel management why we suddenly wanted separate rooms."

"Very true. It seems it's best to remain as we are. It *is* only one more night."

"Precisely. While you were dressing, I inquired about train schedules. We should be able to depart tomorrow morning."

"Perfect."

They were in agreement about everything, it seemed. They even requested the same dish when a serving girl came by to take their dinner order. Conversation, however, came in short, stilted bursts. Their entire discourse consisted of remarks on the continually dreary weather and discussion of the food.

Nora forced a smile. "The service here has been exceptionally pleasing." Good heavens, she sounded as formal as one of the elderly matrons who sometimes took tea with her mother.

"Indeed," Owen replied, with equal gravity. "I will see that everyone is well compensated."

Nora pushed the mashed potatoes around on her plate without eating them. What was wrong? Surely they ought to be better at conversing than this. Or had they never truly talked about anything outside of work? His business troubles. Her work on his shoulder. Was that the extent of their relationship? Or had their friendship fizzled out due to the strange sexual tension between them?

A sick feeling that it was all her fault settled in the pit of Nora's stomach. She stared down into her food, appetite gone. Her life was fixing things. If only she could fix her life.

24

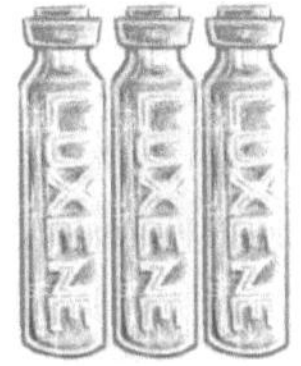

OWEN HADN'T BEEN PREPARED for the sight of Nora in a dress. Or rather, *that* dress. The way it hugged her breasts was every bit as enticing as the way her trousers hugged her bottom. He could avoid the distraction of the latter by not standing behind her. Unfortunately, talking to her meant looking at the front of her.

He wanted to smack himself. He wasn't usually like this. He was fond of women, certainly, but he didn't ogle them. With Nora, tamping down his lust had become a constant struggle. One made all the more difficult by the newfound knowledge of how perfectly her body molded to his. Of the way she had seemed comforted, rather than intimidated, by his size.

He toyed with the cuffs of the too-small shirt as she ascended the stairs ahead of him. She held her skirts clenched in both fists, lifted several inches off the ground. She hadn't explicitly stated that she feared tripping over the hem, but Owen preferred to stay behind her on the stairs, just in case. If she fell, he'd catch her. His repaired arm was plenty strong now.

She reached the top of the stairs and dropped her skirts. Giving a sigh of relief, she strode off toward the room, her steps faster and more confident.

He definitely preferred her in trousers. It suited her personality and her habits. Still, he wouldn't be sad to see her dressed up in a curve-hugging ballgown at other times in the future.

"What future?" he grumbled to himself. *You're putting her on a damned train tomorrow, or have you forgotten?*

No, he hadn't forgotten. He'd made a number of phone calls after their late-afternoon dinner, and the arrangements were all made. He'd be returning to St. Louis. She'd be heading to Savannah. His household staff would pack up her belongings and have them sent after her promptly.

Tonight would be their last night together. Never mind that the thought made him want to punch something. It was the right decision. He had to keep her safe and let her return to her work and her life. Right now, though, he was damn well going to ensure they had a pleasant evening. He would ease some of Nora's fears. Make her smile. How, he wasn't sure.

"You know what?" he said.

Nora paused and turned around. "What?"

"We should look for something to do. Instead of sitting in the room staring at the walls until we grow tired. There must be some books or games in this hotel. You make yourself comfortable. I'll find a way to pass the time, and perhaps a bottle of wine."

Nora's eyebrows rose, then crinkled together. "Is this some sort of date?"

"Only if you want it to be." The words were out of Owen's mouth before he thought better of them. When she didn't answer right away, panic began to set in. Had that been the wrong thing to say?

Owen didn't arrange dates with ladies. That sort of thing was for proper courtship, and he didn't have time for courting. He arranged liaisons with lusty widows. He'd never seen the need for anything else. And now he'd gone and opened his mouth and he'd look a fool in front of Nora.

"That... um, could be nice," Nora said at last.

She wasn't laughing at him. Positive. But she was still

anxious. "Good, good," Owen replied. He would put her at ease. He would make her smile. He *would*, dammit. "I'll, uh, go see what I can find. I'll only be a few minutes."

Sadly, his few minutes turned into nearly half an hour of tromping around the hotel, finding nothing. More convinced than ever of his foolishness, he abandoned his futile quest and trudged up to the room with his meager findings.

Owen opened the door and reeled in shock, the wine bottle nearly slipping from his hand. Nora sat cross-legged atop the bed, dressed in nothing but a man's shirt. *His* shirt. He took a single step across the threshold into this strange, erotic fantasy.

"Hi," she greeted him. "I hope you don't mind me borrowing your clothes. Mine aren't quite dry, and as you can see..." She gestured at the gown now lying atop the bed, a huge tear slashing through the skirt. "I stepped on the hem. But it was too tight, anyway. If you need the shirt back, you're welcome to it. I can use the bedsheets again."

"No." Owen managed to choke the word out. "It's fine." He set the wine bottle onto the table, along with a pair of plain but serviceable glasses. Good God did he need a drink. "I found wine. Everything else..." He dropped the other items he'd carried tucked under his arm. "I found a Bible and a waterlogged deck of cards I think Darling might have left behind."

Nora stared at the sad, soggy offering and burst out laughing.

A grin tugged at the corners of Owen's mouth. Task one: complete. She'd smiled. Maybe he hadn't entirely failed after all.

"This leaves us with a few options," Owen said, shrugging out of the painfully small jacket and taking a seat at the table. "Attempt to gamble with cards that are either stuck together or falling to pieces, read scripture passages and sermonize on them, or tell each other jokes."

Nora laughed again and swung her legs over the edge of

the bed, exposing her silk stockings. Owen poured himself a large glass of wine.

"Definitely jokes." Greatly to Owen's relief, Nora swiftly took the seat opposite him, hiding much of her body. Mercifully, his shirt wasn't thin enough to see what she did or didn't have on beneath.

"Jokes it is." Owen poured a second glass of wine and passed it across the table. Nora took a small sip.

"We'll have to make a game of it," she decided. "We go back and forth, one joke at a time. First person to laugh loses."

"Multiple rounds?"

"Most likely. Unless all your jokes are so terrible you don't think you can cause anything but a cringe or a groan."

Owen held back a chuckle, steeling himself for the competition. "Sometimes the worst jokes are also the best. May the cleverest punster win." He held his wine glass aloft, and Nora clinked hers against it. "Ladies first."

"Hmm." Nora's lips twisted in an adorable little grimace as she thought. "Okay. I'll take it easy on you to begin. 'Man: My heart beats for you alone. Woman: Nonsense. That's your watch ticking.'"

Owen's lips curved, but he didn't laugh. "I actually like that. Here's one in the same vein. 'Man: My dear, tell me honestly what you think of me. Woman: Oh, I would, sir, but in truth I rarely think of you at all.'"

"Ouch! Poor man." Nora shook her head, fighting a smile. "Though, clearly they are not suited. She is too sharp and witty, and he is, I fear, rather dull."

Owen chuckled. "I thought we were meant to tell the jokes, not analyze them. Or does that earn us bonus points?"

Nora's hand shot out, pointing an accusatory finger. "You laughed! Round one to me."

It took Owen a moment to process her words. "What? Wait. I didn't laugh at any joke. You can't possibly credit that as a victory. I only laughed because you were critically pondering what was obviously meant to be a quick gag."

Nora folded her arms beneath her breasts, pressing the cloth of the shirt into her curves and giving Owen the distinct impression she wore absolutely nothing underneath. His mouth went dry and he took a gulp of wine.

"I will cede you this round," he said, fighting for composure. "But only if you agree that moving forward, we award points based specifically on jokes and not any other outside conversation."

"So picky." Nora took a dainty sip of wine. "I accept. As the current leader, I will give you the honor of beginning the next round. Go."

Owen thought a moment. "'Why are bachelors bad grammarians? Because when asked to conjugate they invariably decline.'"

Nora nodded, straight-faced. "I rather like that one. Try this: 'Fortune-Teller: You will be very poor until you are thirty-five years of age. Poet, eagerly: And after then? Fortune-Teller: You will get used to it.'"

"Poets, eh? 'Well, I heard rifles that can shoot five miles have been invented. I mention this to recommend to poets the advisability of sending their contributions by post.'"

A short laugh escaped Nora's throat. She clapped a hand to her mouth to smother it, finally succumbing to a fit of giggles. "Oh, the poor, aspiring poets! No one has a care for their feelings. Point to you, Mr. Cassidy." She saluted him with her glass and took another drink.

Nora's laughter broke whatever tension had existed between them. The jokes began to fly, laughter coming faster and harder as the level of wine dropped lower and lower.

Some time deep into their second bottle Nora asked, "'Why is a person listening to these jokes like a man condemned to a military execution?'" Owen didn't think it was even her turn, but since he couldn't remember the score, either, it didn't seem to matter.

"He's receiving corporal *pun*-ishment?"

"No. 'Because he is sure to be riddled to death.'"

Owen winced. "Good God. That's almost as bad as the one about what Neptune would say if the seas all dried up."

Nora's brow crinkled. "What would he say?"

"I really haven't got a notion."

She snorted and Owen lost all composure. He leaned on the table to support himself, shaking with laughter until his sides hurt. Across the table, Nora did likewise. Her cheeks were flushed, her chest heaving, and she had never looked so beautiful.

"'Why is kissing your sweetheart like eating soup with a fork?'" Owen quoted. "'Because it takes a long time to get enough of it.'"

Nora stilled. Her expression turned wary, but a spark of interest danced in her eyes. Owen met her gaze unflinchingly, a sudden rush of hope bubbling inside him.

"I want to kiss you, Nora." Where moments ago laughter had rung from the walls, all was now silent, serious. "Desperately. Almost painfully. But only if you want it too."

"I don't know if I'm brave enough for that," she replied.

"Could you tell me what was wrong with our first kiss?" He hadn't meant to ask so baldly. Perhaps it was the wine loosening his tongue. Or maybe simple desperation.

"It was too fast."

Nora's matter-of-fact answer startled him. Why hadn't they had this conversation ages ago? They could have avoided days of uncomfortable interactions. He could have made amends immediately and kissed her a dozen or more times by now.

"What if I kiss you very slowly and gently?" he asked.

She took her time answering. "I think I might like that. But I also think I've had too much to drink and should go to bed. I liked the cuddling."

Owen downed the last of the wine, straight from the bottle. "I will cuddle you all night. And maybe kiss you tomorrow."

"Yes. Maybe tomorrow." She stood up and swayed unsteadily, grabbing the chair for support.

Owen hopped from his seat to assist her. He'd neglected to consider how much smaller she was. He couldn't expect her to match him drink-for-drink all evening. The room spun around him and he had to pause several seconds for the dizziness to pass. Perhaps they'd both had a bit more than was prudent.

Doing his best impression of an entirely sober person, he offered Nora his arm and led her the thankfully few steps to the bed, helping her up before climbing in beside her. She burrowed against his chest, and he wrapped an arm around her. She smelled of wine and a floral soap that must have come from the ladies' washroom. Sweet. Smart. Fun.

He was going to kiss her again. Not now. But some time. Some day.

Maybe tomorrow.

25

Nora groaned and reached for the watch sitting on the bedside table. It was no worse for wear following their rainy arrival, thankfully. She flipped it open, holding it in the shaft of bright sunlight slanting across the bed. She nudged Owen, who made a sleepy grunt but didn't move.

"Owen, we need to get up. It's half past seven. When is your train?"

He muttered something Nora couldn't quite hear. A curse, she assumed.

"Your head isn't hurting, is it? I know you drank more than I did, but I didn't think it was as much as all that."

He pushed himself up with one arm. "Head's fine. Just tired. Didn't sleep well. Train's in an hour."

Odd. She'd slept wonderfully. Their silly game and the wine had left her more relaxed than she'd been in ages. Owen was cozier than her warmest quilt back home. Her only complaint this morning was that she couldn't remain snuggled up beside him indefinitely.

Nora clambered out of the bed, gathered up her now-dry clothing, and headed out to the washroom to change. Her clothing was wrinkled and dirt-stained, but it felt good to have it back. It would only be for the day. By evening they'd be back in St. Louis, where she could bathe and then relax in a clean nightgown.

But you'll have no more excuse to sleep beside Owen.

Or would she? Perhaps she could simply ask. It hadn't seemed difficult last night. And she was seriously considering letting him kiss her again. Why not suggest they share a bed at his house? Perhaps a few more days of this would increase her comfort with her body's response to him.

"Don't be daft, Nora," she chided herself. "His mother and brother are there."

They would have to contact the police for updates on the investigation into the break-in. Get a security update from Owen's people and the cameras on the house and his facilities. Check in with the Pinkertons. Last night may have been a brief respite, but her focus needed to be on helping Owen identify and stop his enemy.

Determined not to let herself become distracted again, she hurried back to the room to return Owen's shirt. He sat on the edge of the bed, waiting half-dressed. Nora tossed the shirt at him and turned away.

No distractions.

"Did you happen to recognize the voice of any of those men shouting when we escaped the riverboat?" she asked. Best to make use of their moment of privacy. They wouldn't have much opportunity for discussion on a public train.

"Huh?" Owen sounded so confused that Nora almost turned around. "Voices? Not that I recall. Why? Did you notice something?"

"No. But when they had me locked in that cell, they spoke to me through a telephonic device. I didn't have the opportunity to investigate it in detail, but it distorted the voice of the speaker on the other end."

"An attempt to remain anonymous?" Owen speculated. "You can turn around now. I'm covered."

Nora turned to find him buttoning his vest. A hint of disappointment that she couldn't see his naked body mingled with an appreciation for how good he looked in a properly-fitted suit.

"Ah…" she began, her brain momentarily shutting down. "I think he wanted to prevent me from recognizing him by voice. Not some possible time in the future, but right in that moment. I think he must be someone I've met before."

Owen frowned. "An enemy of yours, rather than mine?"

"I don't have any enemies. No, this was your enemy. He mentioned you by name and made it clear I was only a means to get at you. It has to have been someone I met in St. Louis. Which means it must be someone close to you."

Pain flashed across his features, but he composed himself quickly. "It could be any of hundreds of men."

"Possibly, but I don't think so. It must be someone with the resources to orchestrate these attacks. It must be someone I've spoken with long enough that I would be able to recall their voice. I thought about it for a long time that night, and only a handful of men fit both categories." Nora began to tick off the list on her fingers. "One: Evan Tagget, who we both agreed was unlikely to be the perpetrator. We should be able to easily confirm if he went to Michigan as he claimed."

"I can make a phone call tonight."

"Good. Number two: Mr. Cardot at the mine. Number three: Mr. Jameson at the refinery. Number four: the man who helped salvage the luxene barrels."

"Atwater. And it can't be any of them. I've known all those men for years. Never had any issue. They're all friends."

Nora ignored Owen's indignant tone and continued on. "Number five: Timothy."

"My brother? You can't be serious!"

"I am. He's brilliant, he has what I can only assume to be a generous allowance to work with, and he's desperate to prove himself your equal."

"He's a boy."

"He's not. He's a young man, yes, but a grown man

nonetheless, and he wants to be treated like one. He can't be ruled out. I'm sorry, Owen. I don't want it to be one of these men any more than you do, but they have become our primary suspects. If you can't accept that yet, I can talk to the Pinkertons when we reach St. Louis to discuss it. You needn't be involved until you've had time to adjust. And you have every right to feel hurt. You're allowed to grieve."

Owen put both hands on his hips and glared down at her. With anyone else, she might have shied away, but she'd spent the night in his gentle, protective embrace. She'd seen him pet a mechanical kitten. He could loom and growl all he wanted, but she would never fear him.

"You're not discussing anything with the Pinkertons because you're not going back to St. Louis," he retorted. "You're headed home to Savannah."

Nora rocked back on her heels. "What?"

"I booked your passage home. We'll ride together as far as the Mt. Vernon station. Then I'll head west to St. Louis and you'll head east."

"Excuse me?"

"It's gotten too dangerous. This isn't your concern, and I don't want you to come to harm because of it. The kidnapping made things perfectly clear. You're heading home."

Nora clenched her fists, fighting the urge to slap him across the face. "How dare you! What gives you the right to decide where I do or do not go? You do not get to control me, Owen Cassidy. I am not your employee, I am not an automaton to do your bidding, and I am not some sycophant who will jump at your every word."

"It's for your protection."

"I don't need your protection. If you'll remember, I was in the process of escaping when you came to break me out and I almost took your head off because of it."

"I don't want to see you hurt."

"And I don't want to *be* hurt. But only I get to make decisions about what risks I will and will not accept."

Owen ran a hand over his short hair. "Nora, be reasonable."

"Reasonable?" Her faced flushed with fury. "*You* are unreasonable. You are a thoughtless, controlling, overbearing lout. *This* is why your brother is a suspect. And I *kissed* you. Ugh!" She spun away from him. "Excuse me. I have a train to catch."

26

Sitting for hours alongside a furious man while he pretended to read the newspaper was not Nora's idea of a good time. By the time they changed trains in Marion, she had made a list of fifteen reasons she ought to walk away and leave him to his fate. By the time the train pulled into the station in Mt. Vernon, she'd decided the best punishment was to stick by his side and prove to him exactly how wrong he was. Also, it would prevent him from getting himself killed out of stubbornness.

Nora half ran to keep pace with Owen's long stride as he headed straight to the ticket counter. He gave his name, and the man behind the counter shuffled a few papers before passing a pair of tickets through the slot. Owen silently handed one to Nora, but she didn't even glance at it before slapping it back down on the counter.

"This ticket is incorrect."

The ticket clerk stared at her and adjusted his glasses. "Incorrect, ma'am?"

Nora stabbed a finger into the paper. "This ticket is for an eastbound train. I need to go west to St. Louis."

Owen snatched the ticket away. "There's no error," he stated firmly. "The lady is headed east. Please excuse us."

"No." Nora placed both hands on the counter. "I am going to St. Louis. I need a corrected ticket. My companion here is mistaken."

"No mistake," Owen growled, speaking right over her head. "I paid for the tickets and I know precisely what I wanted. The lady is heading east and that is the end of it."

"This man has no right to speak for me," Nora persisted. "One ticket to St. Louis, please."

The man behind the counter glanced back and forth between Nora and Owen. "Uh, the gentleman paid for the tickets, ma'am. I can give you a new ticket, but only if you pay the fare."

Nora's jaw clenched. She didn't have more than a few coins in her pocket. Certainly not enough to buy a ticket to St. Louis. She'd anticipated this problem, but at least she'd given it a try. She already had an alternate plan in mind.

"Would you like to purchase the ticket, ma'am?"

"I'm afraid I don't have enough money," Nora replied. "Thank you."

They walked away from the counter, and Owen handed her the unwanted ticket. He was smart enough not to say anything. They took side-by-side seats on a hard, wooden bench, close enough that no one could sit between them, but far enough to make their displeasure apparent to anyone who looked their way. Two different elderly women shook their heads in pity as they passed.

Nearly half an hour ticked by in utter silence until the whistle of an approaching train made Owen rise from his seat. "That would be my train," he said. "You have your ticket home. Be safe, Nora. I'm sorry for upsetting you."

"But not sorry for making decisions for me."

"I can't allow you to risk your life. I'm sure you can understand. I'd like to part on better terms." The pleading look in his eyes tugged at her heart, but she refused to be swayed.

"Well, I'm sorry, but we can't."

He stared at her a few moments more with his sad-puppy-dog expression, then sighed and turned away. Nora stayed frozen in her seat, watching as he joined the crowd boarding the train. As he stepped up onto the first step, he cast a glance back in her direction. She neither acknowledged him nor smiled, and he turned again and disappeared into the train car.

Nora counted to thirty, her gaze focused on the windows in the car Owen had entered. No man who resembled him appeared anywhere she could see. She hopped up from her seat and jogged down the platform to the rear of the train, mingling with a group of boarding passengers. She climbed aboard as casually as any of them, then walked one car down from where she'd entered and took a seat.

The train wasn't crowded, but neither was it empty, and a wide enough variety of people had boarded that no one paid a great deal of attention to the woman in trousers. Nora pulled out the newspaper she'd swiped from Owen's collection during the last leg of their journey and wedged beneath her vest. She had no particular interest in reading it, but it hid her face from view and made her seem just another boring passenger. With the upper half of her body shielded, she expected most of the people nearby would mistake her for a man. She scanned the headlines for anything worth reading, and cast surreptitious peeks around the car.

When the whistle blew and the train started forward, Nora let out a breath of relief. She'd made it past the first barrier. She had many stops to go and a difficult plan to execute, but she was on the right train, headed in the right direction. And if all else failed, she could play confused and try to garner sympathy. Since most men treated her as if she hadn't a brain in her head, she didn't think they'd be especially difficult to fool.

Time crawled, minutes seeming to drag into hours, before at long last a ticket-taker entered the far end of the train car. Nora waited until he had turned to talk to a passenger, then slipped from her seat and ducked out the rear door. The ladies' room was just inside the next car and she locked herself inside, leaning against the door to hear what was happening on the opposite side.

Sweat gathered between her breasts and trickled down her back. She rolled her shoulders and flexed her fingers, trying to unclench her muscles. Relaxation proved impossible. She settled for resting her head against the door and taking long, deep breaths.

"Tickets, please," a muffled voice said, eons later.

Nora froze. She pressed her ear against the door, trying to catch his every word and movement. Would someone knock or try to open the door to check for anyone inside? Would she end up stranded at a random station in Illinois with no money, clothing, or friends to help?

The voice grew fainter. He was moving on. Nora waited a while longer, then abandoned her hiding spot. She walked right past the seat she'd occupied before, further down the train, beyond the next ladies' room. She'd survived another obstacle.

Hours passed. At every station Nora changed seats, twice even hopping off the train and reboarding a different car. Over and over, she lurked behind her newspaper, avoided the ticket-takers, and hid herself in the washroom, until she thought she might collapse from the exhaustion of it all. Still, when her feet touched the ground in St. Louis, a smile of triumph spread across her face and a new rush of energy put a spring in her step. She was almost home.

Union Station was the largest and busiest railway station in the entire world, so avoiding Owen in the crowd was trivially simple. Nora wove her way through the throng and wandered out into the cool evening air, where she took a deep breath and gave herself a moment to gather herself. For tonight, she would return to Owen's house, but in the morning she would need to decide whether to remain there or try to find other accommodations. With her originally planned visit long over, she didn't want to impose on her brother's family. Which meant looking into hotels or boarding houses.

Or maybe Owen had repented and was ready to beg her

forgiveness. Maybe he'd spent the entire train ride missing her and lamenting over how foolish he'd been. One could hope.

The change in her pocket was enough to hire a cab to convey her to Owen's townhouse, and a short time later, Nora alit from the vehicle in a familiar posh neighborhood, ready for a good meal, a warm bath, and a long night's sleep.

She was right on time, it seemed. Owen stood at the bottom of his stairs, illuminated by the single electric bulb beside his door, peering at something on the stoop. Nora moved silently closer to see what it was preventing him from entering.

"You again?" Owen sighed.

The same little kitten-dragon they'd seen before wandered across the porch in front of him, moving in fits and starts—a sign its fuel supply was nearly exhausted. Owen bent and scooped it up, carefully folding down its wings before petting it atop the head.

"Poor little thing," he cooed. "I'll get you all fueled back up, and then we'll put a notice in the paper and see if we can't find your owner."

I will not be swayed, Nora repeated to herself. *I will not be swayed.*

He could be as adorable as he liked. It wouldn't change the fact that she was furious with him, and she intended to remain furious until he relented and apologized properly.

Owen rapped on the door, and a moment later it swung open. Nora darted forward, catching the door before it swung closed and letting herself in. Both Owen and his piratical butler whirled around, their jaws dropping simultaneously.

"Nora!" Owen exclaimed. "What are you doing? How on earth did you get here?"

"I walked, obviously."

The most confused crinkle appeared in the middle of his forehead. "You didn't have a ticket." His voice held no anger, only bafflement.

"Oh, yes. I haven't forgotten that."

"Dr. Taylor?" the butler interrupted, sounding as puzzled as his employer. "I don't understand. I thought you were on your way home. We only just sent all your things on."

"My things?" Her eyes darted toward Owen. "Wait. What have you done?"

The kitten made a forlorn mewling sound in his arms, its body gone limp. "I need luxene," Owen blurted.

Nora started toward him. "No, no no. What's this about—"

"Owen!" a distraught woman's voice rang out. His mother scampered into the room, her eyes red and a handkerchief clenched in her hand. "Oh, Owen, you're home. Thank goodness. I know you'll make it all right."

"Make what right, Mother? What's happened?"

She clutched Owen's arm. "I just received a phone call from your brother. He's been arrested."

27

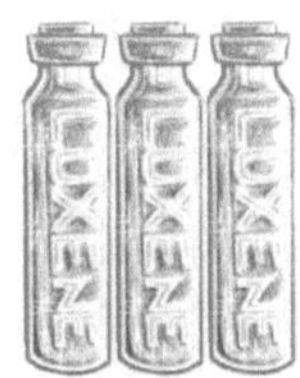

Spending four hours alone on a train second-guessing his every decision was apparently only the first phase of what was shaping up to be a sweeping retribution for all his myriad sins. Nora stood before him like an avenging angel, brought to his home through forces beyond his imagining to exact justice. Meanwhile, her trunks were enroute to Savannah, his butler was moving rapidly from confused to angry, his mother was in hysterics, the poor mechanical kitten was dying in his arms, and he was almost certainly responsible for turning his brother into a criminal.

"I need luxene," Owen rambled again, because it seemed to be the only problem he could actually solve. He started for his study, where he kept a small stash in a safe, along with a bit of money he would almost certainly need to bail his brother out. Owen supposed he ought to have adjusted by now to the fact that his life was falling apart, but he hadn't.

"What did you do with my things?" Nora shouted, following.

"We were informed you were headed home, ma'am," Trask replied. His civilized words held an edge. Most days the butler enjoyed the prim, unperturbed persona he'd cultivated during his years on Owen's staff, but the old miner did have a temper, and had been known to occasionally explode with a, "Cassidy, you fucking imbecile!"

"I'm not," Nora stated. "Fetch my belongings back at once."

Trask looked to Owen. Dammit, he didn't have time to fight about this. "Make the necessary calls. Fetch her things. We can discuss the matter further tomorrow."

"Yes, sir." Trask nodded and walked off, muttering something suspiciously like, "fucking imbecile."

Owen spun the dial on his safe. The kitten-dragon made another pathetic noise, this one weaker than the last. He wouldn't let it run out of fuel. Some dragons could be damaged if the fuel ran out, and even if this cat were better made then that, it would likely forget him if it shut down entirely.

"There won't be any discussion tomorrow," Nora stated, her tone frostier than an Alaskan winter. "I do what I want and you don't get any say in it. There. The discussion is over."

The safe door swung open, and Owen grabbed the bottle of luxene. He carried it to his desk and turned the kitten over a few times, looking for access to the internal workings.

"Here, let me," Nora said. She took the dragon from his hands, looked at it for no more than ten seconds, then pressed somewhere to make a panel in the cat's belly spring open. "Hand me that luxene." She uncorked the bottle, tipped a small amount of the glowing green fuel into the kitten's fuel tube, then closed everything up and handed back both bottle and kitten. "There. All better. Now, what are we going to do about your brother?"

"*We* are doing nothing. I'm heading to the police station to talk to him and bring him home." Owen turned away to place the luxene in the safe, but the movement was more an excuse to look away from Nora than anything else.

He had no idea what to say to her. During the lonely train ride with nothing to do but think, he'd had to admit her suspicions had merit. Try as he might, he could think of no one more likely. And now whatever trouble Timothy had gotten into had Owen terrified.

He returned the bottle, pulled out a wad of cash, and closed the safe. The refueled kitten purred contentedly in his arms. He petted it absently as he turned back to face the room. Any faint hope Nora might have left while his back was turned or some of her anger had faded was instantly dashed. She stood with her arms crossed, glaring at him.

"Feel free to rest up," Owen said, ignoring her fury and the churning it caused in his gut. "My staff can get you something to eat. I hope to return with Timothy before long."

Nora said nothing, but she followed as he walked toward the door. Owen longed to talk to her. He wanted to ask how she was and see to her needs. Get her the food she surely needed. Perhaps a bath. Unfortunately, it was his fault she had no clean clothing.

How had she even gotten here? She'd had an eastbound ticket and no money. He wanted to talk about that too. It would be an interesting story, he suspected.

"If you need something to wear before your personal effects are retrieved, feel free to ask anyone on my staff. Trask can send for something. I will, of course, cover any expense."

Nora rolled her eyes toward the ceiling. "Enough, Owen. We both know I'm not going to sit around here and pamper myself while you run off to handle yet another crisis. Who are you trying to convince? Me or yourself?"

"I'm not taking you with me," he insisted.

"No, you're not. You don't get to take me anywhere. I'm *going* with you."

"Nora, please. What if you were right? What if Timothy *is* the one causing this trouble? There could be danger. And I don't…"

Don't want you to see what a wreck I would become if it were true. Please, God, don't let it be true.

The kitten mewled questioningly, and Owen realized he'd been squeezing her too hard. He relaxed his grip and she fluttered her wings.

"If there's danger, I don't think your little dragon will be much help." Nora gestured at the cat. "He's rather tiny."

"She."

Nora paused and her brow furrowed. "You think it's a girl kitten? How can you tell?"

"It's obvious."

"How can it be obvious? It's a machine. It's not as if they come in male and female."

"Of course not. But she's obviously a she. You can just tell."

Nora crossed her arms over her chest again, but her icy demeanor had thawed and she regarded him now with affectionate exasperation. "You've named her, haven't you?"

"Don't be ridiculous. I can't name her. I have to return her to her owner, who surely has a name for her already."

Spark. Her name is Spark.

He would not admit to that. Nor would he admit he hoped the ad he intended to place in the paper would go unanswered. The kitten was the only nice thing he had in his life at the moment.

"Uh-huh," Nora replied.

The conversation had carried them all the way out to the car, and Owen didn't bother to object when she climbed into the passenger seat. He couldn't stop her from following him. If he refused to drive her, she'd hop in a cab. And to be honest, he liked having her near. The train ride had been hell, thinking he'd never see her again.

Keep her close. Keep her safe. The two ideas warred with one another. Nothing close to him was safe. The moment he had Timothy back home, he'd be making arrangements for a long vacation. Tim and their mother would enjoy seeing New York, perhaps. Or maybe California. San Francisco was a wreck, sadly, after the terrible earthquake and fire, but they could go further north, or to the southern part of the state.

The drive to the police station was conducted in silence, to no one's surprise. Owen gripped the wheel with white-knuckled fingers, growing tenser and angrier with every block. When had he started hating silence?

He longed for the companionship and laughter of the night before. Every memory that flitted through his mind only further soured his mood. They could never reforge the bond they'd briefly shared. Not unless he apologized for trying to send her home, and he couldn't do that. Her safety had to be the priority. If he'd consulted with her before making plans, all she would've done was disagree. He'd made the only sensible choice. Right?

Owen yanked too hard on the handbrake as he pulled up in front of the police station, causing the entire car to jerk to an ungainly stop, shaking its occupants and causing the kitten-dragon to topple into Nora's lap.

Owen grimaced. "Sorry."

Nora raised her eyebrows at him. He wasn't sure whether to interpret the expression as *Are you really sorry?* or *You might be sorry for this, but not sorry for what matters.*

He left the car parked directly in front of the building, which might have been illegal, but he didn't especially care at the moment. Inside, the rosy-cheeked man behind the desk tucked away a liquor flask before acknowledging them. His eyes were a little red as well. Not confidence inspiring.

"My name is Owen Cassidy. I understand you have my brother, Mr. Timothy Cassidy, in custody here?"

"Mmm." The man consulted some sort of list. "Yup. I can take you to see him, but the lady will have to wait here."

"I'm a doctor," Nora replied. "I've come to confirm Mr. Cassidy's well-being."

The boozy officer snorted. "Well, *Doctor*, rule is only one visitor. You can wait here. And you have to leave that thing here, too." He pointed at Spark. "No machines in the cells. Can't have anyone using a dragon to break out."

Owen snorted. "What could she possibly do? Gnaw through the bars?"

"Heard a story once out of Paris where a station was destroyed using dragons and exploding luxene. You want to see your brother? You leave the lady doctor and the wind-up toy here."

Owen reluctantly handed Spark over to Nora. "Dr. Taylor, would you please give us a few minutes?"

Her jaw was clenched, but she nodded.

"Thank you."

The police officer led Owen through the station to a large cell occupied by four men. One drunk man wandered in circles, singing and stumbling over the pair of men sleeping on the floor. Timothy sat huddled in the corner, hugging his knees to his chest. He sprang to his feet when he spotted Owen.

"Owen! You're here!"

"Yes. The question is, why are *you* here?"

Tim's gaze dropped to the floor. "I, uh, was breaking into the house."

Of all the possible answers Owen had imagined, that was not among them. "You were what?"

"I tried to explain that it was my house, but the patrol officer didn't know me and I was holding a dismantled security camera, so it looked bad, I guess."

"You were breaking into the house," Owen repeated, trying and failing to make sense of the situation. "*Our* house?"

"Yes."

"Why?"

Timothy mumbled something unintelligible.

"What was that?"

"I was trying to replicate the break-in at Mother's house."

Owen gaped at his brother, at a loss for words. This didn't seem like the behavior of a man who was trying to destroy his business, but nothing about it made sense, either. "Wh-why?" he managed at last.

Tim sighed. "I wanted to solve the crime. To show you I'm not just the whiny brat you think I am."

"I don't think you're a whiny brat. I'm questioning whether you have a lick of sense in your head, though."

"You never let me do anything, Owen," Tim said, his spine straightening and his expression growing fierce. "You have this idea in your head of what's good for me, and you refuse to let me deviate from that idea in any way. I would say it's because you're so much older and you still see me as a child, but I think that's only part of it. You do this to everyone. You think you're the only competent person in the entire world and if everyone else isn't told exactly what to do and supervised 'round the clock, all life is going to devolve into chaos.

"Well, I'll tell you a secret, big brother. There was a world before you, and it didn't collapse. Most people in this country? They don't give a fuck about you or what you think. If you hadn't discovered luxene, someone else would have. Maybe not then, and maybe they wouldn't have done it all the same, but you're not the most special person in the world.

"So try letting other people run their own lives once in a while. They might actually be better at it than you are."

"Fine. Get yourself out of jail, if that's how you want to be."

Timothy crossed his arms over his chest and glared defiantly at Owen. "I'll do that. It was my house and I didn't do anything illegal. They'll have to let me go as soon as it's verified."

"Then why did you call Mother begging for help?"

"I didn't beg for help. I wanted to let her know what had happened so she didn't think I was dead or kidnapped when she couldn't find me."

"I see."

"I messed up, Owen. I did something stupid. But I'm willing to admit it and I'm big enough to accept the consequences. I don't need you to help me or coddle me. Let me handle me. If I need help, I'll ask for it."

"Fine. Enjoy your night in the drunk tank." Owen began to turn away, but caught himself halfway. "By the way, where were you last night?"

Timothy frowned. "At home. Why? And where were *you*? You and Dr. Taylor vanished for two whole days. I'd started wondering if you'd eloped."

The words felt like a kick in the ribs. Nora didn't even want to talk to him, much less marry him.

"Don't be daft," Owen retorted.

"I'd have to be daft not to have thought of it, with the way you two are always so cozy together."

Another kick. Coziness was a thing of the past. Owen turned away before he could say anything to make the entire situation worse. "Goodnight, Timothy," he called over his shoulder. "You *will* let me know if you need anything, won't you?"

"For God's sake, Owen, let it go. For once in your life stop trying to control everything. Maybe then people will actually *like* you."

Owen walked away, keeping his stride casual, though what he really wanted was to storm down the hall in a raging fury. He swept right past Nora, waving at her to follow without saying a word. She sprang from her seat.

"What happened? Weren't you able to get Tim released? Why was he arrested?"

Owen didn't speak until they were outside, climbing into the car. "It was a foolish misunderstanding. He insists he wants to handle it himself. Fine. If he wants to spend all night in a stinking cell full of drunken louts, he can."

"Well, it can't be too terrible or you wouldn't be leaving him."

"No, of course not. Because I control everything and everyone." He slammed a fist on the steering wheel. "Goddammit! My own brother hates me!"

"No, he doesn't."

"He made it perfectly clear he thinks I'm a complete ass."

Nora laughed. "You are an ass. But that doesn't mean he hates you."

Owen winced at her matter-of-fact confirmation of his boorish status. "At this point I might honestly believe he's the one who's been causing all the trouble, except he said he was home yesterday, and presumably the night before, and that should be trivial to confirm." He let his head drop onto the steering wheel. "Am I really as awful as all that? Is everyone I thought was a friend merely tolerating me?"

"Owen." Nora's hand settled on his biomechanical shoulder, where he could sense the weight of her touch but none of the warmth. Empty comfort. Tolerated, but not liked. "You're not awful."

"Then why is someone tormenting me? Someone close to me in all likelihood? I must have done something to deserve it."

"No." The fierceness in Nora's voice made him sit up. "No, you don't deserve it. You're not perfect, clearly. No one is. But whoever has done these things to you is at fault. Not you. You are the victim. He and only he is responsible." She paused and touched a finger to her lips, frowning in thought. "Or she, perhaps? The person on the riverboat sounded to me like a man, but perhaps the voice distorter drops the pitch enough that it could have been a woman. Do you know any women who might hold a grudge against you?"

"No," Owen sighed. "I know no one with a grudge. Your theory about the suspects is all we have and it's seeming more and more true with every passing moment."

"What about a former lover?"

Owen turned almost entirely sideways to gape at her. "Don't be ridiculous!"

"Why is it ridiculous? A love affair gone wrong is a classic cause of trouble."

"In sensation novels, perhaps."

"In real life!" Nora twisted in her seat to look him in the eye. "It's all over literature, music, art. Because it resonates with people. People have romantic entanglements that don't work out. Most times both parties move on and that's the end of it. But sometimes anger and resentment linger. Sometimes so strongly revenge is sought with violence. You know it's true."

"I'm sure it is, but I have never had a relationship with a lady go sour."

Nora made a small huffing sound.

"Except, perhaps, with you, if we can call a single kiss and one chaste night in bed a relationship." He turned his attention to the road and set the car in motion.

They'd driven almost a block before Nora spoke again. "What if your confidence is misplaced. What if you hurt a woman unwittingly?"

"It's impossible."

"What, are you the world's greatest lover?" she scoffed.

Owen gritted his teeth. The last thing he wanted right now was to discuss his previous liaisons with Nora. "I'm sure I'm not, but I'm also sure I never left anyone heartbroken."

"I really don't see how that can possibly be true."

"Look, can we not discuss this right now? I'm trying to drive, and I don't want to crash the car because we're arguing."

"Of course. We can discuss it when we reach your house. Probably best to do it in private, anyway, to avoid the possibility of anyone eavesdropping." She turned to stare straight ahead, settling Spark securely in her lap and folding her hands primly. Owen settled in for another torturous silent journey.

Trask greeted them at the door when they arrived, making an obsequious bow to Nora. "Dr. Taylor, your belongings are on their way back to the house and should be returned to you by morning. For tonight, a nightgown and grooming essentials have been left in your room for your use."

"Thank you. Would it be possible to have a few snacks sent up to the room and a bath drawn up perhaps fifteen minutes from now? I must have a conversation with Mr. Cassidy, but after that I believe I would like to wash and retire for the night."

"Of course, ma'am." He bowed again and scurried off to do her bidding.

"See?" Owen waved a hand at his butler's departing back. "My own staff prefers you to me. I'm unlikeable. I simply never realized it. And we have nothing further to discuss. I'll speak with the Pinkertons tomorrow and pray they have a better idea for suspects."

"We *do* have things to discuss, and you're being melodramatic. Now, shall we go to the study, or will you tell me all about your former lovers right here in the atrium?"

Owen looked to the ceiling, but no divine help materialized. Exhaustion weighed on his body, and the implications of his recent conversations weighed even more heavily on his heart.

"Look, Nora," he sighed. "The reason there is no possibility of resentment or heartbreak among the women with whom I've been intimate is that I don't engage in romance. There's no wooing, no talk of love. I have businesslike, temporary relationships with like-minded women who aren't looking for anything more than mutual sexual gratification. There, are you satisfied?"

A sudden flush colored her cheeks. Damn. He'd phrased that last question rather poorly and turned it into a horrible innuendo.

"No," Nora replied, sounding her usual calm self despite the embarrassment written on her face. "No, I'm not. Goodnight, Owen." She rushed off, leaving him standing in the front hall with only a mechanical kitten for companionship.

"Best go write up that ad now," he said to the dragon. "Doubt you want to be stuck with me, either."

Spark purred and followed him down the hall.

28

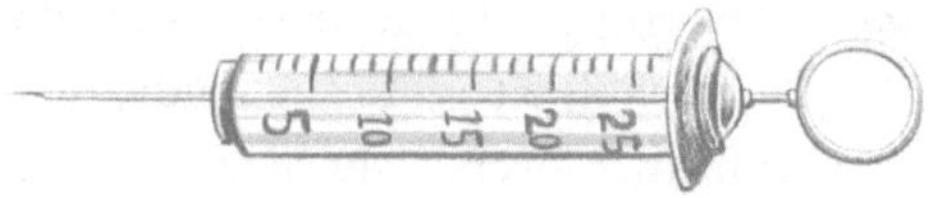

“That's my plan, then. Investigate on my own, since he refuses to see reason.” Nora leaned back in her seat and adjusted the telephone receiver.

“Do keep in mind that much of his resistance is a natural reaction to the pain of betrayal by an intimate companion,” Catalina Navarro replied in her psychological therapist voice. “His reluctance to accept the truth is his way of protecting himself, and will take some time to break down, even with logical evidence presented. The human mind, I'm sad to say, is highly illogical.”

“Yes. Yes, it is.”

“So you're not returning to Savannah any time soon, then? I haven't heard of anyone banging down your door demanding biomechanics, so I don't think it's a problem. But it would be good to know in case anyone asks.”

“No scheduled time to return,” Nora replied. “I think I need to see this mystery solved before I can move on. Owen has become a sort of friend, and I wouldn't feel right leaving him. Even if he'd prefer I go far, far away.”

“Oh?” A note of curiosity touched Lina's voice.

Nora sighed and looked up at the ceiling. “He thinks I'm not safe near him. He wants to protect me.”

“Aww. That's sweet.”

Nora dug a toe into the carpet. “It's annoying.”

"I think he's crushing on you."

"I think I'm hanging up."

Lina laughed. "Stopping. But you will let me know what happens, correct?"

"Yes. I'll call again if anything important happens, or in a few days to check in."

"Excellent. And I'll go over the notes I made on your criminal and see if I can glean any information about what sort of man—or woman—we might be looking for."

A knock on the door prevented Nora from replying.

"Dr. Taylor?" a voice called. "There's a woman here to see you."

"My appointment has arrived," Nora said into the telephone. "Be well, Lina. I'll talk with you again soon."

"Goodbye, Nora."

The line went dead with a click. Nora replaced the receiver, rose from the desk, and crossed the room to open the door.

"The woman is waiting for you in the front hall," the housemaid informed Nora. "Would you like to speak with her here in the study, or shall I arrange for tea and coffee in the parlor?"

"Tea and coffee sounds lovely," Nora replied. "Thank you."

Instead of waiting in the parlor for someone to bring her guest in, Nora walked to the atrium to greet the woman herself. Mrs. Allen was a tall, plump woman in her early thirties. Her vibrant purple dress was styled to show off her figure, and a two-foot diameter riot of flowers, feathers, and ribbon sat perched on her brunette curls.

"Mrs. Allen?" Nora inquired to confirm the visitor's identity.

"Please, call me Bonnie. And you are Dr. Eleanor Taylor?"

"I am, indeed. Nora, to my friends."

"Of whom I hope to be one," Bonnie replied cheerily.

"That's very kind of you. If you'd follow me, please, we can take some tea or coffee in the parlor."

"That would be lovely, thank you."

Bonnie bounced when she walked, her smile never wavered, and her head was on a constant swivel, taking in everything around her. She plopped herself on the plushest sofa, gleefully accepted a steaming cup of coffee, and sighed with pleasure when she sipped it.

Nora wanted to keep an open mind, but it was difficult to imagine this artless woman as the orchestrator of Owen's woes. Nora hadn't had much success tracking down Owen's former paramours. Since he wouldn't give any names, she'd been forced to rely on rumors and mentions in the papers. Bonnie Allen had been the only woman Nora had been able to both confirm and locate, but with luck, Bonnie would be able to point her toward other, more likely suspects.

"So, what brings me here?" Bonnie asked. "Are you interested in millinery, or did Owen need something?"

Millinery. Dear God. Mrs. Allen ran her own hat shop, and while Nora applauded her entrepreneurial spirit, she wanted nothing to do with hats that in any way resembled the concoction Bonnie sported this afternoon.

"Ah, well, you might say I wished to speak to you on behalf of Owen," Nora answered.

Bonnie laughed. "Well, of course! That man wouldn't ever ask for help all on his own. Stubborn as my Tommy was, back in the day. It's why I like him. And also that big love staff of his."

Nora choked on her tea.

"Knows how to use it, too. Gives a girl a good time, right?" Bonnie paused when she noticed Nora's coughing. "Oh, dear. Are you all right, Dr. Taylor?"

"Fine," Nora gasped. "Took too large a sip."

"You're also somewhat red." Her brows knit together. "You *are* Owen's mistress, aren't you?"

Nora finally managed to draw a proper breath. "No."

"Oh. Well, I do highly recommend you give it a try. He's quite considerate. And as I said, big everywhere."

"Yes, I know."

"Do you? Well, you must be heading in the right direction, then. No need for my help. Unless you had questions as to his likes and dislikes, that sort of thing?"

"No." Heaven help her. "I, uh, have a personal question of a different nature."

"Ah! How not to get in the family way? But you're a doctor, you'll know that sort of thing. Or… Oh, my, are you a virgin? Goodness. Yes, I can see you are from your expression. Well, Owen is a good choice for your first. Considerate. And patient. He'll be gentle with you."

"This has nothing to do with intercourse!" Nora burst out, desperate to end the line of discussion. She took a moment to compose herself. "Well, not directly. I wanted to ask whether you were aware of any women Mr. Cassidy may have had relations with who do not remember him as fondly as you do."

"Not remember him fondly?" Bonnie laughed. "Can't imagine there are too many like that. He's the sort who cares about a lady's pleasure. And he prefers widows like me, looking to warm an otherwise cold bed after our husbands have gone. My Tommy wouldn't want me to go without all my life, that's for sure. He was the sweetest. If you ever marry, dear, find yourself a sweet man."

Nora could only nod in response. "Er, yes, but about my question…"

"Ah, yes. Who doesn't like Owen. Let me think. Certainly wouldn't be Lucy or Pearl. They both speak well of him." She drummed her fingers on the arm of the couch. "Not too terribly many to choose from. He goes long periods without any women. Busy, busy with his work all the time. Hmm. I'm trying to think what I know of the women he might have seen when he was younger. He didn't talk about it much, of course, but I always like to ask, you know. Best to know what a man's gotten himself into before he gets into you, right?"

"Um…" Once again the conversation had taken an uncomfortable turn. Nora's lack of knowledge and experience left her feeling painfully childish next to a woman a number of years younger than herself. But if she ever needed advice, she now had a good idea where to turn.

"But I've wandered off topic again. I believe there was one young lady from ages back, when his business was new and he wasn't rich. Wanted to marry him but he only wanted casual and short-term. I never heard there were hard feelings between them, though. Only that she moved on and married someone else." Bonnie drummed her fingers once more. "I don't know if I ever knew her name, but I'll think on it."

"Thank you. And of course, anything else you might think of—"

A knock interrupted Nora mid-sentence. Owen stood in the doorway, a wary expression furrowing his brow.

"Nora?" he called. "I was told we have a visitor?"

"Owen, darling!" Bonnie cooed. "How are you? It's been what, now, three years?"

He walked into the room. Or perhaps stalked. His body was tense, and his gaze darted here and there, as if looking for potential enemies.

"Closer to four, probably," he answered. "Bonnie, what are you doing here?"

She waved a hand at Nora. "Your sweetheart invited me. She wants to know all about your previous lovers. Highly sensible, if you ask me. Can't go about getting diseases and the like, and no one wants to get serious with a man if he doesn't treat women right. I think you'll both be just fine. You must be fretting, I'm sure, about bedding a virgin, but she's a doctor, so she knows how it all works, and you know how to be gentle."

Nora had seen Owen look startled before, but never had his eyes been so wide or so round. "What?" he exclaimed.

"But I should probably leave you two to talk now." Bonnie hopped up from her seat. "Nora, it was so lovely to meet you. I hope everything goes well for you, and if you have any more questions, just give me a call or drop in at the shop. We'll find the Bonnie's Bonnet that's perfect for you. And I want to hear all about you two." She waggled her finger back and forth, pointing from Nora to Owen.

"It was a pleasure, Bonnie," Nora replied. And truly, it was. She had no intention of sharing intimate details of anything she might hypothetically do with Owen, and she had no idea how to respond to Bonnie's wildly shameless sex talk, but Mrs. Allen was funny and cheerful and delightfully honest. They could be friends. "I'll be sure to come by the shop one of these days." Out of morbid curiosity, if nothing else. And if she did happen to leave with a horrifying hat, she could always give it as a gift to one of her fashionable sisters.

"Wonderful! I'll start thinking of ideas of what might work with that adorable haircut of yours!" Bonnie rushed over to Nora and flung both arms around her.

Nora went rigid. Never in her life had she even considered enthusiastically embracing an acquaintance of less than a half-hour's duration. When the initial shock passed, she gave Bonnie a gentle pat on the back.

Bonnie released her, still grinning, then turned to Owen. "Bring her along to the shop, Cassidy. I can tell this isn't your usual, and you need to practice your wooing. Take her out for chocolates and a new hat. Adieu, lovebirds!" She swished from the room in a whirl of purple silk, leaving Nora a bit bewildered, but oddly cheerful.

"What is going on?" Owen demanded. His eyes were still unusually large, and his voice lacked its customary authority.

"I think I made a new friend," Nora replied. "An unconventional one, and not at all what I was expecting, but I quite liked her."

"Bonnie is a lovely person," Owen replied, his tone

becoming clipped as his surprise began to wane. "She'd never harm a soul. I told you there are no grudges. What the hell do you think you're doing?"

Nora put her hands on her hips. "Exploring every avenue. Since you're too pigheaded to tell me anything, I have to investigate for myself."

"There is nothing to find!"

"So you say. But Bonnie did mention something about a young lady who wanted to marry you, once? That sort of rejection could leave lingering animosity."

He shook his head. "Addison is dead. I really don't think her ghost is haunting me."

"Oh." The urge to argue whooshed out of Nora like air from a collapsing balloon. "I'm sorry."

"You couldn't have known."

Part of her wanted to point out that the not-knowing was his fault, but her suddenly somber mood kept her silent.

"The Pinkertons have been conducting interviews," Owen said, turning his back to her and facing out the window. "The men seem happy to cooperate. They want this solved as much as I do. Several have left for other companies, saying they can't risk not being there for their families. I suspect many others would leave, as well, if they could find positions elsewhere."

When Nora didn't reply, he continued on. "While I didn't go into details about what happened to you, I did tell them something of your thoughts about the perpetrator being someone relatively close to me. They have no firm leads yet.

"In better news, Timothy is out of jail and back at school today. I've been considering sending him and my mother on a vacation."

"You might want to ask their opinion of that plan before you execute it," Nora suggested.

"Yes. I've been made aware of that fact." From behind she couldn't see his clenched jaw, but every word came out tight. "I trust your personal items have been returned to you?"

Nora glanced down at her clothing. The same thing she'd been wearing the day she'd rescued him. It now seemed ages ago. Neither of them were quite the same person they'd been on that day. "Yes. Thank you."

He huffed. "You're welcome. Though I doubt I deserve thanks for fixing my own asinine mistake." He continued staring out the window, his shoulders hunched forward, hands clenched on the sill.

"I want to help," Nora said, walking toward him. "You don't have to do this alone." She laid a hand on his left shoulder. "Please, Owen, let me help you."

He whirled around at her touch. Nora inhaled sharply. Her hand had fallen away when he moved, but even without the physical contact, electric sparks jolted through her body. She relived every sensation of their night together. The way her body had curled so naturally against his. His strong, yet tender embrace. The heat it generated inside her. The longing to explore, despite her uncertainty.

"Nora," Owen murmured. His head bent toward hers.

She lifted up on her toes, ready—eager—to try again.

"Nora," he repeated. He touched a hand to her cheek, his thumb barely grazing her skin. "Is it true, what Bonnie said? You... lack experience?"

She sank back down. "Yes." And Owen liked lusty widows. Perhaps they were simply incompatible.

"No wonder I scared you off." His light caress moved lower, until the pad of his thumb slid across the corner of her bottom lip.

A peculiar urge to lick him seized hold of Nora, but her ignorance kept her frozen. Would that be exactly the right thing to do? Or exactly the wrong thing?

Liquid bronze eyes smoldered down at her, so fiery in their intensity she feared she might combust if he kissed her. Or if he didn't.

"Would you perhaps permit me to try again?" he asked, softly.

Nora raised up on her toes once more, leaning in now, bringing their bodies into glorious contact. She meant to say yes. To tell him she wasn't afraid this time. What she actually did was grab hold of his lapels and press her lips against his.

29

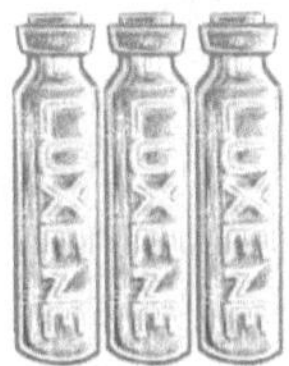

HE WAS SUPPOSED TO take this slowly. He'd meant to take it slowly. Nora, though, seemed to have other ideas. Her grip on his jacket was like iron, crushing him against the ample bosom he longed to free from her neatly laced vest. Owen wrapped both arms around her, supporting her weight so she didn't have to hold herself up on her toes. If he'd planned this, they would have been sitting to minimize the height difference.

If he'd planned this, he'd have some idea what the hell he was supposed to do.

Maybe he would have started by kissing her hand. Turning it over to press another kiss into her palm before moving down to her wrist. Then he would have tried tiny, teasing kisses to the corner of her mouth before covering her lips with his own. Taking his time coaxing her to open for him.

Nora made an insistent mewling noise against his mouth, pressing her lips more firmly to his. Owen's head whirled. His body screamed at him to nudge her lips apart, taste deeply of her, let his hands wander up and down and explore every part of her. His mind told him he needed to be gentle, careful. Protective.

Nora's lips slid over his, sipping, almost nibbling. Her tongue flicked out in a tiny, experimental motion.

To hell with it.

Owen groaned and followed her lead, unleashing his hunger as he sampled every part of her lips, from the pointed corners to the plump centers and back. She licked at him again, and he opened for her, offering himself up to whatever probing she desired. She thrust into him. Taking. Possessing. And he loved it.

Nothing he'd ever tasted had been as sweet as Nora. He thanked God he hadn't planned this, because nothing he could have orchestrated could match the beauty of her untutored passion. She kissed greedily, honestly, with no pretense, no expectations. Only her wants. Her desires.

Every movement of her mouth, every squirm of her body against his mingled bliss and torture in exquisite harmony. Longing burned through Owen's veins. He followed everywhere she led, deepening the kiss when she angled for more, and drawing back when she paused for breath. When she dove in again with renewed enthusiasm, he went with her.

They kissed for hours. Days. Owen would have been content to remain as they were, kissing forever, learning one another, savoring one another.

"Ahem."

At first the sound made no sense to Owen and he simply ignored it, uninterested in anything but the way Nora's tongue was tangling with his own. Then the intruder cleared his throat again and Nora gasped in alarm. She sprang back, out of Owen's arms.

The loss of her heat and excitement left him bereft. Empty. And uncomfortably aroused.

"I beg your pardon, sir," Trask said stiffly from the doorway. "You have a visitor. I did not realize you were... otherwise engaged."

"You're directly in front of the window, Cassidy." Atwater, who had never been one to stand on ceremony, wandered into the room unannounced. His eyebrows twitched in amusement.

"I'd suggest finding a better place for your canoodling. Though I can't blame you for losing your head over such a lovely woman."

Nora's cheeks were flaming, but she kept her composure. "What brings you calling, Mr. Atwater?"

"I received a message stating that all business associates of Mr. Cassidy and his mining operation are asked to submit to an interview as part of the investigation into the recent accidents. I was in the area, so I decided to stop by in the hopes of making things as simple as possible. Who do I need to speak to, and where?"

Anyone, anywhere else but here.

"I'll send the Pinkertons to your factory at your convenience," Owen said aloud. At any other time he would have invited Atwater to share a drink and maybe a game of chess or backgammon. Right now, he only wanted the man gone.

I'm being a terrible friend. I'll have to find some way to make it up to him.

"Nine a.m. tomorrow?" Atwater suggested.

Owen nodded. "They'll be there." He shifted, trying to keep himself shielded behind Nora, in case his 'situation' was apparent. He needed to adjust his damned trousers.

"Excellent. You had no trouble with the salvaged barrels, I presume?"

"None."

"Is there anything else I can do for you? All the machines are back in order? I can make arrangements for the manufacture of a replacement for any where repairs were not adequate."

Would he never leave? "We're fine, thank you. Everything seems to be operating as it should. I will, of course, let you know should the situation change."

"Wonderful." Atwater gave them a nod. "Good day to you both." He grinned roguishly. "And do remember to close the drapes." He started off, but turned back as he passed through the doorway. "Oh, and was that your dragon-cat wandering the front hall? You might want to keep a closer eye on it. I nearly stepped on it." He tipped his hat. "Cassidy. Dr. Taylor."

Trask closed the parlor door the moment Atwater disappeared, leaving Owen and Nora alone, but the mood had been broken. They stared at one another, awkward silence filling the air between them. The evidence of their passion lingered in Nora's swollen, red lips, and the answering tingle in his own.

"Nora…" As usual, words failed him. He knew business. He knew informal, uncomplicated lust. He didn't know this. Whatever it was.

Nora broke the silence. "That was rather nice." Was she forcing the cheery tone into her voice? "Until the interruption, that is. I hope it was okay for you?"

Nice? Okay? Try breathtaking. Earth-shattering. Had he failed miserably once again? He'd thought she'd been truly enjoying herself.

"Er, yes," he mumbled, like a fool. "Very pleasant."

"Good." She shifted, only a tiny bit, but the discomfort in the movement made his chest constrict. Why? Why was everything with this woman so difficult?

Say something reassuring, you ass. Woo *her.*

"I'm sorry, Nora, for making those decisions on your behalf. It was wrong of me. I… I can't stop wanting to keep you safe, but I have no right to force your hand. I hope I can make it up to you." Not very romantic, but the words were necessary. He still longed to protect her, but he had to be truthful with himself. He had no right. The trick would be remembering that. "I hope the kiss is an indication that you do not, in fact, hate me?"

Her smile—her *genuine* smile—warmed him deep inside. "No, I don't hate you."

"Dare I hope for a repeat performance?"

"I would like that." She glanced out the window and then at the remains of the tea and coffee she'd taken with Bonnie. "But perhaps not in the parlor by the window with the door open."

"Right." *Perhaps in the bedroom.*

No. Not the bedroom. He was taking this slowly. He was letting her set the pace.

Now that he no longer sported a massive erection, Owen felt comfortable moving toward the door. With all the distractions, he'd forgotten he had more phone calls to make. More work to do. "I should get back to work, but perhaps we can talk over dinner?"

He considered asking her out to a restaurant or to the theater. Was that moving too fast? Perhaps chocolates, as Bonnie had suggested.

"That sounds lovely, thank you. I'll get back to my own investigations."

Owen managed not to wince until he'd turned away. Yes, he had work to do. He needed to solve this before she put herself in even more danger. And he desperately needed some advice on courtship.

"TELL ME, DR. TAYLOR," Owen's mother said brightly from across the dining room table, "how is Owen's shoulder faring? Has the physical therapy had the intended effect? I would ask him, but you know he would only grunt and tell me that it's 'fine.'"

Nora chuckled, but her amusement was short-lived. She'd been hoping for dinner alone with Owen now that she'd had time to process that stupendous kiss this afternoon. They needed to talk about what might happen next. Owen preferred businesslike affairs. She could be businesslike. She had a plan all laid out in her head for what she would say to him.

Sadly, the talk would have to wait, because currently she was sitting at a table with Owen, his mother, Timothy, and Mr. Jones and Mr. Smith, the Pinkertons. Mrs. Cassidy had invited them to dinner when they'd arrived to give Owen a report on today's progress. They didn't strike Nora as the type of men who ever said no to a free meal.

"I'm pleased to say that if Mr. Cassidy told you his shoulder was fine he would be telling the absolute truth," Nora replied. "In my professional opinion, he has recovered both full range of motion and his usual strength."

Strength. Yes. She'd felt that strength first-hand during their kiss, when his arms had wrapped around her, holding her securely, supporting all her weight as easily as if she'd been a doll. She'd felt it in the solidness of his chest as her breasts crushed against him. And yet he'd been so gentle. So willing to let her make her own discoveries. He'd never pushed her or made her uncomfortable, and she'd known without a doubt he would stop whenever she asked.

Would they have stopped, had they not been interrupted? Their night in bed had given her enough comfort with him and his body not only to try kissing again, but to kiss more deeply and wildly than she'd thought herself capable of. How far was she ready to go?

The thought of renewed kissing caused Nora's skin to heat, and she cooled herself with a sip of her iced tea. The beverage had become hugely popular across the country since its widespread sale and promotion at the World's Fair here two years ago. Restaurants were serving it all over town, but this was her first sampling.

She was about to remark on how much she liked it, when Mrs. Cassidy said, "Oh! Does this mean you'll be leaving us soon?"

Nora's brain took a moment to shift back to the conversation. Before the tea, she'd been thinking of kissing, and then… Oh, yes. It was the comments about Owen's rehabilitation that had sent her train of thought veering off track.

"Ah, no." She groped for a plausible reason to remain in town besides, *I can't leave until I've made love to Owen or decided I don't want to go any further.*

"Due to the nature of the surgery," Owen spoke up, "it is advisable that I remain under observation for another week or two. And I have, naturally, extended the invitation for Dr. Taylor to remain here, as she has no residence in town. I apologize, of course, for my mistaken belief she would be departing simply because I felt back to my old self."

"No hard feelings," Nora replied. The moment the words were out of her mouth she took another large gulp of tea. She'd definitely felt something hard while they'd been kissing.

At the time, it had all been part of the excitement. Now it was unsettling. "This tea is excellent," she added hurriedly.

"Yes, so refreshing," Mrs. Cassidy agreed. "It will be even better when the weather turns hotter."

Nora nodded. She couldn't have cared less about turns in the weather, but the turn in the conversation was a vast relief. She sipped more of her tea and left the others to carry on talking.

Somehow, she managed to speak very little during the remainder of dinner. Keeping her thoughts off Owen and the kiss, however, proved impossible. A shiver would run down her spine when his fork touched his lips. Or he would smile in her direction and her skin would grow hot. Twice she caught herself almost touching her own lips in response.

"We can talk in my study, gentlemen," Owen said to the Pinkertons, when the dishes had been cleared away. He glanced at Nora, but said nothing to her.

As usual, she followed, choosing her favorite chair and declining the offer of a drink. Owen continued to steal glances at her, always frowning, but not commenting on her presence. He didn't want her involving herself in the investigation, but he had restrained himself from telling her what to do. Nora wanted to thank him with another kiss. She would, the moment the Pinkertons left.

The meeting began with a brief summary of the interviews conducted that day. Nothing had been overtly suspicious, but the detectives promised to review their notes and conduct followups on anything unusual.

"Preliminary interviews and investigations are finished at the mine," said one of the Pinkertons. Nora wasn't sure which was which, but she decided to call him Mr. Jones.

"Tomorrow we will call on Atwater, talk to him, the men who conducted the salvage operation, and any engineers who may have been involved in the building of any of your machines," Mr. Smith continued.

"And, naturally, we will give you another report like this one when we finish." Jones grinned. "Will your mother be hosting dinner tomorrow night as well?"

Smith rolled his eyes at his partner. "Before we leave, we have a more hopeful bit of news for you. We have a good lead on the source of that malicious article in the newspaper. Can't name any names yet, but there's a man on it and I trust him to follow the trail as far as it goes."

"No guarantees, of course," Jones added. "But I do like our chances."

The detectives rose from their seats in movements so synchronized Nora wondered if they practiced. Owen quickly followed and the men shook hands. Nora stood as well, shook hands with the Pinkertons, and thanked them. A moment later, she and Owen were alone again.

"They're doing a fine job, don't you think?" Owen asked.

"They seem relatively efficient," she replied.

"And this new lead could be exactly what we need."

Nora sighed. "No, Owen, I'm not going to sit on my ass while you men do all the work."

"Well, I had to try something." He rubbed his hand over his head and turned away from her. "I can't stand the thought of you getting hurt. Especially not on my behalf."

"I'll be fine. I promise I'm not itching to throw myself in harm's way."

He sighed and turned back. "I know. I'll stop arguing. It's growing late and I should let you get to bed."

Bed. Where she didn't get to snuggle up with him any longer. Was this the time to talk? Frantically, she tried to recall the details of her prepared speech. She needed to say she was nervous and uncertain but she didn't want him to worry that it was a sign of lack of interest. She was ready for more kisses. The rest...

I'll let you know.

"Owen." She took a step toward him. "I..."

He walked right up to her. "Goodnight, Nora." He bent and pressed a gentle, lingering kiss to her lips. "Sleep well."

As he walked away, Nora traced her lips with a single finger. She'd be lucky to sleep at all.

Nora stared up at the ceiling, unable to shut down her racing brain or cool her overstimulated body. She'd been foolish to drink so much tea at dinner, knowing full well the effects of caffeine on a body. And then she'd ended her night with a kiss just powerful enough to set her desire ablaze, but nowhere near enough to quench it. Assuming anything could. She was beginning to wonder.

Nora cupped her breasts, teasing her nipples through the thin cotton of her nightgown until she felt the accompanying rush of wetness between her thighs. Contrary to prevailing medical opinions—mostly written by men, of course—Nora firmly believed masturbation caused no ill effects. In fact, she believed it to have a number of health benefits, including muscle relaxation, stress reduction, and—most importantly to her at the moment—improved sleep. The fact it was physically pleasurable was simply an additional benefit.

Usually very little intruded on her thoughts during self-pleasure. She had never needed or used imaginings of other people to help her along. Tonight, however, with the memory of her kisses with Owen heating her blood, she found him infiltrating her customary solitude.

She recalled the taste of his lips, the slight roughness of his tongue sliding against hers, and she kneaded her breasts, enjoying her body's reaction to the memories. What would Owen's hands feel like on her?

Nora swiftly shucked her nightgown and touched herself again, skin-to-skin, sighing in pleasure. Owen's hands would be warm. His large palms would be the perfect size to hold her ample breasts. She thought about the way his thumb had so carefully grazed her cheeks and lips, and tried to replicate the feather-light touch across her stiff nipples.

A groan escaped her throat. Already she was drenched. She slid a hand between her legs, stroking herself, rubbing teasing circles across her clit. She could do this for Owen. Show him where to touch her. Exactly how she liked it. He would fondle her and caress her. Perhaps use his mouth on her, the way she'd read about.

Nora's left hand dropped down to join the right, and she slid two fingers inside herself, curling them to stroke her most sensitive spot as she thrust in and out. She didn't have the polished wooden phallus she often used at home, but she was so wildly aroused she knew she wouldn't need it. Instead, she pictured Owen's unclothed body as her fingers worked magic. She imagined him above her. Her legs spread wider as she contemplated allowing him inside her, letting him fill her, thrusting faster and faster until she broke.

She swirled her fingertip hard against her clit, her other hand pumping furiously, pushing herself over the edge. "Owen," she gasped as the climax slammed through her.

Spent and breathing hard, Nora slowly withdrew her fingers, wiping them clean on the sheets. Heavens, but that had been a good orgasm. Now a languid relaxation spread throughout her body, bringing with it a blissful sleepiness. And along with that came a newfound confidence. She could do this with Owen.

She would.

31

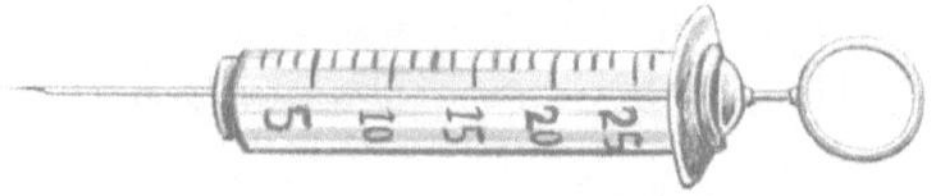

Nora bounded cheerfully down the stairs, fully prepared
to present Owen with her businesslike proposal for an intimate
liaison. She strode into the breakfast room, hoping to catch
him alone, only to discover he'd already eaten. He caught her
eye as he rose from his seat and gave her a grim half-smile.

"Nora. Good morning. I'm sorry I can't linger, but I have
a great deal of work to catch up on. I will be back in time for
dinner. I'm hoping the Pinkertons will have more news by then.
You will, uh, have some way to occupy yourself for the day?"

"Oh, I'll find something to do."

He grimaced. "Please be safe."

Nora stared him straight in the eye. "You too."

Owen gave a brusque nod and hurried away.

Nora sighed and pulled out a chair. "So much for plan A.
I guess it's back to investigation, then."

Sadly, investigation proved nothing but frustrating. A full
morning scouring old newspapers and making phone calls
brought her no closer to learning anything about Owen's past
lovers. Not wanting to declare this line of questioning dead
quite yet, she hopped a cab to the upscale shopping district
where Bonnie's Bonnets was located.

Inside, the shop was an explosion of color, with premade
hats covering the walls and glass cabinets stuffed with ribbons,
feathers, and other ornaments for custom commissions. Bonnie,

whose current hat sported a nest of ribbon and an entire stuffed bird, waved to her from behind the counter.

"Nora! Hello! I hope you like the shop. I try to have something for everyone, so do take a look around and ask me anything at all if you have questions!"

"Thank you. You have quite the collection here."

Not all the hats were terrifying, Nora noted with pleasure. After a bit of perusing, she found a cute, bell-shaped hat with a narrow brim that turned up in the back. She lifted it from the rack.

"Oh, you must try that one on!" Bonnie exclaimed, rushing out from behind the counter with a large hand-mirror.

Nora obliged, and set the hat on her head. It provided just enough shade for her eyes and showed off her short-cropped hair.

"With that black base, I can swap out the ribbon for any color you like," Bonnie suggested.

Nora studied her reflection, fingering the wool. The hat was top quality, and just the right weight to be worn year-round. "Do you have anything in lavender?"

"Of course!"

While Bonnie pulled out ribbons of differing widths and shades, Nora updated her on the morning's failed efforts to learn any new information. "Is there any chance you remembered anything else? Either about other women or more information about the woman who had wanted to marry Owen? I did ask him about it, but he said only that the lady had passed away. Her given name was Addison."

"Addison, hmm? No, that doesn't spark any recollection. I'm not certain I ever knew her name. I do know she was already married by the time I met Owen. To one of his friends."

"A friend?" Nora's head snapped up from her perusal of the ribbons. "A close friend, by any chance?"

"Oh, yes. Someone he saw regularly. He didn't speak much

about it, of course, being the way he is. Only a mention here and there."

"Hmm." Bits of ideas swirled through Nora's mind. She could assemble no firm conclusions, but a new avenue of investigation had opened for her. "Thank you. That's helpful."

Nora selected an inch-wide ribbon that matched her parasol and watched as Bonnie skillfully wrapped it around the hat in three overlapping layers, affixing them neatly in place with swift, perfect stitches.

"There you are," she said when she was satisfied with the result. "Perfect. It will look spectacular on you. Owen will love it."

Nora smiled, a little thrill rushing through her at the thought of enticing him with her new purchase. He could tip the hat up and kiss her. Perhaps knock it to the floor when they grew excited. She would plan it as their celebration after she'd made significant progress in her investigation.

After paying and thanking Bonnie, Nora departed with her new hat on her head and a definite course of action. She settled herself in Owen's office, a glass of iced tea and some snacks to fuel her and Owen's mechanical kitten purring at her feet. A few phone calls later, she had her answer. Addison Atwater, nee Browne. Date of marriage, sixth of June, 1897. Date of death, seventeenth of January, 1904.

"Atwater," Nora murmured. He hadn't seemed particularly suspicious, and she couldn't think of a reason he would have any animosity toward Owen, but the fact that he'd been married to the one woman who might have thought badly of Owen didn't sit well with Nora. "Owen's not going to like this, but he's going to have to talk about it when he comes home."

He wasn't unreasonable. Since they'd returned to St. Louis, he'd been fighting his own instincts to let Nora make her own decisions. She would be able to convince him to talk. And then she could soothe him with kisses and perhaps some wandering hands.

She glanced at the clock. He likely wouldn't be home for another two or three hours. In the meantime, she would dig back through the old newspapers she'd collected and look for any mention of Atwater Manufacturing, and particularly their collaboration with Cassidy Mining.

Nora was seated on the floor, papers spread all around her, when a phone call interrupted her reading. She doubted the call was meant for her, but she answered anyway, unable to leave the phone ringing indefinitely.

"This is Dr. Eleanor Taylor," she said into the receiver. "You've reached the home of Mr. Owen Cassidy."

"Nora, it's me," Owen's deep voice sounded in her ear. "I've had word from the Pinkertons. They've tracked down the man who paid for the newspaper article. They don't want to divulge any information over the phone, but I'm heading downtown now to meet with them. This could be the end of things. I'd like for you to be there."

A nervous shiver raced down her spine. The end of the investigation? Would the police soon make an arrest? Or had they already? Would Atwater somehow be connected, or were her findings no more than an odd coincidence?

One final question haunted her more than any other. If the investigation were truly at an end, would she have any reason to continue her association with Owen?

"I will meet you there," Nora promised. Whatever happened, she wanted to be with him for it.

Finding paper and a pen in his desk drawer, she jotted down the address and hurried out to hail a cab. Gray clouds blotted out the sun, and a light drizzle had begun to fall. She shielded herself beneath a borrowed umbrella and waited.

It felt like forever before a cab materialized, so anxious was she to reach the meeting point and hear the news. It took all her effort not to bounce in her seat as the dragon-pulled carriage rumbled through the busy streets.

By the time the vehicle pulled up at the correct address, the drizzle had developed into a downpour. Nora stepped down from the carriage, umbrella poised above her, and dashed for the door, head ducked, trying her best to avoid splashing through puddles. A doorman held open the door for her, and she raced inside.

"Thank you," she said, pulling the umbrella closed and looking around for a rack or bucket in which to place it. "I'm Dr. T—"

"Yes, we know who you are, Doctor," a distorted and eerily familiar voice said. "Thank you so much for joining us this afternoon."

Nora whirled around, reaching for the umbrella in the hope of defending herself, but she was too late. The doorman gave her a gap-toothed grin as his meaty hand closed around her wrist. She'd seen him before, she thought, as a second man seized her from the other side. She didn't know where, but she suspected she'd know soon. She could only hope it wouldn't be the last thing she ever learned.

32

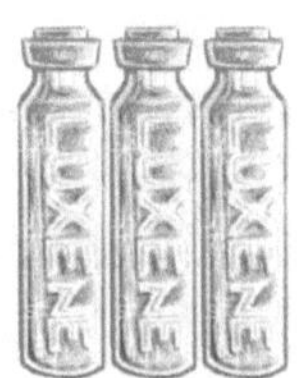

THE DOOR TO THE darkened chamber flew open, and one of the goons flung Nora inside. Owen caught her before she could fall, getting only a glimpse of her furious countenance before the slamming door plunged them into darkness.

"Goddammit," he cursed under his breath. He released Nora the moment she'd found her footing. He'd done this. He'd summoned her here. Right into the jaws of a trap.

The clanks and groans of a machine stirring to life sounded all around him. The floor shuddered beneath their feet.

"An elevator," Nora observed. "And not the usual steam lift. I think we're headed down."

How could she sound so calm? Owen was boiling with rage, wanting nothing better than to plant his fist in his enemy's face and demand he let Nora go. Whatever complaint he had, whatever incomprehensible sin Owen had committed to infuriate him, she was innocent.

"Owen?" Nora's groping hand found his arm in the darkness and grabbed hold, her fingers not even circling half of his biceps. "Are you okay? You're not hurt, are you?"

"No, I'm fine."

He'd been taken entirely by surprise. By the time he'd realized this wasn't the sort of place a Pinkerton would choose for a meeting, a thug had his arm twisted painfully behind his back while a second pointed a revolver at his heart. Now he was trapped, and Nora with him.

"You're trembling," Nora pointed out.

Owen broke away from her. "You shouldn't be here," he growled.

He heard her huff of breath and imagined the look of annoyance on her face. "I came here of my own free will."

"But I was the fool who asked you to come." He slammed his fist into the elevator wall, welcoming the sharp burst of pain. "It shouldn't be like this. This shouldn't be happening. Why? Why would he do this?"

Nora's hand brushed his arm again. "Owen? Do you know who's behind this? I recognized the man upstairs, posing as the doorman, but I can't place him."

"I didn't even look at him when I entered the building," Owen lamented. "What have I become, to be a man who dismisses a working man so casually?"

Maybe he did deserve this. Maybe he'd become so obsessed with his own concerns he'd hurt someone and not even realized it. Hurt a friend.

Nausea churned in his stomach. The deeper he fell into this trap, the more certain he became of his enemy's identity. The address. The peculiar elevator. The elaborate set up. All pointed to the same man.

No. No, it can't be.

The elevator jerked to a halt. Doors slid open in front of them, but beyond was only more darkness. Above them, the hum of machinery continued unabated. Owen stuck a hand out, feeling through the opening and finding nothing. He leaned out and listened.

"Shall we venture out?" Nora asked. "Or remain here? I'm not sure it matters when we can't see our hands in front of our faces."

"No," Owen agreed. He straightened up and smashed his head on the ceiling. "Ow!"

"Owen? Are you okay?"

"What the hell?" He reached up a hand, thinking he must have struck the top of the doorway, but the ceiling of the elevator pressed down against him, forcing him to bend over. "Shit!" He pushed Nora out into the gaping blackness. "Go, go, get out. The ceiling's coming down!"

He scrambled out after her, knocking into her and sending them both tumbling to the floor. Together they clambered to their feet. Owen found her hand and gripped it firmly, pulling her onward several steps until he was certain they were away from the elevator. The grinding of gears filled the air until with a painful clash of metal on metal, the floor and ceiling of the elevator met.

Silence fell. Dim electric lights winked on, providing just enough illumination to show them a long, empty hall. The open elevator doors were blocked now by a solid steel wall.

"Welcome to the labyrinth," an unidentifiable voice echoed.

Owen spun in a circle, but everywhere around him was bare concrete. Nora tipped her head down the hall. He nodded and they walked on, hand-in-hand.

The corridor sloped downward and ran on for perhaps one hundred feet before opening onto a large, square room. Overhead, man-sized tunnels of coiled wire criss-crossed the ceiling. Odd-shaped entryways dotted the walls, some only large enough to crawl through. A spattering of tinted lightbulbs cast eerie pools of color just bright enough for Owen to make out the far wall.

A brighter light flared behind that wall, revealing a wide, rectangular window set into the concrete. Leslie Atwater stood on the opposite side, something small and metallic tucked into the crook of his arm.

Owen's heart shattered. The pain and rage that had been building inside him since his capture broke free. Giving a roar of fury, he hurled himself at the glass, slamming against it with the full force of his weight. The window didn't even shudder and he crumpled to the ground.

"Owen!" Nora rushed to his side and helped him up. He brushed her off, too furious to care about the pain. She probed his shoulder anyway. "Don't make me have to redo this."

Owen slammed both hands on the glass. "Why?" he shouted. "Tell me why, you son of a whore!"

Behind the impenetrable window, Atwater chuckled. "Frustrated, Cassidy?" His voice sounded distant and tinny through whatever phonographic device he was using to project it. His smile, though, was perfectly clear. The smile that had once been the single ray of sunshine in the life of a heartbroken teenaged boy toiling in the mines.

> *"We'll get out of here." The older boy grinned at Owen. "I'm brilliant, you know."*
>
> *Owen had no idea what to say to that sort of statement. He glanced nervously around, not wanting the supervisors to catch him chatting during working hours. He was over six feet tall and still growing, but these men were muscled and angry and not hesitant to use their fists.*
>
> *"You are too." The lanky blond boy carefully cleaned the dirt from beneath his fingernails. A peculiar habit, since he'd be dirty again the moment he started back to work. "I saw you reading."*
>
> *Owen had to read. Books from the circulating library were now his only chance to get the education his father had so valued. Working here was the only way to get his precious baby brother to a real university someday.*
>
> *"I built the new air pump," the peculiar boy continued. "I'm gonna steal parts from things they throw out and build more machines. Maybe mining automata to replace us."*
>
> *"No!" Owen dropped his shovel. "I need this job!"*
>
> *"You'll get a better job. Be in charge of something. Haven't you noticed? The other boys, they all follow you."*

Owen shrugged, getting back to work clearing rubble from the newly blasted tunnel. Two other boys toiled nearby, exactly following the instructions he'd given them this morning. Owen liked organization and efficiency. He was the biggest of the youngsters. Of course they listened when he made suggestions.

"You can be my head supervisor when I open my factory," the blond boy offered. "We'll make a great team." He finally picked up his own shovel and started scooping.

"Keep talking," Owen said. He needed the dream of a better future. Needed the hope.

"Atwater and Cassidy," the boy replied. "Architects of the automated mining revolution. We'll be rich. Everyone will know our names."

"And we won't beat our workers."

"Someday we won't need workers. We'll have automata instead. We'll sit and relax and give orders while machine servants deliver coffee and build more machines to do all the work."

The idea was ridiculous, but Atwater's smile was so sincere and excited Owen found himself smiling in return. Smiling for the first time in months. He mimed raising a glass. "Here's to the future."

· · · ◊◊◊ · · ·

"Why?" Owen repeated. They'd been fast friends. Best friends for so many years. They'd escaped a life of drudgery together and achieved success as wild as Atwater's childhood fantasies. Owen wanted to sink to his knees and weep. To scream and smash things and beg for an explanation.

"You really don't know, do you." Atwater gave a slight shake of the head. "Typical."

"So it *is* you." Nora's tone was thoughtful. "I remember now. The man upstairs was the one operating the salvage machine. That was a ruse, to make yourself look helpful."

"Naturally."

Owen banged on the window once more. "Let Dr. Taylor go. Whatever reason you have for this madness, you can have it out with me, man-to-man. She has no part in this."

Atwater laughed again. "Ah. I'm afraid that's impossible, Cassidy. She chose to meddle in this affair, and she was getting far too close." He loosened his hold on the object he held. It fluttered its delicate wings and let out a mewl. A little metal paw reached toward the glass.

Owen reeled. "Spark?"

Atwater turned the kitten upside down and opened a hatch on her belly. "So good of you to take in a poor little stray, Cassidy." He pulled a thin coil of paper from somewhere inside the dragon. "Allowed me to hear so many interesting things. Ingenious, don't you think? I stole the design from Tagget's spy machines."

"I hope he sues you," Owen spat.

"So much anger," Atwater continued, his voice eerily calm. "If you're mad at anyone, be mad at your sweetheart. I didn't want it to come to this. I would have been perfectly content to continue as we were, making you struggle as you so richly deserve. But your biomechanologist paramour decided she couldn't leave well enough alone. So now you will struggle together. Enjoy my creation."

The light clicked off and Atwater vanished, the window now only reflecting Owen's own image back at him in the dim, colored light.

"Bastard stole my cat," he snarled, trying not to dwell on the reason he'd had the cat in the first place. The betrayal made him physically ill.

Nora placed a hand on his right shoulder, rubbing gently. He felt the strokes of her fingers as soft whorls of pressure, a sensation still alien enough to make him shudder. Nora quickly pulled away. "I'm sorry, Owen."

He spun to face her. "No, don't be. I want you to touch me. I want to learn to be comfortable with my body as it is."

She reached for him again, her touch now a tender caress. "I meant I'm sorry about Spark. We'll get her back. Atwater will go to jail for everything he's done."

Owen wished he had her confidence. If she even believed what she was saying. Maybe she was only trying to soothe him. Her hand hadn't stopped stroking him, and even the odd half-feelings in his mechanical shoulder were sending pangs of arousal throughout his body.

"Be brave," Nora whispered. "Whatever happens, I'll be there to fix it."

Owen yanked her into his arms, moaning her name. Maybe everything had gone to hell. Maybe they would never leave this godforsaken cellar alive. But, by God, he was going to seize the opportunity to kiss this magnificent woman.

His lips had just brushed hers when a terrifying keening reverberated through the chamber. Owen and Nora whirled together. A dozen or more metal dog-creatures streamed from a pair of holes in the wall. Long steel claws clacked on the ground, and they threw back their heads to howl their mechanical cries. Fluorescent pink foam dripped from their gaping maws. When the liquid hit the floor, it sizzled and smoked, eating into the concrete.

"Run!" Owen shouted. He grabbed for Nora's hand and they tore across the room toward the largest of the passages on the opposite side. Owen ducked through the opening into the small room beyond. The floor was rough and uneven, and he stumbled his way through to a narrow, curved passage on the other side.

In the cramped space, Nora had no difficulty matching his pace. He clung to her hand as the passages twisted and turned, branching and reconnecting like the natural tunnels of a cave. As they ran, the fear of becoming separated replaced the fear of the machines chasing them, and Owen slowed.

"This way," Nora said, tugging on his hand.

The passage she'd chosen was low enough that he couldn't see what was on the other side, but he trusted her judgment and dropped down to crawl through the opening. He emerged in a forest of steel trees, lit by bare green bulbs. Light glinted off of polished tiles inset into concrete walls with neither door nor hole. Somewhere behind them, the nasty dragons screamed.

"Dead end. Dammit!" He ducked to scurry back through the hole before it was too late, but Nora seized the back of his jacket.

"Look up," she said, pointing.

More of the coiled metal tunnels like he'd seen in the first room ran across the ceiling, weaving through the steel branches. Directly over Nora's head, one tube curved downward, leaving an open end big enough for a man to crawl through. An ordinary sized man, at least.

"This way," Nora ordered. She grabbed a branch above her head, jabbed her toe into a small foothold in the tree, and hauled herself up and into the tunnel opening. "Don't worry, you'll fit."

Easy for her to say. Owen began to climb, praying she was right. He'd already had one horrible news article about him. He didn't want his obituary to be even worse.

Mad luxene magnate Owen Cassidy was mauled to death by a pack of rabid mechanical dogs while stuck half-way inside a giant spring. He leaves behind millions of useless dollars, a traitorous pet cat-dragon, and a mother and brother who are probably better off without him.

The internal diameter of the tunnel was almost exactly the width of his shoulders. Owen squeezed and wriggled his way inside, crawling after Nora as quickly as he could manage. Which was to say, not very. The hard steel scraped his legs and banged against his knees, he bashed his head half a dozen times, and he held his breath with every bend and curve, certain this time he wouldn't make it through.

Up, around, and over they went, turning down branching pathways until he was thoroughly lost. Owen had worked in mines for two decades. He'd never been claustrophobic. Yet the longer he crawled, the less certain he became he would ever get out. His heart rate quickened, his breaths became rapid and gasping. The distance between himself and Nora stretched ever wider.

"This way," she called, disappearing around a corner.

Owen forced a deep breath into his lungs and dragged himself ahead with aching limbs. Sharp pains shot down his arm from the repaired shoulder. Maybe it wasn't quite as well-healed as he'd thought it to be. He rounded the corner where Nora had vanished and tumbled into a domed room barely large enough for him to sit comfortably upright. The small space had only two exits: the coiled duct they'd crawled through, and a matching tunnel on the opposite side. Temporary relief.

"Thank God," he moaned. He stretched out his legs and neck and sank back against the curved wall, closing his eyes and letting his pounding heart slow to normal speed.

"Owen, are you all right?"

He cracked his eyelids to see Nora kneeling in front of him, peering into his face. He loved the concerned crinkle she got just above her nose. She grasped his right arm and began to manipulate it, stretching him this way and that, testing his range of motion. He also loved the unflappable, methodical manner in which she went about her work.

"Tell me if anything hurts," she instructed.

"Everything hurts. Life is pain. You should have left me to the dogs."

"Nonsense. I would never abandon anyone like that."

Owen smiled. The bumps and bruises remained, and he would definitely need to give the shoulder a rest, but he was remarkably well, all things considered. "Of course you wouldn't," he replied. "You are a natural-born helper. You might be the most caring person I've ever met."

He loved that, too. Maybe he just loved *her*. The thought was less terrifying than he would have expected. Perhaps being chased by razor-clawed canine dragons and locked in an incomprehensible maze by a madman put the rest of life into perspective.

Nora released his arm. "That's very kind of you to say. I don't think the shoulder needs any major repair, but you should rest it as much as possible. I will do a more thorough inspection when we're out of here—wherever here is."

"Below Atwater's factory, I think." Owen sighed. "The building we entered was just across the street. It made so much sense to me to meet the Pinkertons there, since they'd gone to the factory to conduct interviews today. I never even thought to question it. I'm so sorry."

"You don't have to apologize. It's *not your fault*. And I'm going to keep telling you that until you believe me. Atwater knew everything we were doing. He used his knowledge to lay a perfect trap. He's obviously been planning his revenge for years. Look at this place." She waved a hand. "I can't even imagine how much time and money he put into building this. The man is obsessed."

Owen clutched his stomach, fighting the urge to vomit or burst into tears. Or both. "I don't understand." Leslie had always been odd and given to flights of fancy, but they'd been a team. He'd inspired Owen to dream big. They'd still had years of potential ahead of them. "I can't understand why he hates me."

"I don't know," Nora murmured gently. "I began to suspect him when I learned he was the man who married your former sweetheart Addison Browne. Maybe something between the three of you sparked the animosity. Maybe he killed her."

"No. She died of pneumonia."

"Probably not, then. But if he thought you and Addison were reconnecting behind his back—"

"I would never!" Owen cried. "Besides, she loved him."

"People believe irrational things all the time. And feelings like love and lust seem to me to be especially conducive to illogical behavior. I'm honestly not certain they make any sense at all."

Owen stared at Nora. The single, bare bulb hanging outside the entrance to the metal pod cast light and shadow across her beautiful face. There was absolutely a logic to his feelings. A raw, unambiguous logic. Find perfect woman. Fall in love. Desire. Kissing. Fucking. Hold her forever. Simple. Or maybe not. He couldn't seem to untwist the loving and lusting from one another.

Nora reached a hand out of the pod, sliding her fingers up between the coils of the entrance tunnel until she touched the lightbulb. She twisted until it winked out, bathing their small oasis in darkness.

Speaking of illogical… "What did you do that for?" Owen wondered.

"Atwater might have spy devices."

"Yes. And?"

"And he doesn't need to see this." She clambered into Owen's lap and kissed him.

33

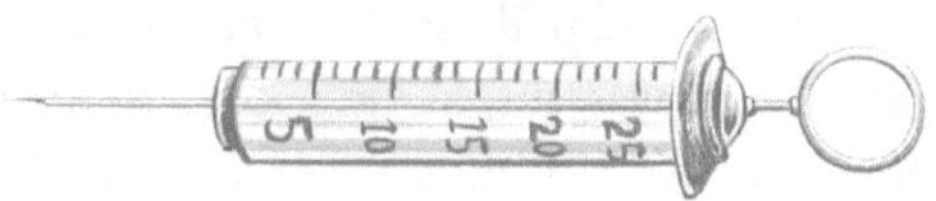

THEY *WOULD* GET OUT OF HERE. Any other option was unacceptable. Nora wouldn't allow this to be the last time she kissed Owen. She would escape, whatever it took. She would get him into a soft, warm bed and kiss him until they were both fully and properly satisfied. Nothing and no one would stop her. She had no guarantee she would ever experience these types of feelings again, and she wasn't going to lose the opportunity.

Her body was not so optimistic. Every nerve seemed on fire, screaming at her that *this* was her opportunity, *now* was her only chance. Well. Now she knew how she reacted to Owen during a time of stress.

Now, now, now. Comfort him. Take him. Claim him.

Nora tumbled into the whirlwind of sensation, lips and tongue tasting while bodies collided and rubbed together. She'd kissed him quite fiercely this time, and he'd been more aggressive in response, sucking and nibbling on her lips, swirling his tongue deep inside her, urging her to mimic his every motion.

In the darkness, she ran her hands through the fuzz of his short hair as she thrust her tongue into him, over and over. He must have liked it, because he made a low, hungry growl.

The sound sent a jolt of pleasure through her. His grunts of pain and sorrow were gone, replaced by desire. He needed to be held, soothed, cared for. Nora could do that for him. Her body would be his balm.

Her own need to touch him flared higher. Her body ached everywhere with wanting this, wanting to be the one to give Owen solace and pleasure. The one he turned to.

If only she could have done it with the light on. It would be so much easier to gauge his reactions if she could see the expressions on his face.

And she wanted him to have no uncertainty about what she desired, as well.

The possibility of spy holes or secret cameras snapping photos of them left her no choice, however. This wasn't something she was willing to share. Not with Atwater, not with whatever goons might be watching for him, not with a random person on the street. She wanted this between Owen and herself and for nothing to come between them.

Nora trailed her fingers down the back of his neck and across his shoulders, copying the downward motion with her mouth. She kissed his stubbled jaw, then his neck, tasting the salt of his skin and inhaling the scent of him. He rasped her name and grasped her waist, but didn't grope or reach for any of her more intimate places. Waiting for her lead.

Nora sat back and fumbled with the laces of her vest. She couldn't pinpoint the moment when her pleasure and his had become intertwined. She only knew they couldn't be untangled. It had become imperative that she both touch him and be touched. She wasn't confident enough in her ability to properly express her desires to tell him with words, but she could tell him with her body.

She shrugged out of the vest and slid back into his embrace, this time straddling him. The bulge of his erection pressed against her sex, sending tingles of excitement up her spine. She leaned in to kiss him again, then reached for his hands.

Owen didn't require much encouragement. A little tug to bring his hands to her breasts, and then he was cupping and squeezing and flicking her nipples into hard, needy points. Nora undid the buttons of his vest and shirt and explored him in return. Her fingers ran up and down his naked torso, enjoying the ridges of muscle and the tickle of chest hair, so different than her own body. His small nipples stiffened and poked out when she rubbed them, much like hers had done beneath his touch.

He opened the top button of her shirt. "More?" he asked. "Yes."

He made swift work of the remaining buttons, then gave her a ravenous kiss as his hands fondled bare skin. Little moans sprang from her lips. The roughness of his calloused hands and the contrasting gentleness of his touch drove her wild. She ground her hips against him, needing the friction against her aching clit.

"Yes." This time she gasped the word. Owen's mouth pulled away from hers, but before she could even protest the loss, he tipped her backward, his lips grazing one sensitive nipple. "Oh, yes."

Nora arched into Owen as he lavished attention on one breast and then the other. She rocked back and forth atop him, setting a rhythm with her hips, picking up the pace as the tension built higher and higher. Owen's stiff cock felt like heaven sliding against her.

"God, Nora," he groaned. He straightened up, his hands grasping her waist, thrusting to meet her every movement. "Nora, I can't—"

The climax hit her in a sudden rush, and her entire body jerked and spasmed in ecstasy. She clung to him as wave after wave crashed over her, until she collapsed against his chest, utterly drained.

Chests heaving, they sank together to the floor, holding one another close, the way they had that night at the hotel. Slowly, reality came back into focus. They were in a small metal pod in a villain's playground. Her trousers were damp, and so were his. Her vest was… somewhere.

"I should, uh, try to clean up," Owen murmured apologetically.

"Er, yes." Nora sat up and did her best to put her clothing to rights, while Owen scrubbed himself clean with a handkerchief. Or at least that's what she assumed the rustling of cloth in the darkness was. Should she apologize? She'd gotten so swept up in their passion that she'd given no thought to the consequences. Now her nagging uncertainty was creeping back in, pushing aside the haze of happy pleasure. "Shall we move on? Or rest here?"

Owen's hand found hers in the darkness. "Whatever pleases you. As long as we stay together."

You please me, Nora wanted to say. "Resting seems sensible," she replied.

"Yes. We are safe for the moment. Best to take advantage."

Nora scooted into Owen's arms, snuggling up to him once again. Though she wasn't sure of the exact time, she suspected it was rather early for sleep. Still, she would do her best to doze while she could. She listened to Owen's steady breathing, letting her body relax.

"This pleases me," she whispered.

His arms tightened around her.

34

Owen rubbed his shoulder. It ached right where the flesh and metal melded together, which probably wasn't a good sign. Too much twisting and turning through tight spaces. At least they were out of the tangle of tunnels. This new corridor was dim and narrow, perhaps five feet wide, with an arched ceiling and bare walls. Maybe it didn't lead anywhere, but he could walk upright and even stretch a bit.

He tried rolling the injured shoulder, fighting a wince. He would've much rather had Nora massaging it, but after what had happened in the pod, he didn't think letting her touch him was a good idea.

He'd been utterly out of his head from the moment she climbed into his lap. This was no sort of place for a passionate encounter. Nora deserved silk sheets, roses and chocolates, slow, sweet seduction. Not half-clothed humping in a factory basement.

Owen shuddered. Just the thought of the way she'd ridden him had him primed to spend in his pants again. Her throaty moans echoed in his mind. He could almost feel the wild abandon of her thrusting hips. He wanted to see her face the next time she came. He wanted to be inside her when it happened. And yet, he wouldn't say no to an exact repeat of tonight's activities. He was a bastard.

Nora had been quiet ever since. Back to her cool, professional self. Owen feared she regretted what they'd done. Or worse, that she found the entire interlude insignificant. They'd been unusually passionate during a tense moment and it wasn't worth fussing over.

He didn't realize he'd grunted until Nora stopped walking and asked, "Are you okay?"

"Fine." More or less. In a physical sense. Crawling through the tunnels again had hurt, but since they'd found an exit only the throbbing in his shoulder bothered him. And the bruised knuckles from punching the elevator. And maybe one of his knees.

"Is that man-talk for 'I will continue on through terrible agony because to show the slightest bit of human frailty clashes with the socially-constructed and entirely arbitrary definition of masculinity'?"

This was what came of educating women. They read psychological studies and suffrage pamphlets and pointed out when you were being a fool. Owen decided then and there, that in the unlikely event he ever had a daughter, he would make sure she had her pick of universities.

"I am physically capable of continuing on without debilitating pain," Owen replied. "Is that better?"

She smiled at him and his heart skipped a beat. "Yes. And mentally? How are you? I can't heal the hurt of a betrayal, much as I wish I could. But I will listen if you need to talk."

He sighed. "I'm… still in shock, I think. Best we continue on."

Not that they had much choice. The passageway had no doors or branches. The floor sloped upward, taking them to a new level of Leslie's Labyrinth. Owen didn't dare hope it might lead to the factory itself and a way out.

A faint plop caught his attention, and he paused. It happened again. He sniffed the air, catching a trace of mustiness.

"Is something dripping?"

"I don't know," Nora answered. "But water would be welcome. I'm parched." She picked up her pace.

The corridor ended at yet another square room, and the moment they stepped inside, a metal door slammed down behind them, preventing any retreat. Blue lights illuminated the space, and wave-like patterns of molded concrete covered the walls. Water dripped from somewhere overhead, forming small puddles on the uneven floor. Wide, rust-stained pipes ran across the ceiling, disappearing out the single exit on the opposite side of the room.

"I suppose we ought to head that way," Owen said. He stepped over a puddle. "I doubt this is safe to drink, unfortunately."

"No. But maybe if we follow the pipes, we'll find something better."

Again, she made him smile in the midst of a crisis. "I do admire your optimistic outlook."

He walked to the exit, taking the lead now to give her a rest. This hall was barely lit, and sloped steeply downward. So much for his hope of going up until they reached the factory. He wished he had any sense of how deep the elevator had taken them or how much higher they'd climbed since.

"Do you think this goes all the way b—" He jerked to a halt, throwing his arms wide to block Nora's path. Not one yard in front of him, the ground sheared away, opening onto a gaping pit. A trickle of water ran over the edge, tumbling into the yawning blackness. A terrifying premonition seized hold of him.

Owen spun around, pushing Nora. "Back. Go back up. Quickly. Get off this slope."

He didn't know if she'd seen the pit, but she obeyed, sprinting uphill toward the water room. They reached the room only seconds before hell broke loose. The pipes overhead burst open. Sections of the wall gave way, unleashing massive jets of water. The flood knocked Owen and Nora to the floor, sending them tumbling toward the hill and likely death beyond.

"Nora!" Owen bellowed her name, catching her with one hand as the rushing water carried her past. He pulled her to his chest, clutching her, stretching his body to its full height. That corridor was no more than five feet wide. As long as he stayed perpendicular to the opening, he wouldn't fit through.

His boots hit the corner of the doorway. His shoulders slammed against the wall on the opposite side, and he barely managed to keep his head from doing the same. Gallon after gallon of water battered him as he braced himself, clinging to Nora and holding his breath.

His chest ached. One foot slipped, loosening his precarious hold. This was it. This was the end. If he kept Nora atop himself as they fell, perhaps she would live. He would make this his last, desperate attempt to protect her.

Owen felt a sudden break in the rush of water against his face and instinctively sucked in a great lungful of air. The roaring around him lessened, and his eyes flew open. The deluge had abated. The jets in the walls subsided to a trickle. The pipes overhead rotated, closing hatches and cutting off the flow of water.

"Goddamn," he gasped. He wasn't dead. Somehow, he wasn't dead.

Nora's chest heaved with every deep, precious breath. He'd saved her. For once, he'd done something right. He smoothed a hand over her dripping hair, then pressed a kiss to her brow.

"Are you all right?" he asked.

She wriggled from his arms, putting enough space between them for him to gaze into her ocean-colored eyes. An affectionate smile spread over her lips. "My hero," she said.

His heart swelled. For perhaps the first time in his life he was one hundred percent happy with his towering size. Every childhood taunt of "How's the weather up there," every doorway he'd ducked through, and every bed his feet had stuck out of was worth it.

Owen returned her smile. "You saved my life once before, Doctor. Now we're even."

Slowly, he climbed to his feet, his sodden clothes heavy and dripping. He helped Nora up, then peeled off his jacket and cast it aside. Her eyes widened, stopping him from removing his vest as well. He didn't want her thinking he meant to strip naked, and this was absolutely not the place to attempt to recreate their passionate interlude.

He took her arm and guided her to the corner of the room, the safest place they could stand, for now. "Wait here. I'll try to pry open that door and we can go back the way we came."

The dazed expression faded from Nora's eyes, and she shook her head. "Owen, not even you are strong enough to do that."

"We can't stay here, waiting to die." He had to do something. He had to get Nora out, at the very least. "Atwater!" he shouted, hoping his former friend had some sort of listening device in the area. "You've failed, you bastard! I'm still alive! If you want to kill me, come down here and do it yourself, you gutless son of a bitch!"

The only response was the slow *drip, drip, drip* from the pipes above. Even the air seemed to hold its breath, waiting.

Owen sagged against the wall. "I have to try to open that door. It's the only way."

"You could lift me up onto the pipes," Nora suggested. I'm small enough to crawl over the top. I might be able to get out and open the door from the other side."

"And if they open up again while you're up there? You'll be swept to your death. No way."

"Are you giving me orders again, Owen Cassidy?"

"Dammit, Nora—"

Peals of laughter interrupted the argument. "Really, Cassidy, you don't think I would truly end such entertainment with your untimely death, do you?" Atwater's crackling voice taunted. "Pity you found the water chamber so quickly. I'm told I missed a rather heroic attempt to save your lady. I would have liked to watch that, but it *is* after midnight, you know. Do try to be a bit more considerate next time. I'll see you in the morning."

Every light in the room went out. Owen opened his mouth to shout again, but then bright lights flared at the far end of the sloped hall. From down inside the pit.

He and Nora glanced at each other and started down together. Owen slowed his pace well before the edge, stepping gingerly on the slippery floor and keeping Nora behind him. He wasn't sure he could believe Atwater's claim to not want him dead. Not when this had all begun with him nearly losing an arm.

Nora ducked right under that very same arm to peer over the edge, and it took all of Owen's self-control to not grab the back of her shirt and haul her away. He leaned over just enough to take in the sight below. How deep the shaft was, he couldn't tell. The bottom remained unlit, an inky, slightly shimmering surface that could have been a pool of water or a hard, wet floor. Well above that, however, no more than ten feet below where he stood, a net stretched the width of the pit. Anyone tumbling over the edge would be caught on its springy surface. This entire elaborate device had been designed to terrorize, and then to taunt the victim as they lay there, stunned to be alive. In Atwater's mind, it was all a big joke.

Owen dropped down onto the net, reaching up to help Nora down after him. His teeth clenched and his muscles tensed, sending new spasms of pain through his biomechanical shoulder. He hadn't survived. He hadn't escaped. He was a helpless dupe. A toy. He crawled through a small opening in the wall into a warm, dry room. Just where Atwater meant him to go, no doubt. It wasn't as if Owen had a choice.

The room was small, but cozy, with a thick carpet, a pair of round, plush stools, and a washstand with fresh water and a chamber pot. Soft electric lights added to the sense of warmth. A rack of clean clothing lined one wall.

He could dry off. Wash. Change clothes. Another non-choice. If he'd had more energy, perhaps he would have torn the suits from the rack, rent them to pieces, and flung them down the pit, screaming that he would be no man's dress-up doll. But what use was a tirade? He sank down onto one of the stools—no doubt put here expressly for this purpose—and put his head in his hands.

"I'm sorry, Nora," he moaned. "I'm so sorry. You ought to have left me on the street that day."

She walked up to him and wrapped her arms around him. Sitting as he was put him at the precise height to pillow his head on her shoulder. She was soaked to the bone, smelling of stale water and rusty pipes, but even cold and bedraggled, her embrace was everything he ever wanted.

"You are *still* my hero," Nora vowed, her tone daring the world to defy her.

Owen buried his face against her shirt and wept.

35

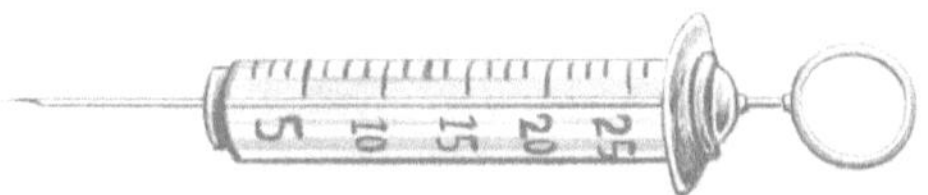

Aʟʟ ᴛʜᴇ ᴄʟᴏᴛʜᴇs in the chamber were sized to fit Owen. Nora knotted the necktie around her waist, turning the shirt she'd adopted as a nightgown into a very short dress. None of the trousers were of any use to her, unfortunately, but the woolen stockings covered her up to her thighs. Barring any more surprise drenchings, she would stay warm, at least. Her boots were still damp, but they would have to do. She couldn't possibly roam this hell-factory unshod.

She checked her vest again. She'd pressed and squeezed and wrung it out as best she could, but a few hours hanging hadn't been enough to dry it out. She would have to leave it behind.

Nora finished adjusting her clothing before kneeling to give Owen a gentle shake. She hated to wake him. He looked peaceful, relaxed, and he deserved a good long respite from his torment at Atwater's hands.

If only Lina were here. She was good at coaxing patients to talk through their problems. She had dozens of techniques suited to different personalities, and she knew how to read people and apply them. Nora only knew enough to realize how ineffectual her knowledge was. And she despised problems she couldn't fix.

"Owen," she whispered, shaking his uninjured shoulder. "It's time to wake up."

He reached out for her, mumbling something she couldn't understand.

"Owen."

His eyes fluttered open and he groaned. "Fuck. It wasn't a nightmare."

"I'm afraid not. It's been several hours since we went to sleep. We need to get moving again."

He rolled away from her. "Why? It's not as if we're going anywhere. Rats in a maze. And we don't even get any damned cheese at the end of it."

Nora climbed right over him to force him to look her in the eye. "We're smarter than rats. We've been on the defensive this whole time. That changes now. This time, we're attacking."

Owen's bleak expression made Nora want to hug him and stroke his hair and whisper soothing things. None of that would get them out, however, and she didn't think he could truly begin to heal until he'd left this place behind.

"I ought to lay here and make love to you until he decides to finally kill me. Then at least I can die knowing I've touched a piece of heaven."

Nora placed a hand on his forehead. Was he feverish to be spouting such nonsense? He didn't seem hot. It had to be the combination of physical and emotional pain affecting his mental state.

"Owen," she said in her calmest doctor voice. "You are going to get up and we are going to leave this room. There are ways out of this labyrinth, and we are going to find them. If you are in too much pain to do this, tell me now. I can go myself and bring back the police to rescue you."

A familiar grunt accompanied an abrupt rise from his prone state. "I can't let you do that."

"I thought not. Let's go."

"Dammit, Nora…"

A tiny smile touched her lips. She was becoming fond of that particular outburst of his.

"My thoughts are this," she began, before he could come up with any further arguments. "Atwater must have spy holes or cameras placed at various locations throughout. Which means there must be a way to access them. Other tunnels and corridors that run along, above, or below these. With all the odd twists and turns they are easy to conceal unless you are some sort of spatial relations genius."

"I'm not."

"Nor am I. But we can still guess where these places might be using other clues. We can knock on walls for hollow sounds. Feel for cracks or holes that might hide spy devices. That sort of thing."

"And if we find a parallel tunnel? Then what? We can't break through concrete or steel."

"No. But there must be doors between the two areas. How did these clothes get here? Not dragged through all the mess we crawled through."

Owen nodded, rubbing his chin and gazing at her with an intensity that made her go hot all over. She couldn't quite decipher his expression, but it made her want things. To kiss the stubble growing on his jaw, for instance. Or lower, where the open collar of his shirt revealed his throat. She wanted to touch him again, but this time in the light, where she could look her fill.

"You think there's a secret door nearby," he said.

"I do."

"In that case." He waved a hand at the plain wooden door leading from their temporary sanctuary. "I am at my lady's service."

The low rumble of his voice caused a flutter in her belly. Goodness, but it was… sensual. How had she never noticed until this moment? She'd never found a man's voice arousing before. She wanted to ask him to read something to her. A bit of erotic verse, perhaps.

"Shall we?" He extended a hand.

Nora grasped it, forcing herself to remain calm, businesslike. His hand was warm around hers. The touch of his skin sparked memories of all the places he'd touched her earlier, only adding to her lust. She focused on her plan. Find a door. Find a way out. Only then would she have the opportunity to explore these feelings.

The search dragged on. Back and forth they went, along stepped, blocky tunnels that looked to have been built from old shipping crates. The ceiling was so low in most places Nora could only stand perhaps a third of the time. Owen couldn't stand at all. He crawled, ducked, shuffled, and grunted. And with each grunt he sounded more forlorn. More in pain.

Nora eyed his right arm, hanging limply at his side. He'd damaged the shoulder for certain. Not the inner workings, she suspected, but the fragile, newly-healed skin grafted to it. The muscles and tendons that had begun to adjust were now protesting. She'd seen it happen before, when patients pushed themselves too hard or neglected their exercises. Owen was strong, and a fast healer. But he was still human.

She would have to stay at least three more weeks, perhaps as much as a full month to be sure he didn't do anything else to undo all her efforts. Plenty of time to indulge in a businesslike exploratory affair. The perfect amount of time. He wasn't likely to be interested in anything longer.

The sudden pang in her chest confused her. If wasn't as if she would lose him when they parted ways. He was her friend. Bonnie still thought of him affectionately, though they were no longer intimate. Nora could see no logical reason it wouldn't be the same for her. He would only ever be a phone call away if she wished to chat.

Owen had sat down on the bottom crate of a stepped section, taking the opportunity to stretch his cramped body. "Please, Nora, let's return to the room. This is hopeless. We can sleep. Let me hold you a little longer."

Tempting. Very tempting. Her own body was plenty

sore. She was too old for hour upon hour spent climbing and scrambling like a child. They hadn't eaten in… how long? A mere few hours sleep couldn't possibly provide enough rest. She could curl up in his arms and leave the world behind. It sounded glorious.

"You can hold me as soon as we find a proper bed and I have a proper nightgown." She gestured at her improvised ensemble.

One side of his mouth quirked. "I rather like your improper style. I wouldn't complain if you replaced your entire wardrobe with nothing but my discarded shirts."

This was the perfect opening for her prepared speech on the sensible reasons they should embark on a sexual relationship and the entirely logical way they ought to go about it—far more logical than their frenzied grappling earlier that night— but the words Nora had rehearsed entirely escaped her mind. Everything escaped her mind except the way he was staring at her. At her legs, at her breasts, at her mouth.

"If you find the way out of here before I do, you can strip this one off of me," she challenged.

· · · 000 · · ·

Ten minutes. That was all the time it had taken after issuing her challenge for Nora to find the door, dashing any fantasies Owen might have had about pulling off that shirt and pressing her body against his, skin-to-skin. Perhaps less than ten minutes. He wasn't certain his watch was functioning anymore after their dousing. What was it about this woman that led them to repeated mutual soakings?

He needed to take her to the ocean. That would be the proper place for it. Somewhere along the California coast. They'd find a secluded section of beach, strip naked, and frolic in the waves.

Owen rubbed his temple. Christ, he was losing his mind. He didn't frolic. Nor did he cavort or gambol. And he didn't take seaside vacations. He had work to do. A business to run. A former friend to hand over to the authorities.

"It's definitely locked from the other side," Nora sighed, straightening up from her inspection of the section of wall she'd declared to be a hidden door. "Perhaps we could ram it with a piece of the clothing rack, but this passage is too narrow to get much leverage." Her eyes flicked to his shoulder. She would never say it. Her medical training wouldn't allow her to suggest he try ramming the door down with his shoulder. But they were both thinking it.

"What sort of lock is it?"

"I'm not sure." She ran a finger down the tight seam in the wall, almost invisible in the poor light.

"Well, I suppose there's one way to find out." He flattened his back against the opposite wall, as best he could with his head ducked, positioning himself directly across from the crack where door met jamb.

"Owen—" Nora started to protest.

She needn't have worried. He had no intention of further abusing his already throbbing shoulder. He lifted one booted foot and kicked with all his might. Wood splintered and the door swung outward into a darkened hall.

"Not the sort of lock designed to keep out a two hundred fifty pound man," he remarked.

An instant later, an alarm began to wail.

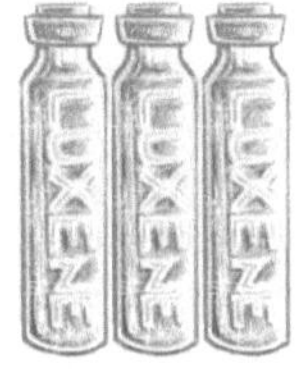

36

OWEN AND NORA tore down the dark, but blessedly ordinary corridor. The ceilings were no longer so low he had to crouch, nothing peculiar jutted from the walls or jumped out at him, and the floorboards were smooth, even, and flat.

The alarm screamed on. It was only a matter of time before the hired muscle Atwater had guarding them appeared. But this time, Owen was ready.

Electric lights winked on, blinding him momentarily. Nora crashed into him from behind. Owen squinted and shielded his eyes, spreading his feet wide and bracing for attack. A thug careened down the hall. He was a big man, near six feet, and solidly built. Not solid enough.

"Duck," Owen ordered.

"What?" Nora sounded confused.

"Duck!"

Owen lowered his left shoulder, dove straight at the onrushing enemy's midsection, and sent him flying up and over Nora's crouching form. Owen grabbed her hand and raced on.

"I might not have gone to college," he said, "but I've played my share of football matches. Everyone wants a 'big fella' to block for them."

The corridor ended in a flight of stairs. His legs were plenty long to take them two or three at a time, but then he'd lose Nora. He spun around and grabbed her by the waist.

"Sorry about this," he apologized, then picked her up and slung her over his good shoulder.

Owen flew up the stairs, his hands clamped tightly around Nora's calves. He was touching a new part of her and couldn't even stop to enjoy it. Another thing Atwater had to answer for.

Owen didn't set her down when he reached the top, choosing instead to use his long strides to carry her swiftly across a section of factory floor. He knew this area. He'd visited when Atwater had first installed his fantastical mechanical transports. The center of the room was an open shaft, stretching up six floors to the roof. A pair of wide metal slides spiraled down from the ceiling. To send a part down, you let gravity do the work. And if you needed a part to go up, a flip of a switch turned the slide into a twisting conveyor belt.

Atwater had been so proud that day. He'd taken Owen on a ride up to the very top, then shut the machine off and gone sliding down with all the glee of a young boy. Owen almost stumbled to a halt, rocked by the force of the memory.

"Owen, behind you!"

He glanced back at Nora's cry. Five men, some armed, charged at him. A door banged open in front of him and more goons burst through. Owen cursed. He had only one option left. He bounded up onto the nearest slide and slammed the lever to the fastest speed.

The machine roared to life so quickly that Owen toppled, pinning Nora beneath him. They spun up the spiraling apparatus, around and around, flying so fast he feared they might be thrown over the edge. He wasn't certain it was meant to be used at this speed.

"What is this?" Nora shouted over the buzz of machinery.

"Parts lift. Sends things up to any floor you need."

"I think I'm going to be sick."

The lift jerked to a halt. Owen splayed his arms and legs to stop himself from sliding down. His head was spinning, but he could see how close they were to the next floor—whichever it was.

"Can you climb?"

Nora didn't answer, just twisted herself around, grabbed hold of the sides of the metal chute, and began to walk up. A short time later, they were standing on the fourth floor, looking down at the enemies below.

"Stairs." Owen pointed. "We can get out on the roof and jump to the next building over."

They clasped hands again and broke into a run. Wordlessly, they moved together, up and out, climbing rooftop to rooftop until they raced down a fire escape to the streets below.

Their running slowed to a brisk walk. Still, they didn't speak. Nora didn't berate him for having carried her about like a sack of potatoes. He didn't pause to ask if she needed help, or wanted to slow down. He knew she didn't.

They were partners. Each contributing as they were able. Trusting one another to handle their part. Stepping back when it was the other's turn. Owen had had countless employees and associates over the years. Ones he relied on and trusted. But he'd always been in charge. He'd always had the final say. He'd never had a partner.

"Don't go home," Nora commanded, the first words either of them had spoken since the factory. "Don't go anywhere Atwater might expect you to go. Not until we can rest up and contact the police."

Her turn. Owen nodded and obeyed. He knew just the place.

37

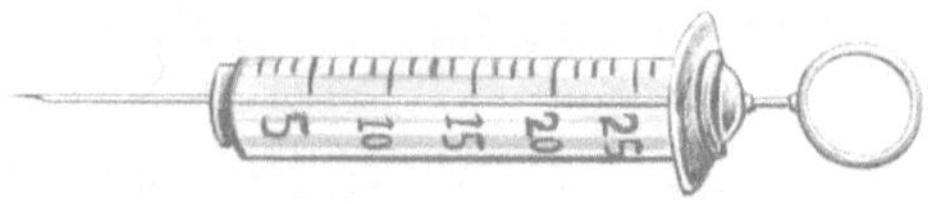

IF NORA HAD EVER been asked to name one place where she was least likely to spend a night—or day—she might have said a brothel. She'd been wrong.

The room was cheerful now, with the heavy curtains pulled back to let in the afternoon sunshine. Photographs and brightly colored illustrations decorated the yellow walls—all erotic images, of course, but the smiles and expressions of pleasure on the faces of the people gave the space a happy, festive air.

At least, that's how it felt to Nora. She couldn't deny that she didn't seem to view these things the way most people did. The images intrigued her, both as a doctor and a curious observer, but they didn't arouse her. The naked men and women were simply… naked. As all people were at various points in their lives. Nothing special.

She paused in front of the drawing of a woman straddling a man. The subject of the picture was partially dressed, her breasts exposed and her skirts hiked up. Her head was tipped back, her mouth open as if crying out.

"Good heavens," Nora murmured. Was that how she'd looked yesterday, in the tiny chamber below the factory, when she'd rocked herself to climax atop Owen?

Now *that* thought was arousing. The thought of trying any of these things with him was arousing. Not with anyone else. Just him.

Nora left off her perusal of the lurid decor and turned to the pile of clothing that had been brought to her to replace the torn and dirtied stockings and shirt she still wore. Like the bedsheets, they'd been freshly laundered and pressed. This was no squalid, back-alley establishment. Nor was it an opulent, gilded shrine to debauchery. It was simple, clean, welcoming. Not at all what she'd imagined a brothel to be.

Owen apparently knew the proprietress. The exceedingly pretty, raven-haired woman had whisked them inside and seen them settled in a room with the same brisk efficiency Owen exhibited in his own business dealings. Nora had been too exhausted to ask questions, and they both had barely managed to stumble into bed. She'd woken well after noon to a plate of food, a pile of clothing, and a message from Owen saying he'd gone downstairs to ask about making phone calls.

Nora discarded a bright red dress without a second look. Not her color. A green dress with an abundance of frills followed. The remaining items, she began to separate into piles to inspect more thoroughly. Somewhere near the bottom, much to her pleasure, she discovered a pair of trousers.

Well, bloomers or knickers, technically. Meant to be worn as undergarments, they were a uniform beige color, with a drawstring waist and a simple ruffle where they ended mid-calf. Nora immediately shucked her old clothing and tugged them on. Perhaps refined ladies would faint at the sight of her, but she was every bit as covered and comfortable as she was in her usual trousers. Excellent.

She found a blue front-lacing bodice to complete the outfit. The top was comfortable and supportive, but showed even more skin than the ballgown she'd worn at the hotel in Grand Tower. She had to tug it up to cover her areolae, and sleeves were so small and sheer they may as well not have been there. Nothing else in the pile was any more concealing. These were garments for the women who worked here: meant to entice.

You could entice Owen. The thought bounced around her head. *Seduce him right here. Right now.*

The very idea should have been laughable. Her, seduce someone. Peculiar Nora who didn't experience sexual attraction, except for a few, rare instances when she had inexplicable desires toward a friend. Inexperienced, virgin Nora, who'd had her first kiss at thirty-seven. Anyone would think it ridiculous for her to seduce a sensible, worldly man like Owen Cassidy.

Well. She'd show them.

Nora tidied up the pile of discarded clothing, polished off the last few crumbs of food, and returned to scrutinizing the erotic artwork. A few of the positions looked extremely uncomfortable and she absolutely did not want to try them. And some of the anatomy...

"I think this man ought to see a doctor," she commented, frowning at the poor fellow's enormous scrotum. "That looks like a medical condition."

A knock sounded at the door.

"Nora?" Owen called. "Are you up?"

She glanced over her shoulder as he entered, but didn't turn away from the wall. "I want to start with this one."

"Excuse me?"

"This picture." She pointed at a photograph. A fully naked woman lay on a bed, her hand between her legs. Nearby stood an equally unclothed man, his hand curled around his erection. "This is what I'd like to do first."

Nora counted to three before she turned. Owen stared at her, slack-jawed, then coughed and looked determinedly away from her nearly-exposed breasts.

"Do we need to go anywhere urgently?" she asked.

He turned to close the door and stayed there, his hand on the knob. His shoulders rose and fell as he breathed deeply. "No. I phoned the police and they advised me to keep my whereabouts unknown. We should remain here until I hear back. And I asked my brother to escort our mother on a vacation of her choosing. They're leaving immediately."

"You didn't tell them where to go?"

"No. I…" He exhaled audibly. "I told Timothy he was in charge and I trusted him to be responsible."

Nora's whole body vibrated. She didn't think she'd ever wanted to kiss him more. "And what did he say to that?"

"He said—" Owen cleared his throat. "He said, 'Thank you. Be safe. I love you.'"

Nora couldn't stand it any longer. She ran across the room and threw her arms around him.

"Nora." His voice was low, thick.

She smoothed her hands across his chest, resting her cheek against his back. "You are such a good man."

His large hands covered hers. "No. I'm a wreck. I'm flawed. So very flawed."

"We all are. But you care. And you try." She pressed her whole body into him. "I am proud to call you my friend. I would be proud to call you my lover, as well."

"Dammit, Nora," he murmured, but this time the phrase swelled with longing. "You know all my weaknesses."

"Turn around," she instructed, relaxing her grip on him. "I want you to see my outfit. I thought you would like it."

"I do." He took his time turning around, but now his gaze remained fixed on her. Nora took a few steps back, allowing him to look his fill. "I definitely do."

"Good." A nervous excitement burbled in her belly. She sat down on the edge of the bed. She was no sophisticated courtesan. Not even an experienced widow like Bonnie. She couldn't coyly flirt or confidently flaunt her sexuality. All she could do was be herself. "I'd like to copy that photograph. To your left."

Owen dragged his eyes away from her to glance at the picture. "With the woman on the bed and the man standing?"

"Yes. I think it's nice. They're just looking. I'd like to look at you."

Owen's hot gaze swept over her, lingering on her upthrust breasts. Nora glanced down. The top had slipped just enough that the dusky edge of one areola peeked out. Instinctively, her hand reached to adjust the bodice, but she stopped herself before her fingers met fabric. She wanted him to see.

He began to unbutton his shirt. "I thought you'd already seen all of me."

"Yes," she admitted. "But that was before I was interested. It's different now."

Another button. His brow furrowed. "I'm not sure I understand."

"I'm not usually attracted to, well, anyone. A few stirrings when I was a young woman. Rare enough I thought maybe I'd imagined them. And then once, very strong, a number of years ago. It didn't work out. And then you."

Nora had no idea what sort of reaction to expect. She didn't ordinarily talk about this. She'd never talked about it with anyone, in fact, except Lina, who'd told her all about the complexities of the brain and how she oughtn't worry about it. And she didn't, most days. Nora didn't mind being different. She only minded people thinking she was broken.

"I am honored," Owen said. His tone was almost reverent.

Nora's jaw slackened. Of all the things he might have said, that was not one she'd imagined. "Y-you are?"

"Attraction is so rare and precious a thing for you, and *I* am its beneficiary? Me? How could I possibly be anything but honored? I'm not worthy, Nora." He finished with his buttons, pulled the shirt off, and tossed it aside.

"Yes, you are." She untied the bow on her bodice, loosening the laces. The top shifted, and both her breasts popped free. It wasn't at all how she'd meant to undress, but Owen didn't seem to mind. He grinned at her. A hungry, wolfish grin that made her blood heat.

"I amend my earlier statement. I don't like that outfit. I *love* that outfit."

Nora laughed. He laughed in return, and in that instant all her lingering uncertainty vanished. She yanked off the top and began to wriggle out of the bloomers.

In a flash, her imaginings came to life. She was looking, and he was looking, she sprawled atop the sheets, propped up by pillows, he standing at the foot of the bed, gazing down at her. He was beautiful. Nora loved that he was tall, broad, and brawny. Never too big in her eyes. She liked the hair on his chest and arms and legs, and the thicker patch at his groin. She liked how his eyes seemed to melt when he was aroused, becoming translucent liquid pools. When he gripped his cock and rasped her name in his seductive voice, she felt such an intense rush of arousal, she thought she might orgasm from even the tiniest touch. She slid her hand between her legs, stroking herself, sighing in pleasure.

"Nice." Owen's voice dripped with arousal. His fingers tightened, his hand pumping up and down. "You thought this would be nice."

"Yes," Nora gasped. She had to force her eyes to stay open, because she wanted to keep looking at him. Every tiny touch of her fingers sent jolts of pleasure radiating through her body, until she thought she might go mad from bliss. "So nice. Oh, God, so nice."

Owen stroked himself faster, his chest rising and falling rapidly. He bit his lower lip and groaned. "Dammit, Nora, you're going to kill me. You're going to kill me and I'm going to love it."

"Owen," she moaned in response. She was so close. She pumped two fingers inside herself.

"Yes. Show me. Please, God, show me how you make yourself come."

Nora was in heaven. She spread her legs wider, arching her back to give him a better view. She worked herself up to the edge, then back, on and on, higher and higher, propelled by his body and his face and every delicious noise that sprang from his throat.

The orgasm hit her like a thunderbolt, spearing down every nerve in her body, making her writhe and cry out. She couldn't keep her eyes open any longer, but she didn't care. She worked her clit hard, drawing out the climax until she couldn't stand it any longer. Her arms fell limp at her sides, and she lay gasping, undone. She cracked her eyelids just in time to see Owen's face contort, almost as if in agony, his thick, white seminal fluid spurting onto his fingers.

"That," he said hoarsely, "was the most erotic thing I've ever seen in my life."

· · ▬▬▭▬·· ·

Goosebumps had begun to form on Nora's skin, but she didn't want to pull the sheets up over her body. Not while Owen lay beside her, smiling at her as though she were the most beautiful thing he'd ever seen. Perhaps a quarter of an hour had passed since he'd joined her in the bed, lying close, but not touching. They'd exchanged a few words of mutual satisfaction, but mostly they'd smiled at one another.

Owen had the most glorious smile, made all the more special by its rarity. He unleashed it more often than when they'd first met, but rarely at its full force. Now his dimples were deep, his eyes gleaming. A faint pink shine highlighted his cheekbones. So beautiful. The only question was whether to stare at him forever or kiss him.

"So, beautiful." It took Nora a moment to realize he was addressing her rather than echoing her thoughts. "Which naughty picture would you like to recreate next?"

"One with lots of kissing," she replied immediately.

He scooted to bring their bodies together, dipping his head to brush his lips over hers. "That sounds delightful."

Nora rolled toward him, wrapping her arms around his

neck and kissing him back. "And one that ends with you inside me," she added boldly.

"That sounds exceedingly delightful," Owen replied. He gave his hips a thrust.

Nora gasped at the sensation of his fully erect penis against her bare thigh. How was he ready again so quickly? She'd thought a period of recovery was necessary after a man spent his seed. She wriggled against him, both fascinated and excited by the thick, hard length of him. He made a low growling noise.

"Shouldn't you, er, wait some time before engaging in another bout of sexual excess?"

His whole chest rumbled when he laughed. "I've waited long enough." He gave another small thrust. "In case you hadn't noticed."

Nora squirmed again. "Oh, I noticed. I just don't want you to injure yourself. Prevailing medical opinion holds that ejaculations occurring too close together..." She broke off when Owen turned his head and smothered his laughter in the pillows. "Not true?"

"Never hurt me," he laughed.

"Hmm. In that case, I suspect the information might be coming from the same unreliable sources who think masturbation will kill you."

Owen's hand found her breast and his lips grazed her neck. "And we both know that's utter horseshit."

"Kiss me," Nora commanded.

He did, sweeping his tongue over hers in greedy, demanding strokes. Nora responded in kind, eagerly delving between his lips. She loved this hot, wet, hungry clashing of mouths. Loved the sensation of being inside him and letting him inside her. Loved the way the rest of her body responded.

Owen rolled her onto her back, straddling her. Nora wrapped her arms around his neck and kissed him harder. There was no fear here, beneath him, no sense of being crushed or confined. Only the comfort of being warm, protected, desired.

When he palmed her breasts and rubbed his thumbs across her nipples she moaned into his mouth.

Yes, yes. Her body remained sensitive from her earlier climax, and it took only moments before she was arching against Owen, begging for more. His big hand skimmed down her body, stroking over her hip and thigh on its way to her sex.

Nora let out an inelegant squeak. No hand but her own had ever explored this most intimate part of her.

Owen froze. "Too much?"

"No." It felt good. Simply different. She tilted her hips to press herself against Owen's hand. "Not enough."

She closed her eyes, allowing herself to savor the new and thrilling sensations of Owen's gentle touch. His fingers stroked through her folds, learning the dips and curves of her. He rubbed tiny, delicate circles over her clit, making her gasp with delight.

"Owen," she sighed.

"Good?" he asked. The hint of uncertainty in his question was adorable. Sweet, caring, lovely man.

"Yes."

Little by little, he increased the speed and pressure, teasing her toward orgasm until she was writhing, her body begging for more.

"Perfect," she gasped, surrendering to the climax.

Owen pressed a kiss to her temple. "I was watching you earlier." Another kiss. "Thank you for the demonstration."

Nora laughed and clutched him, kissing wherever she could reach: his upper chest, his neck. His shoulder, where flesh and metal merged seamlessly. She spread her legs wide, tugging him close, ready for what came next. His cock nudged at her core, but he didn't thrust into her. He lifted his head.

"Nora…" He frowned down at her. "Are you certain?"

"Yes." She flexed her hips to tell him with her body as well as her words.

"I've never been with a virgin," he admitted. "I don't want to hurt you."

She caressed his chest. "Oh, don't worry. You're not any bigger than the wooden phallus I use when I pleasure myself at home."

His entire body jerked. He gaped at her for a second or two, then gave her one of his radiant smiles. "Oh, Nora, you are sensational. I…" He paused for a moment, a faraway look in his eyes.

"You what?"

He kissed her again, a soft, barely-there kiss that nonetheless caused shivers of pleasure to run through her body. "I must be the luckiest man in the world. I admire everything about you. Your wit, your spirit, your kind heart. This sweet, sweet body of yours and your willingness to share it with me."

Nora sighed. His affectionate words were every bit as arousing as his beautiful body. "Owen. I want you. Now."

Once again she felt a nudge against her entrance. They moved together, and he slid inside her, filling and stretching her exactly the way she desired. His thrusts began slowly, carefully, as they learned this pleasure together.

Soon they found a rhythm. He drove into her in long, steady strokes, picking up speed at her urging. Tension twisted inside her. Her eyes closed and her back arched.

Yes. Yes.

She couldn't make coherent speech anymore, so she didn't try, just rocked her hips in time to Owen's thrusting while she teased her clit with a single finger. Every grunt and groan he made pushed her to move faster, to take him deeper and harder. She wanted to drive him wild. Wanted them to be wild together.

Owen's hands fisted in the sheets on either side of her. "Nora…" he choked out. "I—"

Harder. Faster. More. Please.

He matched her frantic movements with swift, powerful thrusts. One. Two. Th—

Nora broke, crying out at the force of yet another stunning orgasm. Owen jerked free from her, spurting across her belly with a strangled cry of his own. He rolled off her and dragged her into his embrace.

"Nora, my Nora," he sighed.

"Yes," she whispered, nuzzling into his chest. *Yes, I'm yours.*

It couldn't be forever. It wouldn't be for long. But in the time they had, she would be his. And she'd make him hers.

38

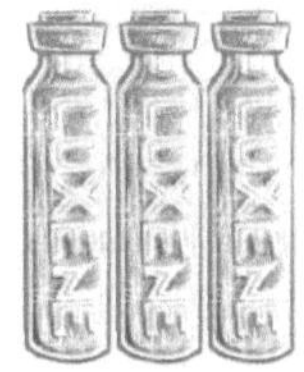

No doubt about it. Owen Cassidy had fallen deeply, passionately, irrevocably in love. He'd nearly blurted out the words during their lovemaking. Thank goodness he hadn't. Nora was a straight-forward, practical sort of woman. God only knew how she'd react to a sudden, impassioned declaration from a man she'd known less than a month. She might well think him daft, and he wasn't about to do anything that might ruin what they had now.

Owen wasn't sure how long they'd been lying there, cuddling and kissing. Nora had given no sign she wanted it to end, and unless she did, he had no intention of stopping. He could stay here for hours, soaking up her happiness, reveling in the sheer joy of the embrace.

He'd never experienced anything like this. Had never expected to. He'd occasionally enjoyed a moment or two of cuddling after sex. A few kisses. Perhaps a "thank you, that was lovely." But not this. Not this potent, lingering euphoria.

He meant to savor it. He would treasure every delightful second of her sweet affection.

Remember this is temporary, he scolded himself. Nora had her own life. She was fiercely independent. Once Atwater was behind bars and Owen's shoulder was properly functional, she would have no reason to remain.

She made the most adorable sighing noise as they exchanged another tiny kiss. His heart lurched. He wanted this moment to stretch into forever. Nora wanted him, despite his flaws. She genuinely cared about his well-being. He would cling to any hope she could someday reciprocate his feelings. He would do all he could to woo her.

Nora ran her hands along the edge of his biomechanics, where the flesh joined metal. "I hope our exertions didn't hurt," she said. She pressed her soft lips to the place her fingers had just skimmed. Owen shivered.

"No. It didn't hurt."

He wouldn't have cared if it had. He could have broken the damned thing entirely and still not cared. It would be worth it for this time spent in her arms.

"Good. I want to do a full evaluation, but as long as it's not bothering you, it can wait until we're able to return to your house." Her hand made another slow caress over the shoulder.

"I hope the evaluation involves lots of kissing."

Nora laughed. "More likely I'll leave you growling and in pain. But then I can give you a kiss to soothe you."

"Sensible, as always. Now tell me, my lovely, sensible doctor, which of these educational illustrations shall we act out next?"

Owen's cock swelled as he scanned the array of erotic pictures on the wall. His vote was for the pencil drawing of the woman sitting on a desk while a man knelt between her legs, but he'd do whatever Nora wanted.

"Um…" Her smile turned shy. "I would have to investigate. I—" A knock on the door interrupted her.

"Owen?" a familiar sing-song voice called. "Are you, ah, occupied in there?"

"Yes!" he shouted back. Yes, he was. He was cuddling and flirting with his sweetheart, and he didn't appreciate the interruption.

"Just how occupied? It's rather urgent."

"Give me a moment, Cynthia," he snarled.

Her laugh tinkled like bells. "Of course. Feel free to finish up."

"Another ex-lover of yours?" Nora asked. There was no jealousy in her tone, only curiosity.

"God, no!" he blurted. Outside the door, Cyn's musical laughter rang again. Dammit. What else had she eavesdropped on? "She's my cousin," he explained.

"Oh," Nora replied. "Well, it isn't unheard of for—"

"No," Owen interrupted. Let other people think of Cynthia that way. To him she was too much like a sister. "No."

Out in the hallway, the laughter grew louder. Owen reached down from the bed, scooped up a discarded boot and hurled it at the door. "Quit laughing, Cyn!"

Nora peered at him curiously. "Well, this is an interesting side of you."

Owen tumbled out of bed, grumbling under his breath. He didn't see Cynthia often. Almost no one knew about their relationship. But in the rare times they did meet, they always seemed to settle into their old adolescent banter. It was familiar. Comfortable. Except now Nora had witnessed him acting like a child. *Not* the way to woo a woman.

He struggled into his trousers on his way to the door. It wasn't locked. Cynthia wouldn't allow locks on any of the internal doors so none of her employees would ever feel trapped. She had no tolerance for misbehaving clients. One of many reasons her business was both highly profitable and well-respected.

Owen opened the door only enough to peer out into the hall, blocking Nora from the view of anyone on the other side. "What's the trouble?"

"There's a..." Cynthia's face went white. "Dear God, what happened to you?"

"What?" Oh, hell. His shoulder. "Uh..."

She pushed the door wider, stepping closer to look, then cringing away. "What *is* that?"

"It's a biomechanical joint," Nora's voice rang out. She padded over to the door, wrapped in nothing but a sheet. "It replaced a severely damaged shoulder and restores full function and strength. Conventional medical treatment would have required amputation. Mr. Cassidy is a complete, whole person who happens to have a medical prosthesis. He is not a machine, a monster, or in any way inferior. And if you have a problem with that, you can answer to me."

Cynthia shuddered. "It's horrifying. But I like your girl, Owen. She's fierce."

She's so much more than that.

"What did you want from me?" Owen asked his cousin.

She'd composed herself, but she was definitely avoiding looking at his shoulder. "There's a police inspector here to see you."

Owen started. "What? Already?" A shiver of dread ran down his spine. "I'll be right down."

He closed the door and scrambled for the remainder of his clothes. Nora yanked on her bloomers and reached for the revealing bodice she'd been wearing earlier.

"Something is wrong," she said. It wasn't a question.

"I hope not."

"But you think so. You're anxious. Your muscles are tense and you have a worried crinkle in your forehead."

A thrill shot through him. She paid enough attention to him to pick up such minute details. That had to mean something. He would grab even the smallest glimmer of hope.

Owen forced his thoughts back to his immediate problem. "Yes, I think so. I can't imagine anyone simply knocked on Atwater's door and arrested him. The man I spoke to earlier clearly thought I wasn't in my right mind, and I didn't even tell him all the details of the story. Everything I said is easily verifiable once inside the factory building, but it ought to take some time to gain access, make the investigation, and then take Atwater into custody. If he hasn't fled. Maybe that's it. Maybe he's fled and they're here to tell me they're in pursuit."

Saying the words aloud didn't make him believe them.

Nora yanked the laces of her bodice tight and tied a neat knot. "Let's go find out."

Owen nodded, biting his bottom lip. He wanted to say, "You can't speak to the police dressed like that!" Whatever else he might be, though, he wasn't a complete fool. The choice was hers. He would, however, reserve the right to punch anyone who might insult her because of the revealing outfit.

Cynthia waited for them downstairs. She ushered them into her small office, where a stern-faced man sat drumming his fingers on her desk. He eyed Owen and Nora, but his expression didn't change.

"The walls are thick enough here you won't be overheard if you speak quietly," Cynthia told them. She stepped out and shut the door behind her.

"Cassidy?" the man inquired.

Owen answered with a curt nod.

"I'm Inspector Banks. Who's the girl?"

Owen glanced at Nora. She smiled at Banks, even though he didn't deserve it.

"'The girl' is Dr. Eleanor Taylor, biomechanologist," she said. "I am Mr. Cassidy's partner in this matter and was with him during the events at Mr. Atwater's manufactory. I can corroborate his report and will testify if necessary."

"I see." Banks steepled his fingers. "Mr. Cassidy, I cannot speak to this matter with Mr. Atwater. That investigation I believe to be ongoing, and I am not a part of it. I must inform you, however, that it is probable you are mistaken about his involvement in this case."

Owen's gut clenched. "I am *not* mistaken."

"I am here to inform you that the information passed on to our department from the Pinkerton agents has led us to the source of the unflattering newspaper article regarding you and your business. The letter containing the details in the article was mailed to the paper from a property owned by one Mr. Owen Cassidy."

"Me?"

Banks inclined his head. "Upon further investigation, we have discovered that property to be the habitual residence of a Mrs. Frances Cassidy and a Mr. Timothy Cassidy."

Owen didn't even realize he was trembling until Nora's hand settled on his arm.

"Impossible," Owen rasped.

"I'm afraid not. I have also just learned that those individuals skipped town not half an hour ago, leaving no word as to their destination or when they mean to return. Doesn't that strike you as suspicious?"

Owen's hands balled into fists. "It does not. I sent them away."

"Ah. We had suspected as much." Banks rose from his seat. "They will, of course, be tracked down and interrogated about their involvement in this matter—"

"There is no involvement," Owen interrupted. "They are innocent."

"The courts will make that determination, Mr. Cassidy. Unless you would like to confess to the truth right now?" He withdrew a small, pyramid-shaped device from his pocket and set it on the table. "Owen Cassidy, you are under arrest for defrauding your clients and insurance companies, assault and attempted murder of your employees, and attempted defamation of your associates and competitors. Have you anything to say for yourself?"

Owen swayed on his feet. What in God's name was happening?

Nora's sturdy grip kept him from toppling. "Owen. Breathe."

"Kiss your whore goodbye, Cassidy. Perhaps once you've seen the inside of a cell, you'll have something to say."

Fury rushed in to replace the shock. He had plenty to say. *Go to hell! How dare you insult Nora? If you harm my family, I'll kill you! How much is Atwater paying you? How deep does he have his hooks in your department?*

Owen stared straight at Banks' listening device and said, "I want to speak to my attorney."

39

"You've hardly touched your dinner, Miss Taylor."

Nora glanced at the tray of food sitting beside her on the bed. She had no appetite. Try as she might, she'd been unable to think up a reasonable plan for helping Owen. Who would believe her about Atwater? Who could she trust?

"It's Dr. Taylor," Nora corrected.

Cynthia sniffed. "I don't give much credence to titles."

Nora wasn't sure what to make of the brothel owner. Her revulsion to Owen's biomechanics was sadly common, and she'd been kind and helpful in all other ways. She also appeared genuinely concerned for Owen, though—like him—she didn't express these feelings openly. The cousins also possessed the same blunt manner of speaking and a similar head for business. Like Owen's facilities, Cynthia's establishment was organized, tidy, and populated with loyal employees.

"I wouldn't have expected my title alone to impress you," Nora replied. "I did, however, think you would have some appreciation for a fellow woman of business."

The deep dimples that appeared when Cynthia smiled reminded Nora of Owen, adding to the pang in her gut. Only a few hours they'd been separated, and already she missed him terribly. Was he well? Had he been fed? How was his shoulder holding up? If anyone hurt him…

"Ah. I certainly do have that," Cynthia said. "Men underestimate us badly, don't you think?"

"All the time," Nora agreed.

"They used to offer me pennies for a fuck up against a wall, can you believe it? I didn't have much at the time, but I did have pride. I told everyone who offered I was worth far more. Got laughed at a few times, but now look at me. I doubt any of those boys can afford me."

"Oh?" Once again curiosity got the better of Nora. "How much do you charge?"

Cynthia seemed neither bothered nor surprised by the question. "I offer a variety of services, ranging in price from fifteen to fifty dollars."

"For one night?"

"For an hour."

An hour? Goodness. Nora's gaze trailed over the pictures on the wall, wondering which ones merited the fifty dollar charge. With rates that high, Cynthia probably earned considerably more money than Nora did. Biomechanics were enormously expensive, but her clients were limited in number and she had a habit of working for reduced prices for people in need.

"I can't claim to have money like Owen does, of course," Cynthia replied. "Bastard got lucky finding that green stuff. But I'll never be poor another day in my life. And if I want to retire, I can. Not that I intend to retire anytime soon. When my hair goes gray and my skin loses some of its shine, I will simply cater to older, wiser men. They will appreciate a woman who ages with confidence."

"That seems sensible."

Cynthia grinned. "And I can tell you appreciate sensible. I'm sure that's part of what Owen sees in you. I think we've left him hanging long enough. If you follow me to the office, he's on the phone for you."

"What?" Nora leapt from the bed. "Why didn't you tell me right away?"

Cynthia waved a hand. "Oh, he's fine. He's already home."

"Hmph." Nora strode for the door and barreled down the stairs, Cynthia close behind.

"You really care about him, don't you?"

Nora didn't turn around. "Of course I care! He's my friend."

"Mmm."

Nora ignored the cynical noise and headed straight for the office, lunging for the phone without even sitting down. "Owen?"

"Nora. It's good to hear your voice."

"Are you okay? What happened? Cynthia said you're at home?"

"Yes." He sighed. "My lawyer did what he could. I'm at home, but I'm not supposed to leave."

"I see."

"Yes," he said again, sounding grim. They had no need to elaborate. Atwater knew where Owen lived. Now he likely knew Owen was there. "You can remain with Cynthia as long as you need. I can arrange to have your things delivered to you."

"What about what *you* need?" Nora challenged. "You're in danger."

"I'm fine, Nora. I have Trask and the security devices."

She said nothing.

"Don't come here."

Nora bit back a retort. She took a calming breath and said, in her professional voice, "Thank you for the update. I'm glad you're not hurt or in jail."

"Nora…"

She hung up.

"Well?" Cynthia asked.

"He told me not to come."

"Ah." The two women exchanged a knowing smile. "Shall I hail you a cab?"

"That would be lovely, thank you."

· · · ꝏ · · ·

The screech of an alarm startled Owen from his exhausted near-doze. The drink in his hand sloshed, spattering him with the bourbon he'd hardly touched. He sprang from the armchair and raced across the study to the wall where the alarm had been installed. He quickly silenced it, looking to see which device had triggered it. The back of the house.

Owen set down the drink and doused the lights. If someone was here to attack him, best not to signal exactly where to find him.

He slipped from the study and made his way through the darkness toward the rear of the house. Not a sound reached his ears beyond his own soft footsteps. He paused to listen. Nothing. Either the intruder had fled after triggering the alarm, or he was silent as death.

Owen continued on, taking the rear staircase up to the second floor. From above, he'd have a clear view down into his small garden. The moon was bright enough tonight to provide some illumination. If anyone still lurked out there, he would see if they tried again to enter the house.

He pressed his face to the glass, studying the neatly trimmed foliage, the stately elm, and the seating area he never used. It was a pretty little garden, but he rarely set foot in it. He almost never walked in the beautiful park across the street, either. What the hell was he doing with his life, to be letting such things go to waste? If there was one good thing to come from this debacle with Atwater, it was that it was opening Owen's eyes to exactly how little he'd paid attention to anything outside his business.

Not any longer. He would be taking a hard look at his life. Learning to do better.

Owen stayed by the window for several minutes before giving up on his surveillance. Maybe it had only been an animal triggering the alarm. He plodded up another set of stairs, heading for his bedroom. He needed sleep. His door locked and the security system was operational. He'd be fine, just as he'd told Nora.

Aside from Trask, Owen had given the entire staff time off, so the hearth in his bedroom was cold, and the room entirely unlit. Fortunately, he knew the space well enough not to need the electric lights. It was his best advantage over anyone who might break in. Owen could navigate the house easily in the dark.

He tugged off his boots, leaving them in a corner, then tossed his shirt atop them. He could clean up in the morning. For tonight he only wanted to fall into bed. Maybe he would dream of Nora. Already their afternoon together felt dreamlike. With everything else that had happened, it was difficult to believe he'd ever had a moment of perfection in her arms.

A slight breeze across his bare torso made him shiver. Why was it drafty in here? He never left the window open. He moved to the window and pulled the curtains apart. Moonlight flooded the room. Wind blew in through a small gap beneath the window. Owen yanked the window closed.

"Sorry."

He jumped and whirled around at the sound of Nora's voice. She lay on his bed, dressed again in the seductive clothing from Cynthia's brothel.

"The window sticks. I thought I'd gotten it all the way closed."

Owen rubbed a hand over his head. "Dammit, Nora."

"Yes, I'm glad to see you too."

"What the hell do you think you're doing, sneaking around the house?"

"I assumed if I walked up to the front door and knocked, you wouldn't let me in. I apologize for triggering your alarm. It made a good distraction, though, while I climbed through your window."

He would have let her in. Leaving her out on the street

alone was even worse than having her here. Her secretive method of entry had its benefits, though. Atwater likely didn't know she was here. Owen almost laughed. Maybe Nora was rubbing off on him, if he could find the bright spot in all this.

"How did you manage to reach the window?" he asked, peering out.

"The tree. You have a convenient chair sitting beneath it, so getting up into the branches wasn't difficult."

A branch of the elm did pass beneath the window, but it wasn't large. It would have bowed under Nora's weight as she reached to tug the window open. She would have needed to use both hands. Good God, how close had she been to tumbling to her death? All to break into his house because she thought he needed protection.

"Christ, Nora, that was madness! This goes way beyond your duties as a doctor."

"But not beyond my duties as a friend. You're in danger, Owen. You can't stay here."

He pressed a fist against the pane, wanting to pound something in frustration. "I have to. Legally, I am obligated to. And if I leave, it will be tantamount to an admission of guilt."

Nora sat up and swung her legs over the side of the bed. "Damned if you do, damned if you don't?"

"I can't go breaking the law." He couldn't. He'd always been a by-the-book sort, even as a child. He knew the rules, he followed the rules, and he made certain those around him followed the rules as well. It was how you ran an organized, reliable, and trustworthy business. He didn't deal with criminals. He even squirmed when his clients were men like Tagget, who liked to bend the laws within a hair's breadth of snapping.

"Oh? And what about when you recruited a gambler to help you sneak onto a riverboat to rescue me?"

"Exceptional circumstances." And the most illegal thing he'd ever done in his life. He did not want to repeat that episode. "If I remain here, I can let my lawyer do the work.

We know I'm innocent and we know who's responsible for this. Justice will be served."

"Well." Nora stood and crossed her arms over her chest. Damn that ridiculous, revealing top of hers. All Owen wanted to do was crawl into bed and make love to her again. "You call me optimistic, but you apparently have a great deal more faith in the United States legal system than I do."

"I have a good lawyer." It was a poor argument, and he knew it. Nora was right to be skeptical. He couldn't trust the police anymore. He didn't even dare to phone the Pinkertons, not knowing whether the men he'd trusted to be impartial investigators were in league with Atwater. Surely, though, the courts and the judges would see reason. The charges were nonsense. The irrefutable proof of Owen's story lay beneath Atwater's factory floor.

"I understand your reluctance," Nora said. "You have a reputation to uphold. A duty to your employees to keep the business solvent. You are a man of honesty and integrity, and you don't want to harm yourself or those you care about by blatantly breaking the law. But Owen, this is your *life*. Atwater is unhinged at best, possibly murderous. You *know* you aren't safe here. And since I'm not leaving without you, you know I'm not safe here, either."

Owen rounded on her. So that was how she was playing? She knew he wouldn't leave to protect himself. But to protect her? He'd do anything, and she knew it.

"That was a low blow," he growled.

"Sometimes it's necessary to fight dirty to win."

"I should pick you up, carry you out of this house, and leave you there," he threatened. Somehow the words came out sounding serious. Would she believe him? Or would she laugh because she knew he'd never haul her away against her will? He'd learned that lesson all too well.

Nora's response was a slow smile. Her professional, slightly-smug doctor smile. "Okay." She looked him straight in the eye. "Do it."

Well. If she was going to give him permission...

"Fine. I will." Owen stalked across the room, grabbed her by the waist, and once again slung her over his good shoulder.

"You bastard!" Her fist pounded against his back, but it wasn't an angry blow. She was bluffing and knew he was too.

But maybe he could win this contest regardless. Maybe if he actually walked outside with her, she'd insist they rush back inside to keep him safe. He stomped down the stairs, not relaxing his grip on her for even an instant.

"Trask!" he called. "Hail a cab. Dr. Taylor needs a ride to the train station. And an escort. We might need to call in a few strapping lads to make sure she doesn't run off."

"Don't be ridiculous." Nora gave him another thump on the back. "The airship will be faster."

"Airship?" Owen stopped several paces from his front hallway. His fingers unclenched.

"Correct." Nora slipped from his grasp and faced him with hands on hips. "Pack your bags, Cassidy. We're going to Savannah."

40

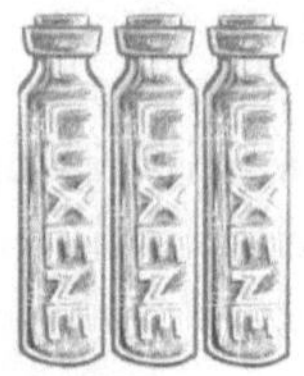

Even the captain's cabin on the small airship was cramped for Owen. The ceiling was six inches shorter than he was, the doorway even lower. The bed was wider than his shoulders, at least, though nearly a foot too short. Nora was bunking with the all-female crew. It made logical sense. She couldn't possibly fit in the tiny bed with him. Which didn't stop Owen from wanting her there anyway.

To no one's surprise, Nora's arrangements were stellar. A closed-top steam cab had ferried them quietly and efficiently to the airfield, where a ship had waited with engines running to whisk them away. The crew would be rotating shifts and flying all night. The captain had given them an expected arrival time of one o'clock p.m. the next afternoon. Much faster than the train.

Owen tried to roll over and banged his head. Much more painful, though. He was accustomed to private train cars with large chairs and all the food and drink a man could want. When he'd first started traveling for business, those cars had been exciting. He'd examined every detail, treasured every moment. All too soon, he'd begun taking those things for granted.

He rolled over again, more carefully this time. There was simply no way to get comfortable in this bed. Even when he willed his body to lie still, his mind raced. What had he done?

He'd knowingly and intentionally skipped town while under house arrest. He was an actual fugitive from the law. Not to mention a fugitive from a madman.

He had called his attorney before leaving and explained the situation. "I fear for Dr. Taylor's life," he'd said. "She knows as much as I do about Atwater's crimes, and I cannot in good conscience allow her to remain in St. Louis. I will be escorting her out of town immediately."

The response Owen had gotten was an unambiguous, "Don't do it," but he didn't see how he had a better choice. Nora had made it perfectly clear she wasn't leaving his side, so the only way to get her to safety was to go with her.

But what had he done? His reputation, already under attack, would be in tatters. What would happen to his business? Would he lose customers? Would more employees quit, or worse, would he be forced to lay them off or slash wages? How would this affect Timothy's education and future? Would his mother find herself ostracized from society and unable to see her friends? Even Cynthia's brothel was in danger.

And Nora... Could he ever be anything to her besides a friend who couldn't seem to do anything but get himself in trouble?

Somehow Owen settled into a pattern of dozing and waking, slipping in and out of unsettling dreams and panicked speculation.

Hours later, he woke with a startled twitch, unable to grasp how he'd managed to fall into a deep slumber. Last he remembered, he'd been twisting and turning, unable to quiet his agitated mind. The sun didn't lie, however. It slanted in through the small window, casting a beam of light right across the center of his naked chest.

"Morning, handsome. Welcome to the land of the living."

Nora stood in the doorway, leaning against the jamb, her legs crossed at the ankles. Cool, casual, confident. Today she had returned to her usual clothing: plain black trousers, white shirt, and a corset-vest. She was ravishing. So deliciously Nora. Owen was every bit as eager for her as when she'd been half-bare at the brothel.

"I was starting to think you'd never wake," she teased.

Owen pushed himself up to a seated position, stretching his cramped legs. "How long have you been standing there watching me?"

"A while. I'd intended to wake you, but you looked peaceful, and I like looking at you. You're gorgeous." Her eyes caressed him, from his mouth to his bare torso, and down to where the sheet rested low on his hips, barely hiding his already semi-erect cock.

He opened his arms. "Come to bed."

Her eyebrows rose. "That seems… impractical."

"We can make it work. I've never made love on an airship before. Actually, I've never been on an airship before. This might be my only chance."

Nora uncrossed her legs and straightened up. "You've never been on an airship? I thought all millionaires used private dirigibles to fly around the country."

"I like trains."

"Hmm. Interesting. Let me take a look at that shoulder." She flicked a switch on the wall, flooding the cabin with the glow of electric lights. Owen squinted.

"Forget the shoulder," he said. "I want to make love."

Nora crossed the tiny room in two swift strides and perched on the edge of the bed beside him. "If I don't examine the shoulder now, it won't happen for at least another day. Better to do it while we have a private room and undisturbed time. So be quiet and let me work."

Owen leaned back against the headboard and closed his eyes. At least she was touching him.

Nora didn't talk as she moved his arm around, probing and massaging the muscles on either side of the shoulder, twisting and turning the joint to assess his range of motion. She did make a wide variety of small noises, however. Little sniffs or grunts when she was displeased, and sounds of satisfaction when she liked something. Owen knew all these noises by now. Could picture the expressions on her face when she made them, even with his eyes closed.

Her remark the other day had been exactly right. He was in pain now, and very close to growling. It was bearable only because her hands were on him and because she was close enough he could smell her. Floral soap. A hint of feminine musk.

"Are you almost done?" he grumbled.

Enough was enough. He wanted to drag her atop him and kiss her senseless. Lose himself inside her. It was the only thing in the world he wanted. The only thing that could make him forget everything that had gone wrong with his life.

"The biomechanics are all sound. A few scratches to the surface, but no damage to the workings, and your face is so pretty it's probably best you have some flaws somewhere."

Owen opened his eyes.

"Unfortunately," Nora continued, "you've strained the surrounding muscles and tendons. Overuse. Doing things they weren't ready for. We'll have to go back to the therapy exercises. The good news is I have an assortment of rubber bands, weights, and machines at my office, so we should be able to get you exactly what you need for a speedy recovery."

Her office. He'd almost forgotten they were headed to her city. Her home.

"Where will I be staying when we reach Savannah?" he asked.

"With me, of course. You don't think I was planning on letting you out of my sight, did you? Besides, I have a plan."

"A plan."

"Yes. A very straight-forward, logical plan that I'm sure will suit your lifestyle and personal preferences."

"Suit my what?" What was she talking about? The only

preference he had at the moment was for kissing instead of planning.

"I mean you won't have to worry it might disrupt your life. Er, well, the life you will return to once Atwater has been brought to justice. You'll be able to continue on as usual. I'm sorry, I'm rambling. As you know, I haven't any experience with this sort of thing, and I'm not following the prepared speech."

She pushed herself up off the bed and clasped her hands behind her back, her posture erect and sober. Owen wanted to rise too, to face her squarely for whatever frank discussion she intended. But with the ceiling so low, he would have to stoop, which would be awkward, uncomfortable, and look ridiculous. Plus he was naked, which generally wasn't considered apropos during a formal discussion.

"It is quite clear," Nora began, "Even more clear than before—that a kind of pull or magnetism exists between us. An unusually strong attraction, on my side certainly, and perhaps something of the sort on yours?"

Unusually strong attraction. What an understatement. "Something of the sort, yes," Owen replied.

"Oh, good." Nora shifted, betraying a touch of nerves beneath her mask of calm. "I have to skip over some bits of the plan, because we already started, and it moved rather faster than I expected. We're already to the part where we're lovers."

Owen's brow furrowed. A spear of pain lanced through his shoulder as his muscles tensed in alarm. She had a plan about *them*? A "straight-forward, logical" plan? He didn't want logical when it came to Nora. He wanted passionate. He wanted spontaneous. He wanted more grappling in the dark and inspiration from erotic artwork. He wanted her to keep surprising him.

"So," Nora went on. "From here the logical progression is to continue with trying new things. I will need your help with suggestions on things to try and what order might be best to try them in, as you are the experienced partner in this matter. Also,

I would be happy to repeat what we've already done. I found it highly enjoyable, and I believe you did also?"

Owen nodded, unable to speak. Part of him wanted to sit down with her at a desk and start writing out a list of everything she might enjoy. The rest of him churned with dread at the direction she was headed.

"I know you like things to remain businesslike and short-term, so don't worry that I'm going to make you try everything we think of. We can try a few things, learn what we like, and hopefully that will last us for a few weeks or a month while your shoulder finishes healing. Is that a good amount of time for you? A month? I hope it's not too long."

He couldn't even make his mouth form the word no. Why couldn't she have kicked him in the balls? It would hurt less.

She gazed down at him, a touch of shyness creeping into her expression as she waited for the approval he couldn't give. His shattered heart pounded against his ribcage, its vigorous pumping mocking him. All his hopes of wooing her were gone. Trampled underfoot and ground to dust. She wanted logical. Casual. Temporary.

"Owen?" Her brow furrowed. "You look unhappy. Is it that bad a plan? Or is something else bothering you? I didn't hurt your shoulder too much, did I?"

"No." So he could speak after all. Barely. God, how could she not understand? How could she not see he was dying inside? "No. I'm fine."

Nora crossed her arms. "'Man-fine' again?"

"Fine-fine." *I'm in agony. I should have stayed in Atwater's dungeon, slowly going mad.*

"Ah." She regarded him suspiciously for a moment, then gave him a flirtatious smile. "Well, I *did* say I would kiss you after the examination to soothe your pain. How do you think we ought to go about that?"

"No," he blurted. He couldn't kiss her now. Not when he felt like his insides had been scooped out and discarded like a jack-o-lantern. No kiss could soothe that. All it could do was remind him of what he couldn't have. Heap more dirt on his sorry grave. "No, you were right. This place is too small and awkward for an intimate encounter. And I need to dress and go up on deck to stretch my legs."

"Oh." A glimmer of disappointment passed over her face. "Another time, then. I'll let you get dressed. Excuse me."

She nodded and scurried out the door, closing it behind her. Owen cursed and pounded his fist into the pillow. Now he'd hurt her, too.

He began to dress for lack of anything better to do, pulling on clean underthings and trousers. He stuck his right arm into the sleeve of his shirt and froze. The metal of his shoulder gleamed beneath the electric lights. He would never be free of her. She was a part of him, grafted right into his body. Owen sank back down onto the bed and put his face in his hands.

41

“**T**HERE'S ONLY ONE BED.”

Of course there was only one bed. Nora lived alone in a small apartment above her office. She never had overnight visitors. A second bed would have been a ridiculous waste of space. Yet Owen seemed stunned by this discovery.

Nora glanced at him again. No, not stunned. Agitated.

“Yes,” she replied. “But I think it's large enough for you. You're not likely to find anything better in a hotel.”

He paced the small bedroom, taking in everything: the lavender walls, hung with photographs of her family. The floor-to-ceiling shelf of books. Her dressing table, covered with creams, lotions, and grooming items she didn't take with her when she traveled.

No one else had ever entered this room, she realized. When family visited, they stayed in hotels and rarely even set foot in her small sitting room. If they came to see her, it was at the office downstairs.

This was her private space, made to be comfortable and welcoming for her alone, and she'd never even thought to share it until now. Strangely enough, she didn't mind sharing with Owen.

He, on the other hand…

“I can't stay here.” He spun in a circle, as if looking for an escape and finding none. “I should never have left.”

Nora couldn't tell exactly what was upsetting him, only that he appeared to be in great distress. He'd been on edge since they'd left St. Louis. When he'd first woken this morning, she'd thought the long night's sleep had done him good. Until her examination and their subsequent conversation had left him worse than ever. She suspected he was suffering some combination of mental and physical pain, but getting him to talk about it was like getting a cat to perform backflips.

A cat.

He'd loved the little kitten-dragon. Maybe she could get him a pet. Pets were soothing and provided companionship. It might help him relax. Ease his mind enough to bring back some smiles.

Nora had hoped to do some soothing herself with kisses, but he'd said no earlier and had been avoiding her touch. She'd obviously gotten something wrong in her plan, though she didn't know what. The whole thing, perhaps, was disagreeable. A reminder that she didn't know what she was doing. Maybe one day with her had been enough?

What a depressing thought.

"There's room for your trunk in the corner, there," Nora said, trying to inflect her voice with calm. "You're not an inconvenience, so there's no need to fret. Now why don't we head back downstairs and start in on some of your exercises."

He nearly sprinted for the door. "Exercises, yes. Maybe I'll go for a jog. A long jog. I've heard Savannah is full of pretty parks and squares."

"If you're going for a jog, we're going together. Isn't that the reason we're here? To protect each other?"

Owen paused with one hand on the banister at the top of the staircase. "Yes. Yes, you're right. It was all about protecting you."

"And you," Nora insisted.

"I know. I know." He started down the stairs, plodding now rather than rushing. "You should just forget me, Nora.

Let me go back home. I've disrupted your life enough. I know you want to help. I know your altruistic heart and your medical code of honor compel you to help, but you don't have to do this. There are others out there you can take care of. Others right here in Savannah, I'm sure."

But they're not my friends, Nora wanted to say. *Not my lover. Not* you.

She kept quiet because she didn't think he wanted to hear her arguments. He had such a terrible opinion of himself, one she suspected had been better before experiencing so much pain and helplessness. Lina would have ideas for therapy. They could make that part of their recovery plan over the next few weeks. In the meantime, Nora would do what she could.

"I want to talk about the trap while we start some exercises," she said.

He looked directly at her for the first time since entering her home. The confusion on his face was an improvement over the haunted look he'd worn all day. "What trap? Did I miss something?"

"Atwater won't wait around in St. Louis forever. Or for long, if anyone heeded our warnings and set out to investigate him. He'll track us down and come after us. But we're not waiting to see what he'll do. We'll set a trap for him. We want him to walk right in, get tangled in the snare, and carted off to jail."

"A literal snare?"

Nora shrugged. "I don't know. You know him best. You're integral to this plan. And it will help." She walked toward him and reached to touch his arm, but he flinched away. "Owen, your life feels like it's spiraling out of control. I see that. This can help. You can *do* something. Seize a chance to take charge. You can be the one to make the rules. Set everything up the way you want it to be. I think this needs to be your trap. Your plan."

He stared at her for a long, silent moment. "I can't possibly make everything the way I want it to be." His chest rose and fell in a great, heaving breath. "But I can help you with this trap business. Show me your therapy tools and we'll get started."

· · ◆ · ·

Doesn't like sausage, Nora added to her lengthy list of entirely random facts about Leslie Atwater. She tapped her pen distractedly against the desk in her office, her eyes once again drawn to Owen's vigorous exercising.

"He thinks there's too much potential for…" Owen grunted as he hefted the two heaviest of Nora's weights with a single hand. "Questionable or unsanitary ingredients."

Nora looked down at her paper and scribbled, the only preventative measure she had to keep herself from gawking at Owen. The office was a comfortable size, large enough to house the exercise machines and still provide room for freedom of movement during rehabilitation work. Yet somehow Owen dominated every inch of available space. He'd stripped to the waist, and his bare torso glistened with perspiration. Every flex of his muscles enthralled her. Maybe this was why people watched prizefighting and wrestling. She would watch Owen wrestle. No boxing, though. She wouldn't like to see his face damaged, and as a medical professional she couldn't endorse any activity involving repeated blows to the head.

Owen set down the weights, though Nora knew by now it wouldn't be for long. He'd thrown himself into his shoulder exercises with such vigor that she'd had to stop him from going for too long or lifting anything too heavy. He'd promptly moved on to working the rest of his body using her equipment: his back, his legs, his good arm. One set after another until she was sure he was aching everywhere.

She couldn't tell him to stop, though. Not when the activity had turned his melancholy into a grim determination. If physical exertion allowed him to feel strong and in control, she couldn't take that from him. He needed it. And if he hurt himself, well, she could give him a dose of laudanum and send him to bed.

He picked up the weights again, beginning another round of fifteen repetitions. "Is any of this at all useful?"

Nora reread her page of notes. A picture of Atwater was coming together. He was a man of fastidious habits. One who craved wealth not for the power it could bring, but for the luxuries it afforded him. Clean clothes and living spaces. Employees to perform any unpleasant tasks. Food prepared exactly to his liking. All of which he could easily afford as a successful business owner. No reason to be jealous of Owen on that account. Nora had yet to puzzle out Atwater's motives.

She drummed with her pen again as she read on. Atwater was also a man given to wild ideas and fantastic visions of the future. One line of her scribbling said, *thinks someday people will do nothing but think up ideas while mechanical servants do all the work.*

"Did I mention the moonship yet?" Owen asked.

Nora glanced back up at him. "No."

"He wants to build a ship that can fly to the moon. And a train that can go from New York to San Francisco in less than a day. He even mentioned an underwater city, once. Some comment about it being nice to lie back and stare up at the fish swimming above you while a serving girl automaton feeds you grapes." Owen paused in his exercises. "Though, to be fair, I think he was only nineteen when he said that, and a mechanical serving girl who caters to your every need sounds lovely to a young man with a face still too boyish and pimply to catch the attention of the ladies."

Nora jotted *moonship* and *underwater city* on her paper. "That is so like you, Owen. The man nearly killed you, tried to ruin your business, trapped you in a diabolical maze, and arranged to have you arrested and disgraced, and you still say, 'to be fair.' Atwater may be a mechanical genius, but he's an utter fool to throw away a friend like you. I can't even comprehend it. Did he truly not know what a rare and precious thing he had?"

Owen set down the weights so abruptly they thudded on the floor. "Nora." He took two powerful strides toward her.

Nora's pen trembled in her hand. The heat was back in his gaze. She'd seen a glimpse of it this morning, before her examination and speech had left him so miserable. Now it burned as brightly as it had at the brothel. And she wasn't even dressed provocatively. Her normal clothes covered her completely. He was tired and achy and dripping with sweat. It seemed a ridiculous time to contemplate kissing.

So, of course she was staring directly at his mouth and reminiscing about the taste of him.

"Nora," he said again. It was simply unfair for a man to possess a voice that deep and rumbly. She had no defense against it. "Is your plan open to negotiation?"

"Uh…" She shook off her surprise at the question. "Of course. I told you I don't precisely know what I'm doing."

"Good. Here are my terms. You make any sort of list you want. Read naughty books. Look at scandalous photographs. Ask whores for suggestions. Whatever you want. Whatever you can think of. I'll please you any way you like. And in return, you don't mention anything about weeks, months, years, or what have you. No talk of endings, departures, none of it. Only here, only now."

That sounded… perfect. To be honest, she didn't like the idea of him packing up after a month and walking out of her life, even if airships and telephones made the hundreds of miles between St. Louis and Savannah a trivial distance. Maybe that's where she'd gone wrong. Maybe passionate affairs weren't suited to a deadline, but simply had to be waited out until they had run their natural course. Owen would know such things, having presumably experienced several passionate affairs over the course of his lifetime.

"Your terms are acceptable," she replied, slightly breathless.

Owen lunged across the desk and kissed her.

Before this affair had started, Nora had had no idea kisses could come in such an astonishing variety. Oh, she'd known there were small, chaste kisses and deep, passionate ones. But Owen had opened up an entire world of possibilities for her. Gentle, coaxing kisses. Wild, desperate kisses in the dark. Hungry preludes to further intimacies and achingly sweet, soft kisses afterward that were possibly more intimate than the act itself.

This kiss was yet another new type. It had something of the desperation of their time in the factory, but slower, more drawn out. As if he were starving, but feared this might be his last meal and wanted to make every bite last as long as possible.

Nora cupped his face in her hands, diving into the kiss even though she had to tip back at a strange angle. It might leave her uncomfortable later, but at the moment she didn't care. She'd been craving his kiss all day and all the previous night. Hours had passed as she lay on the hard, narrow bunk in the airship, cold and alone, missing his warm body and strong arms.

The kiss went on and on, its slow, searing intensity spreading to fill every cell of her body. Nora thought it might last forever, until finally Owen drew back, sighing her name.

He straightened up and ran his fingers through his short hair. "God, I shouldn't be doing this. It's only going to make it worse. But, damnation, Nora, I can't resist you."

Nora pushed her chair away from the desk and rose to her feet. "It's making what worse? Are you hurt? I knew you were over-exerting yourself, but I thought it was easing some of your melancholy. I'm sorry."

He smiled. A touch of sadness remained beneath, but it was a vast improvement over his previous mood. "No, I'm not hurt. A bit sore, perhaps, and I'm sure I'll feel it tomorrow, but I won't require your medical expertise."

"Good. You should wash before dinner. My bathtub should

be large enough to hold you, and it has hot running water. A long soak in the warm water will help your muscles recover."

"And will you scrub my back?"

Her brows rose. "Do you need me to?"

"No." His heated gaze raked over her once again. "But scrubbing my back might lead to scrubbing in other, more invigorating places."

"Oh." Nora's cheeks warmed. "So that sort of thing is done in bathtubs, too? I suppose that's logical, since you're already naked. But I can't try it with you now. Catalina is coming for dinner, so I need to ensure everything is prepared." Nora checked her watch. "We have less than an hour before she arrives."

"Who is Catalina?"

"Catalina Navarro. My friend the psychological therapist. She will help you handle your grief and anxiety. I promise. She's very good, and she has many strategies for coping with traumatic events. It's all very scientific."

Another one of those slightly sad smiles spread across his face. "Darling, Nora. Always kind. Always thinking of me. Thank you. I remain skeptical about this therapy, but I will speak with your friend. And perhaps another time I can show you the fun to be had with nothing more than a bar of soap." He twitched his eyebrows suggestively.

"Yes. I… I think I'd like that. And if you want more kisses after dinner—"

"Yes. Yes, I do."

Nora's smile was broad. He was still hurting, but even a small improvement was a weight off her mind. And perhaps some enthusiastic kissing tonight could help even more.

"Maybe we can snuggle tonight, also?" she suggested.

The pain behind Owen's wry smile stabbed at Nora's heart. She yearned to kiss it away. To hold him forever if that's what it took to heal his wounds.

"We have to snuggle," he replied. "There's only one bed."

42

"HE'S GOING TO BE a tough one," Lina murmured, tipping her head slightly in Owen's direction. The two women watched him disappear down the stairs—off to do another round of exercises before retiring for the night—then settled side-by-side on the velvet-upholstered fainting couch in Nora's sitting room.

Nora slumped against the couch's single, scrolled arm. "Oh, yes. Stubborn."

"I'd say it's less about stubbornness and more about a need for self-sufficiency. He doesn't want to rely on others, and would rather take everything upon himself." Lina tossed her glossy, unbound black hair and glanced in Nora's direction. "I've known people of that sort before."

"Don't look at me like that. I know I'm a bad patient. Years of independence habituate a person into doing everything for herself. And when you don't need help often, help feels… intrusive."

"Exactly."

Nora gave her friend a hard look. "So what you're saying is Owen and I are exactly alike and both impossible."

"Not quite." Lina chuckled. "You do share certain characteristics, though, which accounts for some of the tension between you two."

"He wants to help me, I want to help him, and neither of

us thinks we need help. Is that it? And before you say yes, I would like to point out he needs considerably more help than I do at the moment."

Lina shook her head, laughing again. "Oh, Nora."

"Do you think I'm wrong?"

"No. I don't yet know everything about your situation, of course, but it's clear he's been through a lot. And equally clear he doesn't want to talk about it."

"He did give me a whole page of details about Atwater." Nora reached into her pocket and removed the paper, unfolding it and presenting it to Lina. "Perhaps you might get a sense of his motives from this. I can't understand it, myself."

"I'll give it a look."

"Thank you. The more we can learn, the better we can prepare. If we can get Atwater behind bars, it will be a huge burden off of Owen, and then maybe he'll be able to stop fretting over everything. It's so frustrating when one moment he's clinging to me and the next he's pushing me away."

Lina regarded Nora with raised eyebrows.

"What?"

"This." Lina waved the page of notes. "Has nothing to do with that."

"Of course it does. He doesn't want to let me out of his sight because he thinks he needs to protect me, but then he also thinks he's causing all the danger and wants me to go far, far away."

"It's only a surface manifestation of a much deeper emotional struggle. And this one you can't blame only on him."

Nora shifted on the couch. As helpful as Catalina's observations could be, they could also be highly disconcerting when they forced you to look inward at all your own flaws and quirks. "What do you mean? What did I do?"

"I'm not going to pry into your personal business," Lina said, "but I've been studying human behavior for years. It is patently obvious that a degree of romantic attachment exists between yourself and Mr. Cassidy. A rather strong attachment, I would say, given the way you two look at each other."

"Um…" What did one say to that? Her attraction was "patently obvious"? Nora wasn't certain whether to be embarrassed at being so transparent or pleased she wasn't unconsciously hiding her feelings. She wasn't ashamed of liking Owen, though she certainly wasn't intending to share intimate details of their relationship. That was strictly between the two of them.

"From my professional perspective," Lina went on, "there appears to be great affection between you two, but also tension and uncertainty. So here's my advice: if you want to foster a healthy relationship, you should talk to each other."

"We do talk. We've been working on plans." Nora gestured at the paper of notes about Atwater, but thoughts of their other plan bounced around her brain. Naked bodies. Bathtubs and scrubbings. *I'll please you any way you like.*

"Talk about your *feelings.*"

Oh, Nora had plenty of feelings where Owen was concerned. There was a whole host of *oh, that feels good* and *I love the way you feel.* They didn't so much talk about those as groan and grapple with one another, but they communicated *those* feelings just fine. Unfortunately, Lina was speaking of emotions, and those Nora didn't talk much about. Owen, she suspected, talked about them even less.

"I see," Nora muttered.

Lina smiled and gave her a gentle pat on the arm. "Don't worry. You'll work it out. I have confidence in you. And I'm always here to talk. In the meantime, I'll see what I can discover about your criminal." She rose from the couch.

Nora did likewise. "Thank you. I should get back down to the office and make sure Owen isn't overexerting himself. I think you scared him during dinner when you suggested daily therapy sessions."

"There, that's a good start. Talk about that. Then ask him

what else he's scared of. You tell him what you're scared of in return."

Nora shooed Lina down the stairs. "I'm scared of your meddling questions. Now go, before you ask any more."

Catalina laughed again, a cheerful, friendly sound that lightened Nora's heart. "Tomorrow, ten a.m.?"

"Perfect. Thank you for coming tonight. It's good to see you again."

"It is. And I'm glad to have met your Mr. Cassidy in person."

My Mr. Cassidy. His impassioned words from the other day flashed through her mind. *Nora. My Nora.* What were they to each other? Friends? Lovers? Something else? And how could she talk about any of this with Owen when she hardly knew what to make of it herself?

Nora saw Lina out the door, then stepped into her office to watch Owen at his exercises. He held a large rubber band tightly in his left fist, stretching it as he moved his right arm back and forth the way she'd taught him. He didn't need any instruction, and he wasn't overworking the shoulder, so she waited and watched.

"Just the shoulder tonight," he said when he'd finished the whole series of exercises. He stowed the rubber bands and weights in their proper locations before turning to her. "You never showed me what was through that door." He jerked a thumb toward the locked door opposite her desk.

"My surgery room. I keep it locked whenever I'm not using it. Helps with cleanliness. Antisepsis is vital for preventing infection. If it weren't for Dr. Lister, you'd probably be dead."

"Ah... who?" Owen asked.

"See? This is the trouble. Not enough people know or appreciate the pioneering doctors who did all the things that make surgery safe and biomechanics possible."

He smiled. Not a broad smile, but finally one that didn't

seem weighed down by sorrow. "I'm sure you'll teach me all about it."

"Naturally. Here, I'll open the room and let you see, but we're not going to go inside." She unlocked the door and reached in to turn on the light, but didn't enter.

Owen peered over her shoulder. "So. You *do* have another bed."

Nora turned around, pushing him away from the room before closing it back up. "Patients only."

"I'm a patient."

"Yes. And a very trying one. But that bed is for patients who are in surgery or in the immediate stages of recovery when they cannot yet leave the office. You, as you have demonstrated quite well today, are in excellent health and in no need of immediate medical care or any of the equipment in that room."

He took a step toward her. "Are you absolutely certain of that? Perhaps you'd better perform a thorough examination." He brushed his lips over hers. "Strip me naked and check every part of me."

Nora shivered at the thought. She kissed him back, hard and hungry, until they were both breathless.

"See?" she said. "You're extremely vigorous."

"I don't know." He put a hand to his temple. "I think I may be flushed. Light-headed. Weak at the knees."

Nora put her hands on her hips. "Owen Cassidy, are you trying to talk your way out of snuggling? You said you'd snuggle."

He grinned, and she thought her heart might melt from the force of it. At last, at last.

"On the contrary, Doctor. I'm merely pointing out that you declined to inform me of this alternative sleeping possibility in order to lure me into your bed."

"I like having you close to me." There. That was talking about her feelings, wasn't it?

He wrapped his arms around her, drawing her into a snug

embrace. "I like that too. Take me to bed, Nora. Make me forget everything but you."

"I'll do my best," she promised, and kissed him again.

43

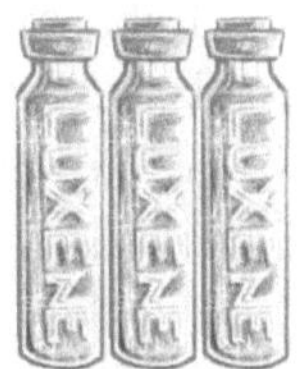

"**W**HAT DO YOU MEAN, you can't ride a bicycle?"

Owen rubbed his temple. "I mean exactly that. I can't ride one. I've never done it in my life, and any bicycle of yours is far too small to even attempt it." He stared at the vehicle she'd wheeled out of the carriage house behind her office, then peered through the door into the shadowy recesses beyond. "You don't have a steam car?"

Nora sighed in exasperation. "Why on earth would I need a steam car when I have a perfectly good bicycle? Here, hold this." She thrust the bicycle into his hands, then disappeared into her carriage house.

"Wait! Nora…" Owen stared down at the contraption she'd shoved at him. Sleek and lightweight, it had two wheels of identical size and a frame with a bar running horizontally from handlebars to seat. A man's bike, or one for a lady who didn't wear skirts. Next to him it was laughably small. If he tried sitting on the thing, he'd have his knees practically up to his chest. Assuming the cycle didn't collapse beneath his weight.

Nora reemerged a moment later, wheeling a second bicycle—an odd-looking one with chunky pipes and cranks and levers jutting out in several places. She stopped next to Owen, considered him for a moment, then began to turn the largest of the cranks.

"This is my adjustable bicycle," she explained. "I keep it here for visiting family." As she cranked, the frame widened, pushing the two wheels further apart, until it stopped with a loud clunk. "This is as large as it gets, I'm afraid, but I'll put the seat and the handlebars all the way up, and that should do."

"I don't know how to ride," Owen insisted.

"It's simple. Sit on the seat, put your feet on the pedals, and go. A child can do it."

"A child doesn't fall as far when he crashes."

Nora finished her adjustments and wheeled the bike back and forth a few times, nodding in satisfaction. "There. Looks good."

It looked like someone had welded together random mechanical bits into a Frankenstein's monster of a bicycle. Owen grimaced. Did the creators not know the dangers of unnatural scientific experimentation?

"You've got to be joking."

Nora pushed the grotesque bicycle toward him. "Try it. We'll go much faster than on foot, and it's part of my plan."

"I thought you wanted *me* to make the plan."

"Yes, I did. Do you have any ideas?"

Owen had to shake his head. "No, I suppose I don't."

"Well, I do. A bit like your security systems, only better."

Better? He'd used the most sophisticated security devices in existence. He raised an eyebrow skeptically. "And it involves bicycles?"

Nora gave him an impish grin. "No. It involves pirates. The bicycles are only to make us highly mobile."

He'd lost his mind. That was the only explanation for why he would be standing here, holding a too-small bicycle in one hand and its ridiculous cousin in the other, his mouth hanging open while Nora talked about pirates. She tugged her bicycle from his hand and mounted it.

"Like this." She placed her right foot on the pedal, leaving her left resting on the ground. "Just do what I do. You should practice now so you'll be comfortable with it later."

Owen stared down at the adjustable bicycle. The seat and handlebars jutted up from the odd-shaped frame like the necks of mechanical giraffes. "You can't be serious. This thing will fall apart beneath me."

"It's sturdier than you think. Give it a try."

"Not until you explain the pirates."

"They're more like smugglers. The crew of our airship and some of their friends."

Oh, God. Not only had he illegally fled St. Louis, he'd done it on a smugglers' ship? This was it. His career was over. He might as well find himself an uncharted desert isle and live out the rest of his days as a hermit. And he'd thought his chances of wooing Nora were bleak before. No way in hell would she want to spend her life hiding in shame from the world.

Owen considered the ugly bicycle again. Why the hell not? It would make Nora happy, and he doubted he'd have more than a handful of days left with her. Might as well spend them watching her smile.

He swung a leg over the bicycle, copying her stance. "Okay. What do I do now?"

"Watch me," Nora replied. In one fluid motion, she pushed the bicycle into motion, lifted her left foot from the ground, and started pedaling. She rode a few yards down the alley, then looped back, pulling up beside Owen and stopping as effortlessly as she'd started. "See? Now you try it."

Owen pushed the bicycle into motion, scooting it along with his left foot while the right remained frozen on the pedal. "I'm going to die."

He lifted his left foot, and the cycle listed to one side. He cursed, slamming his boot back to the ground to catch himself before the bike toppled.

"Good!" Nora applauded. "You almost had it. Try again."

Almost had it? Almost killed himself was more like it. Owen made another attempt, with the same result. "This isn't working. Let's just walk wherever we're going."

"Try pushing the bicycle into motion and then lifting both feet up to get used to the balance," Nora instructed, demonstrating. "Once you start to feel it, the pedaling should come more easily."

Owen gave it a half-hearted attempt, only to discover that it did seem to help after all. Back and forth he went in front of her carriage house, gaining confidence with every cheer and encouraging smile she gave him. The bicycle still seemed dangerously small and fragile beneath him, but he wasn't the utter failure he'd expected. Setting his right foot firmly on the pedal, he kicked off, determined to try again.

His left foot rose to join the right. The handlebars wobbled. And then, suddenly, he was doing it, his churning feet propelling the bike forward, straight and steady. Nora let out a whoop of delight. Owen turned the handlebars, trying to swing around to see her.

The bike tipped. The tires skidded. Owen tumbled to the dirt in a spectacular tangle of limbs and metal, his left shoulder and knee smashing into the ground. That would leave a mark.

"Owen!" Nora leapt from her own bicycle and ran to him. She dropped to her knees and pressed one hand to his temple and one to his chest. "Are you hurt?"

Bruised, certainly, and embarrassed, but it was difficult to feel pain when she was so adorably concerned for him. He moaned theatrically. "I am in utter agony, but it is my manly duty to carry on through the torment and reply that I am 'fine.'"

Nora laughed and pressed a quick kiss to his lips. "I love it when you tease me."

Any actual pain vanished with those glorious words. Owen disentangled himself from the bicycle, hopped up and got back to work. He rode, he teetered, he stopped, he restarted. Back and forth, again and again. Twice more he crashed, and each time Nora rushed to help him up, kissing him and praising his efforts.

With each new tumble, Owen added to his collection of aches and pains, but he couldn't complain. For the first time in a very long time, he was having ordinary, everyday fun. He hopped back onto the bike, starting up smoothly now, and pedaling furiously all the way out of the alley and onto the street in front of her house.

"Where are we going?" he shouted to Nora. "I'll beat you there!" He didn't dare turn around to look at her, but as long as he kept his eyes on the road and the wheel relatively straight, he was confident he could get himself from point A to point B.

Nora came zipping up beside him, entirely at ease on her own cycle. The rush of wind tossed her hair, and her dazzling smile spread from ear to ear. Only the fear of a crash at top speed kept him from staring at her.

"We're headed to the Pirate's House. It's an old tavern frequented by criminals."

Of course. Where else would she take him, but a den of iniquity? Pirates. Smugglers. Criminals. And Nora would stride right into their territory. Sweet, kind, cheerful Nora who always helped and always had a plan.

Reputation be damned. Suddenly Owen didn't care anymore. Maybe it was the exhilaration of the bicycle ride. Maybe it was Nora's brazen optimism rubbing off on him. He was tired of worrying, tired of arguing, tired of always trying to do the right thing. He'd ride this bike straight to hell, if that's where she was leading him. If she wanted to drink with pirates and hire airships full of smugglers, so be it.

· · · ◊◊◊ · · ·

Owen peered into the dimly lit tavern room, trying to see where Nora was pointing. There. The young blond woman who had captained their airship sat at a table in the back of the room, drinking spirits with a group of rough-looking men. She nodded when she caught sight of Owen and Nora, tossed back the rest of her drink, and rose to greet them.

"Doctor," she said to Nora, in a lilting French accent. "You wish to talk here or in the back room?"

"Back room," Nora replied. "I've got a business proposition for you, but I'd like to keep it between us."

"Très bien."

As they crossed the room, several men raised hands or nodded in Nora's direction. She smiled back, even saying hello a few times.

"How does everyone know you?" Owen whispered. "One would think you're a regular here by all the greetings, but I know you're not much of a drinker."

"I'm a professional acquaintance," she answered. "Smuggling and piracy is dangerous work. But it can be lucrative enough to afford top quality medical treatment when you lose a leg or shatter an elbow."

"They're former patients." The pieces fell into place. No wonder she'd been able to hire a smuggler's airship and felt at ease walking into a bar full of thieves. She was admired here. Respected.

Respected enough to be ushered into a small, secret room with a one-way mirror that looked out into the main room of the tavern. Owen tried not to gawk. He'd heard of these fascinating mirrors but had never seen one. From the opposite side, he hadn't even noticed it. It was merely part of the decor on the walls. In the tavern beyond, men drank and talked. How many of them knew they were being watched?

"Owen."

He spun around. "Yes. Your plan. Sorry." He pulled up a chair at the small table, across from Nora and the airship captain.

"I realize I never properly introduced the two of you," Nora said. She waved a hand between Owen and the young woman. "Owen Cassidy, meet the infamous pirate Redbeard."

Owen's mouth turned downward. Was that some sort of joke? The young captain couldn't be older than her early twenties, and Redbeard had been marauding for more than a decade. Not to mention Nora would never associate with a vicious murderer.

"I see you are surprised, Monsieur Cassidy." The young woman grinned at him and stroked her chin. "It must be because my beard is not red."

"Miss Redbeard is an associate of a former patient of mine," Nora explained. "My most difficult project ever. Another rescue, like you." The smile she gave him made his breath hitch. "She became a good friend. I hired Redbeard's ship on her recommendation."

Owen nodded. So she once saved a pirate and now they were friends. That was the Nora he knew and loved.

"To answer the question you do not ask," Redbeard spoke up, "I am the *new* Redbeard. The old Redbeard is no more, and I have taken up the name in his place. And taken the best and smartest of his crew." She winked and grinned smugly. "We fly mostly in Europe, but we had some deliveries in your country. We are honored to help the woman who saved the life of my sworn sister, La Capitaine."

"Thank you," Nora replied. "Here is what we need from you. Regular surveillance over my house. As unobtrusive as possible. An invasion or attack could come at any time. The only certainty is that it will happen. When it does, your crew will move in to engage the enemy with the goal of capturing their leader, Mr. Atwater."

Redbeard's eyes twinkled. "That will be our pleasure, mademoiselle."

Nora drew a paper from her pocket. "This has a description for you of Mr. Atwater's physical attributes. He is likely to be standing back watching while his hirelings do the work. If he doesn't appear during the attack, interrogate his men. We want him brought to the police."

"The surveillance will need to be 'round the clock," Owen added. The words spilled from his mouth in unchecked enthusiasm. Nora's idea was brilliant. Perfect. Atwater would never expect Owen to hire a pirate crew. And who better to protect them? "Atwater has been unpredictable and will be trying to catch us unaware. He may expect us to have security at night and choose to try trickery during the day instead. Nora, can you put together a list of authorized visitors? We should consider anyone else approaching the house suspicious."

Nora beamed at him. "Excellent thinking. Lina will be visiting. I have no plans to see anyone else, but it's possible a friend might come by if word spreads that I am back in town."

Owen pursed his lips. "Any male friends?"

Nora's brow crinkled. "Unlikely. You're by far my closest male friend."

"Perfect." Owen tried to ignore the little fluttering in his chest her statement caused. "Consider any man approaching the house suspicious," he said to Redbeard. "Atwater won't have any women working for him."

The airship captain smirked. "It will be his downfall." She looked to Nora. "I accept your offer, Doctor. And I trust the compensation will be satisfactory."

"It will be significant," Owen promised. He'd pay a million dollars if that's what it took to bring this matter to a close.

Redbeard's answering smile could only be called avaricious. She definitely had some pirate in her. Strangely enough Owen rather liked her for it. He rose from his seat and offered her a hand. Her handshake was firm and enthusiastic. The women shook hands as well, and then all three of them slipped out the small, hidden door into the working area of the tavern, where an employee escorted them back to the main room.

Redbeard returned to her drinking companions, not even nodding a farewell as Owen and Nora walked out the door.

"I forgot about the bicycles," Owen commented, striding

to where they'd left the vehicles propped against the side of the building. "How do they figure into your plan?"

"Anyplace we go, we use them. It makes us fast and maneuverable. If we need to flee Atwater or his men, we'll easily outrace men on foot."

"Well." He slung a leg over his bicycle. "I should practice, then. And maybe we should always keep them locked up or in sight. I'm a bit surprised they weren't stolen."

"No one here is going to steal from me," Nora assured him.

"I suppose no one anywhere is going to steal this monstrosity," he quipped, giving his bike a pat.

She laughed, her eyes sparkling, her smile radiant. "Maybe if you were nicer to it, it would stop throwing you off."

Owen faked a scowl at the bike, then grinned at Nora. "I love it when you tease me," he echoed her words from earlier. "And I love your plan." *I love you.* He wanted to say it. Wanted to shout it. But he was a coward. He kicked the bicycle into motion. "Race you home!"

She would beat him. And tease him. He didn't want it any other way.

44

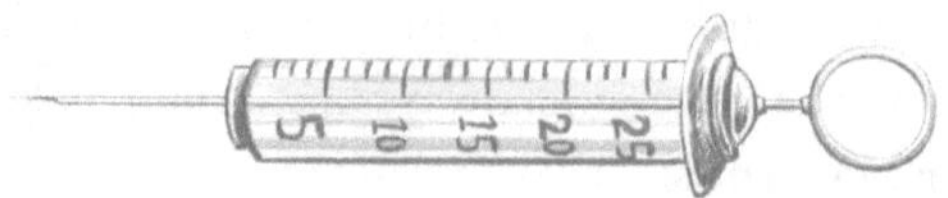

Driving rain pelted the window. Outside, wind whipped through the trees and thick clouds blotted out the sun, turning day into a gloomy, gray twilight. A good day for an ambush. A bad day for her pirate spies.

Nora stared at the water sheeting down the glass. She and Owen wouldn't be getting their daily ride today. In the last three days, the hours they'd spent cycling around town had become her favorite part of the day. The laughter, teasing, and good-natured competition brought as much pleasure to her heart as Owen's touch brought to her body at night. Today, the knowledge they would miss that special time together had her struggling to smile.

Behind her, Owen's grunts of exertion announced he had reached the last and most strenuous of his exercises. Nora didn't need to watch him any more. Since he'd recovered from his miserable first day here, she no longer worried he would overexert himself as a method of distraction. And their bicycle rides had provided the movement and exercise he needed to keep his spirits up. He'd even mentioned the possibility of visiting a bike shop and ordering a custom bicycle built to fit him.

Nora stared out at the empty streets, barely visible through the pouring rain. Would Atwater take advantage of this weather to sneak up on them? Did he even know their location? She hadn't expected to wait this long. She'd assumed he would quickly track them to Savannah and come for them at once.

"Maybe it's part of *his* plan," she mumbled. It would fit with his prior behavior to try to make them nervous and uncomfortable.

"What's that?" Owen asked.

Nora turned around. "I'm worried about Atwater," she admitted. "The weather obstructs our surveillance crew, and he's had plenty of time to get here."

Owen set down his weights and crossed the room to embrace her. "The doors are locked, the windows latched. We're not going anywhere in this rain. And my shoulder is feeling good. I'll keep you safe."

Nora reached up to massage his shoulder. "Don't get any ideas. It's not one hundred percent mended yet."

"Yes, Doctor," he replied, feigning deference. His hands skimmed up and down her back. "Am I allowed to get ideas that involve different body parts?" He bent over to suck on her earlobe, sending a shiver of delight down her spine. "Because I have many, many of those."

"We can't have sex now," she reminded him. "Lina will be here soon for your therapy."

Owen sighed and released her. "I suppose I ought to tidy up, then." He plodded across the room and began to return the equipment to its proper location.

"Are the sessions helping?" Nora asked, picking up one of the rubber bands as Owen hefted one of the heaviest weights.

"A bit. She asks a lot of questions, but she doesn't insist I answer them. Says things like, 'Tell me how you're feeling today,' and, 'What's on your mind?' I suppose she wants me to talk about everything that's bothering me, but..." He shrugged. "I did talk to her about Timothy and some of the difficulties I've had as he's grown older and more independent. She thinks I'm moving in the right direction and has given some suggestions on how to continue improving the relationship."

"Good. I'm glad." *What about our relationship? Have you talked about that?*

Nora's stomach churned. Would he talk about her? What would he say? She couldn't imagine him discussing any intimate details. He was far too private a man for that, and he would be protective with her reputation. But Lina had asked her about it. Told her to talk about her feelings. Nora had to assume she'd said something similar to Owen.

The chime of the doorbell announced Catalina's arrival, and Nora jogged to the front hall to let her friend in out of the rain. Peering through the peephole, she saw Lina huddling beneath an umbrella, a long, dark cloak wrapped around her shoulders. Nora yanked open the door and ushered her inside.

"Please, allow me," Owen said, relieving Lina of the umbrella and shaking it out before propping it against the wall to dry. "Welcome, Miss Navarro. You must be soaked. Can we offer you a towel or a cup of tea?"

Lina shimmied out of the voluminous cloak and stepped out of her tall rubber boots. "That's very kind of you, Mr. Cassidy, but I'm quite well. I enjoy rainy days, and as you can see, I was fully prepared for my short walk. Perhaps you might fetch Dr. Taylor the cup of tea, instead. She has a gloomy sort of look about her today."

Owen's gaze darted to Nora, his brow furrowing. "You have looked unusually somber this morning. Did you want tea? Or anything?"

"I'm fine," Nora answered automatically.

He regarded her skeptically, but then his frown morphed into a devilish smile. "Man-fine?"

With that one simple question, all Nora's gloom evaporated. She burst into laughter.

Owen, still grinning, turned back to Lina. "I don't think she needs any tea."

No. She didn't. Not even a million cups could have soothed

her so completely. She didn't need tea, food, cozy blankets, or anything. Only Owen.

Her heart lurched. Maybe he didn't want to talk about days, weeks, or months, but it still hovered somewhere in the future: the day he would leave her. She didn't want it to come. Not now, not ever. Yes, she would always be his friend, but what if she wanted more? What if she wanted him here, in her home, every day? Sharing the rain and the sunshine. Teasing one another with speedy bicycle races and long, slow kisses. What if this searing desire and inexhaustible affection were symptoms of a deeper affliction? One she suspected would prove incurable.

Owen and Lina disappeared into Nora's office, closing the door for their private chat, but Nora didn't retreat to her sitting room with a book, as she had on previous days. She paced a circle in her small atrium, her mind awhirl. Possibilities danced through her head, the optimistic side of her warring with the practical.

He loves me. We'll marry and have heaps of children.

You're too old for children.

He'll ask me to move to St. Louis and be his permanent mistress.

He's only interested in short affairs.

We'll leave everything behind and fly around the world together on a pirate ship.

Neither of you could stand to abandon your work.

Try as she might, Nora couldn't shut out the visions of a fantastical future. Herself and Owen, leaning over the rail of an airship, pointing down at the Great Pyramid. Bicycling together through Central Park. Walking hand-in-hand along the rim of the Grand Canyon, tugging one another away from the edge. Owen carrying a small boy with big dimples through his refinery, saying, "Someday, my boy, I'll hand this all over to you."

Nora paused by the staircase and sank down onto the bottom step, rubbing her temple.

"Oh no, oh no," she intoned. This would be bad. So bad. Worse than her last infatuation, though perhaps less embarrassing. This would hurt more. This would linger. Break her heart.

Still, the visions continued, enticing her, seducing her optimistic side. This could be good. It could be better than good.

How long she sat there on the stairs, she didn't know, but when the office door finally opened and Owen stepped out, Nora's heart hammered in her chest, bursting with joy at the sight of him, even as her hands trembled. He was smiling, and Nora was suddenly one hundred percent certain no other man on earth could match the beauty of that smile. She hopped up from her seat and hurried to his side.

"How was your talk?"

"Good. We were discussing how you coerced me into riding a bicycle."

"Oh?" He *was* talking about her. And apparently it made him smile. "How did I do it?"

"By being unrelentingly positive and encouraging. A kind word, a smile, a…" He hesitated for a second. "Helping hand."

A kiss. Nora shivered. She hadn't given much thought to those kisses. They'd been entirely spontaneous and natural. Now they felt weightier, more important. As if her body had already known where this was heading and her mind had only now caught up to it.

"Before I leave, I did want to talk to the both of you about Mr. Atwater," Lina said, startling Nora out of her contemplation. "I've read over your notes and pondered a bit. One thing that stood out to me is that he is a man of grand ideas. Often impractical and unrealistic, but grand nonetheless. It makes me wonder if he believes you, Mr. Cassidy, have somehow thwarted his vision for the future. Think on it, if you can. Even the smallest thing that may have derailed a wild plan of his might seem to his mind an unforgivable transgression."

Lina took her cloak down from its peg and slung it around her shoulders before stepping into her boots. "I'm off to brave the rain again. Same time tomorrow?"

Owen looked to Nora, who nodded. "We'll be here."

"Excellent." She picked up her umbrella and pushed the door open. A blast of wind sprayed a cool mist across the tile floor. "Ooh. Getting worse. I won't linger. Stay dry!" She raced off, putting up the umbrella as she ran.

Nora quickly closed the door behind her friend. "I think the chances of getting in a bicycle ride today are about zero."

"Agreed," Owen said from behind her. "We will have to occupy ourselves another way."

Nora turned to face him. "Was that an innuendo? It didn't sound like an innuendo."

"It was a statement of fact," he replied. "But anything can be innuendo if you want it to be."

As she crossed the foyer toward him, he opened his arms, welcoming her into his embrace. "Yes," she said. "I think I do want it to be."

He dropped a kiss on her brow. "Well, then. What sort of vigorous activity shall we try for our indoor recreation? Zealous scrubbing in the bathtub? The dragon riding St. George on the bed?"

"You, naked, on my fainting couch." Nora wasn't sure where the idea had come from, but it seemed right. She wanted him sprawled out before her, to touch and taste as she liked.

"As my lady desires." He steered her toward the stairs, keeping an arm tight about her waist. "In this scenario will you be naked as well?"

"Maybe." That part was less relevant. She didn't need to remove her clothing to explore his body. "When it's your turn."

Once inside her sitting room, Owen quickly began shedding garments. He didn't fling them haphazardly, of course, even in his hurry. Each layer fell one atop the other, in a neat pile set off to one side where no one would trip over it. Silly, perhaps, but Nora loved him for it.

When at last he was down to nothing but skin, he lounged on her couch, taking up the entire thing. He draped his left arm over the back of the couch, and let his right leg dangle over the side, the spread of his legs drawing her attention to his eager, jutting erection.

"Here I am, darling," he drawled, low and sensual. "Yours for the taking."

For a time Nora only looked, slowly undressing herself as her gaze roamed over him. She did want to be naked for this. She wanted her body to rub against his as she kissed and fondled him. Her skin craved his.

Owen either didn't notice or didn't care that her clothing did not end up in a nice, tidy pile. He was too busy staring at her with undisguised desire, his tongue darting out to wet his lips, and a gentle flush of arousal coloring his upper body.

Nora climbed atop him, claiming his mouth with hers. Her hands stroked up and down his arms and across his torso, mapping his muscles, delighting in his strength. She kissed his cheek where his dimple formed, then down along his throat, feeling his groan beneath her tongue.

Slowly, she inched down his body, sliding over him as her lips forged a downward trail. His skin was warm, a smooth, soft coating over his solid bulk. The contrast was delicious. Nora teased one small nipple with the tip of her tongue, drawing it to a tight peak before moving to do the same to the other. She loved the way he was sensitive in so many of the same places she was, yet different in others. His ribs weren't ticklish, like hers were, but she kissed them nonetheless, then further down his abdomen until she could taste his sex, the way so many of the women had in the erotic images at Cynthia's brothel.

The hiss of Owen's sudden breath was all the encouragement Nora needed. He liked this. He liked it a lot.

She licked all along the length of him, from base to tip.

There was nothing poetic about the taste of him. No berries or chocolate. Nothing sweet or spicy. He tasted like man. Like skin and a bit of sweat. Nothing more, nothing less.

Nora loved it anyway. Loved it because she was learning him and giving him pleasure. She swirled her tongue over the head of his cock, tasting the small bead of fluid that welled there. A little bitter. That was different.

"God, Nora," he moaned. "Take me in your mouth. Please."

She spread her lips and sucked gently on the tip of him, unsure what else to do. She couldn't possibly take all of him without choking herself.

Owen grasped her hand and guided it to his cock, urging her to squeeze and stroke. "Like this."

Ah. That made a great deal of sense. Nora experimented a bit until she found a rhythm, licking and sucking as her hand pumped up and down. She darted little glances at Owen as she pleasured him. His eyes were closed, his lips parted, his face a mask of pure rapture. So beautiful. So hers.

He made a strangled noise, his back arching and his hand clenching on the back of the couch. Nora quickened her pace. She was driving him wild, even new and imperfect as she was at this.

"Stop," he gasped.

Nora froze. Had she done something wrong? And just when everything had been going so well.

"Can I," he panted. "Take. My turn. Now?"

Nora lifted up off him. "Oh. You don't want to, well, finish?"

Several seconds passed before his reply came in a thick, husky growl. "Not until I've got you writhing and moaning as thoroughly as I was."

Heat shot through her body. Owen slipped out from beneath her, moving with surprising ease and grace for such a large man. Nora took his place on the couch, spreading herself across the soft fabric, offering herself up to his touch.

Owen grasped her waist and eased her down the couch until her legs dangled over the edge. He knelt between her thighs, nuzzling the sensitive skin there.

"I'll do my best to give as well as you do," he murmured, then put his mouth to her core.

Nora closed her eyes. Her arms dropped to her sides and she surrendered to sensation. Owen's tongue stroked along her folds, tasting all the places his fingers had discovered before, dipping inside her in quick, teasing thrusts that left her breathless. Merciful heavens. No wonder he'd worn that expression of ecstasy. Her face was surely doing something similar.

Her entire body contorted in bliss when he began lavishing attention on her clit, flicking his tongue and sucking. Raw, desperate noises rose in her throat. It was too much, too powerful, yet still not enough. She was falling, falling, falling, until she shattered, bucking against him and calling his name, her fingers scrabbling for something to cling to. His hand found hers, and she seized hold, digging her nails into his skin until the tremors wracking her body finally subsided.

Owen trailed soft kisses down her inner thigh before rising to his feet. "Ready for more, love?" he asked.

Love. He didn't seem to notice the endearment. It fell effortlessly from lips glistening with the evidence of her pleasure. Natural as anything. It sent Nora's heart into wild palpitations, caused her entire body to ache with longing for him. Not because she craved more pleasure, but because she wished to be joined with him. To become as close as their two bodies could be. To share in this passion together.

She opened her arms. "Yes. I'd love more."

Owen embraced her, kissing her hungrily, sliding her up the couch until he could climb between her thighs and fit himself to her.

Nora welcomed him eagerly, wrapping arms and legs around him, holding him to her as he moved inside her.

Yes, yes, more.

She thrilled to the straining of his muscles beneath her hands, the taste of her own sex on his lips, the grunts and groans of his excitement.

All of you, all of you.

Nora could tell from his ragged breathing he was close to the edge. She grasped his backside, driving him into her, wanting him to finish inside her when she hit the edge that hovered so close. She couldn't speak now, could hardly think, but she told him all she could with her body, holding him fast, giving and taking as best she was able.

He shuddered atop her, moaning as he thrust deep, and she was lost, tumbling back into a bliss that shut out the world, where nothing existed but him, her, them.

She drifted back to reality, guided by quiet kisses Owen pressed to her lips and cheeks, over and over. Nora sighed into his mouth, her body relaxing, but still embracing him, still holding him inside her.

"My sweet, magical Nora," he murmured. His words dripped with emotion, washing away her uncertainty and leaving her with only a glittering, glorious hope.

You love me. Say you love me. Please, say it.

He didn't, but he held her and kissed her, and whispered her name. Apparently she had to do this herself.

"I love you, Owen," she vowed.

He toppled off the couch.

45

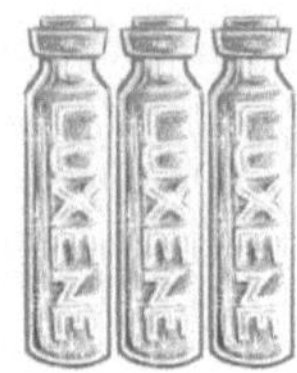

Worried blue-green eyes peered down at him. "Owen?" Her fingers stroked a gentle caress over his brow. "I'm so sorry. I didn't mean to startle you. Did you hit your head?"

He didn't think he had, but he was dazed enough he couldn't be entirely certain. He'd still been reeling from the most glorious orgasm of his life when her whispered words had mowed him down like a steam car at full speed. Maybe he'd misheard. Maybe it had all been in his imagination. But the way she gazed at him, gorgeous eyes brimming with concern, the way her fingers ran through his hair... Those things spoke the truth. She had said those words. And meant them.

"Are you hurt?" Nora asked.

Owen caught the tiny tremor in her voice and lifted a hand to cup her cheek. "No. Falling off the bicycle was much worse."

The worried crinkles around her eyes smoothed out and she smiled at him. For him. The special smile that betrayed all her feelings. How had he never understood it before? He'd been staring at her for hours, days, not speaking her language. And now she'd handed him the Rosetta Stone.

"Oh, good. Teasing is an excellent sign." She held up a single finger. "Follow my finger with your eyes. I want to make certain they're tracking correctly. Even a seemingly minor blow to the head can be dangerous."

Owen laughed. "I'm not hurt, Doctor Nora, only dazzled by your beauty."

"Owen," she admonished.

He watched her finger, tracking it up and down, side-to-side, until she let out a relieved breath. Owen caught her hand, bringing the finger to his lips.

"I love you," he said. Strange, how easily the words came, after all his fretting over them. "I love you desperately."

Nora straddled him, kissing him passionately enough to stir his body from its languid state. She tasted of sunshine and bicycle rides, free and radiant and full of joy. He wanted to claim her again. Make her his. Lose himself inside her again.

Hell and damnation.

"I owe you an apology. I should never have spent inside you. It was careless and inconsiderate and—"

She put her hand to his mouth. "Stop. It was what I wanted. I highly doubt anything will come of it. I'm not exactly in my prime, after all."

Owen pressed a lingering kiss to her palm. "Oh, yes you are. You very, very much are."

He didn't want some young, barely-from-the-schoolroom girl. He wanted Nora. He loved the lines around her eyes and mouth that showed how often she smiled. Loved the years of knowledge she happily shared with all who would listen. He loved her unabashed delight in the things that were still new to her. He loved her heart, overflowing with kindness. Her. Only her.

He probably should have been saying these things aloud. Telling her. Explaining his feelings. His conversations with Miss Navarro had given him a peculiar new perspective. Owen didn't know how good he would be at implementing such changes, but it couldn't hurt to try a little.

He traced a finger along the corner of her mouth. "Your

skin is soft and lovely," he murmured. "But not perfect. You smile so much there's a permanent little line right here. I love it." He cupped her breasts, kneading gently. "Your breasts are full and round, but not exactly the same size. I adore how they feel in my hands. I love exploring the differences between them."

"Owen," she sighed.

He tugged her down atop him, kissing along the column of her neck. "Everything that's different about you, everything that's imperfect, I love. Because it's you."

Nora's hand caressed his shoulder, her fingers sweeping over his biomechanics, touching them not like a doctor, but like a lover. Like he was beloved.

"I understand," she replied. "That's how I feel about you."

And he hadn't even gotten to the part about how she was smart and funny and just damned adorable. Owen sealed his mouth to hers in another searing kiss. He'd been certain this was impossible, certain he would never experience such utter joy. Yet, somehow, here he was. In love. Loved. And about to make love once again to the woman he dreamed of spending his life with.

He cupped her buttocks, positioning her to ride atop him, ready and eager for her. "Nora, I—"

His words were cut short by a blast that shook the entire house and left his ears ringing. Nora shrieked.

"Good God," Owen blurted. "What was that?" It hadn't been a thunderclap. Was the floor still vibrating beneath him? Was that acrid smell stinging his nose… "Christ, is that smoke?"

Nora scrambled to her feet, snatching up her clothing and struggling to cover herself as rapidly as possible. She stepped into her boots without stockings, and clutched her shirt over her breasts, not buttoning it. She went thundering down the stairs, Owen right at her heels, pulling on his own clothing as he went.

At the bottom of the staircase she froze.

Tendrils of ugly, gray smoke twisted and spiraled upward from the open office door. Flickers of light in yellows and oranges told of worse things beyond.

"No!" Nora darted through the office door.

Owen cursed and raced after her, grabbing her by the shoulders and spinning her away from the wreckage. What had once been her pristine surgery room, jutting from the rear of the townhouse, was now a mess of fire and debris. The roof had caved in and flames licked at the half-crumbled walls. Nothing was salvageable, and the rest of the house was in danger of going up with it.

"No!" Nora tried to turn back, but Owen's grip was too strong. He dragged her from the office, all the way out the front door, away from the heat and smoke. Rain beat down upon them as he cradled her to his chest.

"No." She moaned it this time. "No, no, no."

Owen stroked her hair, holding her tight, murmuring words he knew could never take away her pain. "I'm here, love. I have you."

He knew her anguish, knew how it felt to have his life's work attacked, suddenly and viciously. But this was worse. His business had been damaged. Her loss was total. All her equipment, her medicines, her carefully designed workspace, gone in an instant. He'd been in business for years. He knew the cost of restoring her livelihood would be enormous. Quite possibly beyond her means. She would have to begin again, with nothing. And while her years of knowledge and experience were her greatest asset, Owen knew right now they would be little comfort.

Owen wiped a wet strand of hair back from Nora's face. The driving rain had become a blessing that might well be the salvation of the remainder of her home. "We need to summon the fire brigade. Does your neighbor have a phone?"

The neighbor answered Owen's question himself, bursting

from his front door. "The firefighters are on their way!" he shouted. "Is anyone hurt? Is anyone still inside?"

"No. We're safe," Owen replied.

He shielded Nora with his body so she could button up her shirt. Up and down the street, more neighbors poured from their houses, some with umbrellas or overcoats, others shivering in their suits and dresses. Only he and Nora were in any state of undress. Her white shirt was becoming wetter and more transparent by the second, so he hugged her to his chest, protecting her modesty and warming her with his own body.

"Who are you?" the neighbor asked Owen. He surveyed the embracing couple, his brows narrowed in disapproval.

Who are you to be holding that unmarried lady in so scandalous a fashion? was what he meant. *Who is she to have allowed you such liberties?*

Owen's jaw clenched. Nora would get the worst of this. The woman always suffered the most for this. The man often not at all. He had one, single, obvious solution. "I'm her—"

He choked off the sentence. No. No, he couldn't do that. She had made it unambiguously clear she made her own decisions. If he took away her choice, she would be lost to him forever. He tipped her chin up to look her in the eye. "Nora, I love you. Will you marry me?"

She stared up at him in shock, then nodded, slowly, before burrowing against his chest once more.

"There you have it," Owen said to the neighbor man. "I'm her fiancé."

"And we're her bodyguards," a sharp female voice rang out. Owen glanced behind him to see six ferocious ladies with knives and swords converging on them. The neighbors darted away from the pirates, eyes wide and jaws slack.

Redbeard brandished her knife to punctuate her words. "So no one try anything." She stalked up to stand beside Owen and Nora and whispered, in a voice full of compassion, "Let me take you somewhere warm and dry."

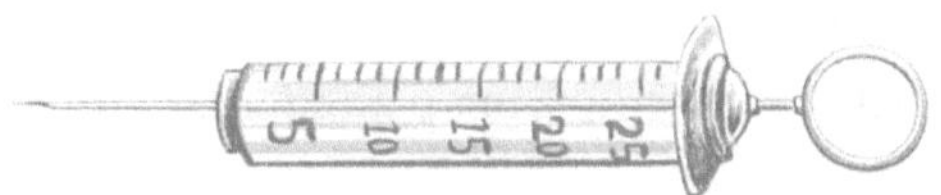

46

Outside, the rain continued, cold and unrelenting, but curled up in a big armchair beside the hearth, wrapped in blankets and with her belly full of tea and hot soup, Nora was warm and protected. All of Catalina's house was cheery and welcoming, but this room—the library—was best of all. It was a room made for reading, with bright lights, cozy chairs, and a carpet plush enough to lie on. Nora couldn't have asked for a better location to recover from her ordeal. Or for better people to have with her.

Owen paced the room like a caged animal. Silent, angry, powerful. Trapped by circumstance, but uncowed. Nora could detect no trace of melancholy in his features, only determination. He looked ready to maul his captor the moment the cage door swung open.

Lina set a fresh cup of tea and a cookie on the small table beside Nora. She pulled up a chair and sat, propping her elbows on her knees and scrutinizing Nora closely.

"How are you doing?" she asked.

"Better. Still horrified, but less in shock. I think a good night's rest will help." Her eyes locked on Owen once again. He would hold her all night. Make her feel safe and loved. And they would be safe here. Redbeard and her crew were patrolling the house, now from above and from the ground. Any attacker would be skewered before he could do harm.

Lina followed Nora's gaze. Owen had said almost nothing since their arrival, but Nora found his looming, scowling presence a deep comfort nonetheless.

"Shall I send him away?" Lina asked quietly.

Nora frowned at her friend. "No, of course not. Why would I want that?"

"He's being rather…" Lina paused, searching for a word. "Menacing."

"He's being protective. It's sweet."

"Ah." Her lips curved in a knowing smile. "You love him, don't you?"

"Yes." Nora worried a bit of blanket between her thumb and forefinger. "I, uh, may have agreed to marry him."

Lina's dark brows arched. "May have?"

"Did."

Lina sat straighter and leaned close, her face impassive and professional. "Tell me why that makes you nervous."

Nora sipped at her tea, watching Owen as he circled past. She wondered if he'd played with knights and castles as a boy. He had a highly chivalric personal code. Friendship, loyalty, honor, duty.

"He offered in order to protect my reputation," Nora explained, once Owen had passed out of earshot.

Lina nodded gravely. Reputation was a fragile thing in gossipy Savannah, particularly for a highly eccentric, unmarried woman living alone.

"He's never seemed the sort to marry," Nora explained. "I wonder whether he wouldn't have preferred something less formal."

"Well, you've never seemed the sort to marry, either," Lina pointed out.

"True." Nora picked up the cookie and took a bite, letting the flaky, sugary confection dissolve slowly on her tongue. "This is delicious."

"Your pirate friend sent a whole box down from her ship.

She's an odd one. Fierce. Angry. But with a hidden soft side. I think she's hungry for affection."

Nora nodded, eating more of the cookie. She'd long since grown accustomed to the fact that Lina analyzed everyone she met. "I don't know her especially well yet. But Sabine vouched for her."

"Ah, Sabine," Catalina sighed. "My favorite patient of yours. I'm still disappointed her interests were limited strictly to the male sex."

"You got over it," Nora pointed out.

"Of course I got over it. I've never been madly in love, only madly in lust. Nothing like you and your..." She glanced at Owen. "Extremely large, grumpy man."

Owen's head swiveled toward the ladies. He must have heard that last statement. He changed directions and crossed the room to stand at Nora's side.

She expected him to make some comment on how they'd been discussing him, but instead he opened his mouth and blurted, "The moonship."

Nora frowned up at him.

"Miss Navarro asked when I might have thwarted one of Atwater's outlandish ideas." Owen folded his arms across his chest and began to pace again, this time back and forth in front of the fireplace. "He was the first person I told when I discovered luxene. I knew I had something special, but I also knew it would require a highly regulated process to make the fuel useful. Too dry and it's explosive. Too dilute and it doesn't work. I asked Atwater to build the machines."

"I would think he would have been grateful for that," Nora replied. "It's how he was able to start his business, I assume?"

"It was. We worked side-by-side. It was a time of great happiness for me. We worked relentlessly, and we were living our dream. The boys from the mines were forging their own paths.

"But Atwater's first version of the refinery equipment had

to be rebuilt. It left the fuel too volatile. It was dangerous to handle and shipment would have been a nightmare. Any device powered by it would have been in constant danger of blowing to pieces. I made him adjust everything until the machines consistently produced luxene in the ratio of water to raw ore I'd determined to be both stable and useful."

"How did that thwart his moonship?" Nora asked.

"I didn't realize it had, at first. He'd talked about the moonship idea since I'd met him. I thought it was no more than his boyhood fantasy. Fly to the moon. It sounded fun and exciting. Then one day, after the refinery equipment was up and running, producing my first saleable product, I went to talk to him. To thank him and see how his own business was faring.

"He had a schematic of his moonship on his office wall. And when I paused to look at it, he said, 'It won't work. Not unless you produce your luxene the way I wanted to. It's the only way to get a fuel both light enough and powerful enough.'" Owen stopped pacing and turned to face Nora. "I told him it wouldn't work even then, because he'd blow himself up. Then I said I was sure he'd find another way. I was laughing. I thought it was only a fun, silly idea. I never thought about it after that, but it was the last time he ever mentioned the moonship."

"Yes, this fits with the man I imagine from your notes," Lina mused. "Not only did you not provide him with the sort of fuel he wanted, but you didn't take his project seriously. My guess is he would have seen that as a double betrayal."

"It's a ridiculous project," Owen argued. "I did the only thing that made sense. Luxene is safe and can power useful machines."

"And cute kittens," Nora added. A wistful look crossed Owen's face. She was damned well going to get that dragon from Atwater. She could offer it to Owen as an engagement gift.

"Ridiculous or not, this is definitely a potential motive or part of a motive," Lina said. "He could be trying to devalue your business to the point where he can buy it himself. Or it could be pure revenge. You ruined his dream, now he will ruin yours."

"Atwater doesn't have the first idea what my dreams are." Owen ran a hand through his hair. "To be honest, I'm not sure I even know what my dreams are. Only that they are… evolving." His gaze settled on Nora. "How are you feeling? Would you like dinner, or do you just want to eat cookies and then go to bed? I'm happy to fetch anything you need, and I promise to take one of the pirate women with me for protection."

Nora held out a hand to him and he grasped it. "That's very sweet of you, and thank you for thinking about protecting yourself, but anything Lina has here is fine. I'm feeling much better now. I'm sure I'll be a wreck again tomorrow when I have to return and survey the damage, but for now I'm content. And I'd rather have you here."

His thumb rubbed gently across her knuckles. "I should buy you a ring. I haven't seen you wear much jewelry. What do you like?"

"Nothing that would interfere when I'm doing surgery. A thin, plain band."

Owen chuckled. "The world will think I'm a skinflint. I can see the headlines now: 'Miserly Luxene Tycoon Won't Buy Fiancée Diamonds.'"

"Oh, don't worry," Nora replied. "I'm sure they'll be at least as obnoxious to me. 'Supposedly Feminist Woman Doctor Engaged to Millionaire: She's Just Like All the Others.'"

Owen's fingers clenched around hers. "I will strangle anyone who says that sort of thing."

"I don't think it will help. Though it's true the world might be better off with one less person who thinks all women are moneygrubbing succubi."

"If I had a gang of pirates, I might call us The Moneygrubbing Succubi," Lina laughed. "And we would only prey on loathsome men. Shall I recommend it to Miss Redbeard?"

Nora looked automatically to the window, though it was

dark enough she couldn't see any of the patrolling women. "Should we invite our guards in for dinner? If they dropped in one-at-a-time, everyone could have a chance to get warm and have a hot meal."

Owen leaned over and planted a kiss in her hair. "That's my Nora. I'll go invite them."

Nora tossed aside her blanket and rose. "I'll go with you."

They'd made it no more than halfway to the front door, when the sounds of a commotion made Nora pause. "Is someone shouting?"

Owen's lips pinched together as he listened. "It's coming from the front of the house."

They jogged the rest of the way to the door. Owen turned the knob slowly and silently, then cracked the door open, positioning himself to shield Nora from any attack. Nora ducked under his arm to look.

The streetlamp cast a misty glow over a trio of tussling figures. As Nora and Owen watched, the small group—two pirates and an irate man—approached the house.

"I'm only a messenger, damn you!" the man cried.

Redbeard jabbed him in the back. "We'll decide that for ourselves, thank you." She and her companion pushed him up the front steps, where she stopped and put a knife to his throat. "Try to harm anyone and it will be the last thing you ever do."

"Only a message," the man choked.

"Then deliver it."

The man fumbled in his pocket. "Are you Cassidy?" he asked Owen.

"Yes. What do you want?"

The man presented a small slip of paper. "You're to telephone this number."

Owen took the paper and peered at it. A series of digits had been neatly written in the center of the otherwise blank page.

"That's it," the man said. "That's the whole message. Can you make this horrid woman release me now?"

"How about you ask her?" Owen suggested. "Nicely."

"Would you let me go, lady?" the messenger begged. "Please?"

Redbeard lowered her knife and gave him a shove. "Go. And don't try anything."

The man dashed off, not looking back.

"Thank you," Owen said to the pirate. "It's comforting to see how vigilant you and your crew are. We'd like to invite you to come inside one-by-one to warm up and have a meal this evening. I want you to know we value your hard work and wish to keep you all in good health and spirits."

Redbeard grinned. "I never turn down dinner when someone else is paying. And all pirates enjoy good spirits." She laughed at her own joke, then nudged her companion. "Brigid, you go first. You were looking cold."

As Lina welcomed the new guest and informed her kitchen staff about the unusual dinner arrangements, Owen and Nora shut themselves in Lina's personal study with the telephone.

"I'm expecting this won't be good news," Owen sighed.

"Likely not," Nora agreed. "But the more we know, the better we can plan our own strategy."

"True. I suppose there's little sense in delaying." Owen lowered himself into the chair behind the desk, and Nora stood by his side, leaning close so they could place the receiver between them.

When the phone call connected, a gruff voice on the other side said, "Who's this?"

"This is Owen Cassidy. Who are you and what do you want?"

A long pause ensued. Long enough Nora began to wonder if anyone would answer.

"Owen?" a familiar voice cut through the silence. "It's Tim. We have a problem."

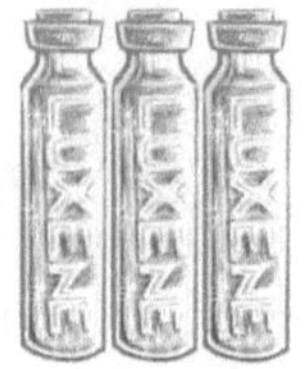

Owen had intended to go slow. To savor every second of what he feared might be his last night with Nora. Perhaps the last night of his life. The moment their lips met, all his good intentions evaporated. He kissed her ravenously, scrambled into bed half-dressed, and made love with a desperation he wouldn't have thought possible. He needed her, more than he'd ever needed anyone, and she understood.

She matched him, kiss for kiss, touch for touch, until their bodies joined and she rode him as hard and as fast as he craved. Until they collapsed in each other's arms, spent and breathless.

Nora drifted off quickly, but Owen lay awake, unable to face the insensibility of sleep. As long as he was awake, he could feel her, hear her, smell her. With her in his arms he could still imagine a future where she was always there. A future where they lived together, traveled together, celebrated each other's successes, and comforted one another after every failure. Perhaps they would have a family. Maybe he would buy a mechanical cat.

It was a dim future, to be sure. He estimated he had approximately three-to-one odds of being killed or captured. But when he held Nora he could still see that future, and he didn't want to let it go. So he cradled her close and he breathed her in, and he fought the sleep he knew he needed.

Dawn broke, sunny and mocking. Owen cursed his body for the hours he'd spent unconscious. Hours he could have had with Nora. Now he had only a handful of minutes remaining before he was forced to leave to meet whatever dire fate lay in store.

Nora deprived him of even that. She woke quickly, hopped up from the bed, and began to dress.

"Nora." He sat up, reaching for her. Exhaustion hung on him like chains of iron. Every bump and bruise he'd acquired over the past weeks ached and throbbed. His limbs were too heavy, his chest too tight.

"Time to get up," was all she replied. She swiftly buttoned her shirt, then wrapped a front-lacing corset around it. Borrowed from Lina, the garment left a three-inch gap down the middle and barely tied, even when laced tightly enough Nora grimaced. "Atwater is going to regret ever crossing me," she said, her voice a growl fine enough to match even Owen's best. "Don't mess with an angry woman in a too-tight corset."

His heart gave a happy flutter. She was his everything. "I hope I'd never be so foolish. Or at the very least, that I would quickly learn my lesson."

She offered him a tiny smile. "Get dressed. You don't want to be late for our appointment."

"*My* appointment," he corrected. "I was told to come alone."

"I highly doubt anyone in the world thinks that's going to happen."

Owen climbed from the bed and crossed the room to take her hands. "Love, this is different. He knows he can't bribe every law enforcement official in the country. He's doomed, sooner or later. But he still has the opportunity to take me down with him. This time he might well mean to kill me."

"All the more reason for me to go with you. I'm a doctor, you know." She released his hand and placed her palm flat against his metal shoulder. "Whatever happens, I *will* save you.

Besides, you are pledged to marry me. You don't break your promises, therefore you can't possibly die before we are wed."

Owen didn't protest further. It was no use. Nora knew her mind, and nothing he said would change it. He couldn't deny he liked having her near. But if everything went to hell, he'd lay down his life for her in an instant.

"We'll take the bicycles as far as we can," Nora suggested. "The carriage house wasn't damaged. We'll get there much faster, and if we have to flee with Tim and your mother, we can ride two to a bike."

Owen wasn't at all certain he could ride a bicycle with a passenger, but he nodded in agreement anyway. Riding there would make him feel as if he meant to ride home afterward. And clinging to those faint images of the future might keep him sane.

The designated meeting location was the Savannah airfield, on the far bank of the river. Nora led him to the docks, where they parked their bicycles and boarded a ferry for the crossing. When they disembarked on the opposite shore, Nora nodded at a small craft anchored nearby. It had one of the new, luxene-powered motors mounted on the back, which meant it belonged to someone with money to spend.

"If we need to flee," Nora whispered, "we'll steal that boat."

He nodded. "Good thinking." A moment later, he realized exactly what he'd said. Dear God, what had happened to his life that he would so casually agree to such a thing? He shook his head. He'd do what needed to be done.

Owen looked to the air as they walked onto the airfield. A large passenger ship hovered only twenty or thirty feet up, taking to the skies. A bit further off, a small pleasure craft was descending. More ships dotted the sky in all directions around the busy port. One of them would be Redbeard and her pirates, moving in to lend support.

The directions Tim had relayed to Owen last night had been troublingly vague. Where in the airfield the rendezvous would occur remained a mystery. He'd received no details of what the aircraft looked like, or even if there was one.

A sudden anger displaced some of his unease. He'd had enough of Atwater's mind games. If Owen had the chance, he was going to put his fist right in Atwater's face. He stalked across the field, Nora matching his pace with furious strides of her own.

They both froze together when they saw it. Owen muttered a curse. Only Atwater could have such a bizarre, fantastical dirigible.

"What even is that?" Nora wondered.

The oblong balloon of the strange airship was more than one hundred feet in length, in Owen's best estimation. The passenger compartment hanging below was nearly as long, and like nothing he'd ever seen. It was neither basket nor ship's hull, but a narrow, metal cylinder, with a pointed nose at one end and something like a tail at the other. Wide metal wings jutted out to either side, giving it a peculiar, bird-like appearance. Portholes ran in a neat row all along the side of the bird-tube. A single door provided access.

"I always knew Atwater had outlandish dreams." Owen shook his head. "I never realized he was actually trying to make them come true. I'm ashamed to say I was probably too busy with my own concerns to notice."

"This isn't his moonship, is it?"

"No. Something else entirely."

"Well." Nora took hold of Owen's hand and gave it a squeeze. "I suppose there's nothing to be done but to go take a closer look."

Hand-in-hand, they crossed the field toward the curious airship. They were perhaps fifty feet away when the door opened and a man stepped out. He pulled a heavy revolver from beneath his coat, waved it to make certain they saw it, then hid it once more.

Owen's stomach clenched. Thank God he hadn't eaten

breakfast. Every second his anxiety worsened, and with it a growing queasiness. He plowed ahead, the firm grip of Nora's hand his beacon of light in the blackness.

Atwater's man flashed the gun again once Owen came within speaking range. "You were told to come alone," he snarled.

Nora beat Owen to a reply. "If Mr. Atwater didn't want me involved, he shouldn't have attacked my property. If he has a problem with that, tell him to come out here and speak to me himself."

The thug drew his revolver, pointing it at Owen. "He said alone."

Owen stalked toward the ship, using his full height to loom over the smaller man. His pulse raced, and sweat gathered at the back of his neck. He remembered nothing about the attack that had ruined his shoulder, but the sight of the weapon aimed at his chest filled him with a bone-deep terror. Put a bullet in the right spot and even Nora couldn't save him.

"You heard the lady." Owen infused the words with every bit of fury he could muster.

"Send her away," the man said, his voice losing some of its swagger as Owen continued to stare him down.

"You want her gone? Talk to her yourself. And prepare for disappointment."

"Let them inside, Sims," Atwater's voice called from beyond the door.

A new burst of rage swelled inside Owen at the sound of his old friend's voice, so calm and dispassionate. As if he were inviting them in for luncheon. The fucking bastard. Owen's hands curled into fists. Too bad he didn't know anatomy like Nora did. He wanted this punch to do damage.

Sims stepped aside, allowing Nora and Owen to enter the airship. Owen had to duck through the door, but once inside, the curved roof was high enough in the center to stand upright.

"Greetings," Atwater said. He looked up at them from the

large leather armchair where he reclined, his feet propped on a footstool and Owen's kitten in his lap. To his right, mounted on a pole, a mechanical hand waved a folding fan, the steady breeze tousling Atwater's sandy locks. Atwater held out a hand and another mechanical device poured a drink for him. He took a swig, then lifted the glass in a toast. "Welcome to air travel of the future."

The interior of the ship was a shrine to idle luxury. Every bit of trim was gilded. A beautiful woven rug, custom made for the unusual space, covered every inch of floor. Owen suspected it was an authentic import from Persia. Chairs and couches upholstered in fine fabrics lined the long, tubular room, many of them with additional mechanical helpers stationed by their sides. Other devices whose purposes Owen could only guess at jutted from the walls or hung from the ceiling.

And at the far end of the space, seated on an elegant horsehair settee, were Owen's mother and brother. At a glance they might have been thought to be honored guests. Until one noticed their bound hands and the guard hovering behind them.

Owen's heart skipped a beat. "Let them go," he demanded. "They have nothing to do with this."

"Now, now, Cassidy," Atwater chided. "Is that any way to greet your old friend?"

The smile that once had brightened Owen's day now stabbed like a knife to the heart. *I loved you*, he screamed internally. *I loved you and you betrayed me! If you'd only asked, I would have done anything I could to help you.*

"Let them go," he repeated through gritted teeth, digging his nails into his palms as he fought the trembling that threatened to overtake him. "This is between you and me."

"Oh?" Atwater cast a significant glance in Nora's direction.

She scowled at him. "You destroyed my livelihood. It's between you and us."

"I'm afraid you have your lover to blame for that, my dear,"

Atwater replied. "He seemed to think he was getting the upper hand by running away with you. But, as you can see, that is not the case." He waved a hand in the direction of Owen's family. "They were even easier to track down than you were."

"Why, Atwater?" Owen stepped closer to his adversary, but held himself back enough not to look threatening. "Tell me why you hate me. What did I do to turn your heart so hard to me?"

Maybe if he could understand he could negotiate. Owen would offer anything in exchange for his loved ones. He only had to know what Atwater desired.

"You really don't know?" Atwater's eyes widened in surprise. He handed his drink back to the machine and sat up straighter. "Truly?"

Owen took another step closer. Spark jumped down from Atwater's lap and trotted over to rub up against Owen's shin. He fought the urge to pick her up and pet her. "I have no idea. Please, tell me."

Atwater's face took on a pained expression. "Of course you don't know. Why would you know? When have you ever paid attention to anyone who wasn't yourself?"

Coming from a man sitting in an airship decked out like a throne room, Owen found the argument less than compelling. Especially when Atwater continued on without even bothering to give Owen time for an answer.

"It was always you, Cassidy. You had to be first. You had to be best. Owen's in charge. Owen tells everyone what to do. Owen's the leader. Did you let it go to your head, the things the boys said? Or did you think it was your due because you were bigger and stronger? And then you stumbled on a treasure. Crawling around in a cave *I* pointed out to you."

"We found the cave together," Owen retorted. "It was your idea to go cave hunting, but we found it as a team. And then you decided it was unsafe to go inside. So I went back later without you. Besides, you didn't want luxene. You wanted to build machines. I gave you exactly what you wanted and it made you filthy rich."

"Lies!" Atwater leapt from his chair, put his hand to Owen's chest and shoved him. Owen barely stumbled. "I was just your hireling. Another person to lord over. It was all about your dreams, not mine. You ignored my projects, denied me the fuel I needed, made everything *your* way. Everything we did together, I was just a sad second place."

"That's not true. I wanted you to succeed. I wanted you to be happy. I've promoted your business to some of the wealthiest clients in the world. I was overjoyed when Addison…"

Atwater shoved Owen with two hands this time, knocking him back a step. "Don't you say her name! You ruined everything. Everything! Even with her, I was second place. You were the one she wanted. She only turned to me after you rejected her!"

"No." Owen could empathize with this fear. He remembered with crystal clarity the ache in his heart when thinking Nora would never love him. "Leslie," he said softly, hoping the use of his former friend's given name would reach him through the anger. "She loved you. Dearly. She told me often how lucky the two of you were to have found each other. I swear to you. You were her one and only."

Mixed grief and fury flashed in Atwater's eyes. "Then why did she leave me?" He hammered with a fist on Owen's chest. "Why didn't she stay?"

The last of Owen's anger subsided. He only wanted to hug his friend. To tell him how terribly sorry he was. To promise he would always be there with a shoulder to cry on. Even if it was biomechanical.

"It was pneumonia, Leslie," Owen said softly. "It was bad luck. She fought as hard as she could. She wanted forever with you." In that moment, he would have offered a truce. Forgiven everything, if they could return to the way things had once been.

"Stop lying," Atwater spat, and Owen's heart broke again.

He was beyond rescue. Fallen too deep into the abyss of revenge. "You ruined her. You ruin everything. Even my spy-cat likes you better than me!"

Spark only purred.

"You need to learn, Cassidy." Atwater's eyes were wild now, his cheeks burning red. "You need to learn what it's like to be second best. To have someone else control your life. You ruined my dreams, Owen. Now I'm going to destroy yours. But I'm more considerate than you ever were to me. I'll only take a small piece." He waved a hand in a theatrical sweep. "Here are three people who mean something to you. You are free to leave and take two of them with you. The third is mine." He dug inside his coat and withdrew what looked like a revolver with a large, square barrel and a tiny glass tube of luxene affixed to the top.

Nora sucked in a sudden, horrified breath.

"Ah, I see the doctor recognizes this weapon." Atwater's mirthless laugh sent stabs of ice through Owen's veins. "Yes, this gun is responsible for your shoulder. I relieved my minion of it after that incident. It seems he took the command to 'injure' to mean 'maim.' But now I have it, and I will use it. Either you take two companions and leave this ship, or I begin shooting and we dump the bodies somewhere over the Atlantic. The boy, the old woman, and your lady love. You get two. Make your choice."

48

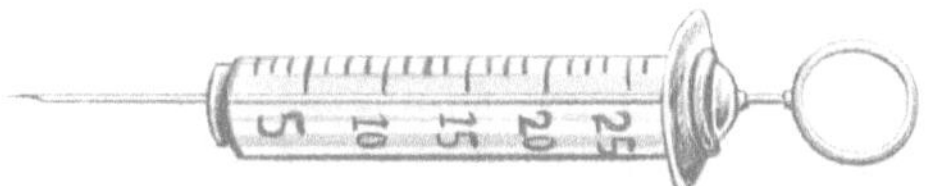

All the blood had drained from Owen's face. Nora shuffled back a step, putting herself in the best position possible in case he fainted. She couldn't catch him, but she could at least guide his fall so he wouldn't hit his head. At the moment it was the outcome she was hoping for. Because if he didn't faint, she feared he would try to wrestle the gun away from Atwater. And a direct blast to the torso at such close range would be well beyond anything Nora could repair.

Don't attack him, don't attack him, she pleaded silently. *Please, Owen. Take a step backward. Tell him you'll choose. You can leave me behind.*

Spark mewled and nudged Owen with her head. He jolted from his stupor. "Take me," he offered.

"No." Atwater wisely stepped back out of Owen's reach. "No, that's you giving orders again, Cassidy. This is my time. My orders. Now choose. Or shall I shoot your pretty little mistress?"

Owen stepped between Atwater and Nora, cutting off her view of the entire situation. "She is my *fiancée*," he growled. Nora took a step to the side to see past his shoulder.

"Oh, even better! Well, I'm sure she'll be happy to be my wife instead. I'll be relocating to a remote island in the near future, and I'll have need of companionship. And her medical skills would be useful. Or would you prefer to leave behind your brother, perhaps? I could use a strapping lad to do heavy lifting, and we both know he resents you, so I'm sure it won't be too hard to teach him to see things my way."

"That is quite enough!"

Every occupant of the airship jumped at Mrs. Cassidy's sudden outburst. She hopped up from her seat and marched toward Owen and Atwater, despite her bound hands and the armed guard behind her.

"There is only one sensible decision here. I am an old woman. I've had a long life and seen my two fine boys grow into good, strong men. You youngsters have years ahead of you. Bright futures. You will leave this ship together and I will remain behind. I'll cook his food and wash his clothes on his silly desert island and be content knowing you're all well."

"Mother," Owen protested.

"Don't you say anything, Owen James. You may be a fancy millionaire businessman, but you are still my baby boy, and you will do as I say."

Atwater burst into raucous laughter. "Ah, Mrs. Cassidy, what a delight you are! Such a strong lady. To reward you for that wonderful speech, I'm going to let you go. Sims, escort Mrs. Cassidy outside and then close the door."

Sims pushed between Owen and Nora, taking Mrs. Cassidy by the arm and walking her toward the door, revolver clutched tightly in his opposite hand.

"You won't get away with this, you fiend!" Mrs. Cassidy shouted.

Owen turned slowly, watching them go. "Fetch the police, Mother. Tell them everything."

Nora stood frozen in place, not daring to move lest she provoke Atwater or one of the goons. Or worse, provoke Owen into a foolish action.

Owen's mother continued to shout as Sims pushed her out of the vehicle. "My boys will beat your sorry behinds, just you—"

The villain slammed the door.

Owen flinched. He turned back to Atwater. "Mother is right. You won't get away with this."

Atwater only smirked. "You think the police will believe an old woman with an absurd story? Not likely. One down, Cassidy. Now, who's going with her, your brother or your sweetheart?"

Keeping her body as still as possible, Nora let her gaze turn to Timothy, trying to catch his eye. He was standing now, having risen to his feet during his mother's rant. Atwater's second guard hung close behind him.

Look at me, she pleaded silently. *Work with me. Help Owen.*

Tim's eyes met hers. His chin dipped almost imperceptibly. A bead of sweat trickled down between Nora's breasts. Did he understand what she wanted? He was more impulsive than his brother. She couldn't discount the possibility he would attack Atwater himself.

Nora looked from Tim to Atwater, then shook her head. She met Tim's gaze once more, just for an instant, before focusing her attention on Owen.

No violence. No violence. Get as many people out as possible.

They had Redbeard's crew as backup. If they could delay long enough for the pirates to find them, they would have the advantage of numbers.

Atwater waved a hand toward one of his plush armchairs. "Why don't you have a seat, Cassidy? We can discuss this in a civilized fashion." Not relinquishing his hold on his gun, he reached to reclaim his drink from the machine-servant. "Can I interest you in a drink?"

Atwater swallowed the remainder of the liquor, then set the empty glass on a table. A dragon scuttled out from beneath the table, grabbed the glass, and darted away again.

Owen remained frozen in place. His face had a grayish cast, and his jaw was clenched. The only discernible movement was the curling of his fingers in and out of fists. His eyes flicked back and forth, taking in everyone around him, assessing his options. Nora longed to hug him. To whisper to him that she would help.

"Choose, Owen." Nora jumped at Timothy's commanding tone. He sounded more like his brother than she ever would have expected.

The younger man walked toward the center of the airship, the guard trailing behind him.

"It's not a difficult decision. Mother is already safe. You need to take Dr. Taylor and join her."

What? No!

Nora barely caught herself before she blurted the words aloud. Her jaw hung open. This was *not* the plan she'd wanted.

"Leaving me here is by far the best choice," Tim continued. "I'm a fully grown man. I know how to take care of myself. You should protect the ladies first and foremost."

Of all the awful things he could have said. This was exactly the sort of plea that would appeal to Owen's protective, gentlemanly nature. And exactly the wrong choice.

Tim was too young, too prone to rash behavior. He didn't know Atwater as well as Nora did. He knew nothing about Redbeard's crew. All of which combined to make him far more likely to try to fight his way out rather than stall. Nora, though, knew her enemy, especially after their recent encounters and her discussions with Lina. Lately she'd had plenty of practice keeping her patience. And, unknown to anyone else in the room, she was armed.

Owen ignored his brother. Despite his pale cheeks and trembling hands, he stubbornly stared down Atwater. Nora forced herself to breathe, slowly and steadily, in and out, willing her body not to panic. Her hands twitched, wanting to twist the not-so-decorative button on the corset that would release Lina's slim dagger, concealed in the busk. Anything to reduce her sense of helplessness. If only she had some idea, any idea, what Owen might be thinking.

"Let them go, Atwater," Owen said, sounding less commanding and more reasonable this time. "You don't want them. You want me. Haul me off to your island and make me your drudge. You'll have eternity to tyrannize me."

"No." Atwater's tone was angry now. "No, I'm going to do much worse. I'm going to make you suffer, knowing you've lost someone you loved. And it will be your decision that dooms them."

Owen's hands lifted, his fingers flexing. He took a step toward Atwater.

Nora lunged before she had time to think, seizing Owen's arm. "Owen, no! Please don't do anything foolish!"

He turned to look her in the eye, blinking rapidly, devastation lining his face. "I can't leave either of you behind."

"You have to." Nora relaxed her grip, letting her hand stroke along his arm, up to where she could feel his biomechanics beneath his clothing. "It's only a battle," she whispered. "Not the war. Regroup and try again."

He shook his head.

"It'll be okay," she said louder. "You're not alone." *Remember our friends. You don't need to do this yourself.* "You're never alone."

"Nora." He lifted a hand to cup her cheek.

"Make your choice, Cassidy," Atwater snarled. "Or I tell my men to open fire."

"Go ahead," Nora urged gently. "You can leave me. I won't hold it against you."

Tears welled in Owen's eyes. "I love you." He extricated himself from her grip and turned to Atwater. "This isn't over."

Atwater lunged for Nora, yanking her against him and pressing his gun to her temple. "Yes. It is."

49

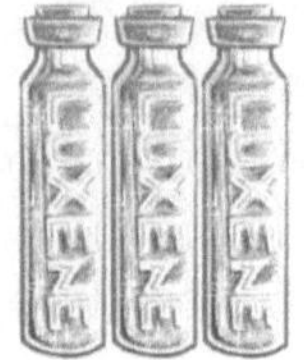

Owen's heart nearly stopped. His entire body had gone cold, frozen in terror at the sight of the hideous weapon touching his beloved.

"Let her go." The words were thick, his tongue like lead in his mouth.

Nora's face, already white with fear, crumbled with sorrow. Pain clenched around Owen's chest. *Oh, my love. I'm so sorry. Please forgive me for what I'm about to do to you.*

"Let her go. I've chosen," Owen said, more clearly this time.

Atwater lowered the gun and Owen's entire body sagged in relief.

"You're saving your fiancée, then?" Atwater asked. "How romantic."

"No."

Nora's eyes widened. A single tear trickled down her cheek.

Owen turned away. He couldn't bear to look. If he saw the hurt in her eyes, it might kill him. "I'm leaving with my brother. Dr. Taylor stays with you."

"What?" Timothy blurted. "Owen, are you insane?"

"The choice is made," Atwater intoned. "Sims, Pauly, escort the men off the ship."

Owen didn't need an escort. He walked to the door under

his own power, his legs somehow moving despite feeling like stone. His brother was ranting behind him, something about how could he possibly abandon a woman. None of it penetrated Owen's shuttered heart. Nora understood the decision. He knew she did, logical-minded as she was. But all the logic in the world couldn't make it less painful to be the one abandoned, the one left behind.

Owen had hardly set one foot outside the doorway when he was rammed into from behind and sent sprawling. His brother landed on top of him. Owen rolled over and shoved him, hard. With Timothy being so much younger than he was, Owen had never gotten into physical altercations with him. Right now, though, he was spoiling for a good fight.

"What the fuck did you do that for?" he shouted.

Timothy swung his hands, still bound together, at Owen's head. "I didn't do it, you jackass. I was pushed!" He swung again, and this time he connected.

Owen pinned Tim on his back and yanked at the ropes until his hands were free. "I want this to be a fair fight," he said, then smashed his fist into his brother's jaw.

Timothy responded with a jab of his own, and the two men tumbled into a mess of flying limbs and shouted curses. They rolled across the grass, punching and kicking, hurling insults at one another, until the tremor of a rising airship knocked them apart. Together they stared as Atwater's craft rose into the air above them, taking Nora away to places unknown.

Owen wiped blood from his lip. He hurt in several places, but the pain was welcome. It provided a small distraction, at least, from the ache in his heart.

"Your nose is bleeding," he said to Timothy.

"Like I fucking care?" his brother shot back. "You're out of your goddamned mind!" He waved a hand at the ship above them. "You said you loved her!"

"I do."

"Then why the hell would you leave her there in the hands of that maniac?"

Owen fought the urge to punch his brother again. "I did the only thing I could do. I made the choice most likely to get us all out alive."

"By leaving your fiancée *alone* with armed men?"

"Better her than you!"

"What's that supposed to mean?"

"Exactly what I said," Owen replied through gritted teeth. "She's a sensible, competent adult. You're a headstrong, insolent, self-absorbed brat."

"And you're a stubborn, high-handed, pompous oaf!" Timothy leapt at Owen once more.

"At least I know I am!" Owen wrestled his brother onto his back, pinning him down. Tim was only a couple of inches shorter, but weighed considerably less. He struggled futilely to escape Owen's grip. "Admit it. You would have done something stupid up there."

"I… Maybe." Tim sighed.

"I hate to interrupt your sweet family moment," crooned a female voice. Owen and Tim both looked up into Redbeard's smirking face. "But what is… this?" She gestured at the two men and then up at Atwater's ascending ship.

Owen leapt to his feet. "Is your ship here? Can it leave at once?"

"Certainly. What do you need?"

"You're pirates, right?" Owen asked. "Real pirates?"

"Oui."

"Good. I need one woman sent to find my mother and ensure she got to the police with her story. Then I need the rest of you, plus weapons for me and my brother." Owen pointed into the air. "We're going to storm that ship."

And then I'll get my fiancée back. If she'll still have me.

50

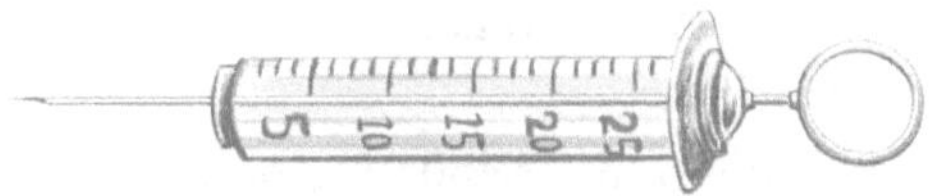

Nora made no attempt to wipe away the wet trails left by the tears of relief that had sprung from her eyes the moment Owen made his choice. She had no shame in them. Besides, Atwater would think she was distraught at being left behind.

Yes, she was scared. But mostly, she was proud. Proud of Owen's strength and character. Proud of herself for being here facing down the enemy. Proud of the relationship she and Owen had built, rooted in friendship and mutual respect. She had never needed, wanted, or expected to fall in love. But life had taken her in this direction, and she would embrace it.

"A drink to soothe your nerves?" Atwater asked. He was smiling again, and his voice was friendly, trying to play the charmer. True to style, he remained in his seat across from her while a mechanical arm offered her a glass.

"You know, Mr. Atwater," Nora replied. "If you never do anything for yourself, your muscles will atrophy and your heart will weaken and you'll lounge your way to an early death."

"Well, fortunately for me, I have your medical knowledge to help me craft an exercise regimen to prevent such a dire fate. Please make it fun, though. None of this lifting weights nonsense. Brisk walks around a lush, tropical island with a beautiful woman on my arm, however…" He gave her a rakish waggle of his eyebrows.

"Save your flirtations, Mr. Atwater. I believe I mentioned before that they are wasted on me."

"Yet you respond to Cassidy's complete lack of them? Peculiar."

Nora scowled. Her finger rubbed across the button that could release her hidden knife. Atwater was hardly the first man to call her peculiar. And it wasn't the worst word men had used when she rebuffed their advances. Still, it roused every bit of her righteous outrage.

"Owen Cassidy is my friend. The only people I have ever been even slightly attracted to are friends. You, Mr. Atwater, are my enemy. I will *never* be interested in your flirtations, your smiles, your compliments, or your luxuries."

"Nonsense. I'm sure you'll learn to appreciate them."

Nora had never before wished she had fangs, but right now she would have liked a full set of nasty, razor-sharp teeth to bare at Atwater. He didn't know it, but all he was doing was reinforcing one of her key reasons for loving Owen. Like everyone, Owen was prone to making mistakes, not understanding, or saying something wrong. But when someone corrected him or explained the world as they saw it, he listened, he cared, and he made an effort to do better. Atwater wouldn't even believe Nora's stated facts about her own person.

She rubbed her finger over the button catch again. She hated waiting.

Nora turned her chair toward the row of small windows to help emphasize her point. If Atwater continued to jabber at her, she would simply ignore him. Outside the airship, the city of Savannah grew smaller and more distant. They were headed inland, taking a westerly course, making Nora wonder if Atwater had lied about his tropical island, or if he intended to fly all the way to somewhere in the middle of the Pacific Ocean.

She spun back around. "Is your pilot hidden up there in the nose of this bird-ship?" she asked. Best to know now how many additional people this craft held. At the moment, all she could see were Atwater and his two goons.

Atwater chuckled. "In a sense. That nose is filled with

complex machinery. One of my best inventions ever. I've already set our destination, and it will fly us there. No human assistance needed."

"What if a storm blows up, or another craft crosses our path?" *What will happen to this ship when the pirates attack?*

Atwater waved a single hand in dismissal. "Nothing to worry about."

Nora bit her lip and turned back to the window. All she could do was wait.

The waiting dragged on for hours, until Nora's hands began to sweat in panic. Where were the pirates? She'd seen no sign of another airship during her vigil by the window. Nor had she heard any sounds to indicate a passing ship. Though that could possibly be because Atwater had flipped a switch and set an autogramophone playing.

Nora ran a finger along Spark's metal back, right between her wings, and the cat made a purring noise. She'd climbed up on Nora's lap about two hours ago and showed no intention of leaving. Nora wondered if Owen had intentionally left the cat-dragon behind to provide her some company.

Atwater had made no attempt to retrieve the kitten. Either he'd decided he wanted nothing more to do with a creature who preferred his enemies, or he thought the gift of a pet might sway Nora to his side. Nora couldn't guess. Atwater was beyond logical reasoning.

At least he had good taste in music. The autogramophone played a pleasant mixture of Sousa marches, current popular hits, and—her personal favorite—ragtime. Even in her state of frustrated anticipation, she couldn't help but dance a little in her seat to "Maple Leaf Rag." It was a quality gramophone, too. Not as tinny as some of them were, and using recordings with enough clarity to hear individual notes.

Nora's entire body went rigid. How was she able to hear

individual notes? The airship was astonishingly quiet. Too quiet. Where was the hum of the steam engine? For that matter, where was the engine at all?

"How is this ship powered?" she asked Atwater, tossing him only a small glance. "I just noticed I haven't seen any of the usual machinery here."

"Ha!" Even in that one syllable he sounded enormously pleased with himself. "My greatest triumph. The high-powered luxene engine."

Nora allowed herself to turn half-way around. "Luxene? No. That's impossible."

"Ah, but it's not, my dear. It's not." His smile faded into a scowl. "Though I shouldn't call my fuel luxene. That's Cassidy's word. Lux. Latin for light. How scholarly. As if he'd actually made it past the seventh grade."

Nora wanted to smack Atwater. Owen's self-education made him more worthy of admiration, not less.

"He was obsessed with making the fuel 'safe,'" Atwater continued. "When what he ought to have been doing was making it more powerful. Utterly ruined my plans. I had to create an entirely new machine in my spare time to take his underpowered luxene and evaporate out the excess water until it was the consistency I wanted."

Nora spun back to the window to hide her face. Her hands shook. Her lower lip trembled. Atwater had recreated the unstable fuel Owen had refused to manufacture. And he'd used it to power this airship. She was sitting aboard a potential bomb. If this ship took too much damage, or even a small hit to the wrong location, it would end in a massive fireball. And Owen and the pirates were headed her way.

No. No. Don't come. Don't do anything. Please. It's too dangerous.

Her only recourse was to pray, which she did with a fervency she never had before.

Don't let them come. Don't let them die.

Atwater's autogramophone seamlessly switched to a new song, a recent hit Nora knew well. It had helped draw folks young and old to Owen's hometown for the World's Fair.

"Meet me in St. Louis, Louis. Meet me at the fair," the singer crooned.

Nora began to weep.

51

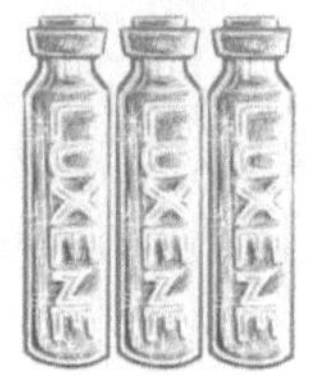

"**D**ON'T TOUCH THAT."

Owen paused with his hand mere inches from the contraption and frowned up at Redbeard—or Yvette, as he'd learned her real name was. The pirate captain wore an identical contraption to the one resting on the deck. She adjusted the position of it on her back, tugging the straps tight. When it was secure, she clicked a button and a pair of canvas wings unfolded, giving her the appearance of a large bird.

No, more of a bat. A creature of stealth. Somehow adorable and terrifying at the same time.

Owen picked up the wing-pack, despite Yvette's protest. "I'm going with you," he insisted.

"Not with the wings, you are not. They are designed to carry eighty kilos, and you are more than that."

Owen paused to do the math in his head. "Quite a bit more," he admitted.

"You will fall like a rock. And then your doctor will have a heart she cannot fix."

"I can't stay here," Owen protested. Already he was going mad. They'd been trailing Atwater's ship for hours, maneuvering into position while plotting their attack. He'd been left out of most of the discussion, which had been conducted in a mix of

French and German. Most of the words he'd recognized had been vulgarities.

Now the ship hovered in the air above Atwater's peculiar vessel and slightly to starboard. In a blind spot, Owen assumed. He couldn't say for certain. He couldn't say anything for certain. Was this how everyone else always felt? As if they were simply being given orders without all the relevant information? No wonder everyone hated him.

"Brigid will lower you in the cargo hoist. She will set you down on the wing of the metal bird, and then you walk along it to where we slice through the roof."

The wing-pack slipped from Owen's hands and clattered to the deck. "Walk?" he choked. "With nothing to support me or catch me if I fall?"

He'd spent years in underground mines and caves. Crawled through Atwater's dark, cramped factory. But standing atop an airship risking a thousand foot to fall to his death? If he could manage a single step without being paralyzed by fear, it would be a miracle.

"Brigid," Yvette called. "He is scared of heights and will need a rope."

Brigid rolled her eyes and muttered something in German. Calling him a coward, no doubt.

Timothy placed a hand on Owen's shoulder. "Don't worry, I—" His hand jerked. "Whoa. That's weird." He patted all along the biomechanics, poking at the metal with his thumb.

"Do you mind?" Owen twisted away.

"Sorry. Never felt anything like it before. Glad I didn't punch you there." He rubbed his knuckles. "Meant to say I'd be with you."

Owen gave his brother the best smile he could manage. It was odd, this working together business, but also comforting. And a damned sight better than beating the snot out of one another, therapeutic as that had been.

Brigid gestured impatiently, and the men hurried to follow her to the cargo hoist.

Tim waggled his eyebrows at the young pirate as she wound the rope around his waist. "I've always wanted to be tied up by a pretty woman," he quipped. She answered with a lascivious grin.

Owen cringed. "Please do not ever tell me anything else about your sexual proclivities."

"Just because you're a stuffy bore—"

"*Ever*," Owen repeated.

Tim shrugged, but continued making eyes at the pirate girl, even when she started tying Owen's safety rope. Looking away didn't help, either. The cargo hoist dangled over the side of the ship, nothing but metal grating and the expanse of air beyond. Owen had never been so uncomfortable in his life.

He kept his gaze resolutely focused on Atwater's craft as the hoist began to lower toward it. A pirate wearing a wing-pack swooped past him, landing gracefully atop the metal bird. Another two quickly followed. Redbeard landed last, a bag of tools clutched in her arms. The women collapsed their wings and formed a tight circle, crouching down atop the ship.

The hoist jerked to a halt and Owen swallowed a terrified yelp. Limbs shaking, he stepped down onto the wing. He sucked in a deep breath, then blew it out. He could do this. For Nora. One foot in front of another, he began the agonizingly long walk. Tim hovered behind, probably worried Owen might fall or start flailing in panic. A distinct possibility.

Light glinted off the array of small windows along the side of the ship. New fear shot through Owen. If Atwater looked out and saw him, they would lose their element of surprise. Worse, he might hurt Nora. Owen's legs began to churn faster, desperate to reach the body of the vehicle, where the women waited to haul him up top.

Two-thirds of the way there, he froze.

Nora.

There she was, sitting by one of the windows, looking out. Her head swiveled in his direction and all the color drained from her face. She clapped her hands over her mouth.

Owen moved faster yet, wishing he could call to her. *I'm here. We're here.*

She shook her head. Tentatively at first, then more emphatically. Owen stared at her as he continued forward, because it helped keep his mind off the fact he was racing across a piece of metal floating hundreds of yards off the ground.

Nora continued to shake her head. She began to wave a hand at him. What was she saying? That looked liked a dismissal. A "go away" sort of gesture. His steps slowed. Why would she do that? Was she worried for his safety? He tugged on the rope to show her he'd taken precautions.

Now she shooed him with both hands. Color had returned to her cheeks. In fact, she was looking a bit red. And her lips were turned down in a furious scowl. Damn. She was angry at him.

His heart stuttered. Oh, God. What had he done?

"Owen," Tim hissed, nudging him from behind. "Go."

Right. Go.

Owen stumbled onward, stunned and confused. He dared another glance at Nora. Her fists were clenched, and she looked as if she wanted to pound on the window. He looked away and hurried the rest of the way. Whatever had happened, however she felt toward him, he couldn't leave her here. Not when her life was in danger. Once he'd gotten her out and safely on the ground, she could yell at him all she wanted. Say anything she wanted. Leave him forever.

He hardly noticed when Yvette and two of her crew pulled him up atop the bird. The driving wind stung his cheeks, but the inside of his body had turned to ice. He had hurt Nora. And he was terrified he'd never be able to atone.

"Hey." Tim gave Owen a small jab with his elbow. "You okay?"

One of the pirates put something in Owen's hand. A small slicing device. Powerful enough to cut through metal. Impossible before luxene. This tool was proof that his life's work was making a difference in people's lives. Creating new technologies. He stared at it. But instead of pride he felt only numbness.

"Owen," Tim whispered. "I know Dr. Taylor looked scared in there, but it's okay. We're going to get her out."

Owen shook his head. "Something's wrong. She wasn't scared. She was angry. I… I don't know. But something's wrong."

Thunk.

The sound of metal-on-metal vibrated up through the cabin beneath him. More thunks quickly followed.

"Que diable?" Yvette blurted.

"Nora." Owen dropped to his knees and pressed a hand to the smooth metal of the bird-ship. "She's trying to tell us something." Either that or something terrible was happening to her, and he couldn't bear to contemplate that.

The noise came again: a loud thunk, followed by a softer tick. Then more thunks. A slight pause.

Thunk-tick. Thunk. Thunk. Thunk.

Thunk-tick. Thunk. Thunk. Thunk.

"Morse code," Timothy said.

Owen grabbed a fistful of his brother's jacket. "What's it mean? What's she saying?"

Thunk-tick.

"N."

Thunk. Thunk. Thunk.

"O."

No? What did she mean, no? What in God's name was going on down there?

"There, Cassidy." Yvette pointed at a spot in the circle she'd scratched with the tip of her knife. "You cut there. When I say. We must all cut together so we are as fast as possible."

"No, wait." The thunking continued unabated. "Nora's telling us not to. Something must be wrong." None of this made sense. She'd known they would be coming for her. Why would she try to stop them?

"It might not be a message," Tim argued. "That was only a guess. She might just be making noise. It's the perfect cover for our break-in."

"Yes," Yvette agreed. "Get ready."

Owen stared down at the tool in his hand. He wanted nothing more in the world than to have Nora in his arms, safe and sound. But that look on her face. Had it been fear mixed with anger? Had Atwater done something to her? Owen couldn't understand any of it.

Thunk-tick. Thunk. Thunk. Thunk.

"I can't," he choked. "I can't do this when she doesn't want it."

Tim grabbed the slicer from Owen's hand.

"Go!" Redbeard ordered.

The devices hummed to life.

52

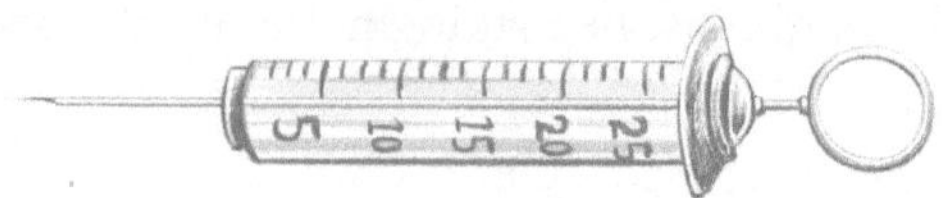

*W*_{HACK!}

The force of the blow vibrated up Nora's arm as she slammed the remains of one of Atwater's servant machines against the side of the cabin.

"Let me out!" she screamed again, her voice hopefully concealing the pattern in her pounding.

Whack-tick. N. Three whacks. O. Surely someone would understand. Surely they would realize she was warning them away.

"Out! Let me out! I can't take it anymore!" She finished her series of whacks, then turned to face Atwater. "Land this ship! Let me out! I can't... I can't do this!"

Whack-tick.

Please. Please, listen. Please go away.

"Let! Me! Out!" Nora punctuated each word with a solid blow, making her letter O.

All this time, Atwater had done nothing but gape at her. He remained in his chair, a drink still in his hand and his mouth hanging open. He thought she was insane. *He* thought *she* was insane.

"Dr. Taylor," he began, finding his voice at last. "If you would try to calm—"

Nora cut him off, swinging for the wall only a few feet from his head. He flinched.

"Sims! Pauly! For God's sake, don't just stand there gaping!" Atwater yelled at his guards. As if he'd done any better himself. "Grab her before she breaks all my machines!"

Nora got in one final series of whacks before the guards seized her arms, wrestling the battered device from her hands and forcing her down into a chair.

"What now?" Sims asked. "Do we tie her—" He broke off abruptly when Atwater held up a hand. A strange hissing filled the now-quiet chamber.

No. Oh, no.

The sound drew four pairs of eyes up to the ceiling, but before anyone could move or even make a sound, a chunk of the roof fell in amid a shower of sparks.

Intruders poured through the hole, hitting the floor with hardly a sound. Four pirates, with pistols and knives in hand and peculiar packs strapped to their backs. The thud of a heavier, less graceful person followed. Timothy. Then Owen.

Nora wanted to weep in anger, fear, and frustration. Why hadn't he heeded her warnings? Why was he here? And with his brother, too! They may as well have stayed on the ship and run at Atwater with their bare hands.

Sims and Pauly released Nora to draw their own weapons. She dove beneath a nearby table, screaming, "Don't shoot!"

Too late. Someone opened fire, the report of the gunshot echoing throughout the enclosed space. Pirates ducked behind chairs and couches. Owen flung himself to the floor. Even Atwater scrambled out of his seat to hide.

"Stop it!" Nora screamed as the two sides exchanged volleys. "Stop, damn you, before you kill us all!"

A bullet shattered a window. Several others poked through the metal body of the ship. Bits of fabric and fluff puffed into the air as projectiles tore into the furniture. One of the pirates cried out in pain, then cursed and let off four shots of her own in rapid succession. Dammit, how many bullets did these people have?

Spark bumped up against Nora's leg, and she pulled the kitten closer. They couldn't die this way. She wouldn't let it happen. She twisted the button on Lina's corset and the thin knife sprang free.

"Stop shooting!" she yelled, putting as much volume behind the words as her lungs could manage. She crawled out of her hiding place to stand in the center of the room, brandishing the dagger, praying no one would fire at her. Spark followed, continuing to nuzzle her, a soothing flicker of normalcy amidst the chaos.

"This ship is powered with a dangerous, highly explosive fuel!" Nora cupped a hand around her mouth to help her voice project. "If you hit the wrong spot, we are all going to die in a giant ball of fire! Now put down your fucking weapons before you send us all to hell!"

The gunfire ceased.

"What's she talking about?" Sims asked.

"His 'special fuel'?" Nora replied. She jabbed the knife in Atwater's direction. "It's not safe."

"It is powerful and perfectly harmless," Atwater snarled. "Kill those invaders. But leave Cassidy for me."

Owen scrambled to his feet to stand behind Nora. "Dr. Taylor knows what she's talking about," he argued. His voice was deep and authoritative. His business voice. "I've seen what that fuel can do. It's highly unstable. Even too large a jolt can set it off. We're lucky we're not dead already."

Nora trembled. All her pounding on the walls had put them at risk. How close had she been to killing them all?

Sims and Pauly peeked out from behind their cover, frowning at Nora and Owen, then exchanging glances.

"To hell with this," Pauly muttered. He leapt to his feet and ran for the door, Sims close on his heels. Pauly reached up to the ceiling and pulled a lever. A folded mechanical apparatus fell to the floor.

"You disloyal oaf!" Atwater screamed.

Sims kicked the door open, then helped Pauly hoist the machine. Together, the two men slung the device on their backs.

"Oh, sorry," Sims snickered. "The escape glider only holds two." He clipped the straps around himself and the two goons jumped from the aircraft.

"It's over, Atwater," Owen said, striding deliberately down the center of the narrow room.

Nora shifted to one side, letting him pass by, but preventing him from doing anything gallantly foolish, like hide her from sight.

Atwater's face had gone crimson and his knuckles were white where he clenched the splatter-gun. "It's not over!" He lifted the weapon and took aim.

Nora didn't even think. She hurled the knife at Atwater, launching herself at Owen at the same moment. She hit Owen directly in the back of the knees knocking his legs out from under him. They went down in a tangled heap.

The gunshot she'd expected from Atwater never materialized. He cursed, clutching his arm where the knife had grazed him, and ran to the nose of the ship. A quick twist of something on the wall popped open a secret door, and he darted through, slamming it behind him.

"It's never over!" Atwater's voice reverberated from a loudspeaker. "This airship does more than you've ever dreamed. I can outrun any other aircraft on the planet, and I have more allies awaiting my arrival. Flee if you like, but you'll never catch me."

Nora wasn't waiting around to hear more. She tugged on Owen's arm, urging him to his feet. "Get out, get out! Before he kills us all!"

"My airglider will be the envy of the world!" Atwater continued to rant.

The entire group scrambled for the hole in the ceiling. The pirates boosted one another through, quickly followed by

Timothy, who needed no assistance. Owen lifted Nora up, then handed Spark to her.

"Hurry!" she yelled, grabbing hold of his arm as he pushed up through the opening. As if she could possibly hold him if he fell.

A sudden bang cracked through the air, and one of the cables holding the balloon to the gondola below sheared off, rocking the ship.

"Fuck me," Tim gasped. "He's cutting the balloon loose!"

Nora's stomach lurched. Atwater was certainly fanatical enough to try it. But could this metal beast even stay in the air without support?

The pirates snapped open their packs to reveal wide, bat-like wings.

"You will have to run," Redbeard said. Her mouth pinched in a grim line, and she gestured at the wing of Atwater's craft. Her own ship hovered just beyond the wingtip, an easy jump to the deck, if one could make it across the wing.

"But we cut the safety ropes." Owen's words came out in an unusually high-pitched squeak.

Tim placed a hand on Nora's shoulder. "He's afraid of heights. Used to freak out when I climbed trees as a boy."

A second explosion shook another cable loose, detaching the balloon entirely from the back of the ship. Nausea roiled in Nora's stomach, but through some miracle the aircraft didn't drop out of the sky.

She shoved Spark into Owen's left hand and took his right firmly in hers. "Run with me."

Together they slid down to the wing. Timothy ran ahead, loping across the wing with an aura of invulnerability only youth could bring. "Run, Owen!" he called. "It's easy!"

Easy? This was hardly the time for casual taunts, but when Nora felt Owen straighten up beside her, she understood. Despite the age gap, their sibling rivalry thrived. This was a challenge between brothers. And you didn't back down from that, afraid or not. Nora had six siblings. She knew. And she wanted to hug Timothy for his quick thinking.

Keeping her fingers tightly entwined with Owen's, she raced along the wing of Atwater's airship. They would make it. They would. She couldn't let herself think anything else.

Halfway to their destination, a third cable burst, sending another tremor through the ship. Owen screamed in absolute terror and nearly stumbled.

"I have you!" Nora cried, squeezing his hand as hard as she could. It didn't matter that she couldn't possibly save him if he fell. Logic would do nothing in this situation. "I'm not letting go!"

Tim had made it to the end and jumped easily over the rail onto Redbeard's airship. The pirates swooped down on their wings, landing gracefully, then racing to their assigned stations. Only Redbeard herself remained, beckoning to Owen and Nora, shouting words of encouragement.

"I have you," Nora repeated. The wing narrowed the further it got from the body of the ship. Owen's gait stiffened and slowed. He needed something more. "And I am very, *very* angry at you," she growled. "If you die before I get to yell at you, I will never forgive you."

He moved faster.

It seemed to take an eternity, but at last they reached the pirate ship, leaping to safety as the last of the cables snapped and the balloon of Atwater's craft drifted off into the sky above. The pirate ship veered away, but his ship continued on, flying straight ahead with its wings alone. Nora stared at it in awe, stunned it didn't simply topple to the earth.

With a flash of light and a sudden roar, the bird-ship rocketed forward, moving faster than anything she'd ever seen.

"My God," Owen gasped. "He was telling the truth."

A shudder ran through Nora's entire body. Atwater had done it. He'd built an uncatchable vehicle. Which meant he'd be back someday. Owen would never be safe.

The airship grew smaller and smaller as she stared at it, flying off to who knew where. It dipped to one side, turning.

And then it faltered. It dropped and shook, slewing back and forth. A second later, it was spiraling out of control, falling, falling, until it slammed into a rocky hillside and burst in a fiery explosion that set the pirate ship rocking.

Nora let out a gasp of shock, horror, and relief, clapping a hand over her mouth. She spun away from the inferno below to find Owen's large body directly behind her. She fell against his chest, her fist beating agitated blows against his biomechanical shoulder.

"I am so mad at you!" she railed. "So, so mad at you! How could you? I told you no. I told you to go away!" Her opposite hand waved at the carnage behind her. "That could have been you!"

Exhaustion crashed down on her and she dissolved in a puddle of tears.

53

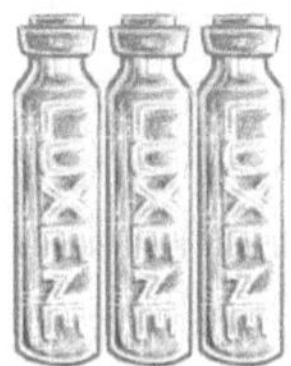

OWEN CARRIED NORA up the stairs of Catalina's townhouse and laid her gently on the bed they'd shared last night.

Damn. Had it really only been last night? It seemed forever. So much had happened, and he could hardly process any of it.

Nora stirred as he removed her boots and untied her corset, but didn't fully wake. When he pulled back the coverlet, she burrowed down into the pillows with a sigh and fell still.

Owen stood rooted to the spot, the blanket clutched in his hand. God, she was beautiful. Even exhausted and haggard from the day's ordeal, she was incomparable. He wanted to run his fingers through her hair, kiss the soft skin of her throat, curl up beside her and soak up her warmth.

Only his uncertainty about what she desired kept him from climbing into the bed. He understood now why she'd tried to warn them away. Because she wanted to keep them all safe. Because she was Nora and she couldn't not help others.

But whether she still wanted him was another matter entirely. Her time left behind with Atwater had to have hurt, regardless of any intellectual understanding that it had been the right decision. And then he had to consider the way he'd proposed to her: at the spur of the moment, when she was in a vulnerable place. They hadn't discussed the matter. Had hardly had time to adjust to the confessions of their feelings.

315

He didn't know whether she truly wanted to marry at all. Had he jeopardized her independence?

A soft knock on the door made him turn around. Tim stood in the open doorway, a frown on his face.

"Owen. There's a pair of men downstairs, asking to speak with you."

Owen draped the coverlet over Nora and followed his brother from the room, closing the door quietly behind him. Good. Whatever this was about, it would prevent him from giving into his longing and flinging himself into Nora's bed. She deserved time to rest. He needed time to… What? Prepare for the worst?

"You look tired," Tim observed. "Or unhappy. Or both."

"Yes, I know, I'm a crotchety old man. Let's see what this is about and then I'm getting a drink."

When Owen spied the two men waiting in the atrium, he nearly bolted. The Pinkertons Smith and Jones stood side-by-side in their austere suits, their expressions unreadable behind their tinted glasses. Owen forced himself to breathe and continue into the room, one step at a time. Yes, he'd broken the law, but he'd been in the right. He'd treat this like a business deal. He could negotiate.

"Mr. Cassidy," said Smith—or maybe that was Jones. "We just received word that an experimental airship belonging to Mr. Atwater crashed near the Georgia/Alabama border earlier today. It is believed Mr. Atwater was aboard at the time."

"Yes, I was aware of the incident," Owen replied.

"It took a bit of doing to track you to this house," the other agent continued, "but we wanted to inform you as quickly as possible that the Pinkerton compromised by Mr. Atwater has been uncovered and taken into custody. Several members of the St. Louis police force have likewise been identified. Mr. Atwater's factory and his subterranean… creation have been closed down for further investigation. You are safe to return home, and no charges are to be pressed against you for your abrupt departure from the city."

Owen let out a relieved breath. "Thank you for your assistance."

"When you return to St. Louis, if you are able to give a final statement for the police, it would be much appreciated."

Would be required.

"If you let my attorney know, he will arrange a time."

The Pinkertons nodded together. "Thank you, Mr. Cassidy," said… one of them. "The only other matter is the break-in at your mother's place of residence. It has been deemed a random event unrelated to Mr. Atwater's machinations. We do not expect it to recur." He nodded. "We will see you again in a few days."

The agents saw themselves out.

"It wasn't random," Tim sighed.

Owen blinked. "Excuse me?"

"The missing things? They're all in the cellar. I staged the break-in."

Owen was too dumbfounded to shout, or even utter a word.

"I was trying to get your attention. I thought I'd orchestrate a crime and then solve it myself to prove my competence to you. I was an ass. I apologize."

They stared at one another for several silent seconds, before Owen pulled his brother into an embrace. "I love you anyway. But don't ever do that again." He released Timothy, who nodded contritely. "And I know you're competent. I'll try never to forget it."

The brothers parted ways for the night, but Owen still couldn't bring himself to disturb Nora, and all the other rooms were taken, with Tim and his mother here for the night. Instead, he settled down in a large chair in Miss Navarro's study with a glass of whiskey.

He slumped in the chair, heaving a weary sigh. Whiskey

wouldn't be enough to ease the pervasive ache of his muddled emotions. Grief at the loss of his boyhood friend twined with lingering rage over Atwater's senseless treachery. Guilt, too, burbled up, because what Owen felt most was relief. It was over. They were safe.

And then there was Nora. Just her name conjured up love, lust, protectiveness, gratitude, warmth… The list went on and on. He closed his eyes and pictured the way she'd looked upstairs. Peaceful. Dreaming. Perhaps of a future with him?

Owen quickly downed the drink and set the empty glass on a side table. Possible futures flittered through his mind, some heartbreaking, some hopeful. What could he do to tip the balance in his favor? Anything? Maybe if he thought all night he could compose a coherent declaration of his feelings and tomorrow give Nora the proposal she truly deserved.

"Owen? Before I head home, I wanted—"

He jolted. "Nora?" His voice was scratchy, his throat dry. And, God, his neck was killing him. He straightened up in the chair. Shit. He'd fallen asleep. All night, if the sunlight behind the drapes was an indication.

She walked closer. "Are you okay? Did you sleep here all night?"

Owen stretched out his cramped limbs and struggled out of the chair. "Uh, yes."

"Oh." Nora crossed her arms over her chest and shifted her weight from one foot to another. Was she nervous?

Owen's empty belly churned. He was making a mess of everything.

"I'm sorry if I disturbed you," she went on. "I only wanted to talk to you for a moment before I head home."

Home. Right. Owen rubbed a hand over hair that had grown longer than he preferred. She had a home here in Savannah, and a business. Yet another issue with his hasty proposal. He'd considered none of the logistics of marriage. They lived in different cities. They both had jobs that were an integral part of their lives. She'd been furious with him yesterday before she'd given in to her exhaustion.

"You wanted to yell at me?" he asked. "Please, go ahead. Or can I avoid any shouting by preemptively apologizing? I didn't understand your warning, and by the time I was fully convinced something was wrong, the others had already begun slicing into the ship."

Nora shook her head. "It's fine. I've had all night to recover, and you had no way to know ahead of time the ship was dangerous."

"If I'd known, I would have found another way. Followed him until he landed, most likely. Somehow I would have come for you."

"I know." She shifted again. "It all worked out in the end. But that wasn't what I wanted to speak with you about."

"Oh." Owen stuffed his hands in his pockets, trying to prevent himself shuffling around the way Nora was doing. Was it his imagination, or was the air in this room stiflingly hot?

"I'm heading home now to take care of everything. I'll have your things brought here, unless you'd like them sent elsewhere? If my house is habitable, I expect I'll remain there while the insurance and rebuilding issues are sorted out."

Owen's heart sank. No invitation to join her. No implication that she wished for anything but to rebuild her old life. But, then, things hadn't exactly been pleasant since she'd met him.

"I will supply any necessary funds for the repair of your office and your business," he offered. "None of this would have happened had it not been for me, and while monetary compensation cannot undo the hurt and disruption to your life, it at least can ensure you have the best of everything as you rebuild."

"You don't have to do that."

He'd anticipated such a response. "But I want to. You helped me out of the goodness of your heart and requested no payment. Please allow me to help in return, in whatever way I can."

Nora's spine straightened. "I will let you know my decision once the full evaluation of the damage is complete."

Owen jabbed a fingernail into his palm. That sounded like a no.

"Is there anything *you* need?" she asked.

You. I need you.

"No. I will be making arrangements to escort my mother and brother back to St. Louis. Their wellbeing is my current priority. As is yours, but you seem to have that well in hand."

"I'm sure Redbeard will fly you all home." Nora fidgeted again. Owen wanted to smack himself for making her so anxious. He wanted to wrap her in his arms and kiss her until they both forgot all their worries.

"We'll take the train," he replied. "I need some time to recover before I'll be ready to fly again."

"Of course."

Silence fell. Owen swallowed hard. He'd slept the night away, leaving him with no fancy declaration of love. No suave proposal. No compromise for how to bring their lives together in a harmonious fashion. With each second that elapsed, he grew more afraid she was slipping away.

He took a single step toward her, prepared to throw himself at her feet and gush about his adoration for her, in whatever muddled fashion he could, just to get it out there. To let her know he was prepared to do whatever he needed to keep her in his life.

"I will not hold you to our engagement," Nora said, on a sudden whoosh of breath.

Owen's own breath caught in his throat.

"I understand that it came about in a moment of difficulty and was done out of your sense of honor, duty, and care for my reputation. But those aren't reasons to upend your life. I don't ever want to be your obligation, Owen." She turned abruptly away. "I won't trap you into anything you don't truly want. Please excuse me."

She was gone before he could open his mouth. He staggered, bracing himself against the wall to stop from sinking to the ground.

"You're not an obligation," he said to the empty room. "You're all I want. You're everything I want."

Did she want him in return? Right now, he truly didn't know. But he damned well was going to find out.

54

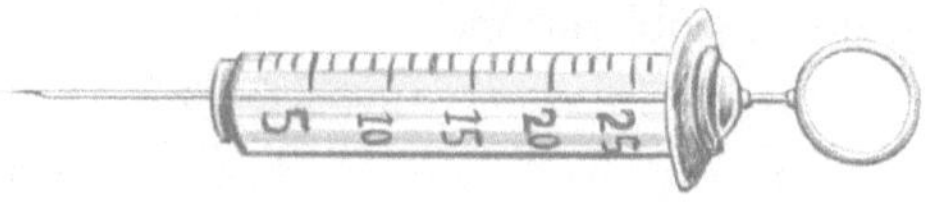

NORA PACED THROUGH the ruins of her surgery room, pausing now and then to pick up a twisted and charred bit of equipment. Tomorrow it would be razed and the rebuilding would begin. The rest of the building remained structurally sound, thankfully. She could continue to occupy her apartment upstairs until the construction finished and she could resume her old life.

She dropped the broken tool she held, fighting tears. She didn't want her old life back. She wanted a new life, with new adventures alongside the man she'd grown to love.

He doesn't want that, Nora. He wants to restore things. He offered to rebuild everything to how it was before. He never truly wanted marriage. But we can still be friends.

The thought offered no comfort. Perhaps at first they would remain close. Continue to be lovers, even. But the long distance was likely to make them grow apart.

And if somehow it didn't? The thought of only seeing him occasionally caused an ache in her heart. They would snatch a few days, here and there, with long, lonely train rides home when they parted. It would hurt them both. Yet the idea of severing the relationship entirely made her blood freeze.

She turned to stare into the house, at her damaged office. She'd sat at that desk, her body heating as she'd watched him exercise. She'd kissed him there, passionately and lovingly. If she lived here alone, those memories would haunt her.

That settled it. She'd fix up the house not to do business in, but to sell. She could be a biomechanologist anywhere. She could settle closer to Owen and perhaps then their relationship could continue more easily.

Or did he not want that either? Perhaps he needed to completely distance himself from everything that had happened, including Nora.

You'll have to ask him. Give him some time to regroup and recover while you take care of matters here. Then you can travel to St. Louis and see if he's still interested in you.

She began to hum the tune of "Meet Me in St. Louis," which had been stuck in her head since hearing it on Atwater's airship. The cheery melody came out slow and somber. She hummed louder, trying to force some optimism into her gloomy mood. She could make this work, couldn't she? She could be happy with a casual relationship and they'd both have plenty of space to continue their work. Right?

"Ugh." The masculine grunt startled her so badly she tripped on a broken bit of brick. "Must you hum that annoying song?"

Nora recovered herself, whirling around to find Owen standing in the lane between the former back of her house and the carriage house beyond. He'd shaved and gotten a haircut. His bespoke suit was immaculately pressed, and his watch fob and cufflinks gleamed as if they'd been polished. Was he all dressed up for her?

He waved a hand behind him. Their bicycles leaned against the door of the carriage house.

"I had your bicycles fetched. My train leaves in two hours, but I thought perhaps we might go for a ride before then?"

Nora rushed toward him, stopping just shy of his reach. "Thank you. That sounds… nice."

He took a step closer. "I've learned something about you, Dr. Eleanor Taylor. When you say 'nice,' it usually means 'wonderful.'"

Happiness burst through her. Yes. Wonderful. They could still be wonderful. She hurried to grab her bike, humming now with genuine cheer.

Owen grimaced. "Could you maybe pick another song?"

She spun back to face him, her hands falling to her hips. "It's a cute and sweet song. It's about a woman who decides she needs something more in her life, so she goes off to get it. But she wants her husband to follow and join her on her adventure. I can imagine them exploring the fair and having fun together. I love it."

"What a way to spring it on a man, though, up and leaving unannounced."

"I expect she had probably talked about it, but he wasn't listening."

Owen's eyebrows lifted, then his expression turned resolute. "I'll listen. Tell me what adventures you want, love, because I know what I want. I want to join in everything you do. I want to go where you go and have fun watching you have fun. I want to cuddle with you at night and smile at you over breakfast in the morning. I want to come home early from work for no other reason than to spend extra time with you. Or drop into your office to surprise you with a picnic luncheon. I want to take time off to travel and see the world with you. I want to try for children and to hell with anyone who tells me to find a younger woman. If we don't have kids we can buy more dragons. I want you, Nora. You and no other, for as long as I live. And if you don't want any of this, just say so. I'll give you whatever you desire. So tell me. I'm listening."

"I…" Nora could hardly speak for joy. "I think all of that sounds *exceptionally* nice."

Owen dropped to one knee. "I still don't have a ring for you. I didn't know what size to buy, and I'm sorry about that. However…" He cleared his throat and began to sing. "Meet me in St. Louis, Nora. Meet me at the fair."

She gasped, tears springing to her eyes as he crooned the

song he had moments ago professed to hate but knew she loved. His voice was rich and smooth, another delightful discovery. A lifetime of such discoveries lay ahead of her.

"Don't tell me the lights are shining any place but there," he sang on. "We can dance the hoochie coochie." Owen paused and gave her a suggestive wink, his eyes tracking up and down her body until she ached with desire.

Nora ran a hand over the short fuzz of his hair. "You can be my darling husband," she sang.

"That's not how the song—"

She pressed a single finger to his lips and finished her new version of the song. "If you will meet me in St. Louis, Owen, I will wed you there."

"Yes," he whispered. "Forever yes." He hauled her into his arms and kissed her until they were both flushed and panting. "Bicycle ride?" he asked. "Or bed?"

Nora drew back. "Two hours, you said?"

He nodded.

"Both."

55

Niagara Falls, New York
One month later

THIS HAD TO BE the most well-attended elopement in history. One word to Nora's brother in St. Louis, and the entire family had trekked to New York to join Owen and his beautiful bride for a brief ceremony by the falls. Mother, father, six siblings, spouses, children, and a handful of others whose relationship to Nora Owen hadn't yet determined had joined Timothy and his own mother in the hastily arranged chairs. In the future, he'd be prepared for such an influx of family.

My family.

It would be an adjustment, joining his tiny family with Nora's enormous one. But she would be by his side to help him through it.

Owen turned to smile at his stunning wife-to-be. She wore white trousers that hugged her hips, a simple white shirt, and one of her cropped corset-vests, also in white, with intricate lace detail. Pearls and tiny flowers adorned her chin-length hair. Perfectly Nora. Perfectly perfect.

She took his hand and squeezed it. "If Becca heads this way, don't let her muss me before the ceremony. She's an enthusiastic hugger."

Owen scanned the crowd. "Who's Becca?"

A flush crept over Nora's cheeks. "Do you remember how I mentioned I only once before felt a strong attraction like this?"

He nodded.

"Well, that was Becca. It was similar to what happened with you and me. We became friends quickly, bonded within weeks, and I began to feel something more. She hugs quite a lot, holds hands, and snuggles. She's a very touch-loving person. I'm usually not, but I responded to her and started to dream of kisses and beyond. Until the day she bounded through my door to announce with great delight that she was marrying my brother."

Owen winced. "Ouch. That must have hurt."

"It did. But the embarrassment was the worst. I felt so foolish. I still do at times. So if I was ever particularly awkward or strange with you—"

"You were wonderful," Owen interrupted. "You *are* wonderful."

She beamed up at him. "Then I suppose we ought to get married."

"I agree."

"I do have one more confession, before we begin." A mischievous twinkle gleamed in her eyes.

"Oh?"

"I'm actually quite excited by your millions of dollars."

Owen wrinkled his nose. "That doesn't sound like you."

"What if I tell you it's because I'll no longer have to concern myself with taking on paying clients and will now be able to devote my practice entirely to providing biomechanical surgery to patients who don't have the means to pay."

Her grin made his heart swell with adoration. With the sun streaming down on her, and one of nature's great beauties as her backdrop, she was the finest thing he'd ever seen. He had to stop himself from leaning in to kiss her. No mussing her until after the ceremony.

"Now, *that* sounds like you. Please, use as many of my millions as you need." He rolled the shoulder that now felt as normal to him as the flesh and blood of the rest of his body. "I love you," he vowed.

"I love you too." She tugged on his hand and led him to the front of the crowd. "Let's get married. I hate waiting."

Epilogue

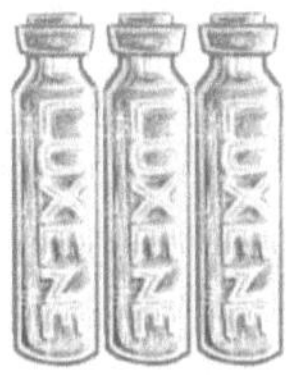

St. Louis, Missouri
Five years later

OWEN WALKED ONE FINAL LAP around his refinery, needing the assurance everything was running smoothly before he boarded the airship for his annual vacation. As usual, he had no idea where they were headed. Even five years on, this still caused a nervous clenching in his gut, but Nora had never led him wrong, and he would never say no to a new adventure with her.

This year, to celebrate their fifth anniversary, the trip was scheduled for an entire month, the longest he'd ever been away. Nora, naturally, hadn't the slightest bit of apprehension. In her absence, Taylor-Cassidy Biomechanical Surgery would be overseen by Dr. Timothy Cassidy, who had finished his degree only eight months prior. True, he'd been Nora's apprentice for years now, but he'd never before had sole responsibility for patients.

Apparently only Owen was concerned about this.

He hadn't said anything. He knew Nora and Tim felt comfortable with the decision, just as he knew Cardot and Jameson would ensure Cassidy Mining continued to thrive while he was away. Owen doubted he'd last more than a week before he telephoned Cardot in a state of semi-panic, begging to be reassured the mines hadn't ceased to exist in the interim. Owen had resigned himself to the fact that this was the best he could manage. Fortunately, his family forgave him for it.

"Daddy, Daddy!"

Owen didn't have time to turn before the small creature hurled herself into him, wrapping her little arms around his leg.

"Daddy, it's time to go!" Beatrice peered up at him with the same blue-green eyes as her mother. Owen suspected those eyes might be magical, because he was every bit as smitten with his daughter as with his wife. Bea was their one and only child—Nora had made certain of that—but the three of them plus Spark were as fine a family as he could imagine.

"I have to finish my walk-though, sweetie," Owen told the little girl, prying her off his leg. "Here. Come with me."

He boosted her up onto his shoulders, identifying equipment for her as he carried her around the room. Nora trailed a few steps behind them, watching everything with an affectionate smile.

"And here the mixer slowly stirs the ore and the water together in exactly the right amount," Owen told his daughter. "When it comes out, it's glowing green like the fuel you see in Spark."

"Wow! Do you drink it, Daddy? Because you're part dragon?" She thumped his mechanical shoulder.

Nora unsuccessfully smothered a snort of laughter. Owen glanced back at her, his own mouth curving as he joined in her amusement.

"No, sweetie, I don't. But I like that description. Part dragon. From now on, that's what I'm going to tell people if they ask about the shoulder." Owen swung Beatrice off his shoulders, gave her a peck on the cheek, and set her down. "That's your tour for today. I hope you liked it, because someday, my girl, I'll hand this all over to you."

"Wow!" she repeated. "Now do we go on the airship?"

"Yes. Now we can go."

Bea whooped and bounded toward the exit. Owen took Nora's hand as they walked after her, more sedate in their excitement but no less joyful.

"Where are we going this time?" he asked. They'd already been to Paris, the Grand Canyon, New York City, and Rome. Maybe this time he would see the pyramids or fly all the way to China or Australia.

Nora shook her head. "You know I never tell you."

"And you know I ask anyway."

She laughed. "You'll see soon enough. Well, the first stop, anyhow. We have an entire month."

They stepped out the door into the clear, sun-warmed air. A quick glance around told Owen no one was watching, so he tugged Nora close for a kiss.

"I've been too busy lately," he murmured against her lips. "Not enough time for this." A slew of new deals and expansion of a section of his mines had had him working late the last few weeks. This time off was a blessing.

"Well." Nora wound her arms around his neck, looking up at the airship hovering above them. "For a journey this long, I made certain to rent a ship with a separate room for Beatrice and an extra large bed for you."

Owen ran a thumb across her cheek. "For us." He claimed her mouth, kissing deep and slow, taking time to savor the softness of her lips, the eager delving of her tongue, and the way her body arched against him, begging for more.

"Mommy! Daddy!" Small arms clamped around his legs once more. "It's time to go!"

Owen reluctantly drew apart from his wife, allowing his daughter to propel him toward the lift that dangled from the airship, ready for them to climb aboard.

"We'll get back to that later," he promised Nora.

She took his hand again, lacing her fingers through his.

Their eyes met, and for an instant life contracted to nothing more than the two of them.

The moment was broken, as it so often was, by the delighted squeals of the child their love had brought into the world.

Nora laughed again. That musical sound never failed to bring a smile to his face. Together, they climbed up into the lift to join their boisterous daughter.

"Later will be lovely," Nora murmured. As the lift ascended, she moved close, rising up on her tiptoes until Owen could feel her warm breath mingle with his. "There will be kisses. I have a plan."

The End

About *the* Author

Award-winning author Catherine Stein believes that everyone deserves love and that Happily Ever After has the power to help, to heal, and to comfort. She writes sassy, sexy romance set during the Victorian and Edwardian eras. Her stories are full of action, adventure, magic, and fantastic technologies.

Catherine lives in Michigan with her husband and three rambunctious kids. She loves steampunk and Oxford commas, and can often be found dressed in Renaissance festival clothing, drinking copious amounts of tea.

Visit Catherine online at
www.catsteinbooks.com
and join her VIP mailing list for a free short story.

Follow her on Twitter @catsteinbooks,
or like her page on Facebook @catsteinbooks.

Also *by* Catherine Stein

Potions and Passions

The Earl on the Train - Book 0.5

How to Seduce a Spy - Book 1

Mishaps & Mistletoe -
A Holiday Novella -Book 1.5

Not a Mourning Person - Book 2

Once a Rake, Always a Rogue - Book 3

Love at Second Sight - Book 4

Sass and Steam

Love is in the Airship - Book 0.5

A Shot to the Heart - Book 0.75

Eden's Voice - Book 1

What Are You Doing New Year's Eve? -
A Holiday Novella - Book 1.5

Priceless - Book 2

Dead Dukes Tell No Tales - Book 3

Arcane Tales

The Scoundrel's New Con - Book 1

The Spinster's Swindle - Book 2

Other Books

Mating Habits - Book 1

Idle Nature - Book 2

Available at your favorite online retailer.
www.catsteinbooks.com

Thank you so much for reading.
If you enjoyed the book and are so inclined, I would love for
you to leave a review. Happy readers make an author's day!

I love hearing from readers,
so feel free to contact me on social media, or email:

catherine@catsteinbooks.com

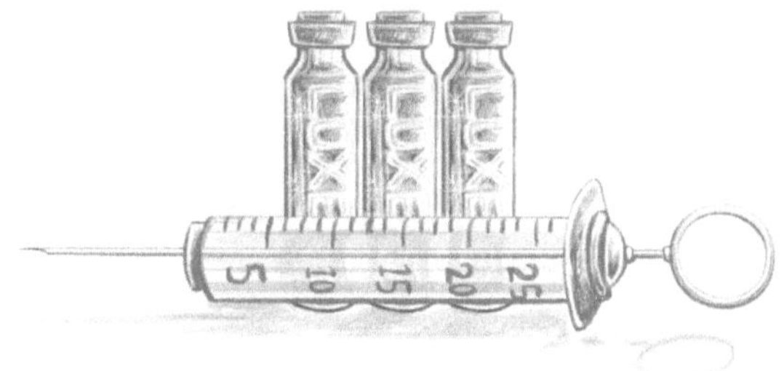